D.H. TREVENNA

Three Daughters of Delockth

Copyright © 2012 by D.H. Trevenna
First Edition – September 2012

ISBN
978-1-4602-0237-1 (Hardcover)
978-1-4602-0238-8 (Paperback)
978-1-4602-0239-5 (eBook)

All rights reserved.

No part of this publication may be reproduced in any form, or by any means, electronic or mechanical, including photocopying, recording, or any information browsing, storage, or retrieval system, without permission in writing from the publisher.

Published by:

FriesenPress
Suite 300 – 852 Fort Street
Victoria, BC, Canada V8W 1H8

www.friesenpress.com

Distributed to the trade by The Ingram Book Company

CHAPTERS

Mixed Emotions

The Tides of War

Castle of Joy

The Aftermath of a Tragedy

The Re-Assignment

Winds of change

The Education of a Queen

The Contest

The One Eyed Gate Keeper

Grannth Mountain (Blood of the Baby)

The Witch's Broom

The Little People Of Dwell

The Volarin Effect

For Love of Country

The Battle for the Plains of Volarin

The Queens in Check

Epilog

CHARACTER LIST

King . . . . Ormund Rex Atlas
Queen . . . . Remarkka Atlas
Princess . . . . Korana Atlas
Princess . . . . Korrin Atlas
Princess . . . . Presta Atlas
The High Wizard . . . . Kem Maththth of Grannth
Koln Killgreth . . . . Dark assassin turned protector and hero
Kathly Killgreth . . . . Wife of Koln
Kill Killgreth . . . . Son of Koln and Kathly
Erin Killgreth. . . . . Adopted son of Kathly and Koln
Marideath. . . . . Dark Lord and Evil Sorcerer
Milonth . . . . Garden servant
Captain of the castle Delockth . . . . Vestran Delrayth
Captain Vargas . . . . Dark Lords black ship Captain
Master Wizard . . . . Woolthen of Delockth
The Dark Wizard . . . . Seth of Andress
Maxx Seneth . . . . Captain of the Guards Marideath's Stronghold.
Eagle place
Romanth . . . . Black ships fetcher and forward scout.
Sabasth O Vectorth . . . . Admiral Delockth Navy
Enndora Maththth of Grannth . . . . Woodland Witch and Kem's mother
Laval of Vectorth. . . . . Spice Trader
Mandth of Delockth . . . . Forward guard
Hangth of Delockth . . . . Forward guard
Rathth of Delockth . . . . Rear guard

Sammth of Delockth	Rear guard
Volzanth	Alpha Wolf spell-trapped wizard
Korell	Volzanth's wolf mate
Dogglopp	Cyclops
Valda	Enndora's flying Broom
Admiral Quantez Levy	Admiral of Marideath's main fleet
Looma	Presta's friend, Village of Dwell
General Mott Mansth	Leader of the Dark Insertion forces: Plains of Volarin
General Bassenth	Queen Korana's army commander
Jimth of Vectorth Isles	Crows man Delockth Navy
Maraculas	Son of Spice Trader Laval

This book is dedicated in loving memory
Of

Charles Haddon Trevenna

(1931-2012)

The most amazing father a boy could have.
"A true artist in every sense of the word."

CHAPTER 1

Mixed Emotions

THERE IN A LAND FAR away and a time most forgotten, was born a set of triplets to an ill-fated Queen. "These blessed girls," were what the common folk called the three daughters of Delockth. Since pre-recorded time in the powerful land of Delockth, only the male heirs could inherit the powerful seat that governed all the eye could see.

Queen Remarkka's time was over with the birth of the three sisters, Presta, Korrin, and Korana who was the largest of the three. The Queen died in labor with horrible screaming pain, as she brought forth one child after the other.

It was said by the midwives, that the first girl to be born arrived silently with eyes open wide. It was as if she knew who she was and where she was. The King was heart heavy and plagued with mixed emotions. He was truly happy for the births, but the loss of his beloved wife was the beginning of his emotional and physical breakdown.

King Ormund Atlas was perched on his throne with a heavy head. All who stood around him stayed silent for fear of the King's temper. He threw back his bejeweled crowned head and yelled in a parched voice, *"Bring me the Lord High Wizard!"*

Two immense guards with twelve-foot pikes spun around and marched away with such vigor: the large wolfhound was startled by the clamor and sat up with a bellowing woof. A lowly servant boy of about eight seasons walked up to the saddened King with a tray extending from his tiny arms. "Wine, my King?"

The King slowly turned his head in the direction of the boy and acted as if he hadn't heard the young lad.

"Wine, my King?" The boy restated his question, but with more bravado.

The King slowly understood and reached out with a trembling hand to grasp the ornate chalice. "Yes...Yes, This is just what I needed. It is indeed late... now be off with you!"

He waved his hand at the wisp of a lad who happily scurried off like a rat smelling a dropped morsel of cheese that had just hit a noisy banquet floor. As the King drowned his sorrows, he looked over the top of the chalice and watched the little boy run towards his bed. He couldn't help asking himself why his garden was so fruitless. How he envied the little boy's father.

Just then, the large doors flew open and the High Wizard entered the room like a sail snapping open from a strong gust of wind. His purple robes billowed in the forward motion of his stride. He fell down on one knee and bowed his head. "You summoned me, your Grace."

The two guards returned to their usual positions. Their pikes hit the floor in unison creating a small explosive sound. The noise reverberated off the large stone-chambered walls. The High Wizard clapped his hands and the noise ceased with a dead silence.

"Thank you," The King quietly stated as he slowly rubbed his temples. He stood and brushed his long robes down to correct his appearance. He walked slowly towards the High Wizard, stopped just short of a few feet from the old man and spoke.

"You know why I summoned you? Don't you?"

The old man kept his gaze on the cold rock floor.

"Yes, my King...I heard of the births and I personally felt the passing of your beloved wife. May she rest in peace."

"DAMN YOU WIZARD! You promised me success this time! I need a son...a legitimate heir to replace me!"

"But the Prophesy, your Grace... I believe the time is at hand."

"PROPHESY! PROPHESY! I don't believe in that...I mean it can't be true."

The King's voice quieted down and he turned back to his throne. He sat down cautiously and grabbed for the chalice, which when he looked into it, was empty. He made a "humph" sort of noise, and under his breath whispered, "Empty...like me."

He looked up at the wizard who was walking toward him. He held out the chalice and wiggled it. The wizard waved his left hand and whispered a small chant. The King felt the weight of the chalice return and tipped his head as thank you to his High Wizard.

"*At least you're successful at parlor tricks.*"

The King took a big gulp and wiped the excess from his mouth with his big red sleeve.

"I think you need rest your majesty. The last thirty-six hours have taken their toll and I fear your judgment may be impaired."

The King looked again into his empty chalice and said, "*I think this time you may be right.*"

"I think before you judge your troubles, you need to look into the eyes of your new daughters."

"*I will...on my way to my chambers.*"

He turned and pointed a finger at the Wizard. "*We are not done! You and I...I will see you…tomorrow.*"

The King shuffled his feet as he headed in the direction of the nursery. His personal body- guards followed him but had the instinct to hang farther back than was required. They had no wish to reap the King's madness at not producing a son. The oil lamps flickered trying to push back the darkness from the seemingly endless corridors of the great castle. The King took note of the large paintings on the stone walls depicting the ancestors of the ancient castle. He drew his robes closer to his body to shield him from the cold, eternal dampness.

The King looked into his ancestor's eyes, he couldn't shake the feeling that they were laughing at him for only producing females. He wondered if they would even allow him a place beside them on the hallowed wall. Up one more flight of curved stairway and he could see the light from the nursery's fireplace. He cautiously rounded the open doorway and stepped in. The midwife was washing her hands and preparing fresh diapers for the new arrivals. She saw the King, curtsied and continued without hesitation. The King took one more step and tried to see in the large crib from where he stood. The midwife seeing this whispered to him," Come on your Highness get closer...they are not going to bite."

The King looked at her and gulped. He quietly placed one slipper in front of the other, which set him directly at the foot of the crib. He peered over the top of the crib and smiled. He turned and began to leave the room. As he was just about out the door, he turned back to the midwife and asked in a solemn tone, *"Where is...she, my beloved?"*

"The palace director has seen that she is taken care of in the traditional manner your grace. She will be able to be seen tomorrow. Tonight they will pack her in a cool place and make her presentable. As protocol states, we will have to say our goodbyes tomorrow. The good Chamberlin is seeing to details."

The midwife feeling that she said too much lowered herself and backed away out of the sight of the King. The good King heard one of the babies gurgle and walked back to the royal crib to investigate.

Three baby girls we lying side by side. On each end was a beautiful dark haired girl, but in the middle was a baby with fire red hair and violet eyes. The baby in the middle wasn't sleeping; she was staring at her father while reaching out with both arms. The King reached in and picked up the child. To his amazement, she started to coo and gurgle as if she was trying to talk. The King turned his head towards the nanny and asked, *"Is this normal for an infant barely four hours old?"*

"I should say not," replied the nanny.

"This one has a mind of her own, I would say. She was the first one born and she damned near pulled herself out...if you know what I mean...begging your royal pardon."

The King's face looked like he had seen a ghost. He turned his attention back to his daughter. *"I shall name you Korana...in our ancient tongue it means "supreme leader."*

He held Korana closer and looked back in the crib. He leaned in, touched the child to the right and said, *"You will be called Presta and you will be called Korrin."* He made the similar gesture on Korrin.

"I hereby...welcome the daughters of King Ormund Rex Atlas"

He turned his attention back to Korana and held her over his head. The six-pound baby girl started to squeal.

Ψ

The Royal funeral was attended by only a select few. The King made sure that Korana was in a bassinette beside him throughout the whole service. Korana never made a sound and seemed to be listening to every echoed word. After the service was complete, the King summoned his High Wizard.

The King could tell by the sound the guards made that his Wizard had arrived. The King waved the servants away wanting to speak most privately.

"How did you like the service for my lady and mother to my girls?"

The King sounded a little bitter and showed the tell-tale signs of inebriation from the strong wine he was gulping down.

"I thought it was to the point and regal. No matter the service the affair should never be judged, not under such sorrow."

"I guess you have a point...Join me this time, old man!"

"Maybe this time I will, friend."

The King was pacing back and forth in front of his fireplace, while the High Wizard found himself a seat facing the radiant heat.

"Here...take a load off and have a seat." The wizard waved his arm and a big chair walked on its four legs close to the King.

"I love those tricks you do." The King said with a distant smile etched on his tired face.

"I told you a long time ago I would teach you but you refused...you called it jokeus rokus or something to that effect."

The King changed subjects abruptly.

"Will you teach her?" He said quietly looking down into his cup of red.

"Have you seen the mark on the back of her neck?" The King just nodded his head.

"Is it the Prophesy you are worried about?"

"Yes!"

"She might not be the one."

"I don't have the mystical powers you possess, but I feel the winds of change blowing. If I'm not to bear a boy child...then I will give her all the help I can to ready her for her trials and tribulations. Will you teach her the mystical ways?"

"I believe she has already shown ability. The mere fact that she is a handful of hours old and is communicating through a childlike form of telepathy makes me believe she will be my teacher someday."

"You will not tell her your true identity."

"No, your majesty, per your command."

The King sat up strait in his chair and looked proud. The encouraging words from his friend gave him hope that his ancestors would approve of his lot in life. The King's face turned a serious shade as he spoke out. *"Wait...if we know...we must assume Marideath knows as well. He will most surely send an assassin, or even a small army to try and stop the chance of the prophesy coming true."*

"Yes...I had already thought of that. I will do my part and set up a fifty-measure perimeter spell. This will at least let us know if any such action is being taken."

"What should I do?"

"Increase the patrol on the great beach and double the nursery guard...wait! I have an idea!" The Wizard poured the King a full chalice of cool red wine and a tiny bit for himself. He raised the chalice to his King and said, "Oh! Your Majesty...I have a wonderful idea."

The Prophesy

Ψ

And a girl shall rise from an age unknown
She will lead a great army against dark forces grown
Against her back two sisters will be
Their strength in numbers grew from three
They with brethren will triumph in deed
Though casualties great will the sisters seed
Never to give up - never to sin
For the fight of the good shall always win

CHAPTER 2

THE TIDES OF WAR

THE WINDS BLEW HARD ACROSS the Shasath Sea, carrying the disturbing news of the heirless King Ormund Atlas. The ruling Lord of the Dark Continent Crestfallen, in the Province of Blackshire was all a glow with the most delicious news. Triplet girls would definitely be the beginning of the end for the Delockth legacy. This twist of fate could be a chance for Marideath to make his long awaited play for the prosperous land of Delockth. Marideath was well aware of the Prophesy but felt he had his own prophesy to fulfill. Three baby girls would not be a challenge…it would be a sport.

Under the great mountain in the Dark Lord's meeting chamber, all the upper echelon were assembled. The floors were littered with straw and discarded human bones. The air was acidic and reeked of fear and palatable horrors. The light torches were lit and the death hounds were tossed handfuls of mystery meat. The sound of the dogs ripping at their food sent shivers through the men waiting for their powerful lord to arrive.

Marideath punched through the large wooden doors blocking the entrance to the cavernous room. As the great doors slammed against the inner walls, the repeating echoes startled the poisonous bat-like creatures that lined the dark cool ceiling. The multitudes started to squeal, adding to the cacophony of the war council's useless chatter. Marideath entered the room with such long strides and vigor that his ominous black cape trailed behind him like a sheet in a wind-storm. He took possession of his enormous stone throne by swirling into its large seat. His thick cape followed shortly after and engulfed his entire body with one commanding tug.

"What is this news that I hear? Someone speak up!"

His voice was gravelly and strong. His eyes glowed red and his face was partially covered by a steel plate. His right hand had been lost in battle and a metal five-fingered claw had been fashioned for him. Many a man had died at the grip of that claw. Marideath stood fifty-five hands tall and looked down on everyone in his dark kingdom. It was common knowledge that he had possessed powers even at the time of his birth.

His pointy chin and long black hair provided him the look he needed to terrify his subordinates and his foul rancid breath was said to be strong enough to kill a man.

Marideath possessed only minor wizards within his army. Any wizards shown to have skills greater than his own, met their death and usually ended up food for his beasts. There was no one more powerful at magic than the Lord of Blackshire. The only exception to this control was the Dark lord's High Wizard, Seth of Andress. On whom he kept a tight rein.

The Lord's most trusted general stood and slammed his fist down hard on the wooden rail in front of him.

"General Trackn...you have something on your mind?" Marideath bellowed.

"Indeed I do Lord! The ancient prophesy is upon us I fear. We believe that with the births of the Atlas bitches...the winds of change are at hand."

"Who is...we...General?"

The general motioned his hand behind and all around him.

"We do lord... my comrades in arms and a few of the gifted seers."

"That's all in good, but doesn't it state that these girls shall be victorious...general?"

"That part must be wrong. There are no women warriors now or ever."

The general rubbed his dirty chin in thought, and then placed both hands on the rail in front of him.

"We must send warriors to eliminate those girls...My Lord!"

Marideath stood abruptly and said, *"Now! That's the first thing you said I agree with."*

He walked closer to the general. He was close enough to catch a faint smell of the Lord's foul exhale. Marideath stood inches away from the general's ear and asked.

"Who shall we send to do such an important task?"

The General was at the point of gagging on the foul stench.

"There can only be one...my lord...Killgreth!"

The benches of the dark chamber sparked alive with the mention of the name Killgreth. Murmurs and whispers filled the empty spaces in the damp air. The large dogs became agitated at the commotion and started to bark and growl. The Dark Lord scraped his long shiny metal fingers along the wooden rail next to him. Bits and splinters of wood flew from their common bond. The noises and commotion in the room ceased instantly.

"Killgreth...Ah! Yes Killgreth. The hero of the Northern Wars."

He turned to a guard stationed beside his throne and barked out the order to have Killgreth sent to his chambers immediately. The battle-dressed guard stomped one foot loudly then turned without hesitation and left the room.

Marideath turned on his heels, looked directly at Trackn and said, *"We will continue this in my chambers."*

Small puffs of moisture resembling smoke escaped from the corners of the Lord's crooked mouth. Marideath turned and pulled on his formidable cape, which covered him in a swirl of heavy fabric.

The cape fell to the floor as Marideath vanished. Then the cape itself disintegrated with a touch of smoke and sparkle. The crowd stood silent and slowly dispersed without a word. One subordinate general turned to the heavily dressed warrior beside him and commented. "You got to admit, he does do a nice exit."

Ψ

Lord Marideath's private chamber

Unusually thick red curtains lined Marideath's private chamber. The cathedral-like ceiling made the space feel strange and foreboding. He was sitting at a great wooden table ripping into an unfamiliar hunk of meat when the General was escorted into his presence by two overdressed and energetic armed guards.

"Sit down, General, we have much to discuss and plan you and me. Please sit down and have something to eat. We are fortunate tonight...for the hunting party downed a massive Luxx beast from the Northern woods."

The Lord gestured to the General to take a seat across from him at the table. The General removed his helmet to reveal a battle-scarred face. Even his beard had lines cut in it. The General wiped his salivating mouth with the back of his weathered hand. With no fineness, he reached in for a large piece of Luxx meat. A wisp of a girl dressed with black flowing cloth entered the room with a large jug of mead. She leaned in and poured the great Lord a full glass of liquid. The mead splashed over the side and the Lord reached out and backhanded the wench across the chest. The jug flew from her hands and in slow motion did a circle in the air. The centrifugal force of the object kept most of the liquid in check. The lord then held his clawed hand directly in the air and recited a small chant.

The jug ceased spinning and sat itself down on the floor right side up. The girl ended up on her behind with a look of terror on her pretty face.

*"PICK IT UP! And see that the thirsty General's glass is full...if his glass should empty during out conversation, this will be your last night with those hands attached to your weak arm*The General's eyes gave away his thought that this was highly unfair and he wanted no part of this subtle mental torture.

The Dark Lord turned his attention from the nervous girl and cast a wary eye on the displeased General. Even though the chalice was too full, the Dark Lord attempted to drink. Pleased with the results, Marideath drew a deep raspy breath and asked the General the important question.

"General Trackn...how long will it take to prepare the army for an all-out invasion on

Delockth?"

The General hesitated then looked into his chalice. Upon taking a long cool drink, he humbly spoke.

"Well my Lord, the truth of the matter...is that our numbers are insufficient, depleted."

He stood from the table and began to pace which forced Marideath to track him with his eyes.

"Our war ships are rotten and not seaworthy. To mobilize the numbers sufficient to overtake Delockth, we would need twenty more ships. We would also have a huge problem with feeding such a large campaign. These are the same problems we have always had, but if we put all our resources to the task... we could be ready in fifteen seasons."

"Fifteen seasons!" The Dark lord stood abruptly and raised his claw, waving the shaking girl from the room. The dog beside the fireplace stood and started to whine.

"Fifteen seasons! That's absurd General. Why do you think it will be so long?"

"We need to grow sustainable crops, while we need to train five- and six-year-old boys to fill our ranks. We also need to build ships. Most of our ships are not seaworthy. The rot has claimed almost all. Just the ships alone would be an insurmountable task, my Lord."

The Dark Lord was deep in thought as he walked over to the great fireplace and grabbed a long iron poker from a rack. He slowly prodded the fire trying to revive its former glory. As soon as he stopped poking at the logs, the fire died down once more. Marideath bowed his head and recited an enchantment, which made the flames appear larger and brighter. There was no extra heat just a bedazzling flame. Marideath turned quickly and in a low growling voice said, *"Make it happen, general…I will wait twelve seasons and not a moment more."*

The Dark Lord stormed out of his own private chambers leaving the General standing there alone. The General watched the Dark Lord leave the room as flames in the fireplace died in a symbiotic gesture. Trackn walked over to the table and reached for a piece of meat. He wondered how many Luxxes would have to be hunted to feed his now growing army. He decided then and there to delegate a troop of men to trap and corral the beasts in hope of being able to raise them like the ancient cattle. He sniffed the meat and threw it in the fireplace. His helmet was pressed over his aged head as he left without pomp and circumstance.

CHAPTER 3

Castle of Joy

A ROYAL BIRTH HAD BEEN A *long time coming. The common people didn't care if the heirs were male or female. The fact that there were triplets sent the land of Delockth spinning joyously upward. Even though the Prophesy was well known, the people all made themselves believe it was a good omen. The good Queen was never far from everyone's mind but the sheer power of the three sisters made the land buzz and sing. The King trying not to succumb to his hideous grief focused on the girls, especially Korana his favorite.*

The King burst into the nursery. "Well...well, well, how are my three little angels?"

As usual, Korana's two sisters were crying and generally acting their age. Korana was sitting up staring into her father's eyes from her crib.

"And how are you this fine morning, little one?" The King looked at the royal nanny and inquired,

"Did she eat already?"

"Twice...your majesty."

"Twice...Well..."

The King looked astounded. He looked at the baby then at the nanny.

The nanny said, "Sit yourself down...if you would your grace... Just watch!"

The nanny softly picked up the child and handed her over to the out stretched arms of the king. The king held the baby as if it were a dripping sack of clothes. The nanny saw his uneasiness and reached out her knowing arms for the return of the child.

The nanny placed Korana in her own crib and propped her upright. She placed the drinking bag of milk on a table in front of the baby and stood back a foot or two. "Watch your Majesty!" The baby stared at the drinking bag and stretched out both arms as if she was trying to reach it. After a few grunts and some serious face contortions, the milk bag left the side table and floated in the air towards the hands of the waiting child. With a gurgle and a squeal, Korana was on her third meal that morning.

The King had a tear in his eye. Never in the land was there a child switched on at such an early age. Truly, Korana was the focus of the Prophesy, the King thought to himself. The King stood slowly and looked into the nanny's eyes. *"Who knows of this...and speak the truth for these girls could be in great danger."*

"This is the first morning where anything out of the ordinary has happened your grace...I swear on my family's lives."

The nanny kissed the amulet she was wearing about her neck.

"We will be needing your silence on these matters good woman, but you and yours will be compensated well."

The nanny bowed her head in cheerful acceptance.

The King took off a small pouch from his belt and tossed it at the nanny. The jingling was profound and the bag heavy. The nanny's cheeks turned a bright tomato red. She curtsied and stayed down until the King turned on his heels and left the nursery. The King turned to the stationed door guards and barked an official order. *"Double the guards here and there...no one is allowed in without my express consent, save for the nanny."*

The guards banged their poles on the stone floor in acknowledgment.

The King continued walking at a quickened rate through the castle corridors. His mind was all atwitter with Korana's future and his own. As he looked up, he swore he could see the pictures of his ancestors smiling. The King's personal guard snapped to attention as the King approached his private chambers. He looked at the guard closest to him and ordered the High Wizard to be brought to him with no delay. The King poured a glass of wine for himself then sat in a big chair facing the grand fireplace. Then he stood and circled the chair, then plopped himself down on the edge of his bed. His mind was mush with dreams of a good life with his daughters at his side. When the High Wizard entered the room, it was with such speed the King thought he was pushed into the chamber.

"Your majesty what is going on...what is the emergency?" The Wizard gave a respectful bow as he tried to catch his breath.

"Kem, my oldest, dearest friend...it is good to see you."

The Wizard immediately thought the King was inebriated.

"Please take a seat!"

Ormund dragged a heavy chair across the cool stone floor. The ungodly noise that emanated from the protesting wooden legs was enough to make the old Wizard wince in pain. "Please! Please! Sit thyself down."

Kem at this point, truly believed that Ormund was off his nut. The King handed an overfull chalice to his old friend and sloshed a bit of wine on his fine flowing garment. Kem tried to ignore this and patiently waited for the giddy King to settle down.

"Dear friend, I need your help...we...need your help! The Prophesy is real...it has begun...she can do things...!"

The Wizard held out a friendly hand in hopes the King would stop his rant and tell him what was going on. The King took a big slurp of wine, which made several drops race down his bearded face.

"Just tell me what has happened?"

"She made her milk move."

"I beg your pardon."

"She looked at her milk pouch...and made it float towards her."

"Which child are we speaking of your grace?"

The wizard leaned closer to enter the King's personal space. The King whispered with a gust of wine-drenched air... "Korana!"

"Well now indeed your grace, that is most interesting news. I don't remember anyone showing signs of magic at such an early age. Even the prophesy doesn't state a prodigy. The fact she is only four months old is quite remarkable...should I test her abilities?"

The old wizard sat up strait in his big chair.

"I want more than that, I want you to teach and mentor her from this day forth."

"I would be honored sire...nothing would please me more."

The wizard waved his hand and the chalices were refilled. With another wave, the fire was stoked and the flames danced higher, licking the sides of the blackened hearth. The two old friends clinked their chalices together, and both this time wore the fruits of their labor.

The days went by as the three sisters settled into a routine. The castle itself seemed to be uplifted by the presence of the three babies. The land was flourishing and the markets were abuzz with hope for the future. The King took precautions in protecting his heirs to the throne and then settled back into his own sadness, with the stark realization that he was alone.

☥

Marideath's Chamber:

Marideath was looking over shipbuilding drafts when his door guard announced Killgreth. The Dark Lord never lifted his head; he just waved him in. Killgreth stood before his lord a massive man. His arms were like tree trunks and his height was staggering. The only contradiction was the kind-looking face he carried about. Flaming red hair protruded from every pore on his face and head. Some people have said he looked like he was on fire in direct sunlight. Black leather and spikes for epaulets seemed to be the fashion of the day. A large broadsword hung beside him, with an evil looking bullwhip as a companion. Marideath looked up from his papers and didn't say a word; he just sat himself down in his ornate chair.

"Well...Killgreth! It is good to see you have survived the Northern Wars in one piece. I have been keeping track of you...you show a lot of promise for bigger and more important things."

Marideath clapped his hands and a small girl carried in a tray of wine goblets and fruit. Killgreth's eyes grew large seeing the fruit. Fruit was so rare; it had to be imported at great peril from across the sea.

"Please be seated."

The Dark Lord pulled the chair closer using his magic. Killgreth couldn't take his eyes off the fruit.

"Please good sir...would you help me eat this fruit?"

Killgreth looked at the Lord, then the fruit, then the Lord.

"Go on then."

Slowly the big man reached for a red apple. He acted as if it would burn him to touch it. He placed the apple in his large hand and drew it closer to his mouth.

"Stop right there! How dare you eat before I do?"

Marideath waved his hands as if he was conducting an orchestra. The apple in Killgreth's hand exploded into applesauce. Killgreth was covered with the flying apple carnage. The big man stood up with mouth agape.

"Sit down! Ha! Ha! Ha! I was just toying with you."

Marideath grabbed a large orange from the plate and tossed it at the assassin.

Killgreth pulled a small waist knife and flicked it at the advancing fruit. It pierced the flying orange, and then with his left hand caught the falling stabbed orange.

"Very impressive…if you are all they say you are…I have a very important mission for you. And if you are successful, I will grant you a peaceful retirement."

This fact alone seemed to light the ears of the famous warrior.

The giant of a man sat and ate his orange without peeling the fruit, while the Lord explained the mission in great detail. After a measure of time, the plan was set and the fruit was eaten. Killgreth exited the chamber and prepared for his great journey. Every detail was revealed to Marideath's great assassin, except the fact that the fruit he consumed was poisoned with magic. If he didn't return successfully, the antidote would not be his.

ᴪ

Castle of Delockth:
The King summoned his great wizard. *"Has the plan been implemented?"*

"Yes your majesty, there are very few in the know as you suggested."

"And Korana, do you think she knows?"

"Well your grace, if she does…she approves."

"Then I will bid you a good night, Kem."

Kem gave the King a gracious deep bow and with one puff of smoke vanished before his eyes.

ᴪ

Beach Gateway, Delockth: Just before three bells

The shoreline of the great sea was bitter cold. Winter had finally taken hold on this chosen country. The sentries that patrolled this beach access to the great castle drew nearer to the fire they had constructed to ward away the evil piercing cold and pitch darkness. The guard being doubled brought no comfort here. A light snowfall had just begun which added to the inherent misery of this post. Three distant bells could be heard emanating from one of the castles towers.

Even the powerful moon itself hesitated in showing its face as it danced between the massive snow clouds that quilted the night sky.

Five guards were the usual numbers patrolling this strip of land, but tonight as all nights to come, the King had ordered extra men in fear that Marideath would try to eliminate the powers to be. More men would create a bigger buffer between The Dark Lord and the King Ormund's precious daughters. He did not foresee Killgreth.

A few more pieces of damp log were haphazardly tossed on the struggling fire. The flame eventually rose but no significant heat was felt. The guards took this sign as a bad omen and all but one kissed the amulet, which was worn by most around their necks. The lowly guard left on the shoreline proper was the youngest of the troop. Being the newest, he received the coldest spot on the watch. The wind was unstoppable and relentless at this particular spot. The young man's designation was Manning of Demoorth. A simple man was he and bravery was not his forte. He had made this detail by drawing straws back at the castle's guard station. He believed it was a stepping stone to an inside detail.

He was starting to regret his decision when he couldn't stop his teeth from rattling in his mouth. He drew his scratchy wool blanket up over his small shoulders to help fight the bitter cold.

The soldier was staring at the three-quarter moon when it slipped behind a sinister night cloud throwing the beach into perpetual darkness once more. A small ripple of a sound caught the patrol guard's attention. He immediately decided that it wasn't worthy of an alarm and assuming it was a fly-eating fish jumping. He slowly turned his body towards the quiet surf. Out of the darkness travelled a blackened arrow; it pierced the young guard's throat and dropped the man dead without a sound. Killgreth pushed his burnt black boat closer to shore and walked slowly from the icy water. He looked over his shoulder towards the ship he had transversed the sea in, heading home under silent oar power. His attention refocused to the beach where he had made his first kill.

Killgreth slung his bow over his shoulder and kneeled beside the dead soldier ensuring a definite kill. He pulled the arrow from the young man's neck and re-quivered the missile.

He held both legs and dragged the dead weight towards a grassy knoll. He then stripped down and exchanged his wet clothing for the guard's. The two men were definitely not of the same proportions, so Killgreth made a few hasty cuts to free his bulk from the tight and restrictive clothing. The scratchy wool blanket the guard was wearing was sopping from the guards open neck wound. Killgreth rubbed wet beach sand over the dreaded stain and nullified the red tinge from the wet patch.

His ears turned to the sound of campfire and merriment of a subdued form. He pulled the blanket over his head and walked into the lion's den, shivering without fear. Without hesitation the assassin walked into camp, sat down opposite the men taking refuge from the cold night and outstretched his hands to warm his thick fingers. None was the wiser. The blanket was a signature piece of Manning of Demoorth. With the wool over his eyes, he was quite pleased with his chameleon trick. There were five men in total sharing the comforting heat. One of the older guards approached who he thought was Manning of Demoorth and generously slapped the young man on the back. *"Ah young buck...What's the matter with ye, can't handle the beach air?"*

The men all threw their heads back in a roaring laughter at the jab the older guard hazed the young man with. Killgreth spun like a child's top in full flight and gutted the large man where he stood with a knife he pulled from his sleeve. Without hesitation or reservation he threw the dangerous knife dripping with fresh blood at the second largest man sitting directly across from him at the fire. The evil knife embedded itself in the upper part of the soldier's right eye ending his life on the spot. The soldier screamed his last breath and fell face first into the licking fire. Sparks filled the night sky around the campfire driving the remaining men to their feet confused and defensive. Killgreth drew his long sword and gracefully leapt over the now stoked fire. With one vicious swing, he removed both heads from the guards to his immediate right. The open-mouthed heads flew in two ghastly directions. Killgreth had a big smile on his face...he was in his element. The moment he landed, he performed a spinning back kick on one of the remaining guards. With the fire dancing a strobe pattern, the sickening scene took on a slow- motion appearance. With a few jagged moves, the assassin was directly in front of the last remaining guard. Without shilly-shallying, he thrust his red-stained sword into the open mouth of the man and severed the top of his head clean off. Killgreth stood back and stepped on the neck of the guard he had kicked down.

A loud crack was heard as he twisted his heavy foot and dispatched yet another inept guard. Three guards were left when he sat down and scooped himself a bowl of whatever the men were eating. The smell of the burning guards face would have made a lesser man heave and toss, but Killgreth was in his arena of expertise...in meant nothing to him...nothing! There were so many battles under his belt. He knew he was dead inside. Within a few moments he rewound all his personal regrets. "Maybe this will be the last battle...just maybe." He thought.

The three guards running into the ungodly scene surrounded the campfire area. The smallest of the three shouted, "*What have you done, Manning? What have you done?*"

Killgreth slowly put the bowl down and stood. He pulled the smelly wool blanket back and let it fall to the ground. "*Killgreth!*" The largest of the three sputtered. The other two answered in unison...in a whisper, "*Killgreth!*"

The three remaining soldiers spread out as their training suggested. They held their swords mid height and danced back and forth. The weapons were clearly shaking in there unsure hands. The flickering firelight added to the surrealistic properties of the visual. The middle-sized man took the initiative and jumped the flames with his sword held high above his head. The assassin went down on one knee and pointed his sharp sword in an upward motion towards the incoming body. The flying soldier didn't have a chance as he skewered himself on the upturned sword of the assassin. Death was instant for the brave man, little reward for such a play. Killgreth booted him off his sword, which made him fall into the fire. This in turn made the flaming logs roll out of their warm bed and travel towards the remaining men. The closest man grabbed the unburnt end of a flaming stick and engaged Killgreth. Killgreth exclaimed. "Ah! Very good...VERY good!" The soldier approach apprehensively with multiple wild swings, while Killgreth repositioned his feet. The assassin pulled another throwing dagger from his waistband and ended the fiery spectacle. The smallest soldier started to run towards the castle. Killgreth walked over to where he had placed his bow and strung a missile in its notch.

Without realizing it, he grabbed a signal arrow and took aim at the fleeing man. The running soldier could hear his heart pound and his cold feet hit the partially snow-covered ground. Then it came... a faint whistling sound...it got louder and louder...then.

Killgreth stood over the fallen man; he placed his foot on the man's back and retrieved his arrow. He looked at the arrow and thought, *"This was a mistake... this could have given away the fact I am here and jeopardized the whole mission.* He was not pleased with himself. He would not make another mistake. As he walked back to the patrols camp, he heard the man he just downed moan. He decisively turned around and knelt down he pulled his knife and slit the man's throat. He angrily shoved the knife back in its sheath and turned back to the fire. As he walked, he could hear the gurgling sound of blood leaving the man's open neck wound. All traces of his personal presence were taken back. The only things he forgot were his original landing clothes. He sat back down and finished his bowl of whatever it was. He took a few deep breaths and adjusted his clothing. He knew he didn't have much time before the sun came to life, so he turned on his heels and headed for the castle to finish this important mission.

Korana opened her violet eyes for she somehow knew a danger was approaching. She could feel her two sisters close by and could hear them breathing. She could do nothing to warn her protectors, for she needed to visualize the object to move it. If she did manage to make something fall, she still could not communicate at this early age anyway. The radiating body heat from her two siblings proved too much for Korana at this time of the night. She succumbed to the warmth and closed her eyes once again.

Killgreth was still a good measure away from the daunting castle when he stopped dead in his tracks. He looked behind him and all around, for he felt a presence, a feeling that someone was watching him. This feeling gave him a chill he had never known. He touched his amulet and continued on his path of destruction.

The castle loomed near; its shadowy outline was etched in the awakening sky of morning. Time was running out and the element of surprise was fleeting. Several of the distant turrets were lit with pot fires.

This helped Killgreth get his bearings on the large structure. He rubbed black grease on his face and hands to help with his invisibility. The moon would occasionally pop out to reveal any reflective surface it wished to awash. Closer and closer he crawled like a giant snake on his belly. He was not used to killing innocent babies, but this was his way out. This was what was owed him. The gift of a permanent retirement would be granted to him if this mission was successful. The thought that recurred in his mind was, "If I don't look at what I'm doing...maybe the girl's death won't haunt my sleep for the remainder of my life."

Killgreth moved like a grass snake to the edge of the castle's moat. He then figured he had a cycle and a half before the sun took away his edge and possibly his escape. Not knowing whether there were serpents in the moat, Killgreth slid into the icy water. With only his head above the water, he breaststrokes to the middle of the moat before he was pulled under by a violent tug on his right leg. The icy fluid covered his head like a shroud. Killgreth pulled his waist knife and started to slash at whatever was pulling him down to the bottom. After a few short jabs, he bobbed to the surface. He took a big breath and did a front crawl to get out of the water as fast as he could. He could feel the pain swell in his right leg as he was using it to propel him through the water. The heavy gear was an extra burden to his life-saving swim.

He pulled himself up onto a small ledge against the castle wall. He took a few moments to inspect and wrap his teeth-punctured leg. He pulled a small vial from his pouch and ingested the powder inside. With a handful of water, he swallowed the substance. He looked at the vial and tossed it in the moat. The cold was starting to catch hold of the big man's body. Parts of him were feeling numb but he knew instinctively he had to press on.

Killgreth crept silently along the ledge. When he reached the drawbridge opening, he twirled and threw a small hook that was attached to a thin rope. The hook caught on the top of the drawbridge and held fast. Slowly and silently, he scaled the side of the castle in hope of finding a better position. Killgreth perched himself on top and surveyed the area. He crouched low; the wall sentries were numerous. The pot fires lit them generously and there were many who neglected their duties for the grateful warmth. This would not be an easy breach, he thought.

The assassin readied his blowgun and the poison darts. "Bluthhoo! Bluthhoo!"

Two darts struck the two nearest guards. The needles pierced their throats and they dropped like sacks of potatoes.

Killgreth Jumped from the ledge and quickly ran over to the two dead guards. He then dragged the two guards off to one side, covering them with whatever he could find. He pulled some material from a pole. The Kings regal banner had to do. As his adrenalin started to diminish, Killgreth started to feel the adverse affects of the wet and the cold. He decided to shed his clothes once more for one of the guards he had just relieved of his vital signs. He chose a more suitable size this time and he needed no alterations. He quickly placed his pouches, his knives, and sword on his new uniform. He then re-hid the body and made his way towards a lighted castle passage.

The passageway felt measurably warmer without the cold wintery winds, and this made the assassin's face smile. The winding staircase down was lined with wall torches that were oil fed. Killgreth was amazed and stretched out his hands in order to steal some of its magical heat. He could feel the heat enter his body through his fingertips. He knew he needed all his faculties to complete this devious mission…even his chunky fingertips.

With his sword drawn, Killgreth downed the last of the stone steps and rounded the well- worn corner. The captain of the tower guards was simultaneously making his way around the same corner. Both men came face to face... weapon to weapon.

The only noise the surprised captain managed to get out was, *"Arrgh..."* before the intruder's sword pierced through the good captain's mouth and out the back of his neck. Quick and silent was the death, just as it had to be. The assassin placed his wet foot on the chest of the departed captain and retrieved his sword with one swift yank. Killgreth paused for a second to look at the man he had just killed. He looked familiar, and this made Killgreth believe he had met this man before, maybe in battle.

The large silent man entered what seemed to be a guard station. He took note of the weapons, which lined the rough walls and of, the large map etched into another. Luckily, the room was void of all guards, this gave the assassin a moment to study and commit to short-term memory, the interior map.

A northern tower was circled in a red dye…Nursery! One more look at the map and then off he ran in the direction of his goal, the three sisters. This was all too easy; where were all the guards? He moved quickly, one more hallway, another corner, another upward staircase. Killgreth ran into a room full of ancient suits of armor. This would have been the former King's trophy room.

The walls were lined with banners of great deeds and battles. He thought he saw movement out of the corner of his eye and stopped quickly. All at once, eight empty suits of armor jumped off their pedestals and lowered their treacherous pikes. A terrible clanking and clatter sound accompanied the supernatural movement. Killgreth turned in a circular pattern as if he was engaging each and every opponent. All the empty suits trained their long weapons on the intruder and advanced their positions. Killgreth knew this was an enchantment of the High Wizard of Delockth. It made him believe they knew someone was coming.

With his shiny sword held high, the very noisy battle began. Slice...parry...thrust! Killgreth was in trouble. The suits seemed to have been given inexhaustible energy and with no human will to demoralize...unstoppable! The only clear way out of the trophy room seemed to be blocked. He reached into his waistband and removed a large black diamond.

He held it high in the air and chanted,

"NOW YOU SEE ME, NOW THERE ARE FOUR
WHICH IS THE REAL ONE WHO ESCAPES OUT A DOOR?"

The black diamond began to pulsate and glow. The radiant light, which was produced exponentially, grew into a mini sun. All the enchanted suits of armor held fast, then with a pop! pop! pop! three exact copies of Killgreth entered the fray. The three copies of Killgreth began to swing wildly at the now advancing tin men. The real Killgreth made a quick exit from the room. He now thanked the Dark Lord for the gift he had received from the victory in the Northern Wars. It was unfortunate the black diamond would only work once. The assassin ran along a few halls then pulled into a dark alcove to recapture his bearings. He closed his eyes and pictured the map on the guard-station wall. "Up and north, yes...up and north," he whispered to himself.

With sword in hand, he dashed out of his hiding spot and directly into the running path of another soldier. "What's all the commotion about?" the soldier said nervously. Killgreth remembered he was in a castle guard's uniform and was taken for a brother in arms.

"There is an intruder in the trophy room." Killgreth said excitedly.

"Where are you going then...it's that way?"

"I was dispatched to the royal nursery"

Without another word, the guard ran off towards the fight in the trophy room. Killgreth couldn't believe his luck and in no time he found himself standing in front of the nursery doors. Before he entered, he retrieved a poison dart from its protective case. He decided that it would be the quickest death for the little princesses. One little prick and the deadly poison would run its course. Upon entering the room, two stationed guards confronted him. Thinking quickly he loudly ordered the two shaken men to help the ongoing battle in the trophy room. They both could hear the distant din and without a second thought ran off together in the direction of the noise.

Killgreth was left standing alone in the nursery holding a small needle. He cautiously surveyed the large room and spotted the crazy large crib at the end of the brightly-colored room. Watchfully, he slid over to the crib and peered in. The three sisters were sound asleep. The assassin hesitated at the beautiful sight just long enough for the nanny to re-enter the chamber behind him. The assassin without reserve swung around and let fly a throwing dagger at the unsuspecting target. The blackened knife buried itself in the woman's throat and she went down into a heap on the cold floor. The assassin turned back to the wicked deed at hand.

One, two and three, all three babies in turn received a prick in the arm. The biggest of the three opened her eyes, but Killgreth covered her whole face with his massive hand. He could not look into her eyes while she slid rapidly from her life. With a few useless squirming movements, she was still. Tics turned to tocks; the great assassin was caught in a trance thinking what he had just done. He spun around in haste to make his seemingly impossible escape just as the High Wizard waved his hand in a mystical pattern. The assassin was switched off and his lights went out.

CHAPTER 4

The AFTERMATH Of a TRADGEDY

THE KING WAS AWAKENED BY *his personal aid shouting and screaming some befuddled nonsense.*

"The girls your majesty...the girls! The poor little darlings what are we..."

The King sat up in bed and tried to shake the sleep from his mind.

"What in the darkness are you jabbering about you noisy little man?"

The High Wizard flew into the room with his bright white morning cape trailing him like a sheet in the wind.

"What in the Dark World is going on...what is all this commotion?"

"Sire the unmentionable has happened."

"What...you got laid?"

The old Wizard took the hit on his character like water off a Relknards wing, and then carried on.

"Very funny sire...no I'm afraid this is a most serious affair. An assassin has breached our defenses, and has successfully murdered the Royal Princesses."

All the color left the King's face. He clutched his heart and simultaneously forgot how to breathe. The High Wizard quickly looked around the room then motioned the King with his open hands to stop.

"My babies! My babies! My whole world...what are we to do? Who could do this? They were only babies!"

The Wizard pointed his finger at the King effectively sealing his mouth with a spell. The King knew right away that something wasn't right about this ghastly information. Kem placed his index finger up to his dry lips and produced a ssshhhhh! sound.

The agitated King swung his cold bare legs around and stood up. His nightgown was somewhere around his portly middle, which made him wrestle the material until it covered most of his hairy legs once more. The angry look on the King's face made the Wizard release the silent spell immediately. The King whispered very loudly.

"Why did you...do that...to me?"

"You were about to spoil the sting we had arranged."

"What are you jabbering about old man?"

"The substitutes..." the great Wizard stopped in his tracks and cast a spell to block out anyone trying to listen to their private conversation.

"I beg your royal pardon...the substitute princesses were assassinated."

"Oh my!" The King sat down slowly on the edge of his large four-poster feather bed.

"How? By whom?"

"Killgreth"

"Killgreth of Delockth, but I thought he was captured in the last Great War between the light and the dark. He was merely a young lad of four I believe at the time."

The King placed his head in his hands and asked... "How did they die?"

"Poison, sire, just a small scratch would instantly send them on to the next realm."

The High Wizard sat himself in a large chair underneath a big window.

"And what of the real Princesses?"

"They are sleeping soundly, my lord."

The King looked up once again, and then stood.

"Their families have done for us the ultimate service. They will be compensated with title and lands."

"I will see to the royal funeral, sire...after all they are supposed to be the real thing. I will also discreetly make the other family compensations, which I am certain won't help them in their infinite grief. You do understand…we must act on this play and go through the motions as if the three sisters have actually perished. The ruse must remain for some time."

"How long?"

"Until we can properly defend ourselves from Marideath's evil intentions."

"I am assuming that the Dark Lord sent Killgreth?"

"I believe so, your grace. Killgreth needs to believe he did his deed just in case he escapes."

The King walked over to the large terrace and looked out on to the white land.

"Where is he, Kem? Is he dead? I want to meet him."

"He is under a constraint spell, sire and I will interrogate him in due time."

"Good ...Good."

"We need to be sad now, sire. The mourning has begun; it is time to act. The people need to grieve and see you grieve. I am sure when this is all over the people will forgive us of this charade we have concocted."

"Well, let us hope they forgive us old friend...let us just hope."

The King put on his royal colors and played his part to a tee. Strong yet emotional was his character, it was well received...the land was officially in mourning. The wind picked up and the land went into a deep freeze.

Ψ

The Interrogation of an Assassin: It was two complete days before anyone opened the door to the assassin's cell. Killgreth was shackled to a small cot in the corner of a very damp cold space. The ceiling was a good 300 hands high with a small barred window way above anyone's reach. The smell in the air was as thick as a quilt and reeked of saturated urine and feces. Many a person has spent his final days within these four walls as attested to by the scratched written messages adorning them.

Morning of the third day leaked through the tiny window way above. Killgreth's eyes were wide open but his consciousness was nowhere to be found. A much too small door in the side of the wall creaked open to bathe a portion of the opposite wall with oil-lit lights. A small- statured man dressed in drab clothes that were much too big for him entered without bending over. He carried a small wooden tray laden with good smelling food and drink. The presence of such fare had never graced these sickening walls before. The High Wizard bent himself in half and followed the tiny man into the deathly chamber.

"Take that waste bucket out of here... 'tis the foul creature that does plague these sorry walls." The tiny man set the tray down on a small rickety table and proceeded to carry the nasty bucket out of the cell. Once through, the man closed the tiny door behind him. A definite "clack" could be heard as he bolted the door from the outside. The noise reverberated and rolled like a crack of thunder throughout the chamber. The Wizard scrunched his nose and waved his arms in the air in a frantic motion. The cell was now scented to his liking, some sort of flowery pot-potpourri. The new smell filled every nook and cranny of the assassin's cell.

"There...that's much better...almost pleasant. Now...to the job at hand."

The High Wizard reached into his large pocket on his purple robe and retrieved a fist full of powder. Without hesitation, he threw the sparkling powder into the face of the assassin, Killgreth. The prisoner immediately regained consciousness. The chains holding the criminal at bay snapped to their lengths end.

"Whoa there big fella! I assure you that you are held fast by those links. It is one of my most famous spells."

Killgreth looked like a trapped animal.

"I only wish to converse with you at this juncture."

Killgreth calmed down somehow knowing the old man in front of him spoke the clear truth. The old man pulled a small stool from the side of the cell closer to the bed and sat down. He straightened his flowing robes out with one pass of his dry hand then pulled on his long white pointy beard to correct its path as well. With all in order and seemingly calm he began.

"Do you know...who you are?" Silence filled the room. Then a far off sound of a prisoner coughing cracked it.

"Do you know where you are?" Still no response, the Wizard waited for a few tics then proceeded on his own.

"Well! Since you're not talking, I will fill in the blanks. You are Killgreth of Delockth." The prisoner turned his head in disbelief of what he was hearing.

"You were sent to this good castle with instructions to relieve the three sisters of their young lives. The three daughters of Delockth. The Dark Lord Marideath is trying to destabilize the power structure of this great country in order to conquer its people and riches. How am I doing so far?"

The Wizard sat back with a smug look on his face. Killgreth, without saying a word sat up in his bed and placed his back against the damp wall. He pulled a leg up and rested an elbow on the knee.

"Well...how do you feel about being the Great Northern war hero and ending the lives of three innocent babies? Does this make you feel proud?"

The old man said with a hint of disdain.

"*I must admit...I am ashamed.*" His voice was low and dry for it cracked once or twice within that short admission.

"Good! Good! You're with us. For a time there I thought you were deaf."

The Wizard stood and fetched the heavily laden tray and set it on the cot beside Killgreth. With a wave and a chant, the chains which bound the big man turned into snakes and slithered away dispersing into thin air. The assassin immediately started to rub his swollen wrists. Killgreth looked into the old Wizard's eyes and spoke. "*For me?*"

The old man nodded his head in approval. Killgreth attacked the food as if it was his last meal and for all he knew it was. Food bits were flying everywhere. The old Wizard pulled his chair back hoping to remove himself from the spray. Once the prisoner was sated, he was allowed to clean himself up before he was to meet the King. The sergeant-at-arms happened to be the same size as Killgreth and set him up with some presentable clothes.

"Your Majesty ...The High Wizard and Killgreth of Delockth! The two men entered the great hallway abreast of each other. The Captain of the guards kept a wary eye on the big brute, while a full squad pulled in directly behind the two men. They both kneeled before the King sitting on his ornate throne high above all.

"*You may rise gentlemen...this is a semi-formal gathering. As you see by my staff, I am not worried for my own preservation but now you Killgreth...you have placed me in an awkward position ...to say the least. I am a merciful King and I will make a deal with you. If you will switch sides and pledge allegiance to me and our country...I will let you live. Live in peace*"

Killgreth was confused because he should have been killed on the spot, maybe even drawn and quartered. There was a ruse going on and he needed to play his part, if he wanted to live.

"I have done you and your country an incredible wrong...I was under the influence of the evil Dark Lord. The Great Wizard, Kem Maththt, has lifted me from his wicked spell and if you are granting me a chance to try to repay the great wrong that I have done...I will gladly accept your request of service. I, Killgreth, pledge allegiance to King and country of Delockth."

Killgreth placed his open hand above his beating heart and humbly bowed his head.

"High Wizard...I assume you have taken the necessary precautions to see that he is telling the truth?"

"Yes, your majesty, I have used all my best charms to, how should I say... to seal the deal."

"Good! Good." The King sat back and assumed a more relaxed posture.

"You may rise...what is your given name?"

"It is Koln, your majesty."

"You know...your father was a friend of mine and a hero in our last Great War against Marideath's father, Maxxwen of Varooth. He fought by my side and saved my young life on several occasions. I suppose that's the main reason I am giving you an opportunity to make amends."

Killgreth never said a word. He just acknowledged the King's words.

"I have discussed this with my staff at great length and we are all agreed that you need to leave for a while, the people of the country...er! Want your head on a stick. So...I am sending you away for a time. You will be sent to your father's village and take on the roll of blacksmith. You will increase my arsenal with as many swords and pikes as you can. You will have my credentials and Sir shall precede your name. I suggest you make haste; these walls have ears and I want my investment alive...for now."

The King waved and the guards opened the great doors. Then they shuffled the newly installed Sir Koln Killgreth of Delockth away. Everyone left except the honor guard and the old Wizard. "Well, old friend, we have set things in motion. I hope...we are right."

"Only time will tell your grace...only time. Why don't we check in on our little princesses?"

"What...right now?"

"Yes! Do you have a better idea?"

CHAPTER 5

The Re-Assignment

SIR KILLGRETH WAS NOT TOLD that he didn't complete his fateful mission. The King gave him an ultimatum to either follow a new master, or relinquish his life. This wasn't much of a choice, so the warrior chose without hesitation. The High Wizard placed some of his most powerful spells on Killgreth in hope of success in his transformation. The Wizard thought it best to give him a real incentive in changing, so he convinced the King to send him back to his original village of birth. The village of Athenza was Killgreth's fathers and father's before him place of birth. It was hoped that the history of a long and proud warrior family would ground the proud beast of a man.

Ψ

It was a particularly rainy spring day when Killgreth rode in on a proud warhorse given to him by the Wizard himself. The 200 plus village of Athenza was not expecting him and its inhabitants scattered like beetles from under a lifted rock. This community was no stranger to warriors, being the most famous region for swords and weapons in the country. With the recent demise of its weapons blacksmith, Killgreth was sent by the King to replace the missing link in the King's Armory. This was not a stretch for the warrior; as he had forged many weapons years back in the Dark Lord's army.

Killgreth's father was said to be the best sword maker ever to have lived in the village. It was generally known that one of his enchanted swords still sits on the King's War belt. One other was displayed above the bar in the local tavern.

The large horse and rider slowly moved into the centre of the village. All the inhabitants within sight of the stranger slammed doors and windows to cower from the scarred monster. Peace had been the order of the day for quite some time and this could be a bad omen. One brave twelve-year-old boy ran up to the tall mounted warrior with a wooden sword in hand. He spoke loudly and demanded, with his toy held proud, "Who are you then...What do you want here?"

Under his breath he whispered, "We don't know you!"

The rain never let up during this one-sided conversation. All of a sudden there was a noise to the left.

The warrior turned his attention towards the sound, ready to react. A door swung open and out stepped a lady wiping her floured hands with a cloth. Killgreth pushed his sword back into his scabbard with a definite resolving click.

"Erin! Erin! Get your skinny arse back inside right now!"

She stood on the edge of the wet porch with her hands solidly placed on her generous hips. Her hair was tousled from working but still managed to frame the face of an angel. The soft blue eyes and full red lips sent Killgreth's pulse racing. She was a breath of spring, thirty-five or more summers have graced her lovely frame and she was enchanting. Killgreth dismounted and tended to his saddlebags trying to retrieve his official papers. Kathly walked sternly over to this large man who was seemingly ignoring her presence. She pointed at the soaked lad and then pointed to the cottage she came from. He scurried off without a solitary word.

Killgreth turned with a scroll in his scarred hand. His dark red hair was plastered to half of his face and he could feel a torrent of rain traveling down the crack of his backside.

"Good day, my lady...was that your offspring I just encountered?"

"He's no mine...his mother is passed and I took him in rightly. What's your business here Sir?...Sir?"

"My business is no concern of yours. What are you, the welcoming committee?"

Killgreth towered over the woman. He had his hand on his sword and the other clutching his important document.

"Where are the village elders?"

"Why...who wants to know?

Killgreth smiled at the ferociousness of the diminutive woman. His gold tooth sparkled for all to see.

"Well, aren't you a spitfire cracker! Maybe you could tell me where a man could get some hot food. Is there a tavern with food and ale in your great town?"

"You're out of luck; the only place is under quarantine then. So you best be off."

The big man grabbed his horse's reins and started to walk deeper into the village. The boy ran out of the cottage with his sword in hand and swung it at the warrior.

"You best listen to your charge boy, before I tear you a new one."

The boy made an abrupt turn and hightailed it back into the cottage. The sun was setting and the woman standing in the rain felt kindly to the large wet beast. "Wait there! Put your horse behind the barn and wash up over there... you may eat with us... Now hurry up, me bread's going to fall and I don't have time for this nonsense."

Killgreth was tired of being wet and hungry, so he followed her directions and decided he would see where this plan would lead. Killgreth opened the front door to the sweet-smelling cottage. He lost his footing as the cottage was sunk about five hands deep. "Agile are we?"

The woman looked amused at Killgreth's poor balance recovery.

"Like a cat," Killgreth added.

"Yes...all be it a drunk one."

This exchange put a full smile on her beautiful face, and Killgreth found himself staring at Kathly. "Here, something for the meal."

He flicked a gold coin at the woman who snatched it from the air with her unused left hand. She bit on the coin without hesitation and put it in her apron pocket.

"I'll be thanking you for the donation, gold is quite rare in this village and this will help.

"Did you wash your mitts? We won't stand for unwashed mitts...now will we Erin?"

Erin understood what she was implying and scooted outside to wash up.

"It smells like nothing I've ever smelled before, what is that?"

"I am the village baker. I make bread and buns for this half of the village anyway. There is another shop...a proper shop...clear on the other side, but I was here first. So I have a good number of loyal, repeat customers."

She nodded her head motioning him to sit down at the large wooden table. He pulled out a wobbly chair and cautiously sat down. Erin flew into the cottage wiping his washed hands on his dirty wet shirt. Without turning her head or looking she yelled at Erin, "change the shirt...you know better!"

Killgreth was starting to warm up, so he dropped his guard and relaxed a bit. Kathly pushed the hair off her face with the back of an open hand and placed a wooden plate of what looked like stew in front of the big man. She then uncovered a fresh round loaf of bread. "Here ya go...it isn't much but is all we got. Would you like a bit of drink?"

Killgreth was too busy cramming the warm food down his throat to answer. Kathly took the silence for a go. She placed a mug of drink, which had a frothy head above it. Killgreth took a big swig between large gulps and burped out loud.

Kathly turned around and exclaimed, "You're welcome, mate!"

Killgreth wiped his mouth with the back of his sleeve and started to belly laugh, which caused him to belch for a second time. This made a second bout of laughter very pleasurable. "Well, I believe...that is the first time in a very long while we have heard solid laugher within these here walls."

The warrior couldn't believe he was laughing. He liked it here...a lot.

Kathly couldn't believe she was laughing; she was starting to like this hulk of a man...a lot.

After supper Killgreth explained the reason he was in the village of his fathers. Kathly informed him she had known the old blacksmith, Hargroveth, and he had been a customer and close friend. Kathly suggested that Killgreth stay the night because he would be shunned away in the night by scared villagers. He graciously accepted and was led by Erin to the upper loft in the horse barn at the back of the cottage. Killgreth said, *"Goodnight"* to Erin. All he could reply was, "I think she likes you...I've never seen her laugh before."

Killgreth lay back on a straw bed and wondered what life would be like with a good woman, a strong woman at his side.

Kathly pulled the scratchy wool blanket up on Erin and blew out his candle. She straightened up and put herself down for the night. While lying there she wondered what life would be like with a good man, a strong man at her side.

The next morning dawned a clear warm day. Killgreth stretched and headed to the jacks. He noticed Erin trying desperately to grease a wagon wheel.

"What are you doing there, lad?"

"Me chores, I need to be greasing this dark wheel here."

"Well I can tell you're having a hard time, because the grease is too thick." Kathly looked out the side window at the scene. Killgreth bent down on one knee and pulled out a small flask from his inside shirt pouch. He uncorked the lid and poured some of its contents into the grease bucket. He then grabbed the grease stick and stirred the nasty smelling concoction. "Here...now try this lad."

The boy found his job much easier and looked at the big man in wonderment. "What was in the thing?" He asked with while scratching his itchy head.

"I call it...my special sauce."

"Oh!"

Killgreth stood up and left the boy to his task.

Killgreth opened the front door to the cottage. Kathly was covered in white flour and when she turned to see who entered she created a big powder cloud. With her hand placed firmly on her hips she spoke out, "Well! What ya looking at then?"

"Well, I tell you now...you're pretty as a new born lamb, you are!"

Kathly blushed right through her powdered face. She tossed her hair back and said, "Oh! You flatterer you are, sit ye down now."

Kathly found time to make a breakfast for Koln and finish her morning's bake orders. Bread wasn't the only thing cooking in this cottage, he thought.

Later that same morning Koln changed most of his warrior clothing for clothes more like the common man. He felt it would scare the population less if he toned it down. Koln made his way into the centre of the busy village. He found the closed and boarded blacksmith shop kitty- corner from the village inn. The medium-sized blackened wood barn stood out from all others as it was the only building with no life. He cautiously pulled the boards off the front door and squeezed himself inside. The wooden window shutter he lifted squeaked and creaked as it was forced open to let in the precious morning sunlight. Once he could see better, he opened all three other portals to try to air out the dark and smelly place. Killgreth grabbed a kiln poker and made a futile attempt to jab at embers of long ago. He haphazardly threw down the poker, which made a plunk and a clink. He then climbed the rickety ladder to the living area in the barn's loft. The inspection was merely a kick and a swipe of an inch of dust and cobwebs. Koln heard a noise from downstairs and wiped his hands together to dislodge the webs. He headed back down to see who or what was there.

"A good day to you sir! And who might you be then?"

An overly dressed portly gentleman stood in the sunlit doorway holding his feathered hat in hand. Two stranger looking lads stood outside in the street and watched.

"Why don't you come in and find out good citizen. I have some official papers from our good King that surely will interest you."

The two boys stood just inside the doorway, which made Killgreth feel they were very afraid. *"Who are the lads?"* Killgreth asked.

"I am sorry, my manners...these are my sons Matth and Patth."

Killgreth nodded at the big boys and then he pulled out a rolled parchment from a leather bag he had earlier placed on a sooty table. Koln unbound the document and handed it over to the older one to research.

"Ah!" The man exclaimed. He looked back at the two young lads bobbing his head in instant approval.

"Very good...Sir Killgreth of Delockth. We have been without a blacksmith and an ear to the King for much too long. I, as self- proclaimed reeve of this shire,...I welcome you with open arms and wish you all the best of luck."

The old man threw his chest out and held on to his lapels with both hands.

"Will you be residing in this." He looked around warily. "Establishment?"

"Yes, I guess eventually. For now, I have taken refuge with Kathly, the baker woman on the edge of town."

The old man cleared his throat. "Well...yes...I see. Well, then we won't be taking any more of your time; we can see you have a lot to do. If there is anything else you be needing...my sons and I reside on the other edge of town... on Shellbark Lane."

"Well, since you offered...I could use the help of a strapping young lad as an apprentice...I am willing to pay one gold piece...a quarter season."

Matth spoke up, "Whoa! Dats lots of coin I have never seen.

Patth is into farming like me father used to be before he became reeve. But I like me ard work. I do it; I'd be pleased to be joining ya."

"Fine, there it is then ...be here tomorrow at sun up; we have a bit of cleaning to do."

The men turned and walked away leaving Killgreth alone with an overused corn broom. He took a few jabs at the biggest cobwebs and laughed to himself.

"Well, if my real mum could see me now."

The rest of his first day was consumed with taking stock and smithy plans. Later that cycle, Killgreth set himself up a workable shop. Not only did he take care of the village needs, but managed to start filling the King's orders for swords and pikes.

The spring Celebration of Renewal was the first village event that Kathly and Koln attended as a couple of interest. All the gossiping women of the village suspected something was happening, but this almost confirmed it. Kathly seemed to play down any seeming relationship for she was scared Koln wouldn't feel the same for her as she felt for him.

With no hint of being turned down, the two fell madly in love. After living atop his shop, Killgreth moved in with Kathly and gave the relationship a real chance to grow. Matth took over the shop loft and was much happier not living under his father's demanding thumb. The beginning of the fall cycle brought much prosperity to the couple. It wasn't long after that Kathly was pregnant. Never in Koln's wildest dreams did he ever expect to live long enough to have a family of his own.

It wasn't much longer after that that Koln got real sick. The village elders called in a healer from far away. The diagnosis was simple; he was poisoned with a spell that had a time delay. The healer figured out it should have happened long before, but Killgreth's size interfered with the timing and release. A normal man would have perished, for certain. The poultices were old medicine and the cost was expensive. The village people got together and helped out. Killgreth was unconscious for the duration of his sickness and didn't remember anything about the scary event. This was one of the reasons Kathly fell deeply in love with the big warrior. The caring and nurturing pulled her closer and closer to him. Koln made a full recovery thirty-four cycles later and was no worse for wear. Marideath's hold on Killgreth was severed.

The couple went forward with their nuptials. The wedding was to happen at the Thank the Harvest Day celebration in the middle of the fall cycle. After the news of the pregnancy, Koln walked to work every day with a humongous smile on his weathered face. Kathly was heard singing while she baked every morning. The wedding was an old tradition held fast by many of the surrounding counties and shires. This was to insure bountiful luck for the new couple and also to feed the whole village who usually attended every wedding. It was a most splendiferous affair. A wild beast was hunted and killed for the wedding. Erin, who was now twelve full seasons old and accompanied Koln in the hunt.

Koln was looking for any excuse to bond with the boy and this event provided the two ample opportunities.

The fire pit was extremely large. Everyone held hands and danced around the fire to some very old tunes played on strangely shaped stringed instruments. This wedding couldn't have happened at a better time. The people of the village needed the party to feel a sense of community after a long period of no weddings or other celebrations.

To everyone's surprise, the great High Wizard, Kem Maththth, attended the festivities. Not to waste any time or money, his trip coincided with the first pick-up of newly forged weapons for the King's armories. He did manage to say they were some of the best weapons he had seen in a long time. This made Killgreth very proud of his new life. After the village settled down into their pre-winter routines, Koln decided he wanted a new and bigger place for his new family. The whole village took part in the house raising and forty-three cycles later they moved into their new place. Killgreth managed to attach a separate room with a bake kiln, so Kathly had a handle on the new born when it arrived.

The winter was one of the worst in memory, but the baby's arrival at the end of spring the following year, seemed to turn the remembrance of the cold into fond memories of hearth and home. A baby boy was born to Kathly and Koln, and was named Killth after Koln's father. He was hoping to resurrect his father's lost memory through name and spirit.

Ψ

The Great Hall, castle Delockth: Korana was bouncing on the King's knee, while her two siblings were fighting over a new toy doll on the imperial designed rug directly in front of the throne. The King noticed the minor squabble and said something angrily to the pair. The two girls in full dispute ignored the express wishes of their father and continued to make argumentative noises. Korana extended her right arm and magically snatched the rag doll from the iron grip of the two sisters. Then by parting her hands, the two sisters were parted as if two unseen hands dragged them apart. The girls started to cry and Korana pursed her lips and placed her finger directly in front of them. "Ssshhhh!" was all that was heard. Then in a squeaky child's voice she said, "Play nice."

The King stopped moving his leg, turned Korana around and looked her square in the face. "Well, little one...you seem to have a grasp on things. You will surely make a very powerful ruler...yes indeed. Then he tenderly kissed her on her forehead and smiled.

The cycles rolled into seasons and seasons rolled into one another. The girls stayed true to form and took all their cues from Korana. She was given the education of a Queen, with all the country's benefits and woes taken into account. Nothing was hidden from the little future Queen. Kem had daily sessions with Korana as well. The girl's identities were strictly guarded and the most loyal attendants were chosen. However, the common folk spoke of the King and the sad fact he had no proper heir to inherit his power. The time for closely guarded secrets was fast running out.

Ψ

High in the tower of the High Wizard: "No! No! That's not what I mean." The old wizard was getting frustrated with Korana. Her character tried desperately to improve every old trick in the book.

"I know I can improve this stupid spell." She stamped her foot.

"Improving it...isn't the point dear...listening is. You need to be able to do the spell, how do I say this...the old fashioned way before you go off on a lark and create something new. Do you understand?"

Kem was clearly frustrated.

Korana put her head down and whispered *"Yes Sir...I understand."*

With that, she picked up a dart using her power, and threw it at the marked board. "There! Right in the bull's eye. Now...was that so hard?"

Korana waved her arms frantically and threw several darts so hard they pierced the board and the four-hand-thick stone wall, too. The darts followed one another in succession through the tiny hole of the first dart. Then they all flew in the open window way down the wall and landed uniformly on the silver plate on which they sat. The old wizard sat down with a thud and called Korana to sit beside him. He stroked her long blond hair and smiled. "Oh child...you do have your mother's temper don't you?"

Korana looked up at him lovingly and asked, *"You knew my mother, what was she like? I mean...I know the maid's stories and also what father told me. But what I want to really know was her person...you know, her ways."*

The old man searched for the right words.

"Well...she was as beautiful as you and she had a temper, too. She kept your poor father on his toes. She would walk through the court garden collecting flowers and singing to herself. Everyone who knew her was touched by her in some way. Of course, she had no magical powers like you. You are one of a kind."

"But...what about my sisters?

"Yes ...yes, they have powers too, but I believe they have borrowed from you during the actual birth. I believe it was a self preservation thing...oh! Never mind that." The old man stroked his long white beard.

"Your mother was a strong woman. I believe she was responsible for pushing your father to make the right battle decisions in the last Great War against the Dark. She had a knack for fighting"

Korana looked down at the floor, then up into the Wizard's eyes.

"They are coming again!"

"I know child, I know...this is why we must prepare. The old man gave the young one a comforting hug.

CHAPTER 6

Winds of change

FOUR YEARS PASSED WITH NO *connection to his former life except for the High Wizard's occasional trips to purchase weapons for the King. Koln and Kathly's family grew close and strong. Little Killth was almost five and quite large for his age. Erin, now in his middle teens, joined Matth at the foundry forging some of the Kings weapons. Koln took to Erin like a son and taught him all he knew about fighting, so one day he would be able to protect his own family. Little Killth was a handful at times for he wanted to be like his big brother Erin. He copied everything the boy did. This brought great amusement to his parents to watch the future warrior in childlike action.*

Out of the blue, on a warm summer's evening while the Killgreth family sat around an outside fire pit contemplating all that's right, six large, dark warriors rode into the village centre. They spotted the village inn and hitched their enormous horses to the outside post. The horses had been ridden hard. Sweat covered each horse while steam was released on every laborious exhale. The large men were dirty and showed the signs of long cycles in the saddle.

The thought of a cool drink made them collectively salivate. They entered the peaceful establishment with weapons on and full battle gear. The first two soldiers entered the inn as the barkeep looked up. The bartender signaled to the bus boy to come within whispering distance. He bent over, "Go get Sir Killgreth...NOW!"

The closest vacant table was near the left side of the small crowded room. Five of the soldiers sat down noisily and placed their swords on the tabletop within hands reach, boldly for all to see and fear. One of the soldiers slammed his scarred fist down on the weak table and barked out loud.

"Bar keep! Bring us some cold drink! Make damn sure it's your best ale."

The others at the table started to chuckle at the standing soldier's uncouth antics. The bar-tender was ahead of the game, for he was already on route to the table in question with a round of large mugs frothing over as he hurried across the straw-covered floor. An older woman pushed through a set of hinged doors with a steaming plate of cooked fowl legs. She unceremoniously plunked the wooden tray down in front of the surprised men.

"Well that's more like it!" One exclaimed.

Another round of laughter commenced. The largest of the soldiers, and the last one to enter the establishment, walked straight over to the bar and stuck an enormous jagged knife in the wooden top of the bar. Its ominous blade quivered from the force of its master's stab.

The bartender couldn't keep his eyes off the menacing blade as it vibrated back and forth as if it was possessed. The barkeep snapped into focus when the large in-charge soldier slammed his metal-gloved fist into the bar. Small pieces of wood flew off in every direction from the force of the blow.

"What ...What...would you like...Sir?"

The barkeep's voice struggled to find a foothold on steadiness.

"Where is the one called Killgreth?"

The eyes of the warrior were red with hate and vengeance. His breath was another terror altogether. All the noises in the inn stopped. It was as if someone froze the moment in time for their own benefit. Slowly the bartender lifted his right hand and pointed in the direction of the front door directly behind the soldier. The large soldier looked confused for a moment, and then slowly and firmly turned around to see what was behind him. Before a word left his foul mouth, a shiny jagged arrowhead pierced the warrior's throat and exited out the back of his neck. This was all the bartender saw...a sliver arrow head with bright red blood dripping from its tip. This action was so fast and stealthy that the other soldiers never broke from their gorging of food and drink.

The large man fell holding his throat. Killgreth stood in the doorway with his power bow still aimed. The soldier crashed on the table directly in his path and with that, came the dark awful noise of alarm. Two of the seated soldiers stood and immediately grabbed at their deadly swords. They were hit with a volley of arrows so fast and accurate, that they didn't have time to know what had killed them. Killgreth calmly put down his hunting bow and walked back outside into the waiting street. Three angry and terrified soldiers burst through the front door and into the street to finish off the job they were sent to do. Killgreth stood in the middle of the street with the tip of his great battle sword piercing the ground just in front of his spread feet. His hands were clasped in front of him and his breathing was slow and calculated.

The mere sight of the calm warrior stopped the three men in their tracks. The largest of the three walked three paces closer to Killgreth and stopped.

"You may not remember me, but we fought together in the great Northern Wars. I envied your skill and courage. Now you disgrace me with your reckless acts of treason and supreme failure. Now as demanded by my Lord...you will die!"

"I don't remember you... because you were a nothing and a no one. How dare you enter my village and endanger my family and people. Now you will join your friends in the next realm...if they will have you."

The soldier turned briefly and made eye contact with his remaining partners. Then he turned and raised his sword high above his head as all three rushed the Great Assassin. The front soldier cried, "You will die, traitor!"

The first man to reach Killgreth lost his head with one circular motion of Killgreth's sword he was transferred to his next life, while his head spun in the air. The next soldier attacked Killgreth and the pair exchanged heavy blows. The battle took on a slow motion ballet of death. The sound of metal on metal cracked the normally peaceful night open. The villagers watching were cowering in fear, but at the same time could not look away. The unattended soldier threw a pointed star, which buried itself deep into Killgreth's leg. With his leg damaged, Killgreth stopped playing with the soldier and thrust his deadly sword through his midsection. Killgreth's leg gave out and he fell. As he fell, his sword released itself from the soldier's stomach. Another star glanced off Killgreth's unprotected head and down the big man went.

Killgreth did not know how much time had passed. He opened his eyes and felt the pain in his head from the star's glancing blow. As his focus slowly returned, he saw what seemed to be a dream. A large warrior with his battle sword raised high above his head poised to strike him down. It all seemed to be in slow motion. He knew that someday the old adage, "live by the sword, die by the sword," would come to pass...was this the day? The moon's light was reflected in the soldier's large blade. So this is it he thought, one quick strike... Then he noticed something was wrong, the soldier's eyes widened and his mouth was agape. Killgreth had to roll immediately to one side so as not to be struck by the falling soldier.

Standing directly behind where the warrior stood was Erin holding one of the shops new pikes. It quivered back and forth covered in bright red blood. Killgreth sat up and asked demandingly, *"Boy! What have you done?"*

"I have just saved the only father I have ever known, I have. Are you angry with me, old man?" Erin dropped the bloody pike and offered Koln his hand in balance and lift.

Killgreth shook his head in amazement and took the boy's hand. He then pulled out the half-buried star and tied his kerchief around his leg to stop the bleeding. Then he noticed the soldier with the stomach wound was moaning.

"Quick! Someone help get this brute inside...I have a few questions."

Koln used Erin as a crutch and hobbled into the chaotic tavern. Three men from the on- looking crowd grabbed the soldier and hauled him inside. Someone cleared a long table with an arm swipe sending cups and plates crashing to the ground. "Ya...throw him there!" someone yelled. With one great heave, the three men tossed the warrior onto the waiting table. Killgreth, still using Erin as a human crutch, made his way to the bar. He propped himself up against it and then sent Erin home to tend to his family's safety. Koln signaled the keep for a shot of whisky. He gingerly poured it over his leg-wound then signaled for another, which he happily ingested on the spot. The mortally wounded warrior could be heard moaning from his table. Killgreth hobbled on one leg over to the dying soldier. He reached over his body and searched the man's pockets and belts for any evidence of whom or where he came from. After a few moments nothing interesting was found, so Killgreth slapped the soldier's upper chest, this woke the prisoner up fast.

"What is your name?" Nothing...no response. The wounded soldier drifted off in his mind......

Marideath Stronghold: Eagle Place (in soldier's memory) The Dark Lord was staring out his ragged window high above in the stone tower he called Eagle Place. One of Marideath's aids burst into his chambers all excited and agitated.

"My Lord! My Lord! We have news."

Marideath slowly turned with his hands still clasped behind his back. His long dark purple robe covered his feet, which gave him the appearance he was floating across the floor in a fluid motion. *"Speak up man, what the Dark is it?"*

The aid started to talk while flailing his arms about in the process.

"A trader to Delockth heard news of a family bragging about gaining lands and title for some service to the King. The trader was curious, so he poked around the taverns and a rumor surfaced that there was a child's death involved."

Marideath started to rub his pointy chin with one hand in contemplation of the mysterious events he was hearing.

"*This is not interesting news!*" Marideath proclaimed. The aid continued uninterrupted.

"Then with more travel, he actually encountered two more families with the same story."

"Now...that is interesting!" exclaimed the Dark Lord.

Marideath flipped the aid a gold coin from his leather-pouched belt and with a slight wave of his bony hand the aid scurried off without looking back. Marideath sat in his big ornate chair covered in baby goat skulls and rubies. "*Three families...how strange...coincidence? I think not!*"

He stood abruptly. "*GUARDS! Get me the Captain of the guards.*"

It wasn't long before Maxx Seneth appeared before Marideath. The Dark Lord was drinking from a skull-shaped goblet when the Captain stood before him. The dark red wine dripped from Marideath's too-white face, giving him the appearance of a bloody Halloween mask. Marideath wiped his face with his large purple sleeve and begged the Captain to stand before him.

"*Come in, my Captain...I have been following your career as of late and I have a special assignment for you.*"

The Captain bowed his head in respect and fear. "Yes! My Lord."

"I want you to choose five of your best men...you're going to..."

The soldier could hear Killgreth's voice clearer and sharper as he returned to the present.

☒

Interrogation of the wounded prisoner: Present time.

"What is your name? Where are you from...speak up!"

Killgreth's leg was throbbing and not helping him to control his anger. The prisoner's eyes opened wider and he spoke, "My...My name is...Hogthm."

"Where did you come from?" No response. Killgreth got closer to the man's head.

"Where did you come from...who sent you?"

"The...the...Dark Lord Marideath sent us."

The soldier passed out from his wound.

"*Wake him up!*" Killgreth yelled. The old lady threw a pot of dirty kitchen water on the soldier's face. The wounded man's head violently tossed from side to side reacting to the splashed water. He then reached for his gut and started to moan loudly. Killgreth leaned in real close to the soldier and asked. "*What was your mission?*"

The soldier could only moan. Killgreth pushed a finger into the man's open wound. "Ok! Okay! I'll tell ye! We were sent here…to kill you."

The soldier tried to sit up but Killgreth held his chest down. "I don't want to…die!"

"*You should have thought of that before you tried to kill me. Why did you come…because I failed my mission?*"

All the locals in the inn looked at Killgreth in disbelief.

"No! I'm not one of them…or well I was…but I'm home now. The King himself has pardoned me!"

"You were supposed to kill…" The wounded soldier was trying to say.

Killgreth spun violently and drove his waist blade into the fatally wounded soldier's heart ending his torment in an instant. Kathly was standing in the doorway to the inn and saw everything. She put both hands up to her mouth in shock, turned and ran home. Killgreth lowered his head, leaving the giant blade in the deceased's chest. He slowly walked away favoring his wounded leg. The inn doors were left swinging as Killgreth hobbled home.

The door to the cottage opened and Koln limped in. Kathly sent the kids to bed and waited with a bowl of water and a clean rag to tend the damaged leg. She looked at him standing there and pointed to Koln's big fireside chair.

"Sit ye down, warrior!"

Koln didn't say a word. He knew he had some explaining to do.

"*It was another time. It was what I was trained to do…as far as I knew…I was born on the Dark land and owed them my existence. I was wrong…but I only know that now.*"

She slapped his arm while she sat there tending his leg wound.

"How could you…I mean, they were only babies." She started to cry.

"I don't really know you!"

"*Yes, you do, I am everything you believe I am…I love you!*"

She got up and went to the bedroom crying. Killgreth turned in his chair; he winced as he stared blankly into the warm fire.

Time moved on slowly in the village. Kathly and Koln eventually learned to push the past behind them enough to carry on raising their son and guiding Erin. Then one day out of the blue, five years later, the High Wizard knocked on Killgreth's cottage door.

"Please come in, your grace."

Killgreth bowed low and long which prompted Kathly to curtsy. The old man found himself a comfortable-looking chair by the fire and rubbed his hands together. Killgreth brought him a cup of mead for his parched throat.

"What brings you,...your grace, to our fair village?"

The old man gave Koln a serious look, a look that Koln feared.

"It is time to repay your debt my son. The winds of change are all about us now and we can't afford to be unprepared."

Koln looked at Kathly with a twist of sadness on his scarred face.

"What will you ask of me and my new family?"

The King requests your presence. He will bestow on you the keeping and safety of his three daughters.

"But...but I?" Koln looked at Kathly once more, this time he was off balance and confused. A single tear rolled down from his eye.

"How could this be...I?"

The Wizard stood and turned to the fire, with his back to the couple. Erin walked into the cottage.

"Not now, son!" Koln pronounced loudly.

"It's okay...this is for all to hear," the High Wizard spoke.

The High Wizard turned towards the couple holding hands.

"You were planted as a decoy. You failed your mission. This is why you were granted a reprieve all those years ago. Now you will repay your marker. You will be the three Princesses' personal bodyguard. The King has made arrangements for your family to join you and live in the castle." Kathly looked at Koln with despair.

"When must we leave? We have commitments and we are firmly entrenched in this community."

"You must be installed in four cycles. The King is firm on this as he is worried."

The Old man walked to the door and turned when he grabbed the door latch.

"This is not a sentence my son...this is an honor."

The Wizard opened the door unceremoniously and left.

"What are we to do?" Kathly's voice clearly gave away the fear she was feeling.

"I must oblige my King. If you wish to join me...it would be an honor."

He took her hand and went down on one knee.

"I would follow you to the ends of time my love!" she said, as she looked deeply into his tear-filled eyes.

The trip wasn't long for Koln and family, but it was filled with sorrow and stress. Kathly was not even a cycle away when she was feeling the loss of Erin and previous routines and convictions. Erin had agreed to stay behind with Matth to make sure the foundry was running. The village still needed to produce weapons for the King and the King was paying handsomely. The village also needed the blacksmith to keep it moving in its daily life cycle. Little Killth seemed to be the only one thriving on this sudden move. His father gave him his own small horse and he loved the feeling of playing warrior on its back. His tiny wooden sword flashed in the sunlight amid whoops and hollers from the mighty child warrior. Once the total shock of a new life settled down, acceptance and happiness would rule the cycle.

It was a wonderful bright and sunny afternoon when the entourage entered the castle walls. The sentries notified the High Wizard who in turn singled out Korana as the official welcoming the party and their pets. The family was supposed to be introduced to the King at a supper function later that evening. The old Wizard was standing there doing his best to smile with nary-a-toot in his head, as Korana spotted Killth and his large wolfhound. The big dog noticed Korana and made a beeline for the little princess. Two of the high perched guards readied their bows as if to put down the beast before it devoured the little future Queen. The Wizard noticed the action and waved his right arm, which made the arrows turn to vines and wither away. This gave Korana enough time to hug the big dog and put everyone's mind at ease... even Killgreth.

"OH! My! What a wonderful creature. What do you call this animal? What's his designation?" Killth looked at his father as if the little girl was cuckoo. Koln just shook his head at Killth to not peruse this thought. In a small boyish tone Killth answered, "Its Killroy, Your highness. But we just call him Roy for short." Killth looked at his father for approval, but he had already dismounted and was hidden by his great steed.

Korana stopped paying attention to the beast and noticed that her hands smelled of wet fur. She turned a wrinkled nose at the problem, and then held up her hands for the old Wizard to rectify. He put a sad face on and obliged with a simple clean-all spell. "You know your highness you really need to get over this dirty hand thing you've grown into as of late. How do you expect the future Queen of Delockth to not get her hands dirty from time to time?"

The tiny princess shrugged her slender shoulders and turned her attention back to Killth who now had dismounted his own ride.

"Come here, little one." Korana ordered.

The boy marched towards the Princess with his head held high and one hand on the hilt of his play sword. He kneeled before the girl and lowered his eyes. Korana looked at Kathly and said, "You have raised him well, Madame...he should be honored to have a mother like you."

Little Killth looked up and Korana noticed a brilliant sparkle in his blue eyes. Korana spoke with authority; "*We will be watching this one...I assure you. He holds great future promise.*" Korana turned to leave and whispered to the Wizard.

"*I want this one in training as soon as you can arrange it...all training, not just fighting. There is something there that all cannot see yet.*"

She put her hand on the Wizards long purple sleeve and walked quickly from the scene. Kathly and Koln walked closer to the High Wizard and paid their respects. Then as if out of the blue, the King walked onto the courtyard steps. Several ragged looking guards followed him who looked as if they were caught by surprise when the King dashed off in a different unscripted direction.

Everyone dropped to one knee when the Royal King walked in unannounced. Even Killth was in awe. As the King drew closer, the old Wizard made an excusable exit back inside the castle. The King stood on the highest step and spoke, "You must be Killth! Such a proud name."IIHhhH fdcdedfKOKJ The little boy's mouth was wide open. "He knows my name, father!" Everyone including the King burst out laughing.

"What a dashing young man, Sir Killgreth. I am so pleased you made it here without incident. I heard about your trials and tribulations in your village...but I'm sure the tale will be different coming from the horse's mouth. Which I am sure we will request from you on some cold and boring night around a flagon of ale. Very good... now walk with me!"

The King gingerly placed his arm around Killgreth and led him towards the garden. Then remembering, he stopped briefly, turned and said, "*Oh! I am terribly sorry, my lady, my aids will look after your every needs.*"

He turned back to Killgreth and led him into the beautiful castle's garden.

"*This was my wife's favorite place,*" he said in a reminiscing tone.

The spot was indeed beautiful. The flowers possessed an illumination rarely seen in this cold and damp part of the country. The red Vulliums and purple Dafondus were spectacular. They must have absorbed a spell or three to thrive in this climate. Killgreth was mesmerized by the intensity of the floral spot. The King sat down on a hand-carved stone bench and patted the spot beside him for Koln to sit. The sun broke through a wisp of a white cloud and shone down directly on the castle and all its inhabitants.

"*There you see even the powerful sun welcomes you. It is good to see your family decided to follow you. I am sorry I had to keep you in the dark for so long about failing your mission. The sting we were playing was meant to draw Marideath out from hiding and confront us in a final battle. I can see now it is working and now I fear for my daughter's lives. The Prophesy is what's driving this next great battle against the dark. We believe Korana was meant to lead the next big war and we need her alive. I need you to swear…you will do all in your power to protect the future Queen of Delockth.*"

"I have been granted and blessed a new and improved life, even though I tried to end the Prophesy. So I will now hereby swear, I Koln of Delockth…will protect the future Queen and her siblings…against the Dark forces." Koln went to one knee and bowed his head. The King put his hand on Killgreth's head.

"*By the power I possess…you will take the position and title of High Protector and all the wealth and lands it entails. Arise! High Protector, Sir Koln Killgreth of Delockth. I believe your family awaits your new fate, Sir Killgreth.*"

"Yes, you're Majesty"

Killgreth was given two complete cycles to settle his family in their new accommodations. The living facilities in the castle were opulent. Compared to their last humble abode, this was like living in a dream. The private kitchen was the best that Kathly had ever seen. The oil-lamps for lighting filled the rooms with a feeling of perpetual daylight. Young Killth loved the inside jacks the best. The warm wooden seats and the fresh linen to wipe his nether regions, almost made him feel like a spoiled Prince. His mother was very impressed that the Princess had given permission for Killth to attend a military-type school. The extra schooling would see him to a higher-ranking position when he was older. The only reservation Koln heard from his wife was that she could bake bread ten times better than the royal bakers could. Killgreth arranged for her to prove her words and got her a job in the royal bakery as head baker. She was so happy; it looked as if her face would crack at times from smiling.

Ψ

First official visit: Koln and the Princesses.

The High Wizard's tower was awash with homemade toys and girls clothes. Upon waking up Kem had the difficult task of wading through the daily destruction and clutter, until he reached the common room, which the girls frequented.

"This unholy mess has got to stop! I can't...move freely."

The old Wizard lifted his foot towards his face while trying to extract a toy caught on his appendage.

"Please, my ladies...try to put things away after you use them."

Korana looked up from what she was doing and stared at the old man. She could tell he was frustrated beyond belief.

"I am...I mean we are quite sorry, Sir. I will try to do better...wont we girls?"

The other two sisters silently nodded. The High Wizard cleared his throat and sputtered, "Well...all right then. It's just that...I can't get around. I'm overwhelmed by your childlike hoarding. Where...did you get all this...stuff?"

"*Daddy!*" All three sounded in unison.

The old wizard put his head back as if he was looking for some tiny little thing on the ceiling. Korana stood up and bowed her head. She raised her hands above her head and the toys and clothes started to rise into the air. Then the debris started to swirl and twist as if it were caught in some sort of invisible cyclonic action. Korana's two sisters played with their toys as if nothing special was happening. After several complete revolutions, the toys were flung with a mystical centrifugal force. They all landed in the right spots on hooks and open cubicles, which lined one complete wall. The Wizard's mouth was open, while he tried to figure out how she was accomplishing this impressive feat. When all the wee bits were back in place the old man spoke. "When did you...How did you? My sweet girl, you've really outdone yourself. Your father will be so pleased...yes indeed."

The smiling girl looked the old man straight in the eye and asked, *"Are you happy too, Master?"* The old Wizard put his weathered hand on her head. "Oh, yes child...you will be a very powerful Queen someday."

"Oh goody, can I play now?"

"No not yet...for today is a special day. You and your sisters will be introduced to your new...how should I say this...life protector. Now all of you come here...stand right here. Presta straighten your dress and hair please, you look like something a catlor dragged in."

The three sisters stood abreast waiting for their guest to arrive. The High Wizard turned around with a wave and pushed open the great circular wooden door. Through the portal walked Killgreth in full battle regalia. The girls were very impressed with all the shiny weapons and leather. Presta couldn't take her eyes off his knee-high riding boots. Korrin noticed his hurt leg and whispered to Presta. Killgreth drew his sword in military greeting fashion. Two of the sisters stepped back while Korana took a step forward and curtsied in respect. When Killgreth saw this, he lowered his mighty sword and kneeled before his future Queen. The extremely large man bowed very low and respectfully. His whitening beard made him look like a toy bear, Korrin thought. When he bowed, his sword hilt caught the old Wizard between the legs, which made the girls laugh and the old man wince.

"I am your servant, Sir Koln Killgreth of Delockth."

Korana took another step forward and addressed the half-folded warrior.

"Have met briefly before?

Killgreth stood and held out a hand towards the princess.

"No, I don't believe so my lady."

"Have you been a bad boy?"

"Korana! That's not polite!" Kem was short with the learning Queen. Koln put a hand up to the Wizard.

"It's quite alright." He turned back to face the little Queen.

"Yes, I'm sure you heard of my ill deed and I am truly sorry. My direction in life was false. Your father has seen need to forgive me...in time...I hope you will do the same." Killgreth bowed once more. Korana boldly walked straight up to the large man and placed her tiny hand on his bare head. She closed her eyes and concentrated. A small glow formed between her tiny hand and his greasy head.

The Wizard looked worried not knowing what she would do. After several ticks, she released her hand and stepped back a few paces.

"I believe you, Sir Killgreth of Delockth, and I do believe...we will be much safer in your presence than not."

Killgreth looked at the Wizard, "what just happened?"

The Wizard exhaled a full bellow of air and shook his head. "We know not of her total powers, for all you and I know she might be able to read minds, or implant desires and wishes into people's minds." The old man shrugged his frail shoulders.

"If she feels safe with you, then you passed the test...that's all I know. I have been helping her in many different fields and mind reading is one. I've seen her read a servant's mind from several measures away...very impressive."

Killgreth nodded his head in agreement.

"So how did you know…I wasn't a sleeper…waiting just for the right time to fulfill my dark duty?" He asked the Wizard.

"I read minds too, just not as well as my little Queen here."

The girls were starting to look impatient, so the Wizard ended the introduction.

"Excuse me! Sir Killgreth, was that your boy with the enchanting eyes I saw earlier?"

"Yes, my lady...he goes by the name Killth. His friends call him Kill."

"We are highly amused."

With that said, all three girls ran off giggling and acting their age.

The two men in the room smiled at each other.

"Do the other sisters have any powers I should know of?"

"Korrin, the one with the white dress can heal by touch. Her sister Presta can disappear for up to ten intervals, if she holds your hand you will become invisible too, but the time in which this phenomenon occurs diminishes."

"Korrin can heal...my word...that's a gift."

"There is a problem we have encountered though; whatever the affliction the wounded has, in transference becomes hers. She might one day be able to restore life itself, but we believe at the cost of her own."

"What of the strong one then, she seems to be dominant?"

The High Wizard called Korana back from the toy shelf and asked Koln to stand firm. "My dear would you oblige Sir Killgreth with a demonstration?"

"Yes, Sir."

57

"Brace yourself my boy for a push."

Koln looked amused himself. The little girl held out her right hand palm out, fingers up, and lowered her head. Without sound or warning, Killgreth flew through the room backwards as if a great, unseen wind picked him up and tossed him like a stuffed doll. Killgreth slammed into the main door to the chamber with a solid boom. He immediately slid down the door to rest on his rear laughing out loud.

"That was spectacular! Well I've never seen…I mean wow! How hard did you push, on a scale of one- ten?" The large man picked himself up and dusted of his uniform. The little girl put a finger to her lips and contemplated the question.

"Hhmmm! One! Yes…definitely a one."

"Maybe one day…you can protect me, your grace?"

"Maybe one day she will protect us all," said the old man.

"That will be enough, my dear. Now gather your sisters, it's time for your lunch."

The High Wizard pulled the warrior aside hopefully out of earshot. "You understand, Sir Killgreth, this is a secret weapon."

"Yes! Yes! I truly understand."

"This could be the thing that tips the next war in our balance some day."

"She is so young to have such a talent."

"We have never in our existence seen anything like this, but the Prophesy seems to be guiding her."

"Are you sure she needs my help…I mean?"

"This coming conflict, Good against Dark, will be fought on two fronts, magic and old fashion sword-in-your-face. She…I mean they, will need an experienced warrior at their backs. Marideath is almost ready to make his play and the girls won't have much time left to hone their skills. We are certain he will try to eliminate the girls at all cost and try to destabilize the King's power in the country."

"I understand when you put it that way."

"How long before you think the Dark Lord might strike?" asked the High Wizard.

"Well, when I left the Dark realm not so long ago. All his ships were all rotten and his man numbers extremely low. The food situation was in ruins. If he builds an army, he will need to feed them, and then most of the lumber for new ships has to be imported. It could be quite a while before he is truly ready. It seems like a lot of time, but it actually isn't. How close are we to being ready to receive the Dark Lord.?"

"By all estimates we could be four complete seasons away."

Killgreth bent down and picked up a toy doll and shook it about.

"So what's the game plan now, Sir Wizard?"

"My name is Kem. Feel free to call me by my given name. Now we begin the girl's training. I will see to the Wizardly skills and you will give formal instruction to the military end of things, fighting, strategy and such."

Killgreth placed the doll on a table and followed the old man into the common area where the girls were engaged in a full-blown food fight.

CHAPTER 7

The Education of a Queen

SPRING WAS TRENDING WARM THIS cycle with an extra radiant sun. Two complete full seasons had passed and the girls we coming along well in their training. The princesses having just turned eight were ready for the equestrian part of their ongoing education. Kill was excelling at his training and was actually allowed to instruct other young people his age. The King took a special liking to the boy and treated him as if he was his own. This bothered Kathly a bit, but she let it pass because Kill appreciated the extra attention, especially from the King himself. Presta was having a hard time relating to the sheer size of her horse, but Korrin rode like a veteran of two wars. Korana's ability to see into the mind of whomever she touched grew by leaps and bounds. Connecting with her animal was on a different plane never before seen. Korana tried to help Presta, but ....Presta wanted to get this on her own and stubbornly worked out some kind of controlling influence with her horse.

It was on the thirteenth day of spring when Killgreth took the three princesses out for their first fox hunt. The first fox to be spotted eluded the hunters and disappeared as if by magic. The second fox was a large red fox and seemed to enjoy being hunted. Killgreth led the chase and all three girls followed in succession. Even Roy the dog managed to keep up somehow. His long gangly strides were almost comical to watch. Korana came from the back and managed to speed ahead of the pack. Her horse was running as if its life depended on it and depending on what Korana told the horse, it probably thought it did. Korana rode like the wind. Her horse followed the fox closely and chose dangerous paths that normally riders went around. Korana, confronted with a large fallen tree decided to jump the dead wood instead of circling around. Killgreth followed suit not wanting to be out maneuvered by a child. Presta wasn't ready for such a feat and her horse stopped suddenly to avoid a hard jump. Presta was airborne for a good ninety-five hands long. She came down hard and rolled inhumanly. Korrin managed a full stop and ran over to Presta. It wasn't long before the whole party was at her side; even Roy gave her tearful face a lick. Killgreth stood slightly back and watched the surrounding area. *"Oh, my angel, are you all right?"* Korana lifted the fallen girl's head and poured some fresh water from the skin flask that was around her chest. Presta responded to the cool liquid and opened her eyes. "Oh, sister! It hurts so." Korana could clearly see the bone jutting out of the sleeve on her tiny arm.

"I know sweetie...I can feel your pain."

Presta sat up with some assistance from Korrin. Korrin looked at Korana and Killgreth, and then she turned her attention to her fallen sister.

"May I try and help you?" Korrin asked. Presta nodded her head.

"You must not take this on yourself sister." Korana was worried about the residual effects of Korrin's healing technique.

"It's all right ...I won't go all the way...don't worry."

Korrin rubbed her hands together rapidly then placed them over the damaged area. After a few ticks the area between her hands started to glow a brilliant red. Then slowly turned to yellow, and then settled on a powder blue. Presta moved her arm in several different ways and was happy for the regained mobility. Korrin's head dropped with the assumed pain and slumped to one side. Killgreth expected something to happen, so he leaned in and laid Korrin down. The pain on Korrin's face told the whole story.

"You are very brave, but you went too far. I will have to ask uncle to help you ward off the pain. I will help you for now," Korana said.

Korana put her hands on Korrin's head. The color came back into Korrin's face as the pain was blocked by her sister's will power. "Thank you, Korana... that feels better."

"It's time you two girls went home." Killgreth commanded the two guards that followed them to see the two princesses back to the castle and tend to the wounds. Korana wanted to finish what she had started, so Koln and she tried to pick up on the fox's scent.

The two were side by side with the afternoon sun beating down on them. Their horses were appreciating the slower trot they assumed and would toss their heads from time to time to show their appreciation. The hillside was green with all kinds of wild colorful flowers everywhere. Killgreth leaned over and scooped a large red and white flower for Korana.

"For me! Oh, it is beautiful...thank you." She hungrily put it to her nose and inhaled the pungent nectar.

"Ah! Marydays...my favorite flower, how did you know?"

"I read your mind."

They both started to laugh. *"How clever you are."*

"So...Korrin's magic is very special. What a great power to be able to heal."

"Yes, but at a terrible expense. Sometimes I worry about her."

"What is your expense my lady?"

"Well, I've never told anyone before...but I get headaches...terrible headaches from moving objects, especially the large heavy ones."

"Why haven't you told anyone about this?

"Its...it's because they expect so much from me, I can't let them down. What about you, Sir Killgreth? What's keeping you from your original Dark programming?"

"Family...true family. I never thought I would be alive to have one. My son and my wife mean the world to me. If the Dark Lord needs to be destroyed to keep them safe, then I will choke the life out of him myself...with these bare hands. Listen your highness...I am enjoying our talk, but I am feeling uneasy here and having the three of you separated like this is dangerous. You know your military teachings, divide and conquer. We must be making our way back now."

"Very good, Sir Killgreth...I concur and also I am feeling a bit of the chafe from this grating saddle. Killgreth snickered a bit as he wheeled his horse around in the direction of the castle. The little princess made a difficult barrel turn and bolted off in the same direction. Her horsemanship was excellent and Killgreth had to use all his skills to keep up with the little fireball.

As the pair neared the castle, Killgreth noticed that something was amiss. The tower guards were doubled and the infantry was beginning to mobilize. The obvious abnormality to everyday castle life was that the Captain of the guards was waiting for the couple outside the closed main gate on his battle horse. As the couple crossed the drawbridge, the Captain met then half way.

"What's going on Captain...did a war start whilst we were away?"

Killgreth was struggling with his steed to settle down. The run back to the castle pumped the horse up for action. "Whoa! Big fella!"

"Is everything all right?" Korana begged to know.

"Princess your father our King has taken ill. The physician requests your presence right away.

Your two sisters are already there."

Killgreth asked, "Is he all right?"

"We do not know...the doctor isn't saying much. I felt it prudent to place the army on battle-ready stations just in case any party might think we are weak."

"Very good, Captain, I will stay with my charge...if you should need me, you know where I am."

"Open the main door!" the Captain yelled.

A pair of disoriented soldiers looked over the gate wall to verify the petitioners. *"Open the gate!"* a muffled voice was heard from behind the great door. The main door protested with its squeaking and groaning as it lifted. Once the horses could clear, both riders ducked under the bottom and made strait for the main steps leading into the grand foyer. Korana didn't bother to tether her horse. She dismounted like a traveling circus rider from the rear of the animal and ran into the castle. Killgreth wasn't far behind. He did think to himself that he might be getting too old for all this running. When the winded girl ran past the King's personal guards, she skidded into the room and saw a somber scene. Her two sisters flanked their father while the High Wizard stood back and watched. Korana stood motionless at the foot of her father's great four-poster bed. The exiting physician stopped briefly to place his warm hand on the princess's small shoulder. She looked at him with big watery eyes as he swayed his head in a negative motion. Korana looked back at the scene taking place on the bed and wiped her eyes with her sleeve. She slowly walked around to the left side of the bed and stroked Korrin's hair. Korrin turned to Korana and said, "I want to heal daddy...but the Wizard won't let me. He says it's too dangerous...but I don't care."

Korana looked into her eyes and softly spoke. *"We need to be strong now sweetheart...I don't believe this is what you were meant to do with your gift. Daddy is naturally near the end of his time here and our time has arrived. I need the two of you strong to keep all of us safe. I can't do this alone."*

Korana leaned in closer and placed her right hand on the King's clammy head and heard:

"I am sorry to be leaving you little one. You need to be strong for your sisters and your country. I truly wish I could have seen you grow up to be the beautiful woman you will be. Your dear mother would have been so proud of you. I didn't want to leave such a big responsibility on such young shoulders. I have entrusted the High Wizard to raise you and with Killgreth at your side, I will rest more comfortably. I love you all..."

And with that Korana released her hand from her father's head. The good King never regained consciousness and slowly fell from one world to another.

Long live the Queen!

Ψ

Spring Time should have been a happy time for the people of Delockth. The Royal funeral and the transference of power to a Queen, whom they thought had been murdered, put a bad taste in their mouths, which they couldn't rinse away. This killed the virtual essence of spring. The thought of impending war also pushed the good people to the edge of tolerance for their new monarch. Korana had been the first out of her mother's womb and thus was the rightful heir to the Throne. No one physically opposed her rightful place or authority. Her two sisters never wished for the seat of power and were happy with their sister's ascension. Spring turned to summer, which begot fall. As fall turned to winter, the people seemed to accept the strange turn of events, which led to Queen Korana's Reign.

Four complete full cycles had passed and the fear of war was on the good Queen's doorstep. The sisters grew up to be beautiful and Korana's power grew immensely stronger. Day after day, the good Queen practiced her special skills.

"Now put the boulder down your majesty," demanded the great Wizard.

The Queen set the boulder down and placed her hands on her tender hips.

"*This isn't fun...it's all too easy! It's just child's play!*" yelled the Queen Korana.

"Well the last time I looked, you were a child your Grace. Thirteen does make you still a child."

"See here... I'm not a child...I am a Queen."

"Yes! Yes! Well then if you're a Queen, then do something Queenly."

The old Wizard was thoroughly amused with the little Queen's temper. Korana chose the largest boulder she could find, approximately the size of a small cottage and threw it clear out of sight. The Wizard's face reflected astonishment mixed with disapproval. Korana grabbed her head knowing that a headache would soon follow.

"I hope you're pleased with yourself, young lady. While I am impressed with your strength, I am not so pleased with your judgment and your aim leaves a little to be desired. That small hill you just heaved, landed somewhere near the village of Heepth."

All the Queen could do was gasp. She quickly kneeled down and put her hand on the fresh earth. *"No! I feel no adverse effects. I missed the village by a hectare of land."*

She sat down abruptly and grabbed her aching head. *"I am so sorry!"*

"No need to apologize child, you must control your temper. No harm, no foul. I am curious...could you be accurate if you concentrated?" She looked up at the old man. *"I think I can. Can I try again?"*

"Only if your head is better."

"It is."

The Wizard found a very large outcrop of boulders over the next hill and set his sights on the largest of the lot. "Ok, my love,...take that one there and throw it at the old dockyard at the beach."

"But...that's over fifteen measures away. I can barely see it from here."

"I know, I just need to know your limitations, sweetheart."

"Ok, Sir...I will try."

Korana lowered her head then rolled it from side to side as if she was trying to relieve a sore neck muscle. Slowly both hands stretched upward. Her fingers started to wiggle furiously and then she directed her mental energy at the very large boulder. It struggled trying to free itself from the wanting ground. The very earth beneath their feet began to vibrate. Then with a jolt, the boulder relieved itself and flew like a missile towards the direction of the bay. Tumbling and turning...dropping pieces of small rock that were attached by dirt from its gray sides. Korana lifted her head in order to aim the boulder. She dropped her left hand and the huge boulder started its decent. Then like a whip, she dropped her right hand just as the boulder dropped directly on the old dilapidated boathouse on the beach. The old structure exploded into a thousand pieces as the boulder skipped gaily across the water a good three times before settling down in its new home at the bottom of the bay.

"Remarkable! Simply remarkable," was all the High Wizard could say while clapping his weathered hands together.

"Nothing in the Prophesy declared that the heir to the throne would have such powers." The realization of what the High Wizard just said made the little Queen blush.

Ψ

3rd. Day of harvest, (Middle of fall) Castle garden:
"Well, you do have a way with flowers, don't you, Korrin?"

Korana pulled a fresh red rose off a bush that was almost seven hands high. She lifted it to her slender nose and breathed deeply.

"Ahhh!" I can't believe you managed this fine bush so late in the growing season. What is your secret, sister?"

"It seems to be a part of my very make up, dear sister. What I touch I heal, what I touch I grow. I'm quite used to it now and I never give it a second thought."

"It still makes me wish I could heal, instead of throwing damn stones."

"Oh don't you fret, big sister, for I am sure someday you will take that wish back. OH! Here comes Presta now."

"Oh, good! We shall all have hot cinnamon tea. Milonth,....will you be so kind and have some hot tea brought round for me and my sisters...thank you, my dear... oh! And make that cinnamon, please, that's a good girl."

The three sisters enjoyed their surprise garden party. They sat on a beautiful family quilt and drank their tea and boskets. They held hands and laughed and sang songs, which reminded them of their dearly departed parents. Being triplets connected them in many unexplained ways. Time flew by on a gorgeous afternoon. Presta looked over Korana's back and noticed the Captain of the guards running towards them, clearly knocked for six and out of wind. She pointed to him and indicated how handsome he was all flushed and red.

The other girls turned to look. Korana instinctively knew something was afoot. She stood suddenly and struck a Queenly pose of authority. The Captain removed his helmet before he arrived.

"You're Majesty! You're Majesty!" He bowed respectfully.

"There is a situation that needs your urgent attention."

"What is it, good Captain?"

Presta couldn't help but blush three shades of red when the Captain noticed her craning her slender neck for a better look at him. She giggled a bit then whispered something to her ever curious sister.

"There is a Black ship off in the distance and it is headed for our port. It is a four-master, Black Warship your grace.

"Just one ship, good Captain...I don't see..."

"Excuse me your Grace; it is one of The Dark Lord's flagships." He looked forlorn as if all was lost.

"But it's still only one ship, Captain. Why don't you send a ship out to intercept the darn thing...if you're so worried?"

"It could be seen as an aggressive act on our part to..."

"Nonsense!" She lifted her voice to a commanding pitch.

"Find Killgreth and send him to me...right now!"

She clapped her hands twice to make a statement. The Captain ran off in the direction whence he came.

Only moments passed and Killgreth arrived at the spoiled tea party.

"Ah! Sir Killgreth...can you shed some light on this dreadful subject."

"I met the Captain in the court yard and he is right my Queen. We must wait to see what their intentions are before we show even the slightest interest in their obvious presence."

"How long before the clearly unwanted quests arrive?"

Killgreth looked at the wind and weather conditions more closely. "I should say four or five bells your majesty."

"Well, that's close to supper and sunset ...that should make for an interesting disadvantage. Wouldn't you say? Very well then, Sir, I will heed your fine as ever advice and do keep us informed. And if you should need us...we will be taking our afternoon stroll in the village."

"Be sure to take the palace guards, your Grace, these are perilous times."

"Yes! Yes! I will do as my protector requests...good aft to you...Sir Killgreth." Killgreth executed a quick bow and raced off to find the Captain.

The Captain was at his command post hovering over the charts of the harbor. Killgreth bounded into the room.

"Well...what do you think they want?" Killgreth asked.

"I don't know, but they have had enough time to sufficiently prepare for an invasion."

"Well...normally the first thing you send are scouts...am I right?"

"Yes, but you don't do this in broad daylight...unless you plan to make an ultimatum or use this ship as a smoke screen for something else. Don't forget

Sir Killgreth, Marideath is a black Wizard of measurable strength. I think we need to be very vigilant on that beachfront. What say you, sir?"

"I agree we need a beachfront. Even if it's just to greet and find out what they want."

"Agreed!"

Ψ

The Queen stirs the pot:
"How long before landfall, Captain Vargas?"

The Dark Wizard, Seth of Andress was getting impatient with the two-week voyage. He longed for solid ground to plant his feet on. His old stomach hadn't been the same since they set sail. The Captain looked into the sky. "Four or five bells Sir."

"Four or five bells? In the name of all that's ungood, why is there no wind?"

The Dark Wizard walked the length of the ship with his hands clasped behind his back. All the men stayed clear of the Wizard, for he was known to practice new spells on unsuspecting crew, which led to their extinction. In the fourteen-day voyage, three crew members vanished off the roster. The evil one eventually stood on the bow section and cast a watchful eye on the distant but nearing shore. The Lieutenant of the soldiers that traveled with the Wizard stood beside the old man and spoke soundly.

"Do you expect much resistance...., my Lord?"

The Dark Wizard looked down on the soldier and answered.

"I am not your Lord,... Lieutenant."

"Sorry Sir."

He paused then answered nonchalantly, while twirling one hand.

"Yes, I expect they will test our abilities and intentions," he said with a large exhale.

"Do you mean…your magical abilities, Sir?"

"I suppose."

3 cycles later:
Behind the two men conversing, the ship's Captain shouted out fresh orders to secure forward sails. The Dark Wizard turned without warning and disappeared in a puff of black sooty smoke. The Lieutenant under his breath said, "Hmmm! Impressive indeed."

The Black Warship Icaria dropped anchor in the bay of Sails, Port of Delockth. The ship was no more than a short rowing distance from the King's beach. The top of one of the towers could be seen with a spyglass from the main crow's-nest aboard the Icaria.

Ψ

Above King's Beach:
Korana could see the big black ship anchored in the Bay of Sails. It was much too close for her liking, just a short row from the vessel to the King's beach. The Wizard and Presta were beside Korana on the grassy hill watching and waiting for any important movement. The cooler fall sun was not more than an hour from setting into the great bay. The season of fall was being true to itself and its nature. Korana was starting to cool down, so she pulled her sweater over her slender shoulders.

"It won't be long now before we know." Korana interjected into a quiet reflective moment.

"Know what sister?" said Presta.

"What they are actually here for. I am assuming it's no good."

"I don't feel Marideath's ominous presence, if that relaxes you any... my Queen."

The High Wizard put his hands in the air as if he was being arrested.

"But I do feel a dark presence emanating from that direction."

The old man pointed to the bay area. The five-man Queen's personal guard lit a fire to warm up the trio of dignitaries. The dancing flames crackled and popped casting unusual shadows like night creatures and dark things. Korana put her arm around Presta for some extra comfort and care.

Ψ

On The Black Ship Icaria:
The Dark Wizard, Seth of Andress, demanded the Captain's presence. The Captain carefully knocked on the Evil Wizard's cabin door, in the bowels of the black ship. The door opened on its own power with a formidable creak. This wearing noise didn't ease the Captains tension in the least. The Wizard's voice was low and deep, resounding and rattled with portentous overtones. *"Come in, Captain!"*

The smell of the room robbed the Captain of any oxygen he had left in his weak lungs. The whole area was redolent with sage and rotten cabbage. The blend made the Captain's stomach do cartwheels like an un-trained circus performer.

"What's wrong, my green skinned Captain? Do ye not be fond of the scent of magic?"

The Wizard's voice reached out from the darkest corner of the room.

"Well I...Well I don't want to intrude, Sir, but did you request my presence?"

"Yes, I did!"

The old Wizard approached the Captain from the shadows. The closer he got the more tension the ship's Captain felt.

"Yes, I did...We arrived late thanks to you, and now we must sit here like a stupid water fowl bobbing to and fro, waiting for dawn to make a play."

"But...I!" The old man's face was now a hand away from the Captain's. It was weathered and sagging. The Dark moles that grew from the man's nose told tales of tormenting woes and ageless fears. The scared Captain stopped breathing, for the fowl stench he thought was the room was the Wizard's rotten teeth. The Wizard turned and shuffled back a few paces to his favorite seat.

"Your incompetence is a little hard to digest. Let me put it in a way you might appreciate. If I didn't need you to get this stinking ship back whence we came, I would split you in two with merely a thought."

The Captain stood silent for he did not know what to say. The Dark Wizard stood once more. "I am going to send one man to shore in the darkness of night, to see what he can see. Make sure he is a good swimmer and can be trusted to do my bidding. Dress this man in black and send him to me...at once! Now Go! Before I change my mind and turn you into fish food."

The Captain high-tailed it out of the putrid-smelling room.

No more than ten tics later, there came a light rap on the Dark Wizard's cabin door. A muffled, "Enter," was heard through the wooden door. A young lad of no more than sixteen full season cycles appeared before the scary old man. He was dressed in black deck clothes and had black pitch rubbed into his face.

"You wish to see me, my Lord?"

"Arrgh! I'm not your lord, and yes you may be the one I need."

The young man immediately noticed the foul taint to the cabin's air. He wrinkled his nose in hopes of blocking the stench. The old man looked closer, squinting his wrinkly eyes.

"You seem to be quite young. Can you swim boy?"

"Yes sir...I am the ships fetcher." The boy spoke his position on the ship with a slight tone of pride.

"Fetcher?" The Wizard cocked his head.

"Yes sir...I fetch things that have blown or dropped mistakenly over side... sir. You know like wood or barrels, and oh ya...men who lose their balance and do what we call, the big splash." The Wizard knew he was referring to his careless spells that constantly were chucking innocent men overboard.

The Wizard cleared his dry throat. "Well then,...here is what I request of you lad. You will swim ashore under the cover of darkness and assess the Delockth strength. Take your time as not to be found and report back to me personally. You have four cycles to complete this mission. If you do this for me...I will see you have favor with the Dark Lord. NOW GO!"

As the boy turned to leave, the old man shouted. "Wait! I have a gift for you."

The Wizard waved his hands and chanted a spell. "There ...that will keep you warm on your swim. It won't last more than four cycles, so be on time."

The Wizard stroked his wisp of a beard and produced a powder that he blew directly into the young lad's face. The boy began to sneeze uncontrollably. When the boy stopped, he tried to ask what that was for, but nothing left his flapping lips. "That was a silent dust...if you are caught and tortured for information you will be mute. That will be all...now get your ass out of here!" The old man pointed to the self-opened door. The boy ran out of the Wizard's smelly room.

It wasn't more than a few measures before the boy found himself in the water swimming for the shores of Delockth. The moonlight was the only thing that gave him direction and the Wizard's spell was the only thing that kept him warm.

Ψ

Above King's beach: Perched on a hill overlooking the bay of Sails.

Korana had a few measures left before she was to meet the High Wizard and the Captain of the guards. She pulled her shawl neatly over her white shoulders and strolled down the path toward the beach's shore. The full moon was playing hide and go seek with the shadows, but burned bright when the clouds parted. The cold waves lapped at the shore and the smell of dead fishy things wafted through the air and stung the nose. She found the shore air too brisk for her liking and decided to turn back to the warm fire on the hill. Then with no warning, she saw a figure rise out of the water a short distance away. Korana went to her knees in the sand so as not to be noticed. She kept very quiet and still for she knew not what was happening. She instinctively wanted to scream and sound an alarm, but she was off-guard and scared.

The dark figure had a small frame as if it were a child. The moon jutted out from behind a cloud and Korana could see with more detail that it was a slender young male. He walked upon the water's edge and tried to relieve himself of some of the excess water and seaweed that shared his clothing. She instinctively knew that this boy was no real threat, and possibly was a forward scout for the anchored Black ship. She waited as he passed by her. At two hundred hands away, he was far enough to move from her position, and thus make her way quickly up the side hill towards her people and that warm fire. The single intruder carefully made his way along the path moving from shadow to shadow in hopes of staying invisible. He quickly stopped when he saw a glimpse of firelight atop a grassy cliff to his left. He wanted to know who was there, so he crept closer being very careful not to make any unnatural sounds. He belly crawled up to a grassy knoll and parted the vegetation to take a better look. Just as his focus was adjusting to the firelight, his body was jerked into the air and hovered a good hundred hands up. He didn't make a sound because his voice box wasn't working. The firelight lit up the portions of the boy's face that were not covered in black pitch. One of the guards finally noticed the suspended boy and brought it to the attention of the others present. As all eyes were trained on the boy kite, three blackened figures emerged from the cold bay water. The noise of the young boy's capture blanketed the disturbed water sounds the three special assassins couldn't help but make.

"What in the good Lords! Well, I've never seen..." Korana stepped out from behind the vegetation with one arm in the air controlling the boy like a human kite.

"Are you all right your majesty?"

Korana looked excited, "*Look...Look what I caught!*"

A soldier ran to her position with his sword held at the ready.

"Excuse me, your Majesty, what do you wish to do with the...flying boy?"

Korana twirled the boy around so as to look at all sides of him.

"*He does appear to be unarmed.*" She exclaimed happily.

"*My Queen...he does appear to be soaking wet. He was either swimming or he's from that damned ship.*"

"*I will have you take him to the castle's lower cells and have two guards stationed at the door.*" Korana happily dropped the young boy on his head. With the spell still intact, the boy made no sound except for escaping air from his bellowed lungs. Two guards grabbed the young man by the arms and escorted him away with his feet dragging. Korana turned and looked out to the sea; she felt a cold presence run through her.

She briskly rubbed her arms and moved closer to the dancing fire. Two of her personal guards kept a much closer proximity to the Queen. Killgreth ran into the scene from the castle with all his armament clacking and clinking.

"*Your Highness, what are you doing out here, and why wasn't I informed of your little excursion?*"

"*I am sorry, Sir Killgreth, I didn't think...I*"

"*That's right you didn't think...your majesty. It is my job...my duty to keep you safe. There could be a possible threat to your very person. Please your Highness keep me informed in the future.*

"*I am sorry, Killgreth...it was foolish of me.*"

She fell into his arms for a warm comforting embrace. He paused then pushed her gently away.

"*Are you all right, your Majesty?*"

"*Yes! And I caught a boy.*" She said excitedly.

"*A handsome one too...fresh out of the water, presumably from that Black ship in our bay.*"

"*He is most likely a forward scout for the uninvited guests.*"

Killgreth looked to the ship in the bay and felt a cold chill travel through him. "*We need to get you and your sister back inside.*" Killgreth posted a patrol on the beach itself and doubled the path guard. He then escorted the Queen to the prisoner's cell.

Ψ

Castle Delockth: Lower dungeon, cell four. The High Wizard and the Captain of the guards were waiting outside the captured boy's cell when Korana and Sir Killgreth arrived. Killgreth immediately pulled the Captain aside. "*Do you know what's going on here?*"

"We think this boy might just be a scout for whatever, or should I say… whoever is on that Black ship. It could be the Dark Lord himself on that evil vessel."

"I don't believe it's him." Killgreth added.

"He always likes to make a grand entrance in whatever he is doing. This seems too small for his big head. It could be a test of our strength and resolve for self-preservation."

"What are you saying?" The Captain leaned against a cold stone wall.

"I'm saying…this is just a test. It is his ship, but I believe it might just be his Dark Wizard, like in chess…Knight for a knight."

"And the boy?"

"A mere pawn, a forward scout and not a diversion. If we are challenged, it will be face on." Killgreth made his point with his armored finger in the air. The two men turned back to the Queen and the old Wizard.

Killgreth spoke. "The Captain and I believe this young boy is a pawn sent to find out our strengths and weaknesses. He is not a key player in this scenario. If I do this right…he might be able to tell us the information we need about the mysterious appearance of the Black ship."

"You're not going to torture the boy are you?"

The Queen asked in nervous tone.

"No! Your Majesty…he is merely a child…but I have my ways."

With that said, Killgreth signaled the cell attendant to open the cell door. Killgreth smiled out the corner of his mouth for this was the very same cell he was brought to a while back. The cell door gave its usual groan as the guard pushed on its face. The boy sat up with a start and put his back to the wall while sitting on his nasty cot. All four walked into the room.

Korana made a face as the pungent smell hit her olfactory nerves.

"My Queen, you don't need to be here." Killgreth said.

The High Wizard noticed the Queen's reaction and quickly waved his old hands and the scent of wild flowers took over the room. Even Killgreth turned to the Wizard and said, "You know…I believe that is one of your best spells."

The good Captain also looked relieved.

"How is his condition?" Killgreth asked.

"No worse for wear as I can see. He doesn't even look cold and this room is damp…and he is still wet."

Korana left and fetched a scratchy blanket, which she tenderly draped over the boy's wet legs. He looked at her as if he saw an angel.

The Wizard leaned in. "I believe he has a warm spell on him. There is no need to worry your majesty; I don't believe he is cold. It was possibly attached so he could make the very cold swim."

The Captain went to make the first move, but Killgreth put his strong arm across his armored chest.

"I got this." The Captain nodded and graciously stepped back.

"What do you have to say for yourself, lad?"

The boy started to mouth words in desperation but nothing emanated from the flapping lips. The Wizard leaned forward again and added, "He has a gag spell attached as well. I guess it is so he can't do what you apparently want him to do."

The Captain asked out loud, "Can you reverse this spell, or whatever you call it?"

The old man thought hard for a moment then reached into a bag that was slung over his shoulder. He then pulled out a small cloth sac and emptied its powdery substance into the palm of his open hand. He slowly walked closer to the boy so as not to disturb the fine powder, and then he unceremoniously blew it in the boy's dirty face. "There! That hopefully will rectify that situation."

The boy yelled out, "What are ye to do with me?"

"Ahhh!" Killgreth sighed. "Now we can get somewhere."

Killgreth sat down on the cot beside the boy. The boy realizing he could speak was even more terrified of what the Dark Wizard would do if he found out he talked. Killgreth could see the terror in the boy's eyes and decided to take a different approach. "How old are ye, lad?" The boy's face twisted with wonder. He wasn't expecting this kind of question. "I...I am sixteen full seasons, I think...sirs."

"Are ye hungry, lad?"

"I am...always hungry sir. We don't get much on ship...'cept the gruel,...sir."

The boy sat up straighter and unfolded his arms. Killgreth called out to the cell guards to bring a plate of hot food and fruit and to be sure that it was fit for a King. Killgreth stood and walked over to the others watching from the corner of the cell.

"I think this will work. Whatever the lad knows, we will soon know."

"So they are testing us?" Korana asked.

"Yes, I believe so." The Captain said.

"We have surmised that they have taken their time to repair their ships and to grow and train a massive army. The weather on their continent has changed for the worse and they can no longer feed their people. This is why the birthrate dropped off and their army is depleted. And, of course, it is the main reason that The Dark Lord wishes to vanquish us and take our land. It is either defeat us or perish. This is why he is taking his time...he wants to insure a complete victory."

The Queen looked forlorn and felt the weight of her office for the first time.

"We also believe Marideath is looking for a successor to his seat of power."

Killgreth asked quietly, "How are our numbers, Captain?"

"We have 50 units which will unfold to a strength of 75,000 soldiers. Any more than that, we would not be able to feed or shelter. The one thing we have that they don't know about is the Queen and her sisters. Just the Queen's power could be the turning point of a sudden war." Killgreth stepped forward, "Shall we see what this scout knows?"

The guard walked in with a steaming tray of hot food. Beef was piled high and hot buns lined the tray. There was a small selection of fruit shining off to one side. Killgreth ordered the food to be placed on a rickety table in front of the boy. The boy started talking as soon as the food was within reach.

"I am Romanth,...kind sir." The boy looked befuddled.

"Is it spelled or poison, sir?"

Killgreth thought actions spoke louder than words. He reached over and tore off a piece of cooked meat, then ripped it in half. He popped half in his mouth and threw the other piece at the Captain who ate it readily. The boy seeing this little play dove into the food as if it was his last meal or his first in forever.

"Did you come from the Black ship anchored in our harbor?"

The boy could barely speak with his mouth and cheeks stuffed full of food. "Yuthss!" he said. Killgreth looked at the Wizard and smiled. "Bring this lad some drink!"

The guard rushed in with a big flagon of fresh milk. The boy snatched the drinking vessel and tasted its rewarding nectar. "I have never had this before... what is it?"

"There is plenty more where that came from, me lad."

Once the boy finished his drink, Killgreth took all the food and drink away. The boy sat there wondering what went wrong. The boy clearly looked upset.

"What was your mission, boy?"

The boy's attention was torn between the question and the plate of food.

"I...My mission was to see what you got...sir."

"Did you know we could execute you for spying?" The boy's head hung low.

"If you help us, I will see you safely back and fed."

"What if...I don't want to go back?"

"I am afraid you must go back, we will send you with false information to keep your master happy and misguided. If you do this for us, I will ask the Queen to give you asylum in our prosperous country."

Killgreth placed the warm tray on the boy's wet legs. Without hesitation, he began inhaling the food.

"That poor boy is starved." Korana blurted out.

"Yes, he is your Highness." The Wizard added.

The boy turned with a startled look on his face. "You're a Princess,...mom?"

"Well actually...I'm a..."

Killgreth stopped the direction of the Queens answer, and went for the needed info strait out. "What and who is on that ship?"

While still chewing, the boy answered. "We have a good Captain, we do, and a nasty, nasty Wizard. About thirteen of us left on da crew...Oh ya! And twenty soldiers in the hold...yes that's about it."

"What are you doing here?" The Captain asked.

"I think the Wizard came for a fight, I think." The boy said between gulps.

Killgreth directed everyone out of the cell and left the boy to his meal.

"Can you fill his small head with false information of our readiness and things of that nature?"

The High Wizard stroked his chin. "Yes...I don't see that as a problem...but what I do see...is this other wizard being able to eventually see through it."

"Well, we will have to take our chances," Killgreth said.

The Captain and the High Wizard went back into the cell to prep the boy for his soon to start voyage back to the ship. Korana stood close to Killgreth and asked. *"Should we be worried?"*

"No, my lady...we should be prepared."

Ψ

King's Beach: One bell before dawn.

The young lad was escorted back to the beach. The Captain of the guards personally shook his hand and informed him there was a place for a good man like himself here in Delockth. He also hinted that a place in the royal guards would always be interested in the boy. The boy had a look of foreboding as he entered the frigid waters of the bay. He looked back once more, thinking of the amazing food he had just eaten and how he wanted more. The farther he swam the more nervous he became. What if the Dark Lord finds out he divulged pertinent information...he may never make it back to this land of plenty, and he may never see that beautiful girl again. He bore his head down and began to swim faster. The warm spell was soon to wear off and hypothermia was soon to be his death if he didn't make haste.

When he neared the Black ship, he gave the telltale whistle and a watchful crew member lit the signal candle. He found the side rope and pulled himself up the long side of the Black ship. Rung after rung he strained as he climbed. He arrived just in time for his fingers had started to show signs of numbness. Two shipmates grabbed the boy by his arms and belt and hauled him over the side. Romanth landed on the deck like a large wet fish.

"Your late, mate...The Wiz isn't too happy wit ye. You best be getting yourself dried and ready, I would."

The boy sat on the deck and tried to stop himself from shaking. The Dark Wizard must have known he had arrived and yelled from below for someone to drag that no good carcass to his room...and the sooner the better for all. The Wizard knew the warm spell had ended and recharged the spell from his room. *"There that will help him get here sooner."* The boy could feel his feet and fingers again. He stood on his own power and headed to the Wizard's cabin door.

A few tics had passed before a rap sounded on the Wizard's door. *"It's about time...come in!"*

"You wanted to see me, sir?"

"Yes, I did boy, this is your debriefing. There...sit over there."

The Wizard physically lifted his wobbly chair closer to the boy and sat face to face with him. He casually turned to his right and lit an oil lamp. Lowering the glass the light started to do its dance and cast ever changing dark shadows on the two souls. *"Would you like a drink son? It isn't warm, but I don't expect you're cold right now."*

The Wizard poured a goblet of wine from a large pitcher resting on the nearby table. The boy took the goblet to be polite, but thirst was the farthest thing from his mind at the moment. He was terrified the wine was laced with some sort of magical truth serum, and the scary Wizard would find out he failed his mission. *"Did you enjoy your little swim?"*

"Not really...I don't like the water at night."

The Wizards face changed in the flame's light. His eyebrows arched in a menacing chevron and his eyes turned a crimson red. His voice boomed with terror.

"Now tell me, boy...what did ye see?" The old man's face drew nearer.

"I...I saw...very little action...I mean there wasn't many soldiers patrolling the beach. The castle itself was quiet...I didn't venture in, but there were few guards on the tower's edge,...Sir.

It was very late, sir, I don't know that castle, but I can imagine it sleeps at night."

"Don't think, boy, just tell!"

"I don't know...what to say."

"Of course you don't" The Dark Wizard's face lit up in a crooked smile... he had heard exactly what he wanted to hear. He commanded the boy to lean closer to him. In doing so, the Wizard placed his decrepit hands on the boys head. Then he threw his own head back and stretched his mouth open wide. Steam started to rise from the evil one's open mouth. A gurgling sound emanated from the depths of his bony chest. The young boy started to shake and roll his eyes from side to side, finally to rest white side out.

The Dark Wizard was deep in the boy's conscience. He found himself in a big room with many colored doors. The Wizard walked cautiously towards one white door and turned a brass- colored handle. The door opened and revealed a lake with black shiny water. Steam rose from the black liquid and a bitter sense of being alone permeated the old man's mind. Not understanding or seeing any real benefits, the Wizard turned back into the room of doors and chose a red one. Inside this particular room was an old wooden table with no chairs around it. It was laden with all types of exotic fruit and styles of cheese. *"This silly boy dreams of food"*

The old man turned and slammed the red door behind him. The next several rooms turned up nothing but the same folly. A large door suddenly appeared before the Dark Wizard. He grabbed and turned the heated door latch, which flung open the door to reveal several young and voluptuous females rolling and frolicking on a large circular bed. The room's walls danced with colors never seen before by the Wizard and the sweet scent of exotic flowers permeated everything. The old man suddenly wished for younger days and envied the lad for his great gift...his youth.

The females spotted the guest at the door and were gesturing, even begging for the guest to enter and join them in their wanton abandonment. The Wizard took one more wanting look and slowly closed the door. As he turned around in the boy's mind, he noticed a door behind him with a big padlock on the door. It was the only door he noticed with a lock. The more he turned to see the portal, the more it slipped behind him, conveniently staying out of his direct vision...as if on purpose. This was the door he was looking for. He concentrated further and using all his powers managed to hold the door in front of him. The act of doing so was robbing the Wizard of needed mental powers and he knew it was taking its toll. He had to hurry with his mental investigation. The padlock somehow seemed very familiar to him. Then he remembered his old master's teaching and then he recognized his very old friend's signature. There was a "K" scratched on the face of the pad lock. "Kem" he whispered to himself. The Dark Wizard exploded the lock open with a reverse spell and immediately pushed open the door.

A loud rap sounded throughout the Wizards mind like a series of small explosions. "It be dawn your lordship...it be what you requested." Again...Bang! Bang! Bang! The wizard lets the boy's head go and the boy fell to the cabin's sticky floor. "I...am...not...your Lord!"

The old Wizard slumped forward in his chair drained of all mental energy. *"All right!...All right! If I find the man who disturbed me...he will be our next supper...Arrgh!"*

As the young boy started to come around, the Wizard kicked him in the side and demanded he leave while he still could. The boy understood the meaning of his short rant and crawled out of the stinky room. The old man hobbled over to his cot and threw himself in. It was eight bells before the Captain dared wake the sleeping beast. When he did, he woke as strong as ever.

At eight and a quarter bells, the Captain and the Lieutenant of the small force was summoned to the Dark Wizard's cabin. *"Splendid morning, Captain...Lieutenant."*

The Captain gave the Lieutenant a look of surprise as if he was hearing things. The Wizard appeared outwardly to be jovial and happy.

"Good morning to you, you're lor... er...Master Wizard?" the Captain asked as if it was a question.

"Well,…I will tell you…it is a great day for a visit, don't you think? I want you to prepare the small boat for me and six of your best soldiers…Lieutenant."

The Wizard lightly paced around his small room as he spoke.

"We...or should I say I, will be making our Dark Lord's intentions known. Are there any questions?"

Again, the two men standing in front of the Wizard looked in disbelief at one another.

"Come! Come now! There must be something on your little minds? A query, a question?"

"Well…I might have just one…Sir." The Captain spoke quietly.

"Are we going to have to defend ourselves against the entire standing Delockth forces?"

"Not if I do what I was sent to do. Don't worry Captain Vargas; I will see you back whence we came. As for you Lieutenant...we will be prepared for anything... wont we? That will be all Captain. I wish to speak to the Lieutenant alone."

The Captain tipped his filthy hat and happily exited the dark room.

"How strong is the High Wizard you are about to engage?"

The old man poured two goblets of wine and handed one to the Lieutenant.

"We trained together, him and I long time ago..."

It was about seventy full seasons or more ago when the great Wizard took his two apprentices out on a field trip. Kem was by all accounts favored by the powerful teacher, but I excelled in the fact I would do anything, even break the rules to win my teacher's favor.

Kem was two full seasons older than I and maybe that's all it took to achieve the Master's favor, the Great Woolthen of Delockth. The day was like any other day, except we were to challenge each other to a pulled punch duel. I took the first shot, albeit a cheap one and hit my opponent on a blind side with a mentally tossed rock. Kem complained unfair and the teacher sided in his favor. I was given a warning.

The teacher pulled a green glowing ball from his long sleeve and warned me, "If I ever took liberties with the rules again he would use the green ball and freeze me for an unspecific length of time."

Well, the day ended in a complete waste of time. Several days later the Master's special green ball was misplaced or stolen. He accused me and that was the beginning of the end for Seth of Andress. It wasn't more than half a season before I left for the harsh guidance of the Dark Lord, Marideath.

"Did you take the green ball or whatever it was?"

Seth of Andress lifted the glowing ball from his robe's pocket. "Yes,...Yes, I did."

"What do you need from me?"

The Dark Wizard turned to the lieutenant and quietly said, "Here's what I want you to do."

The landing party was underway by nine and a quarter bells. The Lieutenant stayed behind, but ten of his best men joined the Dark Wizard in the small boat. Four of the biggest men powered the oars, while the others sat patiently holding their weapons. The old man perched himself at the bow of the boat like some kind of wooden figurehead. The Wizard wrenched on a crooked smile for the short trip.

Ψ

The King's Beach: Nine and a quarter bells.

"It looks like the Black ship is finally sending a landing party, Sir Killgreth."

"Thank you, sergeant,...please go and summon the High Wizard. I have a strong feeling that he is going to be directly involved."

The Captain, overhearing the orders asked Koln an obvious question. "Why do you think this is more than a diplomatic visit?"

Koln handed the spyglass in his hand over to the Captain. "See the crest on the banner they fly...It is the banner of the Dark Wizard. I know this crest well."

"Anything else I should know before this begins?"

"Yes...if I were you...I would place several snipers on the ridge there...there... and there."

"Very wise, Sir Killgreth, consider it done."

The Captain started off to make arrangements for the long bows.

"Ah! Captain, if you will?"

The Captain looked in his hand and saw Koln's spyglass.

"Sorry!"

Killgreth smiled a golden tooth.

It wasn't more than ten ticks before the old Wizard galloped in on an old grey stallion. *"Nice ride, Kem...He looks as old as you...Ha ha-ha!"*

"Yes! Dingle nuts and I have been together for over thirty full season cycles. He is the oldest in our stable."

"Why...Dingle nuts, Sir Wizard?"

The old man pointed to the grey horse's undercarriage.

"Oh! Wow! I guess you don't jump many fences...ha-ha!"

"No...never could, but we did sire many a fine colt. okay! So I raced down here, what is my immediate presence needed for?"

The boat was tics away from landing on the King's beach. Koln handed the spyglass to the old Wizard for a look. "Oh!" Was all the old man said.

"It's been a long time." He handed the spyglass back to Koln. The old man sat down on a big rock and told the story of Seth of Andress to Koln. The viewpoint was different, but the sad outcome for his old friend was the same.

CHAPTER 8

The Contest

THE SMALL BOAT MADE A scratchy sound as it hit the wet sand of the beach. The sudden change of inertia nearly toppled over some of the unprepared occupants of the small-sized vessel. A few Dark words seeped from the Wizard's rotten mouth. The soldiers were the first out and tried to steady the boat for the old man to disembark with some sort of quasi grace. The strong beach waves made the task very laborious. When the Dark Wizard finally beached himself, he desperately tried to straighten out his attire. His Wizardly pointy red stocking hat fell off in the miserable landing and he hadn't noticed it missing. When he finally realized the hat was not adorning his balding head, he panicked and starting yelling and shouting. "Get my hat! Get it. Get it now."

One of his underlings rushed to his side clutching the bent object. The Wizard slammed it down on his old head and angrily walked toward the oncoming Captain.

The Queen was escorted back to the castle for her safety, while Killgreth and the High Wizard stood on the grassy hill overlooking the beach. The Captain and a troop of twenty soldiers lined up in a diamond position in front of the uninvited foreign guests. The Captain bowed curiously but cautiously.

"I am Vestran Delrayth, Captain of the King's troops."

The Dark Wizard stood before the Captain in his Black and blood-red robes. His favorite hat was bent on his head. The old Wizard tipped his head ever so slightly and spoke as if he was talking to a low ranking dignitary. *"I bid you a good morn, sir...Er...Captain is it? But let's cut the crap as we say...I know the King is gone."*

"Yes it is! Yes he is, and to what do we owe the pleasure of your unscheduled visit."

"I am Seth of Andress, Dark Wizard to his Lord Marideath of Blackshire."

"State the purpose of your landing, Sir Duck Wizard!"

"That's Dark Wizard... Dark! Not duck you buffoon."

"You should watch your mouth, Sir. You are severely outnumbered and your back is to the sea."

"And your back is to the sand!"

The Wizard raised both hands then pushed them forward in a pushing gesture. With an unseen force, he pushed the Captain and the troop down like pins in an ally.

"Where is your High Wizard? I am here to settle things once and for all."

The remaining soldiers of the Dark Wizard's party armed their crossbows and pinned down the prostrated troops. The Dark Wizard rose into the air a good 500 hands above the whole scene. He threw brilliant blue bolts of lightning at the soldiers. The soldiers who could, scrambled for cover amongst the large crop of boulders nature had placed on the beaches side. The rest stayed motionless and hoped for the best. The High Wizard called out from his overlooking mound and demanded.

"Leave them be... they are not in question here. It's me you want, I presume!"

Seth took a shot at Kem from his position above the beach. Kem matched the shot and ran as fast as his old legs could carry him towards the beach. Once on the beach the two old friends tried to kill each other as if they were still young boys vying for their teacher's love and attention. Kem threw a shot at The Dark Wizard's men. Two of them burst into flames, while the others were protected by some magical force. Seth screamed out, "*I don't care about them...I see you fight as you always did...no focus. It will be your downfall.*"

Seth hit Kem with a clear and precise shot. It made the Wizard spin backwards several times until he righted himself. Kem's return shot was a brilliant red thunderbolt. It made the Dark Wizard's cloak burst into flames. Seth removed his garment quickly, and then landed on the beach with both feet down. Kem landed a good 300 hands down the beach. The scene resembled an old-fashioned gun fight. Two men opposing...drawing down on each other with deadly weapons.

Ψ

Castle Delockth: Rear of the Castle.

While the beach duel raged, three assassins dressed in stealth black scurried up a grassy hill towards the rear of the castle. The diversion that was taking place on the King's beach created the right ingredients for a daytime covert operation. Over the small grass hill lay the castle's moat. The back of the castle sported the narrowest part of the ancient trap. The assassins entered the water silently and used their blowguns to slip completely under while using the tubes to breathe. After a few hundred hands, the three soldiers slithered out of the murky water like some ancient watery serpent.

They rearranged their weapons and made a straight path for the castle's kitchen entrance. The first to fall to their silent skills was Gregth the vegetable peeler. He met his demise with his throat open and exposed to the world. Not a sound was made in his violent undoing. Into the very kitchen itself, the three men dodged and crept. Kathly was sliding a big wooden paddle into an enormous open flat oven trying to extract a large bread. The silent killers were completely on the other side of the kitchen and saw no need in ending her life. Through the kitchen's front entrance, they escaped. Kathly pulled both pieces out of the hot oven and laid them on a table to cool. When she went to place the large paddle back in its wall holder, she almost slipped on some water on the kitchen floor. She walked over to the rear window and yelled for Gregth to come and clean up his mess. She tried twice more to call the lad and ended wiping the spill up herself, all the while cursing his name. She was perplexed; the boy was never like this before.

With everyone's attention focused on the great light show on the Kings Beach. The three assassins managed to make it through most of the castle with great ease. The three found the upper grand staircase and ascended to the royal's bedrooms. The three rounded an oil-lit hallway and stopped suddenly. All three backed up around the corner they had just navigated. The largest of the three peered around the corner and assessed the situation. When he rejoined the others, he communicated in hand signals. Four guards were posted in pairs of two. The overdone uniforms they wore, spoke of a high official being guarded. This was surely one of their intended targets. The three assassins loaded their deadly blowguns. With one simultaneous blow, three guards dropped without a sound. The long darts pierced their throats right through. The fourth guard drew his sword not knowing what had just happened. He knelt beside his comrades to see what befell them. In the matter of a heartbeat, he joined his fallen friends with his throat open wide and a torrent of warm blood signaling his doom. The last killed soldier's grip, released his sword upon his death. The heavy weapon bounced off the stone floor and for all concerned was an alarm sounding. Presta was behind the door brushing her long brunette hair. She heard the noise in the hallway and knew something was amiss, but was not sure exactly what. She stopped brushing and placed the ornate brush on her gilded vanity.

She stood and faced the large wooden door to her chambers. The door handle slowly started to turn. Instinctively she knew she was in peril. The door burst open as two of the three assassins rushed silently into the room. They stopped dead in their tracks, for no one seemed to be occupying the chamber. One threw himself down and looked under the large bed. The other one opened the closet door and poked around the clothes hanging there. They stopped and looked at each other, then quickly left the room. They dragged the four fallen soldier's bodies into the room and closed the door. When Presta materialized again, she was standing before the dead bodies. She had to cover her mouth to keep from screaming and giving away her position. She quickly ran to the door and secured the brass bolt, locking herself inside. Not knowing what to do, she ran over to her window to push open the glass panels. Just as Presta was going to push, a dark figure pushed from the outside and caught Presta before she could dematerialize. Presta jumped back as Korrin jumped through the window. "KORRIN! What are you doing...you almost scared the life out of me?"

"Ssshhhhh!" Korrin put her finger to her pursed lips.

"Someone or something is in the castle. They must be from that Black ship in our waters. That boy I heard about, and that blasted Dark Wizard must have been all a diversion tactic. We need to get Killgreth's attention so we can eradicate the threat without sending an alarm."

"Why don't I make us invisible and we'll just walk out of here?"

"Okay,...it's all we have right now. Let's do it. How much time do you have left before you need to recharge?"

"I have approximately 8 tics left...that's if I am alone. Together the time is cut in half...so I will say 4 tics."

"Okay then,...let's hurry."

The two girls happily joined hands as Presta nodded her head once. The door bolt opened on its own, and then the door opened like magic.

Korana was just back from the beach front and was trying to wash her hands when her chamber door flew open. Her personal guard, people she had known all her life lay strewn across her threshold. She hadn't had time to blink, when a man clad in pitch black clothing leaped the dead bodies and flew into her room. The mysterious man threw a dagger at the Queen before he managed a cat-like landing. Korana had less than a blink to react to the threat. With a head nod she diverted the air-born dagger's path around her. The sharp metal projectile lodged itself into her antique dresser door. She raised both palms and mentally pushed the attacker into the wall with such force, he was rendered unconscious upon impact. A second assailant bounded into the Queens chamber brandishing a blowgun. The Dark soldier brought the bamboo pipe to his lips and was about to exhale into the weapon, when Korana mentally pushed the pipe through the man's mouth and out the other side of his neck. He dropped and clutched his neck in a useless ploy to save his own life. With a few gurgles and twitches he stopped moving. His eyes were open in a deathly surprise. With a few stressful pushes, Korana pushed both assailants into the hallway and closed the door. Her window started to open behind her, for she heard the tell tale squeaks she was so accustomed to each morning when airing out her room. A dark figure tried to jump through the open window, but was pushed backwards in the direction of an ill-fated fall. Behind her, the chamber door smashed open, splinters flew in all directions. Korana spun around once more, this time to see Killgreth with a monstrous battleaxe in his scarred hands. His eyes were glowing red and a demon's focus was etched on his familiar face.

"What are you doing?" she cried.

Killgreth raised the battleaxe high over his head and threw it at the Queen.

Korana quickly squatted down hoping the deadly axe would pass over top of her. She opened her eyes and stood. Killgreth didn't have the axe in his hands. She looked behind herself once more. In the window was the assassin she pushed out moments earlier with an axe buried deep in his chest. In slow motion, the man fell backwards for a second time...this time in certain death. "Are you all right,...your Majesty? I saw the look in your eyes, and I am sorry to have scared you."

"I am now...thanks to you, good Sir. I owe you a great debt."

"You looked at me...like I was going to...strike you."

"For a moment there...I really didn't know what to think...that's probably why I didn't push you through the wall. I didn't want to believe you would hurt me."

"I would never hurt you, your grace. I owe you my life."

"And now I owe you mine, Sir Killgreth...we all do."

There was a moment of silence. Korrin and Presta walked into the room still holding hands. "Well, it looks like you had your own party, sister."

"Yes...but I absolutely hate crashers."

The tension of the moment caused everyone to burst out laughing. When the merriment settled, Korana informed Koln that one of the intruders was only unconscious and needed to be incarcerated. Koln left the room and with orders given, had the unconscious prisoner taken to the cells. The other intruders were whisked away and never seen again. The bodies of the castle's fallen soldiers were also taken away but with proper attention and respect for service given.

Killgreth re-entered the room. "Your highnesses...we need to go immediately. There is still a live battle situation on our beach. Even though we outnumber the intruders, they have a powerful wizard, and I don't want to take any more chances with your safety. We will be leaving for the High Wizard's tower right this tic. I believe it is the safest keep in the castle."

Two big guards escorted Presta and Korrin directly out, while Killgreth walked to the big window with the Queen. He looked way down and saw the assassin lying on his back with the axe still in his chest. Then he directed his attention to the beach area. Red and blue light flashes covered the sky over the beach area.

"Will he be all right?"

"Who?"

"Kem...does he have the power?"

"I don't know little one, he is very old. I need to get back to that beach, your Highness."

"I know." The two left the room together.

Ψ

The Kings Beach: Eleven bells.

As the rain fell hard, so did the effects of the two old Wizards. For energy bolts to be highly effective, they need natural static energy. The torrential downfall washed nearly all away. Their effects in the rain amounted to only a twelve-volt battery charge. During the rain, the Captain's men regrouped and positioned themselves in a close but safer spot.

The Dark Wizard proved himself a force to be respected. The Wizard's light flashes seemed all to be weakening. They both stopped taking useless pot shots and tried another approach.

"I know you talked to the boy I sent...I saw your memory pad lock, or should I say one of our old master's spells."

"So!...he is a good spirit. What did you do with him?"

"He is nothing to me, simply a pawn in our great game. He is unharmed... for now!"

"Seth...what are you doing here. Is it just me you desire?"

"You? You are merely a pawn as well. After I eliminate you, I will topple your little insignificant Queen."

"Don't be so sure of her insignificance. The Prophesy was written for her."

"Prophesy! You are an old fool. That tall tale is just a precursor to war. Unfortunately, the Dark Lord believes it and is willing to risk everything to see it doesn't happen. We are coming old man...and when we do…we will reign supreme for thousands of full seasons and generations.

The two Wizards began walking in a circle opposite to each other while keeping a distance of 300 hands. The Dark Wizard waved his hands and a small sand tornado formed in front of him. With a mental push, he directed it straight at the High Wizard. Kem whirled in one spot Dervish style, and by counter spinning, he eliminated the sandy threat in a small sand explosion. The High Wizard tipped his head down and the Dark Wizard started to sink into the sand as if it was quick sand. Not more than three tics and the Wizard was gone. With a great poof the old man resurfaced and was pitching rocks at the good Wizard. Kem threw up an invisible shield which made the rocks bounce away ineffectively.

Just then the Captain yelled down to the High Wizard. "They are okay... The threat has been nullified!"

"So that's it...this was some sort of diversion and I suppose that young lad was one as well." Seth Pulled a green glowing ball out of his robe's pocket. The orb pulsated as if it was charged with a great energy.

"That's a... you took it all those years ago. The master was right. You were unworthy of his knowledge. I missed you like a brother, but I can see now it was all for naught."

"Yes, I did relieve him of it...he favored you. You were older and he deemed more worthy because of that fact alone. Now I will show you who is more worthy to rule this land." The High Wizard of Delockth rushed the Dark Wizard of Blackshire, but wasn't fast enough to escape the Dark Wizard's play. Seth tossed the orb high into the air at Kem. Before he could dodge or react, the green orb exploded and showered down its contents on the unfortunate good Wizard.

The rain ceased and the sun broke through the black clouds. It was as if someone had waved a hand and moved the storm. The evil Wizard looked at his friend frozen in time. His body was totally green from the spell's effect. The position he statured was one of sadness. His frozen face reflected the regret he was feeling. His out stretched arms in a defensive position cried his frustration at his own inability to defend his Queen and himself. A single green tear rolled down his solid face. Seth looked up at the bright blue sky wondering how the storm could disappear so rapidly when he noticed an enormous volley of deadly arrows raining down on his position. The arrows fell and landed without prejudice. The Old Wizard shielded himself with a quick incantation and a flick of a hand. His comrades didn't fare so well, half the troops he had landed with dropped like human pin cushions. Seth quickly realized he was too weak from the all-out battle with his old friend and decided to retreat. He turned to Kem and said. "Sleep well old friend...I will return. If you are lucky...I will make you a permanent fixture in my new home."

He laughed while he dragged his feet towards the small boat waiting for him. Another volley of arrows was in the middle of an encore performance when the Dark Wizard waved his arm without even looking and changed their trajectory. The Captain gave the order to cease-fire. The Captain and a select few quickly made their way to the High Wizard's side. They watched the Dark Wizard and two soldiers transverse their way over the strong surf.

As the little boat made its way towards the Black four-sailed ship, the Delockth Navy rounded the Bay of Sails. The Admiral, Sabasth O Vectorth placed a clean shot over the bow of the Black ship. This act focused the Dark Wizard's attention in returning quickly to the ship. He had a spell in his cabin he was saving. He knew if he could make it back to the Black ship, he could render the ship invisible for a few bells. He helped the two soldiers row. A second small boat arrived on the watery scene. It too was making its way towards the Black ship.

Killgreth made it to the beach hill as soon as he could. He tied his laboriously breathing horse to a small shrub and yanked the long copper looking spyglass out of a side-saddle pouch. He directed the scope at the fleeing Wizard's boat. As he turned the lens and focused it, he could see the old Wizard feverishly trying to row with the other two soldiers. He shifted his focus to the other mysterious vessel and to his mind-numbing horror, saw Killth his son and three other male children from the castle. Koln had to remove the device from his eye and rub it in hopes it was dirt on the glass that transformed another child's face to Kill's. He repositioned the spyglass on his eye and noticed a ranking officer, possibly a Lieutenant and three other able-bodied soldiers rowing the boat. As he panned, he noticed Kill looking back at him. The other children looked as if they were crying. Koln could feel the bile rising in his dry throat. Korana and four Queen's guards rode up to where Killgreth was standing. The queen expertly dismounted her animal and ran over to Killgreth.

"What's happening here...I'm sorry...I need to know?" She asked excitedly. Killgreth tried to sum it up as directly as he could. "Ok! That green statue on the beach...is the High Wizard. That small boat there...is an escaping Dark Wizard and that smaller boat...right about there...has my son and three other kidnapped kids."

"What!"

With that Korana snatched the looking device from Killgreth's hand and directed it towards the fleeing boats. With the spyglass still on her eye, she asked,

"Oh! My! What do you want to do? We obviously don't have much time or choices."

"Well...the Wiz is on ice...so we can leave him out for now. The escaping Wizard will soon be on the same boat as my son...so...I say we concentrate on the Black ship."

"Well, our navy has taken a shot, but they're still too far away to be effective... would you like me to take a shot?"

"What do you mean your majesty?"

Koln looked perplexed but amused. He knew not to underestimate this little girl's ability. Korana spun her head around looking for something. When she spotted what she was looking for she said, "Watch...I will show you."

Korana spotted a horse size boulder half sticking out of the ground. With seemingly little effort, she extended her hands towards the half-freed boulder. She wiggled all her pretty little fingers and suddenly the boulder started to vibrate violently. The others around could feel the effect traveling up their stationary feet and into their legs. In a few tics, the large boulder was spinning and rotating in the air a good ninety hands high. The dirt side of the boulder shook free the dirt, which caressed its side, for what seemed like an eternity and soon the boulder was a clean projectile ready to be launched. While keeping her hands outstretched, she turned her head towards the fleeing ships and squinted her eyes. With no effort applied, she dropped both arms in the direction of the bay. The spinning boulder shot from the airspace it occupied and flew away in the direction of choice. It flew like a ball from a cannon. The eerie part was that there was no sound to this method. Over and over the large rock turned. All eyes were on the missile and open mouths lit the faces of the on-lookers. Killgreth, out of a visual desperation, tried to track the moving object with his spyglass. The vision was too narrow for him to find, so he watched the Black ship's hull in anticipation.

The boulder smashed down on the bow of the small boat, which held the stolen children. Wood splinters and debris littered the surrounding waters. Water rushed into the small craft as the onlookers could clearly see bodies jumping overboard. There was oooing and ahhing from the fortunate witnesses. Killgreth couldn't figure out what the commotion was about for he saw no occurring event in his trusted spyglass. When he took the device away from his eye and refocused, he saw what they all gasped about. A clear and direct hit on the escaping vessel containing his son Kill. "What are you doing your Grace? You hit the wrong boat."

"Did I, Sir Killgreth? Did I?"

"The Black ship, your Majesty! The Black one!"

"Oh! I am sorry...they all look black from here."

Killgreth knew she was fabricating that bit of information and retrained his seeing device on his son's predicament.

Ψ

Kill Killgreth: I don't know what really happened. I was sleeping in and generally being lazy, when someone roughly placed a smelly, scratchy hood over my sleeping head. I was unceremoniously man-handled down corridors and staircases. For a moment, I thought it was my father playing some sort of learning exercise. I changed my mind when I went to speak. Someone big punched me in the stomach and said, "The next sound will be your last."

The accent was different from around these parts; this made me more confused. My hands were tied behind my back and I heard several more footsteps added to the horrible parade we were forming. I could hear distinctly some young child whimpering. It wasn't long before we were outside the castle and into the elements. If only my hands weren't tied.

Soon the ground turned to sand and I surmised we were headed for the King's Beach and possibly to an awaiting vessel. Why would someone want me?

I served no purpose, except being my father's son. Was that all it was? Leverage for some evil person to fashion his will against our people.

If I get the chance...I will destroy all who dare plot and taint our existence. I swear!

We...and I'm guessing here, were placed into a small water craft. The small jerky movements made me visualize an eight-person rowboat. The instructions by my captor were spoken in a seafaring lilt. I heard the oars protest in their dried out shackles. The surf's waves caused the small boat to rise and fall violently. I had to hang onto my position with my feet jammed underneath the seat in front of me. One of the others with me started full out crying and was stopped dead with a mysterious thud. The sea gradually started to calm down and I could hear the heavy breathing of the men who were rowing the boat. Then out of nowhere, with no warning came a tremendous crash. The boat took a great hit from something big. The person who sounded in charge was yelling out panic orders and his own personal evil thoughts and words.

I shook my head violently and removed the scratchy hood from my sweating head. The light made me see white flashy dots, like fireworks in the summer time. The cold water was now up to my knees. I needed to do something very fast, so I pulled my arms down underneath my behind and pulled my little legs through. My hands were now in front of me. I grabbed a belt knife from the sailor beside me and dove off the side of the small boat. Once in the water, I immediately cut my hands free and put the knife in the waistband of my sleeping wear. I surfaced for as long as it took to catch a full breath of air and I dove down a few hands, hoping to avoid detection. When I resurfaced, the boat was no more. Two sailors and two boys in tow were headed towards a large Black ship not far off in the distance. I instinctively headed towards the beach and hopefully home.

My extremities were starting to get numb real fast. I didn't know how much longer I could stand the cold water. Again without sound or visual warning a large tree splashed down not more than 150 hands away. I knew it was my only chance and I directed my efforts towards the huge tree. I had some initial difficulty climbing aboard, but desperation won in the end. Using my new knife I cut off a small limb and fashioned a crude paddle. I then rowed my tree to shore as fast as my numb arms would let me move.

Ψ

Kings Beach: Worried Father and Queen,
Killgreth's eye was still trained on the watery scene. "Oh!...he's in the water. Wait he's gone! Oh No! The small boat just went under."

Koln pulled the spyglass from his eye and dropped his head. Korana took the spyglass from his limp hand and viewed the scene.

"Wait...I clearly see someone swimming this way...and a few bodies swimming towards the Black ship's direction."

Killgreth grabbed the spyglass from the Queen almost forcefully. "It... Could be him! What can we do? I don't think he will be able to stand the frigid water very long."

"I have an idea." Korana sounded excited with the thought.

The little Queen mounted her horse expertly and headed off towards the castle. Before she hit the moat she turned right towards the wooded area. There she desperately searched for the perfect tree. Korana dismounted and ran towards a big Sycamore tree. The living tree was very old and Korana placed her hand upon its large trunk. *"Do you mind if I use you to save a human life...old man?"*

This was her thoughts and not verbalized. She heard, *"I have been waiting to serve a purpose...please use any and all parts of me."*

With this ancient form of communication taught to her by the High Wizard, Korana felt good about what she had to do. She ran back a hundred hands away and turned towards the magnificent tree. With outstretched hands, she did her magic. Her head lowered and her fingers wiggled. She even felt the urge to wiggle her toes. With one swift move, she uprooted the large Sycamore and threw it on the King's Beach. It came down with a mighty crash, startling half of the soldiers that were now patrolling the sandy area. Korana remounted her steed and raced to her fallen hero. Once she arrived, she wasted no time in picking up the intended tree canoe and launched it. It landed only seventy-five hands away from the person swimming for his life. Feeling her self-worth, she walked with her horse in tow back to join Killgreth at the water's edge.

When she arrived, Killgreth put his arm around her and comforted her. "It's him! It's Him! I saw him. You did a magnificent job. Why couldn't you just pluck him from the water?"

"*He was too far out and Kem told me, just a slight miscalculation could snap a humans spine...I did not want that on my conscience, especially if it was Kill. If you want me to try, I will when he gets closer.*"

The Captain rushed over to the pair half winded. "I...Heard about...the Castle breach my Queen...I am so sorry! I do apologize."

The Captain bowed low to the Queen.

"*It is all right Vestran; we were all caught off guard. There were multiple fronts...I hope we have learned a valuable lesson here not to underestimate our mortal enemy.*"

"You are so right, my Queen, and very wise for your young age. Kem has schooled you well." The Captain bowed again.

"Are the Princesses all right, your Highness?"

"Yes...they are no worse for wear. They handled their aggressors each in their own special way."

The Captain looked at Killgreth. "What are we to do about the fleeing Black ship?"

Killgreth answered with escaping breath.

"Signal the fleet to pursue from a safe distance. I don't want them to engage the Wizard at this time. He might be weak, but he may also have some power on his ship."

The Captain nodded his head, turned on his heels and ran off to implement his orders. Killgreth walked down to inspect the Green Wizard.

"He looks so unreal all in green and standing with his arms in a defensive position. What are we to do with our friend here? I don't know anyone with magical powers that might free our Wizard from his greenish cell casing."

"I might know someone...but first let's get him out of the elements."

Several soldiers were immediately assigned to carry the Wizardly statue to his room high in the Wizard's tower. They struggled, but managed to relocate him in one piece. Killgreth turned his attentions to his boy once more. The two walked to the shore's edge and called out to him.

"*Do you want me to try and pull him in now that he is closer?*"

"No, sweetheart! He now must make it on his own steam for the experience to mean anything real to him. This is a character builder and will strengthen him or kill him." Korana found the reasoning unkind, but respected Koln's fatherly decision.

When Kill got close enough, Koln waded into the cold water to retrieve his exhausted son. Koln pulled his slumped body off the Sycamore and held him tight. "Did...I do...?"

The boy couldn't talk with his teeth chattering. Koln held Kill close to his chest and waded into shore.

"Don't try to speak, son...you did good...very good. I am so proud of you."

The boy's teeth chattered so loudly his father almost started to laugh.

"*Is he all right?*" Korana sounded worried.

"I think so; he just needs his mother's love and warmth right now."

Korana pulled the sweater from her tender shoulders and draped it over the cold wet boy. The big man held his child close and headed for Kathly's awaiting arms.

Later that same evening, Koln, the Queen and her two sisters met at the Green Wizard's chamber in the High Wizard's tower. Kem was placed in front of a warm fire in the futile hope the green coating would simply melt off his person. Korana walked right up to the living statue and placed a tender hand upon his hardened cheek.

"*Is he alive?*"

"I don't know sweetheart...I am not good in these mystical areas." Killgreth answered with a measure of tenderness.

"What are we to do with him?" Korrin asked.

"We can't just leave him here...can we?" Presta sounded truly worried.

"I know of a powerful witch, that my father's village has told many stories about. Some say she is older than the hills and just may have the right spell to rid the High Wizard of his green prison. I think we should take a few men and try to find this person of interest."

Korana looked deep in thought. "*I believe you have something there, Sir. Why don't you make an expedition and do just that.*"

"I will do as you suggest, my Queen."

Korana blushed three shades of red. Presta lifted her voice to a fever pitch.

"Oh! Please can I go? I really need to help Kem."

She looked at her red haired sister and pleaded. "Oh, please, big sister, I really wish to be a part of his healing."

"*If you wish this adventure...who am I to stop you? I am sure you might even be a great help.*"

"Oh, thank you, sister!"

"*No, Presta, thank you. Is this acceptable to you Sir Killgreth?*"

"I would be honored to have the Princess on our quest. It is also well known that she sings very well and has a large repertoire of old songs we might enjoy around our cook fire some nights." Presta blushed and smiled.

"Okay then, we will make preparations to leave in three cycles. I want to be sure that Kill is up for the trip. I believe he will learn much from this kind of adventure as well."

Ψ

The Witch's Glen:

The morning was a crisp fall day. The wind had finally died down and the sun was blinding. The anxious horses exhaled steam as did also all other animals and humans. Koln had recruited four of the best palace guards for the trip. Altogether the party of Koln, Kill, Presta and the four guards were underway. Korana and Korrin were both there to see them off and wave until they were out of sight. Presta looked back as if she had second thoughts, but waved goodbye for the last time and continued on. It was usually a twenty-four-cycle trip to the old village, which would be broken into two trips. With Presta and Kill along, they moved a little slower than a troop of well-trained soldiers. Nine cycles went by and the young ones were getting sore. Kill wasn't fully recovered, so Koln made camp early the first day. The group found a little sheltered stream to camp beside.

"I am hungry, father!"

"Yes, son, what else is new?"

"I guess...I could stand some sustenance as well, Sir Killgreth."

"Listen...your Highness, please...for the sake of this trip...would you please call me Koln and I will call you by your given name. We also don't wish to advertise to anyone that we are traveling with royalty. It's just safer that way."

"Very well Sir...Er! I mean...Koln."

Koln gave her a fatherly smile.

The first night passed by without any trouble. Koln believed the young people were exhausted and didn't even notice the temperature falling. The soldiers kept the central fire blazing to try to ward off the frost. Breakfast was fast and hot and then they were underway around eight bells and headed straight for the old village. Very late in the day they entered the village, two abreast. Koln led the way and happily waved to all who recognized him. He stopped the group in front of his old blacksmith shop.

The sign on the front was new and read, *Killgreth and Sons*. This brought a smile to the father's face. He dismounted and walked into the open shop. He expected to see Erin hard at work. The first thing he noticed was that the smelter pit was burning bright, as if it was just stoked. He slowly walked over to a workbench and inspected some of the swords which lay there. He threw one down and it sounded a loud "clank." There was no one in sight, so he climbed the stairs to his old loft. Also to his surprise, it was vacant. He scanned the area and walked over to the back window in the loft. Then he heard a sound he recognized. He walked down stairs to see Matth shoveling coal into the fire pit. Matth was startled by the unknown man's presence and then he recognized his benefactor.

"Sir Killgreth!"

"Dad!" Koln spun around defensively and before him was Erin, a good foot taller and broad-chested.

"Erin! Me boy, how's ya, too? Come here, me boy."

"I am good, Pa. What are you doing here? Are you with those people outside?"

The two men locked arms and then went for a full hug.

"Yes, I am. How are you, Matth? You look more like your father every day."

"Thank you ...I guess." Matth looked confused.

"What are you doing in the village?"

"I will tell you over a hot supper."

"You must stay in the cottage, Pa. Your soldiers can stay in the barn's loft and the little ones can use the bedrooms. I know you won't mind the space in front of the fireplace. Just like old times, eh Pa? Hey! Let me round up some deer meat and bread."

"No...The meal is on us. We are traveling with the Queen's food and wine... tonight the banquet is on us. Matth you are also invited."

"Thank you, Sir, but I have my wife and kid to feed, Sir Killgreth."

"Okay...if you change your mind... at least let me get you a pouch of wine for your family."

"Thank you, Sir Killgreth," he said with enthusiasm.

Killgreth grabbed Erin's shoulders firmly. "It is good to see you boy, but now I must see to my charge's comfort. We will meet back at the cottage later." Koln smiled and flashed his rarely seen gold tooth.

Ψ

Killgreth Cottage: Nine Bells, dark fall.

A white plume of smoke puffed into the night escaping from the chimney's top. The interior of the cottage was alive again with multiple conversations and smells of home cooked food. The hearth sent a steady glow of warmth, bathing all who dared sit in front of it. Two guards were posted outside, front and back, so Koln could relax. Koln had them rotate every cycle, so all could enjoy the festivities and much-needed warmth. Reflections of the flames danced in the shiny objects that hung from the split-rail ceiling and soon everyone's eyes glowed with the flow of the excellent wine. The large family-sized table was piled high with all types of warm food. Venison and grouse were in abundance. So was the fresh fruit from the Queen's special storehouse. A large wooden bowl full of polished red apples made Erin's eyes widen with delight. Presta helped make a vegetable stew that she had learned from the head cook at the castle. It boiled and bubbled throwing hot scented gasses into the air making everyone drool with anticipation. "Thank you, father, this home hasn't smelled like this since Ma was here."

"Oh, that reminds me!" Koln reached behind him for a satchel. He handed it over to Erin.

"Here, it's from your mother."

"Oh! I know what this is." Erin raised the package to his nose and inhaled sharply. "Yup! Dis is what I'm talking about...Me Ma's bread. I would know that smell anywhere."

"It's the cinnamon," Presta said.

"What!?" Erin said.

"It's the cinnamon she uses. That's what makes it different."

Erin looked at Koln.

"I guess it is time for a formal introduction. Erin of Delockth...I would like to introduce you to Her Royal Highness, Princess Presta Atlas of Delockth."

Presta stood back from the table and tipped her head ever so slightly. Erin's mouth was wide open. "Well I...but I, how was I to know...er."

He pushed his chair back in a rush to get up and lost his balance. Over he went with his feet in the air. Everyone, especially the Princess, burst out in laughter. When he finally made it to his feet, he was as red as a summer beet.

"I don't know what to say," was all he said, when he made it to his feet.

"I am actually disappointed in you Erin. You didn't even recognize your stepbrother Killth." Then it flashed in Erin's mind and he ran over to Kill and gave him a big hug. "Why didn't you say something?"

"I wanted to see how long it would take for you to know me."

"But you're so big...you really take after your father, you do. I am so happy let's eat… everyone."

They all ate their fill. The food and merriment was too much for Kill and he retired to a small room in the back of the cottage and instantly fell sound asleep. Presta couldn't keep her big eyes off of Erin. Koln noticed and it put a smile on his face. After a cycle or two of casual conversation, Koln and Presta cleaned up the mess while Erin checked on the horses. A short while later Presta, Erin and Koln sat by the fire with some wine and brought Erin up to speed on their Quest.

"We are here in search of a powerful witch. The High Wizard to the Queen was encased in a green coating and we need to free him. Our only hope is that we can find someone who can release him. Do you know of such a person? Does she even exist?"

"I remember the King's High Wizard. He was the older authoritative looking man that would accompany the wagons for the weapon's pick-up."

Erin took a big drink of his wine and wiped his face with his sleeve.

"She does, Pa, right she do. I have heard stories, several actually about things she did. Some of them scary and some right strange. But this old witch seems to be real on all accounts."

Erin took another big drink and then poured himself more.

"Do ye like that, boy?"

"What?"

"The wine...do ye like it?"

"Yes, Pa...it surely hits the spot, it does."

Presta started to giggle at Erin's apparent inebriation.

"I will send you a case when we get back. I want you to find out where this witch is. We need to finish this quest in due time."

"If I find out...can I go with you? I have never been on a quest before and I want to help." *"Who will look after the smithy?"*

"Well...Matth of course, he can enlist his brother to help now that the growing season is over, he doesn't do much."

"Ok! You're on son. Now go get some rest."

Koln was actually happy both sons would be with him on this adventure.

"Where am I to sleep?" Presta inquired.

"You can take my room, my lady."

"Please call me, Presta."

Erin took Presta by the hand and led her to the back room. He opened the door and it squeaked on its unoiled hinges.

"This used to be Ma and Pa's room...sorry about the mess you're hi... I mean Presta."

Presta entered the moschatel-smelling room. When she turned around to say goodnight, Erin was already gone. She slowly pushed the sticky door closed.

The next morning, after a hearty breakfast of fresh duck eggs, Erin found his father making the horses ready for the next leg of their journey. "Morning, father."

"Good morn to you, Erin. Did you manage to find a direction for us?"

"Yes I did. Hedgrowth the village Crier spoke of a very powerful witch who resides in Witch's Glen. It's a good four cycle's ride from here. The only thing I don't like...is that we must pass through Wolf Forest."

"This is not a good thing I take it?"

"No...But the other route takes you through swamp lands and they're basically impassable this time of the season...too wet you know."

"Oh, right you are. Do you know how to get us there?"

"I believe I do. The old geezer told me some good information on things to look out for, like outcroppings, rivers and hills with trees on them."

"Okay then, do you have a good horse?"

"Yes, I purchased one last season and it's a black stallion. They say it's the fastest horse in the whole county."

"All right, get your pack on. I want to be on our way soon."

Erin ran off excited about the adventure he was embarking on.

I started the expedition started off a little late. Eleven bells had rung before they had passed the village limits. Two soldiers led the way with Erin close behind making sure we were headed in the right direction. The rest were sandwiched between the last two rear guards.

I convinced Presta to sing a song to lift their mood as we moved along. "Yes Sir Killgreth. I would be happy to oblige."

I have a sweet lassie whose name is farewell
I will always be leaving her back in the dell
Her hair is as bright as the sun on the dew
and her lips are as red as rose petals too
If I could stay long enough I'd take her hand
then I surely would be the happiest man

Koln looked around and everyone was smiling. Erin dropped back and rode beside Presta. "That was a lovely song, my lady...where did you learn a song like that?"

"The vegetable peeler at the castle would sing as he peeled his potatoes and carrots. For some reason...everything I hear I can...just remember. I guess it's another one of my special gifts."

"What do you mean...special gifts?"

"I have a special gift; would you like to see?"

Erin's eyes got real wide. "Sure!"

Presta looked back at Koln. "Can I show him?"

Koln just nodded his head approvingly. Erin's face reflected youthful wonderment when Presta vanished from the top of her horse.

"Wow! Did you see that...or not. What just happened?"

Presta reappeared.

"You must be a wizard or something."

Presta smiled and blushed. Koln pulled up beside Presta and acted the parent. "Please sweetheart, I need you to save your strength. We don't know what's in store for us and surprise could be our best weapon."

Presta understood and nodded her approval. Erin moved back into position but couldn't help looking back every so often at the amazing girl.

The expedition stopped unexpectedly early. Erin informed them that they were only four bells away from the forest and they potentially might not make it all the way through by night-fall. Killgreth took Erin's advice and tried to avoid being in the Wolf Forest at night. They were well warned to expect anything while traveling there. The local folklore was laden with stories of the macabre and strange. Presta asked the most obvious question, if there were any wolves in the forest. Erin told her that he had found out that not only were there wolves but they were very large and in charge. Some packs were seen fifty strong and almost impossible to vanquish.

They made camp near a small stream with a few large deciduous trees around for shelter. The leaves were starting to fall, but the cover was still adequate. It didn't take long for a central fire to be lit with everyone clambering to get close. It turned out that one of the soldiers was an excellent road cook and made a stew from several rabbits Koln and Kill managed to catch. The entire party agreed that it was the best stew they had ever had. The group was quiet, possibly because of the anticipation of the forest trip that was pending the next day. Erin and Presta sat beneath a tree talking and enjoyed each other's company. Koln and Kill practiced some fancy swordplay and constantly searched for dry wood for the camp. The four soldiers did their job and protected the perimeter of the makeshift camp while tending to the animal's needs. The night went by without too much commotion or revelry. The main campfire went out sometime in the early morning, which caused much discomfort for those sleeping on the ground in the cold temperatures. Koln assigned the duty of maintaining the fire to one of the soldiers, so that didn't happen again.

Breakfast came and went in the blink of an eye. The soldiers raised their heads when they felt the subtle vibration in the ground of riders coming their way. As five large men rode into camp, all the men drew their swords not knowing what to expect.

Killgreth stood boldly and spoke loudly, *"What is your purpose here?"*

"Whoa! Friend we mean no challenge. We merely saw your camp smoke and hoped to share some heat. I am, Laval of Vectorth Ils. And these are my business partners. We are spice traders and we are on a long journey to try to find a salt mine to trade with. We believe there is one not fourteen complete cycles from here."

"I am Sir Koln Killgreth of Delockth."

Koln bowed his head but kept his eyes forward. Koln must have believed his story, because he sheathed his sword and offered the travelers comfort. The traders huddled around the fire, which Erin stoked with some dry wood he had found. Presta made a hot drink from a type of chocolate and shared it with the guests. Koln and Erin sat with the traders while the soldiers prepared for the day's trip.

"So Laval, I must ask...why salt." Koln looked inquisitive.

"We need salt to cure our fish. It is our main source of food and if we cannot keep it from rotting, we would starve during the lean months. This salt mine would mean much prosperity for our small island and survival. And you sir, if I may be so bold to ask, what are you doing in the middle of nowhere... with children to boot?"

"*We are on a quest to find a powerful witch. We believe she lives on the other side of the Wolf Forest.*"

"Witch? Why would anyone want to be near a witch?"

"*The great Wizard, Kem of Delockth is in a bind and we were hoping that she could break the spell he is under.*"

"Oh! Interesting." Laval turned to Presta.

"This is wonderful drink...what do you call it?"

Presta leaned over, "We call it hot chocolate."

"Wonderful, simply wonderful." Laval finished his drink and stood rapidly.

"Well, my new friends, I wish you well on your quest and we must continue ours." The traders all mounted their horses and said their goodbyes. Erin spoke out. "Excuse me sir trader...Er! Laval, Sir. Did you know...if you were to pass through Wolf Forest, you could take five full cycles off your journey?"

"How do you know this?"

"We know of the salt mine you speak of and it's that way...but there is a large river you would have to circumvent. If you go this way, through the forest, there is a narrow spot on the river that your horses can swim."

"But where did you get this information?"

"From an old man in my village; we have no reason to disbelieve him."

"Very well then...I feel good about this news and I will change my route."

He looked at the other men and they all agreed. "Which way to the forest, lad?"

"Just over that distant ridge,...Sir."

Laval and all the others tipped their caps and thundered off in search of what they were seeking. Koln turned to Erin. *"Nice one son, you sent a scouting party for us...very nice."* Koln turned away to finish breaking camp. Erin had the biggest smile on his rosy-cheeked face. He turned on a stone and checked to see if his horse was packed tight.

The expedition finally got underway. They made it to the forest's edge at approximately five bells in the afternoon. Killgreth put up his hand and stopped the train. *"I can see the tracks where the spicers entered the forest."*

"Yes, it's pretty clear. Fortunately this is the way I would have taken us," Erin said.

Little Killth pulled up beside his father. "Are we to take the same route?"

"Yes! We will follow who went before, it's safer. We only have few light cycles left and we must make camp again. If we enter now we could be in the dead centre when night falls. We will start early tomorrow."

Just as the party finished supper, it started to lightly snow. The temperature dropped drastically and they had to pull out their woolen clothes. Their tents were set up close to the roaring fire and all but two guards on patrol sat close to the radiant warmth. They sat by the fire until it dimmed listening to Killgreth the warrior weave tales of war and great battles of the past. His recounting of stories of Marideath the Dark Lord was exceptionally vivid and disturbing. The oppressive rule over his people scared Presta the most.

"Boy! I hope he don't come to Delockth any time soon," Kill pleaded with apprehension and worry.

Presta asked, "He is coming...isn't he? I feel a dark wave coming our way."

Koln lowered his head in depression. His voice was low and almost inaudible.

"He has been preparing for an invasion for over ten full cycle seasons. His new ships, I expect will bring a rebuilt fresh army to our shores. He will sail across the great sea like a swarm of disease- spreading locusts and try to devour us...whole."

"What are we to do father?"

Koln raised his head and the flames were reflected in his black eyes.

"We must free our High Wizard if we want a chance of holding them back or even defeating them once more. Now! Off to bed with the lot of ye. We rise early and this time we need to get all the way through the forest."

During the long, cold night, Presta could swear she heard wolves howling, but it could have just been a premonition of what was to happen. She knew she was too far away from the forest to actually hear any animals. So she fell back to an undisturbed sleep.

In the morning, a blanket of freshly fallen snow covered everything. Breath steam was released on every exhale as warm porridge heated their stomachs. It was a welcomed friend to cold fingers as well. No one spoke a word as the horses stomped their hooves in anticipation of another day's ride. They were underway by nine and a half bells and the usual order of procession was in place. Presta gave Erin a warm smile to which he responded with an old-fashioned blush.

Presta Atlas:

The edge of the forest is right where Erin said it would be. He really does ride that horse like a proud warrior. As I looked forward, I noticed that the trees have changed. They now look tall and coniferous. Those wooden soldiers were so tightly grown that it looks like we may never find an opening.

Koln Killgreth:

"What now!?" Koln blurted out.

"Is there a path or an opening in this dark forest?" To watch Erin take to Presta, reminds me of the childhood I never really had. They look so good together... *"If I was a betting man,"* Koln whispered to himself.

"Yes!" Erin shouted back to Koln.

"It's what the old man said to me. He said to find the tallest tree with a red top and the opening will reveal itself to us."

Koln thought, I can't believe |Erin. His mother will be so proud of the way he is handling himself. He will be a great warrior someday..

Erin Killgreth, thinking:

I can see the notable tree. Wow! It sure is a big one. Father just signaled the line to the desired direction. I am a little scared...but for Presta, well, she has been the highlight of my trip so far. I can't believe she can disappear, if that isn't the cat's meow. Okay! Hold yer head up you fool...she could be looking. I must keep my eye on her. If anything should happen, I don't know what I'd do. This could prove to my father that I am worthy of his name.

Killth Killgreth of Delockth, thinking:

I'm feeling something, but I don't know what it is. We have only been traveling a short distance this morning, but already my rear end and inner thighs are throbbing. I really don't know how anyone can get used to this punishment. Oh, great! Now we are going to enter the Wolf Forest. I hate wolves;

they smell so bad when they get wet. I can't wait to make camp again...I hope this is a small forest.

The expedition:

The expedition found the hidden entrance. Koln noticed multiple horse tracks once inside the trees and surmised that the spice traders made it this far. Slowly they entered the bowels of the forest, single file. The first impression the collective felt was an uncertainty, an eerie silence added to the flavor of the moment. No birds, no rabbits, no small rodents of any species, not even a wolf. The trail that lay before them was winding and hilly, making the procession unstable as well as dangerous. Large boulders also dotted the hazardous trail making it increasingly difficult to keep to the etched path. Afternoon cycle sun would poke its head through the treetops every so often, making the scene a dream-like sequence for all who dared to enter. A dusty haze could be seen emanating from the tree tops. No one dared speak...everyone was on a heightened alert. Without warning, Presta's horse stepped in a small sinkhole and broke its leg. The horse went down on his front good leg and threw Presta for a loop. She rolled like a circus performer, but ended up stopping with her pretty head against one of the trail boulders. The whole train went into a panicked high alert. Even the rear soldiers drew their swords in confusion. Erin and Koln arrived at the fallen Princess first, while the others automatically set up a defense perimeter. Koln brushed Presta's hair from her white face. She slowly opened her blue eyes and gave the audience a slight smile.

"How's my Maybell?"

Koln looked to one side. The horse in question was standing, but only on three legs. He looked into Presta's eyes. *"Not good, little one. How are you, love?"*

Presta moved her legs and then she sat up slowly. "I seem...to be...okay."

Erin leaned in close and ripped off a bit of his undershirt. He dabbed the cut on her head and said. "You took quite a spill, my lady. I didn't know you were such an acrobat."

Koln left the two for a minute. Kill was holding the reins of the wounded horse. "What are we to do Father?"

"You know what we need to do, son."

Koln pulled from his saddle his long battle sword. Taking the reins from Kill, he led the horse off the trail and ended the horse's pain with one fierce swing. Presta saw the horse fall without a sound except for the large lifeless body crashing into the underbrush. She lowered her head sadly and wept tears of release. She had never seen this act before, but in her life and all others who relied on horses for transportation; this was a common and humane experience. Erin held the sobbing girl close and was sad for her pain, but was happy for the opportunity to hold the beautiful Princess. The mixed emotions he felt, were like no other he had experienced before. The party passed around a wine skin and everyone calmed down. Presta showed great strength and regained her composure very quickly. Even the hardened soldiers were impressed with her power and fortitude. The train was underway with Presta sitting in front of Erin on the same horse. Erin was happy he had purchased such a large horse and her smile was his personal reward.

They moved through two cycles of almost impassible trail. Four bells came too soon for Koln. He looked at the patchy sky and tried to guess how much light was left in the day. The expedition broke through the edge of the thick forest and headed into a natural clearing the size of a small horse farm. Small trees dotted the clearing and patches of blueberries were abundant. Koln did not want to stop, but he knew all the younger people were cold and tired. He went against his better judgment and called for the party to stop and make Erin dismounted and rushed over to Koln.

"Pa, are ye sure you want to be stopping in the middle of this good forsaken place?"

"Yes, Erin...we need to...we are running out of light and it looks like a fresh campsite over there."

"It must have been them spicers who went before us...right?"

"Yes...that's what I was thinking."

Koln rubbed his hand over Erin's messy hair like he used to do when he was a little kid.

Koln sounded out commands as if he was in the army and the troop responded with precision and an unexplained sense of awareness. The four soldiers set up a fire perimeter surrounding Erin's central campfire. The tents were beside each other and the horses were at the rear of the tents. Presta grabbed a satchel and plopped herself down in a large patch of berries and proceeded to gather something different for their breakfasts. The two brothers scurried off together in search of dry firewood for their fires. Koln made sure they didn't travel too far from the camp's defense perimeter. The troop settled into a rhythm and started to prepare their supper, when all Dark broke loose. It was a little after six bells night when a rider-less horse bolted into their campsite.

☥

Castle Delockth: Queen's Chamber.

Korana didn't feel well after eating, so she went to her bedroom and tried to lie down for a while. Every time she dared close her eyes, they popped open. Something was wrong, this was clear. She shuffled over to her big closed window and threw it open. The reverse air pulled the heat from her room's fireplace and over her milky white shoulders. Something was definitely wrong. She thought it was her indigestion, but in actual fact it was Presta. She knew Presta was in danger. Korana's frustration mounted with the fact that there was nothing she could do about it from that distance.

She had to accept the fact that she trusted Killgreth to protect Presta as if she was his own. With one more distant look, she reached out and closed the big heavy window. Pulled the sweater over her shoulders and went back to the sanctity of her own warm bed.

☥

Main Campsite:

A large rider-less horse charged into the camp like a bat out of the Dark. The poor beast had multiple shoulder wounds and various leg traumas. Even the animal's soft nose was torn from its face. When the horse stopped abruptly, blood could be seen soaked into the tan-colored saddle...human blood! A wave of fear and panic swept through the little camp. To make matters worse, large snowflakes started to fall. Koln was the first to get to the horse. He lunged for the reins to settle the terrified animal. Presta put down her berries and joined the men rallying around the wounded horse.

"I wish I was Korrin...maybe then I could do something to help this poor animal."

"Don't say that. We each make our own contributions when the time arises. You are who you are...and you are special." Koln spoke with passion.

Koln turned back to the fatally wounded horse.

"He will have to be put down."

"Wow! two in one day...that's horrible," Erin said.

Presta started to cry, so Erin placed his arm around her and led her back to the central fire. One of the soldiers noticed large teeth marks and concluded that the horse had been attacked by multiple animals, and didn't receive the wounds from battle between men. Koln confirmed the blood on the saddle was human and recognized the saddle from the spicers earlier that day. Koln turned to the perimeter guards and ordered them to build the fires higher, just in case they needed the light to fight at night. This command didn't make Presta feel any better. She wondered what her sisters were doing right now and truly wished she was with them sitting by a roaring fire, weaving stories and drinking apple juice.

Kill was feeling sick to his stomach. The stress and tension was more than he had ever experienced and he was showing his years. Koln turned to Kill.

"Son...I want you... to put down this proud beast. Relieve this animal and send him on his way."

"I don't...know if I can father."

"This is an order...you must. You will need this skill in the future. Now! Take him into the forest just beyond the tree perimeter and use your short sword just behind the ear...right here."

Koln pointed to the most proper area for the swiftest death.

"One fluid motion and put your everything into it son."

Little Kill grabbed the reins and slowly led the limping horse out of the central camp. Approximately ten tics went by when the whole camp heard the beast fall. The sound meant something different to each soul in the temporary camp. When Kill walked into camp, his eyes were wet with emotion. His short sword was stained bright red from his first humane kill. Koln approached him and gave him a few short, sharp slaps on his small shoulder.

"Clean your blade well before you put it away son. What you did was right."

It was the first time Kill ever drew blood from any beast or foe. How fragile is the heart of a child trying to be a man? Without a spoken word, Kill sat himself down beside Presta. She instinctively knew he needed a loving hug. With her hand on his tiny back, Kill slowly spun his sword in the cleansing fire, round and around. Koln discussed the wounded horse event with his soldiers and decided that a strong offence was better than a surprised defense. They decided that they would trace the horse's tracks back to where the horse trauma happened. They reasoned that whatever happened there could happen where they were. One of the forward guards figured they didn't have much daylight left, so they had to hurry. With quick goodbyes, and last tic instructions the three warriors left to solve a mystery or at least plug a hole.

The Spice Traders Camp:

Koln was surprised how dense the forest actually was. He surmised that a large amount of the wounded horse's wounds were caused by running spooked through the treacherous vegetation. The large bite marks on his rump worried Koln the most.

Thirty tics went by and still no sign of a battle or disturbance. One more corner and one more hill and there it was, a very small clearing, the size of a small cottage appeared in the middle of the dense forest. Koln named it Spicers Clearing. It was soon clear to see that this was the site they were looking for. Body parts and horse parts littered the entire area. The smell of fresh blood was unmistakable to warriors of this nature. If the three had not been as experienced, they would have emptied their stomachs in a heartbeat. The men drew their swords in anticipation of anything sudden.

Half-eaten beasts lay everywhere. Small wolves dying or dead dotted the landscape. As the three warriors moved through the carnage, a distant moaning could faintly be heard. They picked up their pace looking for the hurtful sound. One of the forward guards spotted a human jutting out from under a half-eaten horse. The leg was barely moving. The three warriors converged on the human sound. Two of the guards lifted the horse while Koln carefully pulled on the single leg. Laval was lying there with half a sword-arm missing and obvious trauma to his ribs where the horse fell on him. His breathing was very laborious and it was plain to see by the experienced warriors, that he wasn't going to make it. The loss of blood from the half-chewed arm was enough to put anyone down. The fact he was alive at all attested to his shear willpower. Koln ran back to his saddle and grabbed his drink bladder. "Here friend…drink!"

Koln squeezed the bladder gently and applied a few choice drops of wine to Laval's dry lips. A few of the drops made it down his parched throat. He coughed the fluid up mixed with blood. The nasty mixture trickled down his dirty chin. Koln laid his head back on a rolled up piece of clothing. Laval reached with his one good arm and placed it on Koln's arm. "There were too many my friend, (choke, and cough) they came at us from all sides."

He tried to sit up. "*Take it easy.*"

"Get ye out of this dark place…friend…save those children…you carry."

Koln knew he didn't have much time.

"Is there anything I can do for you, mate?"

"Take my ring back home to...my...son. He will be needing it soon enough."

Laval went to look for the ring but it lay on the hand of his missing arm. His eyes widened...then froze open in death. Koln ran his large open hand over Laval's eyes to close them in respect for a fallen soldier. Koln stood and viewed the scene more closely. *"What in the Dark happened here?"*

The two forward guards rummaged through the carnage trying to find any information on what had actually happened to the traders. They needed to know what they were up against. Koln spotted a severed arm fifteen measures away. He bent down to pick up the limb and noticed the unusually ornate ring on the index finger. He pulled the ring off and tossed the arm to the ground. Upon further inspection, he noticed the ring had an imprint of a dragon on its golden face and a small inscription. Argonnis et Dominata surrounded the Dragon's out stretched wings. Thinking no more of the strangeness of the piece of jewelry, he placed the ring deep inside an inner pocket of his jacket and joined his men.

"Well, what do you want to do with the remains...Sir?"

"Leave them...the forest has a natural way to reclaim flesh, and it's all the time we have anyway. We really need to get back to the camp and secure the site. The young ones could really be in mortal danger."

As the three were heading back to their horses, a lone wolf howled in close proximity. The three hardened warriors drew their swords simultaneously. One of the forward guards ran to his saddle and detached his crossbow. A second wolf howled, then several. The cacophony of wolf war cries was gut wrenching, even for the experienced warriors. From out of the forest's edge, backlit eyes poked through.

"Why are they not charging?"

The forward guard had a nervous twitch in his voice. Koln answered with the obvious. *"They have already fed. They are here for sport or territorial issues. They are going to make sure they can win before they strike. Keep your eyes open!"*

The light of day was fading fast and at the most inopportune time. One large dominant wolf broke through the tree line with speed and agility. He ran into the centre of the clearing and stopped suddenly. The large dog-like creature strengthened his stance while rolling his black lips back, baring his pointy yellow teeth. Then came an evil sounding growl. The hairs on the back of Koln's neck stood at attention. Without another obvious command, thirty to forty small wolf-like creatures raced from the forest straight for the three soldiers. Their teeth were bared and tails were down. At that very moment,... the sun seemed to drop beneath the distant mountain.

Ψ

Expedition's Main campsite:
Kill was pacing back and forth like he was worried about something he couldn't understand.

"Did you hear that? There! That…right there!"

"What?" Erin answered back.

Presta added her two copper coins, "*I didn't hear anything. Stop pacing… you're making me scared.*"

Kill placed his small hand on his sword hilt and craned his neck to hear. Everyone at the central fire joined Kill in listening extra hard, but all anyone could hear was the crackle of the firewood burning. Small sparks shot into the air with each mini explosion.

The sun was almost spent when all this noise started to happen. The main campsite would soon be bathed in full moon illumination.

"It looks like they might not come back tonight. We had better bed the horses and secure the tents for the evening."

Kill was right and the others silently agreed. They all knew what had to be done and started the manual tasks of preparing for dark. Kill was the youngest and the shortest but came across with all the control and tone of his father giving knowledgeable orders. The others always smiled and enjoyed it when he thought he was in charge, but he was right.

The two forward guards left the central fire and started their night patrols along the fiery outer ring of the camp's perimeter. Walking back and forth between the four fires, they occasionally threw fresh wood on the fires to light the area. Little Killth once again spoke in a nervous tone. "There! I heard it again…right there. Did you hear that?" No sooner were his words spoken than three small wolves walked out of the forest's edge heading for the centre of the camp. Erin was the first to spot the three dog-sized animals.

"Over there!" he shouted.

The two perimeter guards ran back towards the young people with swords drawn. Erin grabbed his father's crossbow, which was leaning beside his tent.

He loaded the weapon with a bolt and without hesitation ran back and stood beside Presta. The three wolves stood still and then immediately turned and ran back into the darkening forest. The sunlight was almost gone. Only tics remained before they were all covered in a cold blanket of dark.

Presta exclaimed, *"What do you make of that?"*

One of the forward guards said, "It resembles a forward scouting party, if you ask me."

"What do you think we should do?" Presta asked with a shake in her voice.

Erin spoke up with authority. "Quick...everyone stoke all the fires. We will need fighting light."

"We need to protect the horses!" Kill added.

"Fine! Bring them closer to us and the fire." Erin sounded angry.

One of the forward soldiers was already in the process of gathering the horses together. It was customary for them to protect their animals when danger threatened.

The sun disappeared with a flash. The fires around the camp were the only light they had now. A few large clouds drifted by and saw the moons light tempered. This made everyone a little tenser. When their eyes adjusted to the low lighting, they could all see many sets of eyes peering out from the forest's edge. The people gathered around the central fire hoping it would ward off night animals that feared fire. Presta handed out dry biscuits instead of hot food. She was scared the smell of the cooked food would entice the forest creatures to attack in hunger. *"Will they...attack at night?"* Presta asked with her mouth full of dry food.

"I don't know," Erin answered truthfully.

"Why is father taking so long?" Kill asked.

"I wish I knew," Erin answered grimly. Presta jumped up and screamed, which made everyone jump up and draw their weapons.

"What?" Kill shouted.

"Look!" Presta pointed to the forest's edge just to the right of a large boulder. Small dog like creatures emptied the forest and spilled into The camps fire lit area. They immediately formed a circle formation around the entire camp. Kill handed Presta a short sword and showed her how to stand. She gave him a look and informed him that she came in second in girl's weapon training. Which made Kill scrunch up one side of his face as if to say...what girls?

The humans had their backs to the central fire hoping to give them an advantage. The fire was an equalizer when it came to wild animals or so the young people believed. Erin pointed his father's crossbow at the encroaching doom.

"Wait until I say…go!" Erin interjected into a panic-filled conversation between the two forward guards. Just as the circle of wolves reached the danger zone, they all stopped simultaneously. One extremely large wolf broke through the fur circle and slowly approached the side the young girl was on… then stopped. Erin aimed his weapon and slowly placed his finger over the crossbows trigger. Kill noticed that his teeth were not bared and his tail was between his legs. Kill put up his hand to Erin's weapon.

"Hold yer fire brother, this animal is not going to attack. He is acting like my dog back home…he's acting like he has done something wrong, see his tail."

The large wolf was the size of a small cow. He was dark brown with a white chest. There was no doubt in anyone there that this was the alpha male. The great beast stopped just short of fifty hands away.

The great wolf spoke human words. *"Why are you here…in my forest?"*

Ψ

Koln and the forward guards:
The small sized wolves charged the three warriors with a demeanor that could be seen as only lust for the kill. The three brave men stood their ground and swung their weapons as if they were swatting pesky flies. Dog-sounding cries could be heard throughout the vast forest.

Ψ

Main Camp:
The dominant wolf briefly turned an ear towards the forest, then cocked his head if only slightly.

Ψ

Koln and the forward guards:
The sound of the wolf cries coincided with the swings of the large battle swords the men swung. The cries and yelps could be heard left, right and centre. One of the forward guards had an animal on his back, while another

was making a meal of his leg. The soldier cried out in pain for assistance. Koln was taking his share of ankle biters, but was also managing to stay ahead of the attack. He would dispatch three at a time with one giant swing of his death-delivering sword. The other guard was also managing to stay ahead of the wave with his fearless battle-axe. After a few long tics, the initial first wave was over. The animals seemed to retreat to the edge of the forest. The wounded animals were left by the pack to die in agony alone. Killgreth dropped his guard and wiped his sweaty forehead only to find out it was fresh blood...and not his own. The blood of his new enemy covered him from head to toe. When he looked around he saw his comrade beside him breathing heavy. He lowered his battle-axe and hung his head trying to catch his breath. When he looked behind him, he saw his friend down. Killgreth and the remaining soldier ran to the aid of the third man.

Upon first inspection, they both could see he was badly wounded. Heavy amounts of blood leaked from an open wound on the side of the downed soldier's neck. The wound was the size of a man's fist and it was directly over and through the jugular vein. It was clear now there was no saving him, he was no more.

"Ah! Poor Hangth...Not like this, mate! I knew ye in three wars and why today in this dark place?"

Koln lowered his head, but knew he couldn't grieve long for they were not out of danger by any means. The dead soldier's eyes were open in death. Koln placed his blood-spattered hand over his friend's face and closed his eyes in a final gesture of friendship and honor. Koln's large fingers produced a pattern in blood on his soldier's face. The other soldier leaning over his friend quietly asked a rhetorical question. "Do you think they will return?"

Koln just looked at him and said, *"They are not done. We are still here."*

Killgreth looked for materials dry enough to start a bigger fire. The small one the traders had lit was not for light but for cooking. Within a short time, they had the main fire blazing big enough to throw their friend on and complete his journey to the next realm. Koln and the remaining soldier moved some big logs and debris around to make a high point from which they could have a slight advantage over their canine enemy. They lit several small satellite fires, in hope it would provide sufficient light during a battle.

"What did we do to piss them off?" Koln's friend asked.

"It's not what we did...It's what they did." Koln pointed to the departed spice traders. The two remaining soldiers stood on the freshly made hill back to back. Steam was emanating from their flared nostrils, evidence of the heavy breathing they were maintaining.

"*There!*" Declared Koln. Out of the forest came the dogs of war.

ᚹ

Main camp site:

Presta had to shake her head. For a tic, she thought the large wolf actually spoke like a human.

She turned to Erin, "*Did you hear something or someone speak?*"

"No...Except for the beating of my heart."

"I could have sworn...the big one talked to me."

"What did it say then?"

"He asked what we were doing here."

"Tell him...see if he understands."

She looked at Erin as if he was totally crazy then thought...what have we got to lose.

"*Are you talking to me?*" She pointed to herself as she spoke to the wolf.

"Actually...anyone who will answer," the large wolf replied. "*How is it... that...I can understand you?*"

"I used to be a great wizard before a Dark wizard put a spell on me. And now I exist as a wolf. I live in this ungood forest, leading these good forsaken dog-like creatures. It might have something to do with my large size...I guess."

"*My friends can't hear you as I can and they are very scared right now.*"

"What are you doing in my forest, little one?"

"*I am Presta Atlas...Princess of the throne of Delockth. We are on a quest to find a powerful witch, which we believe is located somewhere on the other side of your forest...as you put it. Our High Wizard was frozen in a green solid by a Dark wizard named Seth.*"

The big wolf tightened his stance and growled sonically loud. All of Presta's comrades jumped fearing the worst. "That's the name of the one...the Dark one who made me this way. If I could only destroy him, my curse might be lifted."

The wolf paused then spoke more gently.

"So it is true...the rumors I hear that a Queen now rules the land and not a King."

"What's he saying?" Kill wanted to know.

Presta told everyone what the wolf had told her and told them to remain calm, there might be a way out of this.

Presta lifted her Royal head and spoke aloud. "*We seem to have a common enemy and I am proposing that we join forces to defeat the Dark wizard and all who control him. Will you let us pass safely, great wolf wizard?*"

"I agree with your proposal and wish to add that if you should ever need my assistance, you need only call."

"*How shall I call you...I know not your name?*"

"I was known as Volzanth, Volzanth of Yelld. You can summon me by three high-pitched whistles. I will send my kind out from the forest towards Delockth so that they will be my ears. It would take me two full cycles to respond. I am sorry...it's the best these four legs can do."

"*A couple of members of our party have been out looking for some spice traders who recently passed through here. Have you heard or seen them? We are getting worried for their safety.*"

"We didn't know they were with you and just for your information; these wolves hear and see everything. I know for a fact it's too late for the ones you call spice traders, but maybe not for your friends."

The large wolf knew what he was hearing while he had his human conversation. He truly feared for Presta's people. He knew he had to find the large pack. The great wolf turned around and howled. After a few tics, he took off and ran at full speed in the direction that Koln and the forward guards took. All the smaller wolves followed in the same direction at a full-out run. Erin put his sword down as if it was very heavy. He blew out a full chest of held air. "What did the beast say, my lady?"

"*I think he said something happened to the traders, but Koln and the guards might be in danger as well.*"

"How come only you got to hear the big dog?" Kill asked as if he was whining.

"*I'm guessing it has something to do with my special abilities. After all, Kem did tell me...well before he was turned to that green solid coating, that I didn't really know how strong I was...I guess that's why.*"

"What do we do now?" Kill asked.

Erin jumped in; "I say we stoke the fires for heat and also for a beacon for the men to find their way back in the dark."

"A wonderful idea...I will put on some warm food. Now that we know we will not attract ravenous wolves, we should be able to cook some food."

Both boys and the rear guards applauded. This made the Princess curtsy. Presta soon stopped her merriment and looked towards the forest's black edge. She ordered an existing fire to be enlarged so the men could put the lifeless carcasses of the wolves atop. She was worried. The snow stopped falling, but not before it blanketed everything in sight. Erin was throwing wood on the central fire when a thought occurred to him, that possibly this night would never end.

Ψ

Koln and Mandth, Forward guard:

As the fearless wild animals moved closer, the night sky began to dump large snowflakes on the Spicer's camp. Each individual flake was the size of a gold coin. The men's visions were impaired with the snow globe effect the falling snowflakes gave. The sound of their demise was similar to being surrounded by snakes. Hisssss! The wolves that watched were strangely silent, calm before the storm. The remaining forward guard broke the eerie silence.

"It was an honor fighting with you, Sir Killgreth. If any of us survive, this story will be told for generations."

"For me as well, Mandth of Delockth, for I could not have chosen a better soldier to die with, if that is the case. You are the best forward commander and scout I have ever had the pleasure to serve with. Please don't count us out yet though, I am just starting to get angry, and I feel the urgent need to dispatch these flea bearing creatures to their next world." The pair strengthened their stances and hardened their focus on the forest's edge. The falling snow nearly concealed the advancing four-legged army. One wolf advanced, then two. They then came exponentially in waves.

The first few climbed the man-made hill and swiftly met their demise with eyes wide. The first blow was struck and the yelps echoed deep into the forest. The scene from the men's point of view played out in dizzy slow motion. With the men being back to back, one front was maintained by each individual fighter. The large swords arched in voluminous swings, while the falling snow played with their visual accuracy. By the time Koln achieved a good down stroke, he had to use the up stroke to kill another. This play seemed to go on for several measures of time when things took a turn for the worst.

Mandth's footing was compromised due to the wet earth on which he was standing. The solidity of the hill gave way and the soldier lost his balance. One last fierce sword swing was enough to send Mandth off balance and off the mound onto his tired back. He fell into a sea of fur and flashing teeth. Koln's ears didn't hear his comrade fall for the blood rushing through them. He kept swinging madly, almost euphoric from the adrenaline racing through his bulging veins. Never hearing his friend fall was the part that Koln never forgot. He repeatedly stabbed and kicked, then punched and stomped. A mental picture of his wife and sons kept flashing through his mind's eye. He had no regrets for himself; only his dying wish to see Killth's dreams fulfilled and become the man he knew he would be. His arms felt like rubber and his legs were aching from multiple teeth bites. Even though all seemed lost, he somehow knew he was going to make it out alive. On a desperate swing, his blood-soaked hand slipped and his mighty sword flew out of his weakening grip. He was pushed from behind by a leaping wolf and he flew head long into a sea of waiting wet fur.

The large wolf broke through the tree line just as Koln disappeared into the cornucopia of wolves. The wolf at full stride pushed off with his powerful legs and landed in the centre of the mayhem. The smaller and less dominant wolves ceased their actions immediately and slowly started to give the great wolf the space he controlled. Slowly the forest wolves stepped backwards with teeth bared.

Koln was on his back with his bloody arms crossed in front of his face in a defensive position. He could tell the animals had stopped their advance, and was confused about why they were stopping.

As a battle strategy, this action made no sense. He now could feel a warm and tainted breath on the back of his blood-covered hands. He wouldn't have admitted this to anyone, but he was scared. Killgreth unfolded his arms and looked at his fate with eyes wide open. A large wolf, the size of a small cow was straddling his body with its face only twenty fingers away from Koln's. The large animal cocked his head, as a domesticated dog would do to his master when he had a question. The large wolf, knowing Koln wouldn't understand as Presta did, tried licking Koln's face and wagging his bushy tail in a sign of friendship and trust. Koln in utter amazement sat up and stroked the animal's head like an old favorite dog. The giant dog sat down and the tension dropped all around Koln. Despite his sudden awareness that he was spared from a gruesome death, his legs told another story. They were bleeding and the pain was starting to drive him into shock. He knew he would have a hard time trying to stand, but stand he must if he wanted to get back to the kids. Koln used the big wolf's head as a brace and lifted himself into a standing position.

"Well...to what do I owe this deed? You have saved my life, sir wolf, and I am eternally grateful. If I ever could repay you...I, Koln Killgreth...am bound to you in debt."

The wolf barked loud signaling as best he could that he somehow understood the promise Killgreth had just made. A few stray wolves looking to challenge the large wolf, tried to reengage the conflict with Koln, but a quick glare from the alpha wolf and a few choice growls stopped them in their tracks. Koln picked up a broken stick and used it as a crutch. He struggled over the white terrain to find his silent friend who he feared took a turn for the worst. Sure enough, Mandth lay there amongst the dead and dying wolves. His body had been torn and mutilated by the ravenous wolves. Koln said a few words to himself then turned towards his horse. Mandth needed no fire to release his soul. He found Mandth's sword and stuck it in the ground next to his tattered corpse. Koln turned away from his comrade and counted his blessings. He mounted his horse in a lot of pain and noticed that Mandth's mount was unharmed. He then gathered the reins of the fallen soldier's horse and started back whence he had come. He stopped just short of the forest's edge and turned around in his saddle. As he looked back at the horrific scene, the great wolf stood on his back legs and howled with his large bushy tail still wagging left and right. He knew he would see that beast again. The ride through the Dark Wolf forest was assisted by the full moon's light. Its light painted an eerie wash over the rough terrain. Koln's legs throbbed and pained with every twist and turn on his ride from the trader's clearing. He stayed alert for he wasn't out of danger yet. The challenging wolves, when separated from the alpha male, seemed to relish their own autonomous desires. Koln reached into his saddlebag and pulled out a skin of moonshine he was saving for a special event. He took a swig then poured the rest over his bloody legs. The fearless warrior cried out in pain.

Erin shouted from the top of his lungs, "Rider, too!"

He pointed to the forest's edge. He raised his still loaded crossbow in readiness for any new threat to spill out of the dark place.

"Wait!" Yelled Kill! "Its father...I recognize his outline."

Presta and Kill ran towards the single rider towing an empty horse. When they arrived at the injured warrior, they stopped with mouths open.

"Where...are the...others?" Presta asked unsure.

"It is only I...who remain...we did battle with..."

"A pack of wolves?" Kill added knowing it was.

"How did you?"

"*They were here too,*" Presta interjected.

"*The large one is called Volzanth. He talked to me and I understood...it has something to do with my special abilities, I am guessing. He is on our side.*"

"Volzanth, why does that name...sound familiar?"

Koln hung his head from the leg trauma he was experiencing.

"*Not now, we must attend to your wounds. I am presuming that some of this blood is actually yours.*"

Presta called the rear guard to help get the big man down from his horse and lay him by the main fire on a blanket.

Presta propped up Koln's head with a removed saddle then handed him a wine skin. After a large drink, Koln wiped his face with his dirty sleeve and smeared old blood across his already dirty face. Presta ripped a piece of her clothing off and dipped it in the pot of boiling water over the fire. She carefully and tenderly wiped Koln's face semi-clean.

"You mean the large wolf...was actually a wizard?"

"*Yes...he said he was turned into a wolf by a Dark wizard...for whatever reason. We never got into that.*"

"That explains a lot... he saved my life, you know. I pledged to repay him some day."

Erin came closer to his step-father. "What of the others?"

"They fought bravely but alas, succumbed to the brutal numbers of our attackers. They will be greatly missed, for we are a long way from home."

"Did you bury them?" Erin asked.

"I had no legs and no time. Besides there wasn't much left to bury."

"Oh! Will you bury me...if I..."

"Erin, stop that! Keep your eyes open and your sword sharp. I will get you and all home... I promise."

Presta was cutting Koln's trousers open to reveal his wounds.

"*Oh my! Sir Killgreth. You have lost a lot of blood.*"

Kill brought the pot of heated water to Presta's side. She dipped her piece of cloth in its warmth and started to wipe Koln's tattered legs. The big man winced in obvious pain, but never made a sound. The last rear guard put his face into the group.

"Are you okay, Sir Killgreth?"

"I will be okay Sammth. Bring me some warm food…if there be any. I will need my strength." Erin left to tend the horses while Kill needed to search for more dry wood. Raththth stood beside Koln and asked respectfully about the demise of his two friends. Koln explained in detail what he wanted to know and commented on their bravery, and to the major contribution they had made to the success of this campaign. The rear guard was satisfied that they would be honored and went back to his guard duties. Koln feeling the guard's immediate sorrow ordered a wine skin to be passed around, hoping it would take the edge off the cold slice of the night.

Presta handed Koln a wooden bowl of road stew. Koln grabbed the bowl eagerly and shoveled the hot contents into his open mouth. Presta turned her attention back to Koln's legs. She managed to tear up one of her underskirts for bandages and proceeded carefully to wrap his legs from thigh to ankle. Once again, she wished she had Korrin's powers of healing, but this time kept it to herself. Presta did a wonderful job of cleaning and wrapping Koln's lacerations and bites. He settled down after eating and managed to sleep through the night. The others settled down around the fire and told stories of their personal feeling of the day's extraordinary and deadly events.

Ψ

Marideath's Castle: personal chamber, "Ah! Seth…I've been expecting you. I need to clear up some rumors I have been chewing on. Sit down old man…here! Let me help you."

Marideath tossed a heavy chair across the room, and then slammed the old wizard into it. "Oh! I am sorry…was I too rough?"

The Dark Wizard just held up his withered hand in surrender. He didn't want to get into a scrap with his overlord. He thought to himself in a hidden fit of rage… "If I ever get the chance to crush this oaf, I would do it without hesitation."

Marideath had a smug look on his face. "How was your trip? Did anything interesting happen…perhaps?"

Marideath paced the cold stone floor holding a drink in one hand and a nasty bullwhip in the other.

"Well I did have..."

"CRACK!" The bull whip broke the sound barrier. Seth stopped mid-sentence and gulped a throat full of spit.

"*Continue,*" Marideath said.

"I...I confronted the High Wizard of Delockth and I have to report he is out of your hair." Seth's knuckles were white from squeezing the arms of the chair.

"*Very interesting...Where is my Lieutenant?*"

"Ah...He didn't make it back."

"CRACK!" The tip of the whip exploded only three small measures from the old man's wrinkled face. His eyes shut with such force it squeezed out tears on both ends.

He sat back fearing a direct hit.

"*And why didn't he make it back?*" The Dark Lord's tone sounded like he was chewing sand.

"It appears that the boat he was on was hit with an exceptionally large flying object...maybe a big boulder."

"A What?"

"A boulder my Lord...a huge rock."

"*I know what a boulder is...you old fool.*"

"That's what the survivors said."

Marideath stopped in his tracks and started to rub his pointy chin. He let the demon whip drop to his side. He whispered to himself... (*They either have one dark of a catapult...or...Someone has my abilities to move matter... I can pick up a big rock...but I can't throw it with that kind of accuracy, Hhmmm!*)

"*I thought you said you put the High Wizard out of commission?*"

"I did your Lordship; he is encased in a green solid."

Marideath turned quickly towards the Dark Wizard.

"*Go to sleep old man...I will be needing your skills again, and I want you at your best. We leave for Delockth in thirty cycles.*"

Marideath pointed to the door. As the old man got up Marideath cracked the whip once more this time taking the wizard's purple pointy hat clean off. All that was left was the old man's bald spot. "No screw-up's old man or this will be your last trip...anywhere. And make sure you get your rest!"

Seth moved a little quicker while headed directly for the door. Marideath yelled at him again. *"Seth! Send in that ship's Captain!"*

Seth never turned around to acknowledge his master's demanding words. He just kept moving until he was out of his sight. The Captain entered the large room.

"A drink...Captain? I have a special assignment for you. Come sit by my fire and warm your bones. I will lay it out for you."

The Captain had a grin from ear to ear as he grabbed the goblet of spirits he was handed.

ᴪ

Main Forest Camp: Morning.

The dawn of a new day broke far too early for all. Sleep was handed out like army rations near the end of a long and hard campaign. Snow fell during the wee cycles and successfully blanketed everything in sight. Even the exposed horses looked as if they had a sugar frosting. Some of the outer rim fire had succumbed to the large volume of snow that fell. The central fire wasn't much to speak of. A tiny plume of smoke escaped from dampened wood.

Kill was the first to leave the semi-protection of his make-shift tent. He knew enough to see to the main firee's rebirth and readily used some of the protected wood the guards had covered up the night before. It wasn't long before the fire was given a second chance to bring heat and light. Once he completed his task, he saw to waking the rear guards and subsequently everyone else in the process. When the guards finally arose, they immediately attended to the horses and all that it entails. Presta managed to get up before Erin and shook his tent violently to awake the snoring beast. The porridge was on and so was the great pot of home brew. Cinnamon and chocolate drifted on the breeze, tickling everyone's nose in the camp. Everyone left Koln alone, hoping he would heal faster with more sleep, however slight. Presta was worried about infection from the animal bites. She was hoping that wherever they ended up, someone would have some herbs and medicine. A cycle later Koln awoke and slowly ached his way to the main fire.

"Report!"

He grumpily barked out, as if he was in the army still.

"Nothing to report...Sir." Sammth said between bites of his steaming hot porridge.

"Very well, then." Koln sat down with a thump.

"How do you feel, father?" Kill asked.

"I've been worse. I think I actually cried the last time I was hit in the ribs. Every time I passed wind, it hurt like the dank dark."

Everyone broke out into laughter. Presta handed Koln a bowl of hot food and a magical chocolate drink.

"I think you spoil me, your highness."

"*Nonsense!*" was all she needed to say.

"When do you want to leave?" Erin stood while scraping out his bowl.

"Give me a cycle to wake up and tend to my wounds, then we can leave…"

He looked into the sky shielding the morning sun from his eyes with his saluting hand.

"At nine bells should be good."

Erin nodded his approval and carried on with his packing. Presta got up from the circle never saying a word. It was just the look on her sweet face that Koln noticed. He turned to her. "Are you all right…your highness?"

She stopped and turned looking at Koln with her eyes but a slightly down turned head. "Yes, Sir Killgreth, I believe I am experiencing …what some may call, homesickness."

"Do you want to return? I can send you with a guard if you wish. I don't think those wolves will bother you."

"No…I will be all right. *What doesn't slay you… makes you stronger.*"

"If this is your wish, we will be glad to have you, my lady."

"*I will be all right; I just need to keep busy.*" This she said with a new vigor.

"We will be leaving shortly. I suggest you dress with some layers. This could be cold and I'm feeling a weather change."

She smiled at him as she let him play a fatherly role. She turned and entered her tent.

The group of adventurers left at ten bells, early rise. The overall mood was somber but the eagerness to conclude the journey was evident. Erin, trying to prove to his father he was his son, suggested a guard in the front and the rear. Koln readily agreed much to Erin's happiness.

Five land measures away, they came upon Spicer's Clearing. Koln advised Presta not to be inquisitive and to move through quickly. Koln noticed that the local wildlife had made short work of the flesh that was hastily left unburied.

He was thankful for that natural exchange. A set of horse ribs poked through the snow and reminded Koln that they were not out of the woods yet.

The rest of the day seemed uneventful in comparison. At approximately five bells, the convoy broke through the forest's edge. A wonderful clearing opened up before the travelers. A few mountains lay in the distance and the snow was nowhere to be seen. It was as if they entered a totally different place this side of Wolf Forest. It didn't take them long to come to a fast and clean-flowing river. The river was about chest deep and 300 paces wide across. The sound of its babble in the shallow parts was a welcome sound. The forest they had just traveled through was very quiet and muffled in comparison.

Koln called out, "Make camp!"

Much to everyone's happiness, Presta lifted her voice and sang out, *"I'm going to take a bath and I don't care if it's cold."* Everyone had a good laugh when Presta let out a little scream. Apparently, the water was cold, much to the delight of all except Presta.

Erin and Kill were assigned to fish up the river as to not disturb the young lady from her private river bath. Neither of the two having fished from a moving river, found the task frustrating. As luck would have it, the boys caught a bountiful supply from the fresh river. It wasn't much longer after that the whole camp site had the distinct smell of fresh cooked fish. The vegetation around the camp was too fresh to burn, so the perimeter fires had to be scrapped. The men did find enough to successfully run the main campfire.

At dinner, he hadn't eaten more than a few mouthfuls, when Kill discovered he loved what the rear guard Sammth called… salmon.

His cheeks were full of the wonderful meat, when he asked Koln how long before they might encounter the mysterious witch.

Koln turned sideways and tried to sound like he knew what he was talking about.

"By my mental map…I do believe we should arrive by mid-afternoon cycle."

"Oooo! That would be nice. I've never met an actual witch before," Presta added.

"Hold on now…I really don't know if she is a good witch or a Dark witch. So don't get too excited, this could turn out to be more trouble than it's worth. We could be walking into a very bad situation." Koln sounded worried.

As the flames danced late into the night sky, a strange sound leapt from the silence. Who! Who! Erin jumped out of his position.

"Wha…what was that?"

Who! Who! "There! That noise again."

The two rear guards stood and drew their swords. They swiveled their heads left and right, then looked at Koln for an answer. Koln looked amused and shrugged his shoulders in response.

Who! Who! Koln reached for his crossbow that was leaning against his tree-stump seat. It was obvious by now that no one in the group had ever heard the hoot of an owl before. The great hunter of the night was perched on a jagged half tree, that lightning had made short work of on a stormy night past.

"*There!*"

Presta honed in on the direction of the sound and saw a great White Horned Owl sitting on a snapped over stump.

"*What is it?*" She sounded excited.

Koln drew his short sword while retaining his crossbow in the other. He walked right up to the unknown bird and taunted him with his sword. The bird stood unmoveable. He slowly blinked his ultra large yellow and black eyes. He acted as if he was above all and saw no direct threat to his well-being. One more hoot and the magnificent bird pushed off the jagged stump and took flight. His large and expansive wings only needed the luxury of two large flaps to distance him from human reach.

"It's gone…it was nothing. Every one stand down." Koln almost sounded disappointed.

"What was it, father?"

"It, my son, was just a strange bird. We are in a strange and enchanted land. From now on keep your eyes and ears open."

The camp settled down and turned in early on Koln's advice. The guards took turns switching on and off so they were rested as well.

Ψ

CHAPTER 9

The One Eyed Gate Keeper

THE GROUP WOKE TO A bright sunny morning. Steam rose from the green and predominantly red vegetation. This local flora seemed to cover every available ground space. The river they camped by moved at its usual meandering speed. The group ate quickly and saddled up. They soon after made their way to the edge of the wide river. Kill was the first to ask the obvious question that was on everyone's mind. "Ya…so how we going to cross this baby. My horse can barely run, so I know it's not going to swim that distance."

Koln sat tall in his horse and looked up and down the ominous river. "Let's go that way," he pointed.

"I'm hoping that around that next bend the river may be crossable… or something." One way was as good as the next to everyone, so they played follow the leader.

As luck would have it, just around the next bend the river narrowed. In the distance, Koln could see a crossable rope and wood bridge spanning the space between sides. Koln looked at the rear guard then the forward guard. "This can't be right, I'm not usually this lucky."

As the excited party neared the opening of the bridge, the forward guard drew his sword and galloped back towards the rest. The guard came to a near sliding stop. He looked nervous and animated at the same time. "Ok…we need to find another way around, or over."

Koln drew his short sword. "What the Dark is wrong with you?"

"I don't know if you'll want to go this way."

"What's wrong with you soldier…speak up. That's an order!"

Koln looked intensely over the guard's armored shoulder. Standing on the bridge at the entrance was the biggest, ugliest Cyclops anyone has ever seen. Koln rubbed his eyes and looked again. These mythical beasts were only heard of in kid's sleepy tales, and now he had to confront one.

The beast stood thirty, maybe forty hands tall, and had one outsized eye situated in the middle of his fivehead. The eye was just above his huge flattened nose. With half his teeth missing the beast wore a diabolical smile. His hands were the size of coal shovels and his feet were bare, except for the large tuffs of hair on the tops and each knuckle. He wore a brown cape and a leather belt, which divided his bulging belly in half. His buckle was the size of a dinner plate. Even the skull design on the buckle struck fear into all who stood before him, or dared oppose him.

Koln looked worried. It might possibly take a whole platoon to physically persuade this giant to stand down. He ordered the group to pull back while he went to parlay with the one eyed monster. If the beast wouldn't let them pass, he might at least tell them of another crossing. The question on everyone's mind was why he was blocking the path. Koln thought he would stay on his horse so he could at least be of formidable size when talking to the giant. As Koln moved closer, the giant raised his crossed swords from waist high to throat high. The Cyclops opened his one eye wider.

"Who dares cross my path…speak up or I shall make you visit death's door."

"I am Sir Koln Killgreth of Delockth. I am here on a Royal mission charged by our Queen Korana Atlas. Will you let us pass?"

"You…cannot…pass!"

"We need access to the Witch's Glen, as we seek advice from a powerful witch."

"The witch you seek is indeed powerful. She is Enndora Maththth Grannth…and you may not pass."

The Cyclops widened his stance and raised his two butterfly swords in a clear statement of readiness.

"You may…not pass!"

"And why the dark not?"

"You must prove yourself worthy!"

"And how do we do that?"

"If you can pass me…all of you may enter."

"If any of us can get past you…we all may enter?"

The beast turned his head in thought.

"Yes…if anyone of you puny, human people passes…you all may enter."

Koln turned around and galloped back to the others.

"What did he say? What happened?" Erin was all excited.

"If any of us can pass by him, we all can cross."

Kill asked. "Can you beat him dad? I bet you can cut him a new one."

"No! I will not take the chance. We will find another way around."

"Wait I have an idea…just hear me out." Presta had a big smile on her face.

"I know what to do." She said giggling like a little schoolgirl.

She pulled up beside Koln and stretched to whisper in his ear. Koln smiled and nodded his head in reluctant approval. She cautiously dismounted her horse and took a deep breath. She put her Royal chin in the air and walked with purpose towards the one-eyed monster. Erin shouted to Koln, "What does she think she's doing?"

Koln put his hands up to silence Erin. She looked back at her troop of friends while she still kept a forward motion towards her fate. The closer she got the more shallow her breathing became.

"STOP! None shall pass!"

"But…I am only a little girl."

The great hulk bent at the waist and looked down at the small girl. He blinked his one eye rapidly in disbelief. "No one shall pass! Not even the pretty little girl."

"Pretty girl…Pretty girl! Why…I am Princess Presta Atlas of Delockth, and I demand you let us pass."

The Cyclops didn't respond, nor did he move, he just calmly blinked his one eye.

"Move aside I say!" Now Presta was getting angry. She felt like running up to him and giving him a swift kick in the shins.

One more giant blink. "I shall not move and none shall pass!"

"If I can get around you…then we all shall pass unharmed…as you put it?"

The beast started to blink rapidly then he positioned himself in a defensive stance with one sword held high over his gruesome head. Koln turned to the two rear guards, "get ready…move forward slowly."

They both calmly drew their swords. Even Kill and Erin prepared for a fight.

"If you can get by me…you all can pass."

"*Fine!*" was all she said with her hand placed firmly on her slender hips.

One tic she was in front of him, three tics later she was behind him. The Cyclops reacted as if he was punched in the lower belly. His big eyelid slammed open and closed. His head turned everywhere looking for her. He even took several useless swings at imaginary foes in every direction but behind him.

"*I am here…Sir giant! Here behind you…past you!*"

The giant turned in total disbelief to see the tiny girl standing there with her hands on her slender hips again, looking very smug. The Cyclops dropped his swords and placed his empty hands on both sides of his head, as if he was trying to block out a terrible noise. "But…But!"

"*But nothing, you were bested by a little, pretty girl…now stand aside!*" The little mouse roared.

The beast fell to one knee and tipped his head in defeat. "I…I have never been beaten before. You must be a powerful wizard. I am at your service, my lady."

He placed his fat fingered hand over his heart.

"*What is your name big one?*" She spoke with an air of royalty.

"I am called Dogglopp."

"*Dogglopp…is that all?*"

"Yes, my lady wizard."

The others made a train and passed by while the giant was exchanging information with Presta. As Erin passed by, he blew Presta a kiss. Her cheeks turned beet red. Presta said her goodbyes to her new servant and rejoined the others on the other side of the bridge.

"Well done, your highness." Koln bowed his head.

"Once more you have shown grace under fire. You are an asset to our quest."

He bowed for the second time. Presta didn't say a word, she just nodded her head. Koln turned to Erin, "Do we know which direction we are now headed?"

"Your guess is as good as mine."

"*We need to head in the direction of Grannth Mountain…there in the distance.*" Presta pointed to a mid-sized mountain in the distance.

"Did one eye tell you that?" Kill asked jokingly.

"*Yes, as a matter of fact he did. We are to follow the road until it branches off towards the mountain. We will find who we seek in the valley…actually a glen, Witch's Glen.*"

Kill dropped back feeling the sting of her words. Presta looked back at the bridge to see her new friend waving like a happy schoolchild.

The group passed through the wet lands without incident and made camp just outside the desired glen. Even though winter seemed to avoid this part of the land, it did; however, get deadly cold at night and for this reason the central campfire was built extra big. The flames twisted and gyrated high into the cool air. The deer were abundant and one of the rear guards showed his skill with a bow by downing a two-point deer, It wasn't long before the fresh meat was turning on a spit over the hot fire. The smell of the game cooking was intoxicating for deer meat was rare in Delockth. Erin and Kill took advantage of the downtime and decided to practice their swordplay, much to the pleasure of their father.

Koln had some immediate chores of his own. He had to re-shoe some of the horses and tend to Presta's worn saddle strap. Meanwhile, Presta had to rearrange her clothing in her travel bag. No one noticed the white owl perched on the tip of Koln's tent. The great silent bird turned his head from left to right then back again. It seemed to blink constantly as if it was sending some kind of animal Morse code. Sometimes, only one eye blinked. When no one was looking, it flew off without being noticed.

"This meat is great. I don't ever remember something like this...for surely, I would have remembered." Kill was thoroughly pleased with the day's catch.

"*We only have deer once or twice a year...usually on special occasions. Sometimes when father had special dignitaries from far away, he would commission a special hunting party. It's not my favorite, but I know for a fact, Korrin could eat her weight of the stuff.*"

Everyone had a good chuckle. The two rear guards must have been hungry for they both ate without saying a word. They just continuously shoveled food into there already full mouths. Kill noticed and elbowed Erin to point it out. Erin was also amused by the pair.

No one saw the large shadow pass over the moon's face. Koln felt the hairs stand at attention on the back of his sweaty neck. He looked around from where he was seating, but the feeling was only brief. Brief was enough for him to send both rear guards to light some perimeter fires. They never asked...they just obeyed. Just as he sat back down from issuing orders, a large unidentified flying object passed directly over the camp. Kill and Erin both stood quickly.

"What was that? Did you see that?"

Presta directed Erin to throw some more fuel on the main fire so to extend their night vision. The horses became agitated and Koln knew something was very wrong. Erin's stallion was on his hind legs looking like a horse on a crest. Erin ran to him and the other horses. Koln told Kill to join him but be careful; spooked horses are very dangerous. Something very dark swooped out of the night sky and with large talons picked up one of the packhorses like it was no effort at all. The poor animal could be heard screeching far off into the distance. Everyone in the camp was now fully armed and looking up.

"What do we do?" Presta was clearly spooked herself.

"What in the dark was that thing, and how many others are there?" Kill was turning left and right, desperately craning his neck looking into the night sky. Koln hated an enemy he couldn't see. He shouted to the boys.

"Bring the remaining horses closer to us!"

The two rear guards took their positions beside Koln with their weapons drawn.

"I'm hoping it's not what I think it was," Sammth said.

"What are you thinking?" Koln asked.

"A Dark dragon."

"That crap is only in fairy tales." Koln didn't sound convincing.

"What do you mean? Didn't we just encounter a Cyclops just a short time ago?" Sammth was pressing his point with a slashing sword.

"Point taken, but still…a dragon…come on, mate."

"Maybe whatever it was…will be satisfied with the meat it just acquired." Sammth started to settle down.

"Let's just hope so." Koln lowered his weapon slightly and stood more relaxed.

"Where do you want them father?" Kill asked.

"Just over there lad…to the right."

Kill had the reins to three horses and Erin towed the rest.

The night passed without any other incidents. The whole party was on edge so Koln ordered a wine skin to be passed around. They had very little sleep in the camp that night. The invisible owl that was perched high in a neighboring tree kept a silent vigil.

The morning arrived on the back of a brilliant sun. It charged the bright landscape with brilliant colors and singing birds. Even the horses looked happy and playful. The group was underway after a lengthy breakfast. A small base camp was left standing in hopes of a swift return for their trip home. Without the stolen packhorse, it was difficult to carry everything anyway.

The valley that opened before them was a wonderful and enchanted place. The predominant tree type seemed to be a version of a lotus blossom. Pink flowers were everywhere and the turquoise sky painted a magnificent background for the full effect. Small hummingbirds were everywhere. The scene was such a sharp contrast to the night before. Kill pointed to a flock of geese flying in a V formation. A path opened up in the natural splendor of the Witch's Glen. They followed the path for a full cycle before they came to rest in a grove of spent apple trees. The only apples left were the ones that gravity had claimed and left on the ground to wither and rot. The twisted apple trees gave the field a sense of danger and doom. Their gnarly branches pointed like wretched fingers on a witch's hand. Just a little ways into the grove, almost directly in the centre stood a generous sized cottage. The roof was thatched and laundry hung from a small tree beside the cottage. A small creek ran off to one side providing water. There were a few barns to the rear. Erin quickly pointed out that there was smoke coming from the main cottage chimney.

Presta exclaimed, "Apples…don't you smell them…apples!"

The look on her face was priceless. Erin turned to Kill, "It's only apples?"

The smell of apples permeated everything.

As the group drew closer, Koln spotted an owl on the cottage rooftop. He pointed to Sammth, then up to the perched bird. The group dismounted with no formal invite or official welcome. Koln signaled the rear guard to be prepared. They tied up their horses at an obvious hitching rail. Erin then realized that there was water and hay for their horses.

"Did someone know we were coming?" was what Koln was thinking.

Slowly they made their way to the quiet cottage. Only Koln drew his weapon.

He arrived at the wooden door and asked Presta to enter first in her invisible state. He slowly knocked with his sword handle. No answer.

He tried again a little louder…still no answer.

He pushed on the door and it opened without a sound. Presta walked in first. The smell of cooked apples almost knocked the two of them over. The main room Presta entered was lit with tall slender candles. There had to be at least fifty of them. Presta guessed that they were made from apples. The floor was covered with freshly laid straw. Koln signaled the others to follow. The hearth had a small fire with a large copper pot braced over the flames. Presta could see apples bobbing in the water of the pot and almost giggled. Across the large central room was a large rear-ended woman bent over a sink in a highly functional kitchen. Her hair was white and a tangled mess at best. She didn't turn around.

"Hello there, young lady, or would you be more comfortable with… your Highness.Presta stopped in her steps."She can't see me," she said to herself.

The old lady reached behind herself and untied her apron, which she neatly folded and placed on the small wooden table beside her.

"I'm glad you're all right. I've been expecting you and your friends."

She turned around and looked straight at Presta.

"Can you see me?"

"Oh, yes, dear and by the heavens, I can smell you too."

Presta was embarrassed for she knew she had not bathed properly the last time. Presta materialized in front of the old lady.

"Ah! My child you are a vision of beauty…just like your mother."

"What…you knew my mother?"

The old lady stepped out of the shadows and into the brighter candlelight.

"There will be time for that later. Please… all may come in and make yourselves at home."

The witch's face was weathered and wrinkly beyond prune. Her eyes were green like Presta's and had the glow of inner goodness. A few of her front teeth went south for the winter, as did her figure. Her face was white as flour and sported a large mole on her chin. She was round as a pumpkin winner and dressed not to flatter. Kill mentioned to Erin, that she looked like the high wizard. Erin in turn elbowed him, to keep it to himself.

"I am Enndora Mathth of Grannth … and you are the sister to the Queen, Korana… Presta Atlas of Delockth." The old lady tried to curtsy and stumbled. Erin rushed in to lend a shoulder.

"Thank ye, lad! I am old and bent from years gone by, I am truly spent."

"How…How did you know?"

Erin helped the old lady into an awaiting chair she commandeered with a hand gesture. The boys looked at each other in amazement.

"How did I know you were coming? Did you meet my bird, Waldo the Owl?"

"You mean…that big eyed white bird we have been noticing?"

"Yes, sweetheart…yes, that's him, my eyes and ears."

Koln looked agitated, being out of the general conversation.

"Oh! Stop fidgeting, Sir Killgreth. Take a seat at the big table…come on! All of you."

Presta turned to Koln. "She knows all our names." Presta was excited.

Koln sat down cautiously at the giant wooden table. He placed his short sword on the top and removed his leather gloves.

"The news on the wind is that you have been searching for me."

"We have indeed…we need your help."

"How did you get by Dogglopp? Did you use that disappearing thing?"

Presta felt akin to the old woman but carried on with the group's business.

"I bet you a bucket of apples he was spun in the head after that."

Koln interjected. "We were told by an elder in Erin's village, you might be able to help us with a grave problem."

"Yes, that would have been Bernarth…an old, old flame of mine. Did I mention old? I'm sorry love…what's this urgent matter?"

She placed her ancient hand on Presta's and the connection was made. Presta looked at her as if she saw a ghost.

Koln spoke out. "My lady…are you okay?"

He stood and reached for his sword.

"It's okay, Sir Killgreth…she just found out I was her grandmother…please sit down. I think we all could use a drink."

Kills eyes lit up for the first time that day.

After the old lady poured apple cider for the lot, she turned to Presta and asked,

"Why? Do you have a problem with graves… that you can't handle yourselves?"

"What?" Koln said while shaking his head.

"No,…No, Our high wizard has lost a challenge with a Dark wizard and now stands in his tower stuck in a green solid casing."

Presta was waving her hands while speaking. Right then and there the old lady's mind took a detour.

"I tell you what, my lady…you take a hot bath and I will feed the lot of them. Then we will get down to business."

Presta just acquiesced and nodded. Koln threw up his hands in defeat.

It didn't take Enndora very long to scare up some food for the travelers. They all scurried and sat down at her large table, sitting on anything that would hold their weight.

"Sorry about the chairs…I don't get company much anymore, not since Wal…" The old lady stopped talking mid-sentence. "Anyway."

Koln left a guard outside against the old lady's recommendation. He didn't want to take a chance, not after that horse incident. She said it was unnecessary because her eyes were everywhere. The great white owl sat on the cottage roof listening to everyone inside. A single tear rolled down his all-knowing feathered face.

ᴪ

Presta Atlas (thinking):
My new-found Grandmother fixed me a hot bath in a grand old wooden tub. She even managed to close off a space in the rear of the cottage to give me the privacy I deserved. I hope Erin doesn't peek through the curtain.

She put her finger to her bottom lip for a private thought.

The water's temperature was perfect and even had the scent of apples and cinnamon. Not really a Princess's fragrance, but a refreshing one indeed. I put my hair up in a bun and put my last clean clothes on a stool beside me.

I cautiously tested the water with a big toe. When I was satisfied I wasn't going to cook, I slid into the wooden tub. Oh my! I forgot too soon the simple pleasures of a hot bath. I think I miss this more than my big bed. As I brought the water line up to my neck, someone burst into my space without warning.

Out of fear, I turned invisible. The old lady…I mean my grandmother, excused herself and grabbed something off a shelf over my head and to the right. While doing so she knocked over two candles and cussed in a tone I haven't heard in a while. It reminded me of the time Korrin and I passed by the soldiers barracks and heard them through an open window. We used to giggle at the vulgarity. When she left I changed back to conserve energy. When I had finished drying myself, I put on my fresh clothes. A beautiful lavender-colored dress and white leg stockings. I pulled my hair down and gave it a brushing with the vigor of a well beaten carpet. I can smell the food, I don't know what it is but I am going to eat it all.

ᴪ

Erin Killgreth (thinking):
Presta opened the curtain at the rear of the cottage and walked towards us. Her head was held high reflecting her office and her new cleanliness. Her dress was so purply and pretty, my mouth froze open. I hope no one notices that I can't breathe

when she is near me. I don't know what that old lady is cooking; I just hope there's enough. Oh, I hope she sits beside me. Maybe her leg might touch mine? Wow! This warm apple drink has a kick. I had better sit down before I make a fool out of myself.

ψ

Koln Killgreth:
Thinking: *My…My! Presta looks like a Queen herself. I sure could use a bath; I must make a point to ask later. In the old days I would go 90 cycles or more with nothing but a shave. The Castle life has made me soft. However, I would settle for soaking my throbbing legs. My goodness…the smell of food is intoxicating or is it this warm apple drink. I don't care…I am hungry as I am assured we all are. I am finding it hard to believe that the old witch is Presta's grandmother.*

The old lady walked up to Koln and pushed her bird's-nest hair out of her eyes. "How are your legs, Sir Killgreth?"

"Please, my lady…address me as Koln."

"I am sorry, Sir, for I am no lady." Her response had a lyrical quality to it.

"As you wish Koln, how are your bloody legs then?"

Koln sat back at the bar-room tone of her voice. He slouched down into his chair in response. "They throb, my good woman. How do you know my legs are wounded?"

"Volzanth used to be a friend of my husband's, Prestas grandfather. Well, that's when he walked with two feet anyway. My eyes and ears are quite extensive, Sir Killgreth the assassin."

She gave Koln a stern look with one bushy eyebrow raised on her wrinkled forehead. All Koln could say was, "Oh! Yes…well."

"No need to explain, I am not judging your past…only your future. May I tend to your legs? My main expertise has always been to heal."

"Yes, I would appreciate that, Enndora."

The old lady gave him a big toothless smile, for she hadn't heard her name spoken in many full Cycles. She knelt before the warrior and rolled back his trouser legs. Kill moved closer to watch what was going on.

"You are very fortunate, Sir; any less attention to your obvious ailment would surely reveal a time line for your death. Ah! Don't you worry now,…Enndora has the stuff, and in no time you will be as good as new."

She pulled herself off the floor with Kill's help and went searching for the desired salve. It wasn't more than a few tics when the old lady returned. She opened a red-colored jar, which sent Kill spinning about twenty hands backwards.

"Hokum! pokum! What is that dark and wretched smell?"

"It is an old, old recipe of this and that. Mostly that…is the part you're reeling from. The old lady started to giggle like a child. She generously smeared the green stinky paste on Koln's wounds. When she was done, she wrapped them tightly in a white cotton material cut into hand- width strips.

"There you go; you'll be right as rain in a few cycles.

She sat back on her haunches and commented, *"It's been a dark of a long time since I touched a man's legs."*

Koln didn't want to know where that was going, so he didn't respond. The paste made his legs feel hot then cold. The sudden relief gave a wave of euphoria that he was enjoying.

"Okay, if you will help this old beast off the floor once more, I will see about the food I know you all are craving…help me up lad."

She held out her weathered hand for Kill to pull.

They finally all settled down to a country feast. Everyone was afraid to ask what it was they were eating, but it tasted so good they were afraid they would stop eating if it was something questionable. The bird on the table was recognizable to all. The pheasant still had its feathers in its tail. Erin thought it was a nice touch. The apple pie was the coupe de grâce. It was the best anyone there had ever consumed.

"Why apples…I've just got to ask?" Erin had his head tilted to one side and a puzzled look on his food-covered face.

"That's an easy one, lad." The old lady wiped her face with her sleeve.

"The apple, or napple as we call it around these parts, gives the magic practitioner her source of chemical power. It's the natural sugars that drive the spells and internal energy."

"Don't other fruit have sweet sugars?" Presta asked.

"Yes, little one, but the apple tree can grow in more places than…say…cherries or grapes. The original napple tree was grafted by a powerful warlock many hundreds of full cycles ago for the express purpose of his craft. The fruit is perfect it's… history…no it's…tradition."

"We don't have many apple trees…I mean napples, where we are from but we still have special powers."

"I understand love. Your powers and your sister's powers are different from each other. It's what makes you special…standout from each other. Korana seems to be the strongest, but she was first born of the three, which makes her dominant and slightly more focused on her powers. If you had more napples in your daily intake, you would all share the same level of power and possibly the exact same abilities. The only thing you can't change is that Korana is the chosen one from the ancient Prophesy…this is written, this is clear."

Presta was in deep thought while everyone else continued to eat as if they were at a strange dinner theater. "What was she like?"

"Who love…your mother? She was like you, sweetheart, beautiful and adventurous. When she left our world, a part of me went with her. She would have been so proud of the three of you. Kem did a good job of tutoring and guiding you. Yes… he is my son and your uncle."

"We didn't know."

Koln stood… "That would make Kem her uncle. Maybe that's why the King made the High Wizard sole custodian to the three sisters…that would make sense. Why did no one tell me? This might be a blessing in disguise; we need all the help we can get if we are going to save Kem and hopefully ourselves in the process." Kill looked at Erin with a big smile on his face. It was obvious he was being entertained by the turn of events.

Koln pushed his plate away and sat back. "Can you help us with your son's predicament?"

"You say he was in a wizard fight and was encased in a green solid…my, my. It definitely sounds like an old friend of Kem's, Seth of Andress. He turned to the Dark after he was recruited by the Dark Lord Marideath when he was young. I can tell you this…Kem is still alive, but not for long. Thirty cycles is all the green solid will allow. Red solid is a full season cycle and blue is one-hundred full-season cycles. How long has it been since my son was defeated?"

Koln looked at the group and hunched his shoulders. "I am guessing… Twenty full cycles past."

You have little time if you want to save your friend. Tomorrow you must leave for Grannth Mountain. There you will climb to the top and retrieve a vial of baby dragon's blood."

The group started to twitch and stare at each other.

"You will then bring the vial to me, and I will craft a spell and a potion that will free our beloved Kem. I believe I have all the other ingredients here."

They all looked stunned, Erin had his mouth open full of food.

Koln stood, "Dragons? Is that what took our pack horse?"

"Sit down, Sir Killgreth. You haven't had you dessert drink."

The old woman got up and quickly as she could, filled his cup with an apple brandy. Koln took a large drink and choked thinking it was apple cider.

"Whoa! That's the grownup nectar."

He sat down by the fire. "Now! How do you propose we get the dragon to give us her baby's blood…ask nicely?"

The old lady went to the back of the cottage and opened an old trunk. She pulled out an object wrapped in a soft tan-colored hide and handed it to Koln.

"This will help you."

Koln unwrapped the cloth to find a small golden bolt. It shimmered with flashy little lights and

felt warm to the touch.

"You want me to kill the…?"

"No killing! The dragon is part of the land's eco system. It is important not to harm either the mother or the baby."

The old woman raised her voice to make a serious point.

"The bolt is a sleeping bolt. It will put down the mother for a full cycle. This will make your task easier, but not without risk. The young one is still a formidable fighter. Luckily, it won't have fire for another two full cycles, but it has very sharp teeth and a skin of plated armor."

Koln spun the beautiful bolt in his fingers then showed his sons briefly. He rewrapped the bolt and placed it on the table beside him.

"I need to know if everyone is still into this. The dynamics have changed and I won't think badly of you if you back away now."

Erin stood, "I'm in…all the way."

Kill stood, "Count me in…I'm a Killgreth."

The guard stood, "Without question, I would follow you anywhere, my Captain."

Presta stood slowly as her chair scraped across the rock floor. "I am not going home…my family needs me and this is my destiny."

"Good! Then it is agreed, we leave tomorrow for Grannth Mountain."

"You will need this."

The old lady handed Koln a glass tube with a thick needle fashioned to the end of it. *"Just put the needle in and it will automatically draw the right amount."*

"You make it sound easy." Koln smirked

They all helped with clearing the table and stoking the fire. Koln changed the guard and gave the other a chance to eat and warm up. Koln sat by the roaring fire and lightly rubbed his throbbing legs. The brandy made his eyelids heavy…very heavy.

The grandmother stroked her granddaughter's hair. *"I know the Dark is heading our way…I can feel it. Maridean is strong…but lacks one important thing. Love…he loves nothing and nothing loves him. You will be stronger to remember this child. Also if you remember nothing …remember this. You are stronger as one."*

Presta thought she meant the group heading to Grannth Mountain. Presta was feeling the effects of the rich food and fell asleep on the old lady's big chair curled into a ball.

Enndora turned her head up to the ceiling trying to hear something. She shrugged it off and turned in. The boys lay down in front of the fire and were soon snoring. The inside guard folded his arms and placed his head on them. Only a two and a half cycles later, the door to the warm cottage flew open and smashed up against the heavy-laden coat rack. "Sir Killgreth…Captain Sir, come quick…I think it's back."

Koln threw off the blanket some kind soul had thrown over him earlier. He sat up not knowing who or where he was. "What…why? Who goes there?"

Sammth stepped inside while still trying to keep his eyes on the night sky. Koln was up and hurried to the door. He turned around before he was there to retrieve his short sword he had placed beside the fireplace.

"What are ye babbling about, mate? Speak up."

Everyone in the cottage was now fully awake and scrambling for either cover or a weapon.

"It's back, I tell ya…the big winged demon. I saw it as clear as day. It was dragon shaped and was black as the Dark it was."

Enndora pulled a shawl around her bare shoulders and entered the front parlor. That's not one of the Grannth Mountain birds. It reeks of Dark and ungood. The old lady stepped outside and looked up to her roof to see if her owl was on guard.

"That's strange…I received no warning from my precious."

She quickly dashed inside the cottage and headed to her big book on a wooden stand.

"*I will need a strong spell to counteract this bird of prey.*"

She feverishly flipped through olde, dusty pages. She took a tic to reach for a ripe-red napple sitting in an ornate fruit bowl only small measures away. She returned to flipping pages while she devoured the napple.

Koln resumed his focus and sent the now fully awake Erin to tend to the spooked horses. "Make sure you always have one of your eyes pointing up, son."

Erin just nodded and grabbed his coat and short sword scabbard. He ran out of the open door towards the back of the cottage.

"Sammth and Kill, I need a few fires lit. Use the wood from the side of the cottage and throw some oil on it. I want them roaring yesterday."

"Right you are, Sir." Sammth replied.

The two bolted out into the night. Rathth stood at the door as if he was waiting to jump off a cliff.

"No not you…I need you here to look after the women. I am going to assess the threat…I will be back."

Koln would have liked to have bounded out of the room like a hero but his legs told him otherwise. He cautiously walked out and closed the thick door behind him. Presta went to the back and put her travel clothes on while Enndora still searched for the proper spell weapon.

The Dark dragon never reappeared. The men came back inside and sat at the big table. The old lady heated up some leftovers and fresh bread. Presta managed to make some of her chocolate and cinnamon hot drinks.

"Well that didn't turn out the way I thought it was going to," Erin said.

"Lucky for us," Kill added.

"Well, something tells me we have not seen the last of that black beast."

"*You are quite right, Sir Killgreth. The only spell I found that might help you is a fog potion. When you break this small glass ball, a great fog will roll in and blanket everything. This I hope…will give you an advantage of escape or diversion.*"

"I hate an enemy I can't see," Koln whispered to himself. He took the glass ball from Enndora and put it in his vest pocket.

"After this food…we need to try again to rest."

No one argued with that. The two guards were stationed outside for the night taking turns, keeping a watchful eye open. Presta curled up against Erin much to his youthful delight in front of the fire. The outdoor fires would flicker and could be seen through small holes in the wall. Enndora rocked in her chair wondering where her owl went, while Kill slept beside Koln who found it impossible to close his eyes.

The Dark dragon stayed high in the sky ever watching the bright fires that lit the witch's property. Waiting for the right moment to do what he was sent to do.

Ψ

CHAPTER 10

Grannth Mountain
(Blood of the Baby)

THE NEXT MORNING BROKE EARLY in *Witch's Glen*. *The rising sun filled their hearts with hope and a collective thought of success. A wonderful array of birds and bushy ground squirrels filled the witch's property with joyous movement and sounds. Through this whirly happiness, they all went about their morning tasks preparing for a new adventure. The horses were tended and the clothes were washed. Even the boys managed to rise early enough to have an ice cold bath. Never was a scream heard, but a few personal comments were made on the effect of shrinkage. This flew over Presta's unknowing head, but made the old woman smile from ear to wart. No one seemed to care about flying dragons or death dealing wolves that morning. Their focus was on completing their new quest.* Enndora went about her usual routine of drawing water and feeding her pets. She seemed to be enjoying the company and attention she was receiving from her guests. She stopped briefly in her tracks and looked up at the cottage's roof top. "What's the matter Grandmother? Do you hear something?"

"No child...It's my bird...I'm scared something has happened to him. It's not like him to be far away, or for long periods of time."

"I'm sure he will turn up."

Presta rubbed her Grandmother's back. The incident with the black dragon was worrying Enndora. The owl was no match for such dark evil.

Koln prepared the last packhorse for the journey and made a detailed personal inspection of his weapons. He even went the extra measure to sharpen the points on his bolts, remembering what the old lady said about the extremely tough, armored hide of the grown dragon.

It wasn't long before the party gathered at the napple tree line and said their thanks and goodbyes.

"Take good care of my granddaughter, Sir Killgreth. I know she is strong…very strong, but so inexperienced."

The old lady had a tear in her wrinkled eye. "And good speed to you all…for Kem's sake." Hugs were shared and waves were a plenty as the group left the witch's property. Overhead flew the missing owl in the direction of the travelers. The old lady was heard from a short distance away, "There you are you naughty bugger! What have you been up to…eh?"

Ψ

Presta Atlas (thinking):

It was shortly after nine bells when we waved goodbye to my Gram. We headed in the direction of the valley searching for the path that will eventually lead to the mountain's cave. I decided the day was too lovely and the mood too somber, so I started to sing.

We're…off to slay the dragon
the wonderful dragon of Grannth
we need to score some dragon's blood
so we can release our Kem
we really need to release our Kem
because the Marideath is coming
he's coming, he's coming, he's coming…

Koln turned his head in disgust and with the sour mask, begged me to stop or at least keep it in my own head. I couldn't help but giggle…just a bit.

The day was warming up nicely as the differences between the two sides of Wolf forest were felt. The Delockth side was racing towards winter, but the Witch's side was bathing in warm summerlike conditions. Strange, to say the least, but highly appreciated by the adventurers. The flowers were in full bloom and the small rivers were spring fed and clearly drinkable. For a brief moment, Presta forgot they were on a dangerous mission to steal blood from a magical beast's newborn. Kill broke Presta's moment when he spotted a dark shadow high overhead. All he said was, "Oh, Oh! Here we go again."

Three Daughters of Delockth

Koln shouted out orders to tighten up the line. A small grove of leafy trees they didn't recognize lay directly ahead of the travelers. Koln bade them to pick up the pace and head directly for cover.

They stayed atop the mounts while one of the guards peered out from under the green protective cover. "The shadow appears to be gone…sir."

The guard walked back to the fold appearing perplexed.

"Ok…now what?" Erin asked while exhaling.

Koln made a gut decision. "Okay, everyone let's keep moving, we are sort of on a time schedule. Please everyone train one eye to the sky. I don't want any more unseen enemies today…Okay?"

Koln put himself at the head of the train and swiveled his head up and down and from side to side as if he had a spring for a neck. They watched the sky so intently, that they never realized the passage of time. It wasn't long when the base of the Grannth Mountain presented itself. The Mountainside that lay directly before them seemed to be unscalable, but this was the way the old woman had directed them to go. Kill found a natural spot to tie the horses and they all agreed. The supplies were moved from the packhorse to the men's backs. Erin had a brainstorm and used the supply of rope they carried to tie themselves together. He said if one should slip, the others would be anchored from a deadly fall. Koln was very pleased with Erin's quick thinking and slapped him on the back, his own signature for endearment. Koln once again put himself in the lead with Presta trailing a close second. Everyone else fell in respectfully. The last rear guard filled in the caboose, as we'd say and ended the train. The climb was very slow and steady. Kill's footing slipped half way up the face of the mountain but he managed to correct his footing without any injury. Koln pulled himself over a small shelf-like plateau much to everyone's excitement. One more ledge lay above the adventurers approximately 300 hands up and right at the dragon's cave opening. The whole group huddled close together on the small shelf, while Koln tried to hatch an attack plan.

"Father…exactly how do we fight a fire breathing dragon?" Kill inquired respectfully.

"I will be honest son of mine…this is a completely new one for me. I don't know." Presta was thinking too and had an interesting thought. "*Maybe I could…*"

"No I won't have it… it's just too dangerous. To bring Kem back, but to lose you in the process is not a fair trade…No way!"

Koln folded his arms like he was done.

"What's more dangerous than sitting on a small ledge, on the side of a Dragon mountain...anyway? I'm not a weak individual and I have authority to..."

"All right! All right! I will hear your idea...Your Highness." Koln tipped his head in respect.

"I will...without being seen, assess the situation. Then I will report back. And then we might be able to fashion a workable plan."

"How long can you keep up your shield?"

"I am well rested mentally...so I should be good for twenty tics. If I add anyone to my effect... the time is cut down considerably, but since I'm alone it should be plenty of time to see what I shall see."

"I don't like it...but very well then, but hurry, little one...ah! Er...your Highness." She fashioned him a great big smile.

"What should I be looking for specifically?"

"We will need an idea of the layout...in and out accesses. Is there a rear door to the cave? Are there any objects to conceal us once we are inside? You know like boulders or alcoves? What is the size of the young one...that would help? And most important, is there sufficient lighting to carry out this task of bloodletting? If we carry torches in...I'm afraid it will surely give away our presence."

"Okay, then...I can see I have my work cut out for me. Well we are not getting anywhere sitting here...so I will be off then."

She turned and smiled at Erin, then vanished right before his eyes.

"I love it when she does that," He exclaimed.

Erin felt a kiss on the cheek. His eyes grew large and his imagination soared. He rubbed the spot where the soft lips had been and tried to kiss the air back. Kill looked at him as if he was a card short of a deck. Koln forgot to detach Presta from the safety rope. He followed the rope until it disappeared, then saw that the rope was suddenly was lying on the ground. All they heard was *"sorry!"* from the thin air.

Koln said, "I will follow you until the next level...then wait for you there. The others will remain here."

Koln tapped the soldier's shoulder and said, "Be alert! I don't know if we are going to put mad this Dark beast."

He turned and immediately started to climb. He could only hope Presta was right in front of him. Measure by measure they climbed to the lip of the next level above them. Koln lifted his eyes above the edge of the shelf and looked over and about. Presta reappeared to save power. A large cave entrance appeared before him and some kind of fresh animal carcass. He dropped back down to where she was waiting. "Ok…the coast is clear of dragons and such. Just watch out for the dead animal. It must have been lunch. I am scared if you touch it, you might begin to smell like a dragon's dinner…so stay clear of the dragon's food."

Presta closed her eyes and she vanished. Koln thought, "I don't like anything I can't see."

"Ok! I am going to push you up and over the lip's edge. I will apologize now for the awkward placement of my hands…you're Highness."

"*Please, Sir Killgreth; this is not the time or place for such protocol.*" Without another word Koln cupped Prestas small derriere in his shovel-like hands and pushed the small girl over the lip and onto the shelf. Her head popped back over the lip and said, "*Your hands were warm.*"

Koln couldn't see her but said back in a whisper. "Your quite welcome, little one." She giggled and turned back to the task at hand. She stood up and walked towards the cave's entrance only briefly hesitating to look down at the ribs sticking out of the dead horse. She stood very still and tried to listen for sounds emanating from the cave, but she could hear nothing. She couldn't even confirm that the cave had any life in it. She started to enter the mouth of the cave when a big puff of steam shot past her. The smell associated with the steam was definitely animal. The next shot of steam was a direct hit on her. The steam silhouetted the little girls frame. It took all she had not to scream. Fortunately, there was no heat accompanying the steam, so she carried on down the grade and around a corner.

Ψ

Presta: Into the Dragons mouth.

Reporting: The smell…that's all I can remember of the first few moments. I was unharmed from the steam but the next shot of steam was more tainted than the first. My stomach did circus flips to be sure. I could describe the smell as sulfur and cabbage. The smell almost suffocated me. I shifted to one side of the cave so as not to run head first into a fire-breathing…you know what. The next corner revealed an orangish-red glow, pulsating from a pile of dirt that resembled a butte. I dared to walk further down the cave's throat and there it was…a real…full-grown…dragon.

It was curled around the small table-like butte as if it was protecting it. I pushed against the wall and escaped another blast of steam that was released from the Mother's nostrils. I found a little alcove in which to duck and thus observe my surroundings.

Just as I was about to put the cave's layout to memory, the baby awoke. His tail spilled over the edge of the mini-butte and in doing so woke the sleeping mother. In an attempt not to be detected, I slowed my breathing down but all that got me was nervous. I did notice in my terror that the walls were strangely lit. The only conclusion was that they were phosphorous and had that mystery glow. It was enough; however, not to need any torches to complete this mission. I'm so glad my Uncle Kem taught us about all kinds of subjects…I hope he's all right.

I was at this point, hoping that the baby didn't have a keen sense of smell. I should have rubbed dragon poo on my sleeve to help mask my human scent. Oh well, too late for that now. Oh My! I totally forgot I was in invisible mode and running out of time. I don't even have one of Grandma's napples to help. I could feel a definite drain on my special energy and felt noticeably tired. Maybe it was just the fact I had just climbed up the face of the mountain. All of a sudden, the mother lifted her head and looked straight at me. Then she quickly lifted her head up to the ceiling as if to stretch her long powerful neck. I thought I was going to soil myself. She then moved her body enough to sufficiently seal me in my alcove with the backside of her body. I was trapped. Her thick skin was four hands away from my face. The smell of the dragon was rather fishy. This was not what I expected and I dared to reach out and touch the armored skin. Now won't my sisters be jealous…that's if I make it back to tell them. As I pulled my hand back, I felt the emptiness and I again was visible.

Ψ

Castle Delockth: Queen's chambers.

Thinking: I was trying to enjoy the moment by trying on some new clothes that were fashioned for me. Anything I could do to take my mind off my departed sister was choice. I was spinning myself around in the reflection of a full-length mirror when my other sister Korrin burst into the room.

"I feel something! I feel something! Our sister is in grave danger."

Korana stopped spinning and looked at the ceiling. It was as if she was trying to focus on a small fly on the high gilded ceiling. *"Yes…there it is I feel it too. I'm sorry Korrin, I was so trying to block out the miserable feeling of her being away, that I blocked her out completely."*

"What's going on…I'm so scared?"

"I really don't know, but I feel her power draining."

"I am worried about her, Korana."

"Don't be, sweetheart, you must trust in her judgment…now come here."

Both sisters benefited from the comforting hug and felt measurably stronger.

Ψ

On the mountain's lip: Grannth Mountain

Erin shouted, "Dad look!"

He pointed upwards to an inbound object. "Oh, No! It could be that dragon. Everyone huddled closer together. Kill use the blanket and cover us… hurry! Hurry son!"

The black dragon had something else in his sights for he missed the blanket-covered dessert, shivering on a small shelf on the mountain. He swooped down with the grace of a falcon and immediately changed course into the bright sun, totally making the beast invisible for another pass.

Inside the cave: Mother Dragon

The half-asleep mother awoke and sensed that something was amiss. She repositioned her large body so she could get her face near her offspring. She pushed the sleeping baby with her big wet snout and took in a few deep sniffs. The baby seemed okay, but something was bothering her. She lifted her head as high as the cave would allow, smelling the air more efficiently.

Mountain side: Blanket of men

Erin popped his head from under the scratchy wool blanket. The smell of sweaty horse saturated the blanket. Erin was glad to be out of the tent, and didn't care if there was a dragon flying around or not. He re-entered the skunk tent.

"We seem to be in the clear."

Everyone together threw off the blanket and filled their lungs freely. Koln drew his short sword. "How long has she been gone?"

The rear guard spoke up. "She's been gone a good 25 tics I would say…Sir."

Koln stood. "We need to get in there, everyone stay sharp; this could be intense."

Koln led the quasi charge up the mountain's face to the staging plateau. When he reached the lip, he peered over as he had just a short time ago. "The coast is clear."

Ψ

Dragon's Cave: *Presta*

The mother dragon was getting agitated. She knew something was wrong in her small world but couldn't figure it out. Presta started to feel like she was going to pass out from thinking, so she held her breath so as not to give away her presence. She took slow and controlled breaths, like her Uncle Kem had taught them. She was going nowhere fast. The mother had her sealed off in this crevasse pretty good. She couldn't readily think of a way out and panic started to set in. She knew the others would eventually try to rescue her and hopefully get the job done at the same time. She was so scared that they all might not make it out of this cave in one piece, or maybe even…charbroiled.

The mother dragon crooked her spiky head then stretched her elongated neck and looked directly towards the front of the cave. She now knew positively what was bothering her…the taunting of a male dragon. So it is told that once a baby dragon is hatched, the male and the female separate never to produce again. The mother will instinctively defend her offspring from the ousted male; in fear that the male would eat the newly hatched young. This was one of those times that she needed to be outside putting up a brave front against an aggressive larger male. The mother's drive made her extra dangerous. She might even take chances she never would when not being challenged or courted.

Steam projected out of her flared nostrils in short, sharp blasts. Presta's heart rate shot up and she was worried the dragon would be able to hear the heart beating in her heaving chest. The large beast turned herself around in the small cave, with the gracefulness of a hippopotamus out of water. She poked the young one with her nose to make sure he was all right, and then proceeded to point her fire-dispensing head towards the exit and venture out in search of a fight.

Ψ

Koln and company: Caves mouth

Koln saw the short burst of sulfur-tainted steam exit the cave's mouth. He instinctively moved to one side and situated himself behind a fair-sized boulder. The others followed suit and were glued to his concerned back. Kill tapped on his father's wide back with enough force to almost make him lose his squatting balance. "What!?" Koln whispered forcefully.

Kill pointed up to the sky. Koln looked up in childlike astonishment.

"Oh my good….!"

The sky was turning black within a matter of tics. Koln knew this was the handy work of some Dark wizard. The patchwork of the sky turned pitch black effectively shredding the rays of the life-giving sun. It was getting increasingly harder to see with the sun's demise. Just as he was staring in amazement, a very large black male dragon broke through the dark clouds and headed straight for their position. The Mother dragon stepped free from the confines of her small cave. She clearly saw the black male approaching her location and focused her gaze. She now stood in a threatening position ready to receive the male and his intentions. Her hind legs were slightly spread for balance and her neck was straight and erect. Her leathery wings were unfolded from her body to appear bigger in size. Short puffs of smoke and flame were released from her open mouth. She shifted her weight from side to side in anticipation.

"Dad is there going to be a fight?" Kill asked all excited.

"I sure hope so, son. Frankly we need the diversion to finish the job."

Koln looked over the top of the boulder at the mother who was watching the circling black dragon. They were only tics away from storming the cave's entrance.

Ψ

The shores of Blackshire: Shipyard

"Aye Aye! Captain, I say we be ready in thirty cycles…maybe even in twenty-six if the weather holds up." The captain looked pleased.

"Very good mate. I shall relay the message to the proper authorities."

The Captain filled his goat faced pipe and tried to light the piece as he was walking away.

Marideath's Chamber:

(Bang! Bang!) *"Enter!"*

"Sorry to disturb you Master." The aid bowed exceptionally low and long.

"The Admiral Quantez Levy is here. Did you send for him?"

"Yes I did, give me a moment then send him in."

The aid never spoke; he just executed a short but respectful bow and closed the doors behind him. After 15 tics the aid standing by the admiral, signaled the officer in.

"Admiral...how very nice to see you. Please come in. Can I get you a cup of ale?"

The admiral new better and didn't refuse the masters good grace, he just nodded his approval. Marideath clapped his hands thunderously twice and a small boy scurried into the room with two large mugs teaming with frothy ale.

"Well...what say you man?" Marideath like to lower himself and sometimes speak the words and phrases of the uneducated style of seafaring people. It was one of his very few pleasures.

"My lord...I will make this brief. Your fleet is ready tomorrow."

"Wow! That was brief. What is the count man...how many floaters do we have?" The general was taken aback by the Dark Lord's childish speech, but chose to ignore it.

"We have successfully salvaged twenty ships from your former fleet and have constructed 150 more for the ready."

"And how many bodies with arms man these floating war horses?"

"We have approximately fifty men per ship and enough weapons for all. That's not counting thirteen crew...per ship."

"Thirteen crew...isn't that an unlucky number, Admiral?"

"I don't know about those things my Lord."

Marideath raised his voice enough to startle the decorated soldier.

"It's your job to know these things... When you get to sea, you will toss one crew member overboard and have everyone understand that this is the fate of anyone who tries to mutiny...do...you...understand?"

The admiral stood there with his mouth agape and momentarily stopped breathing. He eventually nodded his head and gulped a mouthful of spit. Marideath changed his demeanor in a split tic much to the Admiral's amazement.

"Well done, Admiral! If you make it back...I shall personally see that you are well taken care of." The naval officer bowed his head in appreciation, but highly doubted anything in return for a job well done other than another posting in some distant region far from the beaten path. "Well...its official Admiral...we launch tomorrow. I will be on my own ship, the Torrent, somewhere in the middle of the armada. until tomorrow, Admiral…till tomorrow."

Marideath placed his bony hand on the sailor's back and pushed him ever so slightly towards the waiting door. Marideath spun on his heels. He was pleased with himself and felt that the prize of conquering Delockth was well worth the full season cycles he had invested. Delockth would be his and the magnificent young Queen would be his new toy.

℣

Grannth Mountain: Defensive Dragon,

There was no doubt to Koln that the Dark Dragon was just an extension of Seth of Andress, a manifestation of pure evil, but now used against him in the balance of power. The black demon broke through the dangerous clouds and using his powerful wings seemed to hover high in the air. He could see his prey spreading her wings in a gesture of flirtation. He knew she was just baiting him to come closer so she could attack with his guard down. She turned her magnificent head around and took one last look at the cave's entrance as if to say goodbye. Then with powerful legs, pushed off the ledge and headed in the direction of her aggressor.

She soared above the clouds and came in hot hoping to catch him off guard. The sun broke through just at the right time. The bright light in the sky was right behind her, giving her the stealth she needed. She came in hot and with talons outward and ready. The black male misjudged his opponent's ability and took a direct hit to the back of his long neck. Most of his heavy armor held, except for around the edges towards his soft neck's underside. His green dragon blood spattered in a spiral direction. Koln commanded, "NOW!"

The dreaded black dragon spun out of control for several tics, then gathered himself together and shot straight up towards a large black cloud. Koln and the men advanced over the lip of the shelf. They scurried along the shelf looking for sufficient cover to plan their next advance. Kill was watching the sky as he ran and tripped over a piece of deer carcass. He regained his composure and joined the others. Koln just gave him a stern look and never said a word about his focus. Koln was at the head of the line of soldiers sliding along the cave's wall. He tried to speak with hand signals as to avoid detection. Down the slippery slope they moved. Small baby steps towards the central chamber. Koln stopped at the opening of the central chamber. He held up his hand and everyone understood. Erin just under his breath said, "Phew! What is that stink?" Kill responded, "I think it's your breath blowing back in your face."

Erin smacked Kill on the top of the head. Koln raised his fist at the two boys. *"Presta!"* Koln's voice took on a full shouting whisper. There was no answer. *Pr..est...a!* He tried again. This time he cupped his hands together.

Presta couldn't believe her ears. She had thought they were goners when the mother left the cave with a nose full of steam. She was terrified to look around her safe crevasse. Very quietly she whispered back, "I'm here…I'm okay."

Then she bravely waved an arm out from the crevasse she was wedged in.

Koln turned back to Erin directly behind him and said. *"She's okay…I can see her arm wave."* Koln and the men slowly entered the chamber. Koln pointed to the spot she was formally wedged in and Erin went to get her. The others gathered around the sleeping dragon. Sammth was sent back to the front of the cave for obvious reasons. He took Erin's crossbow with him and a few bolts. Once he was back at the mouth, he ducked behind a boulder and watched the sky.

Ψ

Skies over Grannth Mountain:

The fierce and now slightly wounded black dragon flew straight up and into a dark black cloud. He turned and pointed straight down. Pulling his wings in, he fashioned his body into a missile and plummeted straight down using gravity to assist his velocity. He pointed his head at his prey and showed no signs of stopping. Just before he struck he shot a liquid ball of fire at his opponent. The fire exploded from his toothy mouth in a straight line. The female instinctively used her wings to cover her head from the stream of liquid flame, thus leaving her back exposed. The black male opened his talons and made full contact with the female's upper back. It was a sensitive spot right between her wings. The male didn't wait for a result he looped a circle and grabbed the hurt female face on. The two animals locked belly to belly in a spiral fall towards the unforgiving mountainside. The two became one in a certain death plunge.

Ψ

Dragon's Cave:

"How heavy do these creatures sleep?" Erin asked.

Everyone shrugged their shoulders.

"How are we supposed to know?" Kill asked.

Presta spoke, "Do we stick the baby with the arrow?"

Koln rubbed his chin trying to figure out what to do. "I don't know? Let's try and do it without resorting to the charmed arrow."

Erin pulled the special needle out of his shoulder bag and handed it to his father.

"Why me?" Koln asked.

Everyone else present just smiled. Koln snatched the vial needle from Erin's grasp and gave him a scowl. Koln placed the needle in his right hand and reached in towards the sleeping dragon. He tried to stick the needle under one of the young dragon's plates on his back, but the needle didn't even scratch the surface. With no luck on his first attempt he pulled his arm back.

"It won't go through the creature's exterior."

Presta had an idea. "Why don't we try extracting blood from the baby's wing? There seems to be big veins running through the skin…see right there!"

"That might just work." Koln's voice sounded enthusiastic once more.

Koln was clearly impressed with Presta's idea. He turned around and tried again. This time he lifted a part of the wing and found an obvious vein. Slowly and steadily he inserted the needle. The precious glass tube began to turn green with blood.

Ψ

Skies over Grannth Mountain:

The two large beasts spiraled down and showed no signs of breaking their hold on each other. At the last moment before impact the female exhaled a blast of fire directly into the male dragon's face. It was enough of a punch to make the black dragon let go of his deathly grip. The female spread her wings fully and managed an immediate upturn to avoid a collision with the unforgiving ground. The black dragon wasn't so lucky and crashed head first into a stand of small pine trees. The female managed to sustain flight high overhead with much discomfort. The wound she initially received was giving her cause for concern. She waited to see if the black dragon survived the crash landing. Then she heard the most distressing sound she had ever heard. Her baby cried out in pain. She turned her head to focus her hearing.

She decided to break off the fight and head back to her nest. The black dragon shot out of the treetops like a cannon ball bent on destruction of anything that crossed its trajectory. The female had to defend herself despite her baby's cries. She violently veered to the left trying to avoid a ball of searing fire, but was too slow. She was hit broadside and it damaged a wing. She managed a rough landing and then prepared for a second confrontation. Flying in behind her on silent wings came the black dragon male. Merely 100 hands from the ground did he fly. Directly at his target his focus was set. His great talons ripped the female between the wings and flew off. The female tumbled across the mountain landscape head over tail.

Ψ

Dragon's Cave:
As the needle punctured the baby's wing, he woke up. The high-pitched wail that he produced was excruciating at close proximity. Presta and Kill both covered their ears with their hands. Erin made a face as if he had eaten a sour lemon, then left to check on the guard situation. The needle broke off when the baby jerked from the sudden jab. Koln stumbled backwards wincing from the sound of the cry. He yelled at Kill. "Go and get some of that deer meat at the front of the cave…and hurry!"

Kill stood still not really hearing what his father had just said. Koln tried again this time using his big hands. "Go…get…deer meat at…front of…cave. Use short sword."

Kill ran towards the front of the cave while brandishing his short sword. Koln pushed Presta back towards the wall not knowing if the young dragon could produce fire. Koln looked at the special vial in his hand and noticed it was only half-full. He rotated the tube and wondered if it would be enough. He looked at the irritated baby and knew that's all he was going to get from him.

"Well, little one…this will have to do."

Kill ran into the chamber with a hunk of dripping meat. "What do you want me to do with this?"

"What do you think…give it to the hungry dragon."

Kill threw the raw meat at the dragon's front end as if he was an Olympic shot putter. The baby must have smelled the prize because it snapped it right out of the air. Presta took her hands off her ears with much relief. They all stood in amazement and watched as the dragon tried to chew the massive hunk of meat, bones and all. "Ok…that reminds me I'm hungry." Kill said.

They just looked at him as if he was crazy. The baby dragon settled down drastically after the injection of food. Koln placed the precious vial in a protective leather cloth and placed it in his inner vest pocket.

Ψ

Skies over Grannth Mountain:
The large female tried to sit up straight. Her injuries made this simple task hard. She shook her head from side to side while trying to gather her thoughts. She turned her ear towards the mountain's cave but heard no sounds or cries. The silence didn't bring her any comfort. Not knowing what had happened to her baby made her very angry. Meanwhile, the black dragon showing no mercy was preparing for another attack. He flew straight upward to prepare for another high-speed dive. The female focused on the male's pattern of attack and devised a plan. She purposely positioned herself in front of a tree that had been struck by lightning. It was snapped in half and had a sharp edge. She play-limped to the spot and acted as if she was fatally hurt. The black dragon started his decent. He pulled his leathery wings in and committed himself to the dive. Faster and faster, he sliced through the cool mountain air. He narrowed his vision and exhaled all his air hoping to achieve the ultimate speed. This was to be his kill strike. The female stood in a subdued and injured position with head down in a defeated stance…waiting for the right micro tic to make her play.

Ψ

Mountains cave shelf:
The rear guard pointed to the scene that was about to transpire. "See! See! There's that black dragon I told you about."

Erin knew that his father would wish to see this so he ran back into the cave yelling. "Father…father! You need to come and see this."

Koln happened to be already halfway there wondering where Erin was. He broke into a full run and ended up at the entrance within two or three tics.

"Look there!" Erin pointed.

Koln looked up just as the black dragon broke through the black cloud. Presta and Kill arrived to see what all the yelling was about. They were all looking up as the black dragon made a slight course correction and headed directly for the injured female dragon.

The black dragon was coming in hot. Fire was streaming from his alligator looking mouth. The fire was split and being forced to either side of his head by the shear speed he commanded. He managed to open his wings enough to plane out and fly parallel to the ground. He was reaching maximum velocity at an altitude of twenty hands above the ground. 300 measures away…200 measures away…75, 50…25 hands away. The female dragon used her powerful hind legs and sprang out of the way at the exact tic the male was about to strike. She moved, and he saw the jagged stump too late to maneuver away in any direction. He closed his eyes.

Koln pulled his spyglass from his pouch and extended its length to focus the distance. Just as he focused, he saw the female move. Then he saw the large black dragon strike the solid tree stump and tear him from neck to tail. The black dragon exploded in the direction he was flying. Guts and other various internal organs littered the area for 100 hands beyond the deadly stump. A faint sound could be heard from where Koln stood, but he imagined it would have sounded more horrific the closer he was. Some of the dreaded dragon still remained on the unforgiving tree stump. The rest of the dark beast was now the property of the scavengers of the mountainside. Koln turned the glass on the female's face. The gruesome profile showed no expression or satisfaction, just the mask of indifference. He widened his focus and could clearly see a bloody patch between the females retracted wings. He assumed the dragon was flightless for the time being.

From behind Koln a terrible loud screech was reverberating out of the cave. The baby dragon was out of food and hungry again. Koln pulled up his spyglass and refocused on the female. He could tell that she definitely heard the baby's cries as well. The movements she was making, were clearly signs of agitation and anger. A large spray of fire flew from her leathery face. She slowly and uncomfortably tried to fully spread her massive wings. Koln yelled at Erin while still focusing on the mother dragon. *"Erin!...get everyone together. We need to get off this mountain…Now!"*

The angered female pushed off and took to the skies.

Before Presta and the others could make it out of the cave, the mother dragon was hovering only 500 hands in the air above the cave's ledge. Koln and Sammth were the only two exposed at the front of the cave. Sammth had Erin's crossbow and Koln had his short sword. Sammth without a word or a plan rushed to the end of the shelf and aimed the crossbow at the winged beast. The angry female was losing altitude from her sustained injuries. Sammth took a shot and missed. The dragon screeched and doubled the child's volume. This made Sammth wince with pain and drop the bolt he was trying to load. The dragon was losing precious blood and patience. Sammth reloaded and took the second shot. The bolt contacted the underside of the dragon's great tail. The mother swooped in and took her shot. A large ball of insidious fire covered Sammth and dispatched him where he stood. Not a sound did he make. He fell where he stood in a heap of burning flesh. The others behind Koln arrived just as the ball of flames struck their friend. Presta reeled in horror. Kill had to look away. Erin watched in horror to learn.

Koln rushed towards his burning friend. He did a forward summersault and snatched the crossbow from the ground. Part of the handle was on fire but Koln ignored it. Koln yelled at Erin once more.

"Give me the enchanted arrow…for the love of good, hurry lad!"

Erin dropped to one knee and pulled his shoulder bag around from his back. He dug frantically in the leather bag and finally extracted the small shimmering bolt. Koln stood with his back to the dragon and tried to entice Erin with his hands to hurry and throw the bolt to him. Erin tossed the magical bolt, which turned in the air over and over. The bolt's trip through the air, seem to take on a slow motion odyssey. Some of the enchanted dust flew off in every direction, making the toss look magical. Koln caught the bolt only three fingers away from his tired face. The mother dragon flew up behind Koln and spread her wings fully. The sight was Darkness itself. Without hesitation, Koln spun around and simultaneously loaded his crossbow with the special bolt. He dropped to one knee and fired the pointed weapon. The tension was released and the bolt found its target. The female dragon with her last ounce of strength took the hit square in the soft part of her exposed belly and received it deep. The desired effect took only the smallest measure of time.

The dragon started to shimmer the same way the bolt did. She instinctively knew she was beaten, for she flew straight at Koln and the others. Like an airplane running out of fuel, she skidded in for a landing just before the mouth of the cave. Koln and the others managed to dive to one side and let the beast pass. Her spent body came to rest with her front half tucked neatly into the open mouth of her own cave. Presta and the others stood up and started to clap as if they were watching some daring circus performer do an amazing trick. Koln seized the moment and did a bow. Then he remembered that Sammth was no more and sobered up sharply.

Without a solitary word, they all filed past the burnt remains of their friend and helped each other scale down to the lower platform to prepare to leave the dark place. Koln made everyone rest on the plateau while he collected his thoughts and planned the trip back to the witch's cottage. Rathth pulled the last wine skin from his pouch and drained some of the fluid down his parched throat. "Here" Was all he said as he passed the skin to Presta. She didn't feel like refusing on this occasion and guzzled a good portion of the red wine. Koln passed and waved it on to the boys instead. After Kill relieved the skin of a mouthful, he felt the need to be the first to speak. "Wow! That was quite a shot dad."

"*If you only knew how many times I've missed an important shot.*"

Koln looked reflective. His eyes were clearly focused on the past. Presta asked with slightly more than a whisper. "Where is the tube of blood?"

Koln reached into his vest under his leather coat and retrieved the sacred tube. "*Here*"

"Do you think that there's…enough?"

"*I don't know your Highness. I guess only Enndora will know that.*"

He held the precious substance up to the sun that was peeking its face around a dissipating Dark cloud.

"It looks about…just…slightly over half full."

He jiggled it once more and then placed it back in his inner vest pocket. Rathth pulled himself up from the lip of the shelf and sat beside Koln.

"Did you know him well?"

"Who…Sammth?"

"Ya."

"We fought in a few hard campaigns together…way back when."

"Do you think he died a soldier's end?"

"*I thought he was very brave and courageous.*"

"His wife and daughters will greatly miss him."

"*I know…I know. It's the risk we all take as soldiers of fortune. I did pick up his necklace. Maybe you can give it to his wife when we return home.*"

"Will we return…home?"

"Why not?"

"Promise me…if I don't make it home you will tell my girl friend I… love her. You know, she's the blonde one at the King Head Tavern."

Koln slapped Rathth's chest hard.

"Tell her yourself soldier. Okay, everybody up, were getting off this chunk of dragon dung." Everybody laughed.

Erin took the lead and was the first over the side, while Koln held the rope until the last one vanished over the lip of the shelf. Koln took one last look towards the top of the mountain. *"I hope it's the last of this place that I shall see."*

Ψ

The Witch's Glen: Enndora's cottage,

The fog was as thick as pea soup. A person would not be able to inspect his hand five fingers in front of his face. The tired travelers found it very difficult to find their bearings with no visual cues. Kill mumbled to himself, "I don't know…where…or if?"

Erin asked shortly. "What are you going on about now, Sir Whine-a-lot?"

"All right! all right boys keep it down. It's difficult enough without the two of you filling up our ears."

"All I said was…that I'm tired and hungry."

"Well, who isn't" Koln cut him off short.

"Me legs are throbbing…you don't hear me complain."

"Besides father…I really do believe we are traveling in circles."

"Yes…I agree." Koln pulled up beside Erin.

"What shall we do father?"

"We weren't more than a few country measures from the cottage before the blanket fell. I suggest we stop and try to make some sort of…camp and wait until the cloud lifts."

Rathth almost ran his horse into a large out cropping of boulders. They were piled high enough to be considered a hill of boulders. He called out to the others to follow his voice. "This way! …follow my voice…over here!"

It wasn't long before they were all together. They tied the horses to a stake that Koln drove into the ground with his sword hilt and then they all climbed to higher ground. They ended up in a flat place surrounded by many large boulders a good sixty hands from the cold ground. "Wow! This is nice." Erin said. "Is there any wood lying about to start a fire?"

"Ah, warm food, I'm all for that idea." Kill rubbed his hands together vigorously in anticipation.

Killth offered, "I will go and find some wood."

Koln grabbed his shoulder. *"Take Rathth with you…and be prepared for anything."*

"Yes sir." Kill signaled with his head for Rathth to follow him.

The late cycle sun was trying to break through the thick fog. It looked like an insignificant dot in the sky and not the great giver of life. Koln sat on the ground with his back to a big rock. The day's riding had taken its toll on his still healing legs. Presta sat down beside him and snuggled into his arm. "How Long before we are home…do you think?"

"I don't know, little one, but I must state you have been a trooper. I have seen many things in my life…and I know you have much potential to lead your people. I don't think we would have made it this far without your skills and personality."

Koln gave her a peck on the top of her head.

"Ahhh! You're a flatterer, you are, Sir Warrior."

He turned towards her. *"No, I truly mean that, my lady."*

"How are your legs?"

Koln sat back against his boulder. *"Throbbing…they will get us home."*

Kill climbed into the centre of the boulders and threw down several small branches of wood. "Here you go, Pa."

Rathth was right behind him with four or five larger pieces. Koln spoke to Rathth. *"Did you see anything? Any landmarks… perhaps."*

Rathth just shook his head in the negative and proceeded to hack away at some of the bigger pieces of wood he had found with his long sword.

Kill picked up a few of the pieces he threw down and commented. "They aren't the most dry, but if I can get this fire hot enough…it should burn anyway."

Koln tried to get up to help but had trouble straightening out his stiff legs. He made it half the way up then plopped back down hard. Presta stood and wagged a royal finger at Koln. "Stay ye down, Sir Killgreth…you be no good to us on crutches…now would ya?"

Koln had a chuckle at Presta trying to speak like the people from the bay.

"Okay, young lass, I be thinking ye be in the know, and I will heed your words."

Erin looked at the two of them bantering with their bayish lilt with a big smile on his face. He spun on his heels and helped Kill with the night's fire. It wasn't very long before the companions were feasting on wild rabbit and flattened blueberries. The apple cider skin was passed around to everyone's amusement.

Six bells would have sounded and, as suddenly as it came, the fog lifted. It raised enough to successfully get their position and direction. Erin positioned himself on top of the largest boulder and with Koln's spyglass turned himself in a 360 degree circle. "I still can't tell where the dark we are."

Koln stood slowly and walked up to Erin. "*Help me up boy…I want a look.*"

Erin offered him a hand up. Koln did the same rotation but in the opposite direction. "*I…don't see…anything either.*"

Koln threw his hands up in desperation, then with obvious frustration closed the spyglass and reached for Erin's hand in climbing down.

Without warning, a white owl landed on the second highest boulder and flapped his impressive wings.

"Oh look! That's Enndora's bird…isn't it?" Kill sounded truly excited.

"If it is, maybe she knows we're lost?" Presta had to wonder.

The owl departed as fast as it had landed. "Where did it go?" Erin shouted.

"*How am I supposed to know?*" Koln said.

Not more than fifteen tics head passed when they all heard and recognized Dogglopp's voice. "Pretty Lady! Oh Pretty Lady! It's me, Dogglopp…don't be scared…it's me."

Presta climbed up on the edge of a boulder and waved her arms.

"Over here! It's me, Dogglopp! Over here!"

Koln and Rathth both drew their weapons not knowing where this confrontation would lead. Dogglopp walked straight up to the large pile outcrop of boulders and bowed his big ugly head. "I am pleased to be of service, little miss. I am here to guide you home."

"How did you find us?"

"We always knew where you were. It was only when the owl noticed the stress you were feeling, did we know we should intervene. Follow me…your grandmother is waiting."

"Hold on a few…we have to pack up." The Cyclops bowed his head again. They pulled their things together in a hurry and followed the large one-eyed monster to Enndora's door.

Ψ

Enndora's Cottage: Seven and a quarter

"Come in, come in...I'm so glad you're safe. My eyes and ears told me you were coming. But for the life of me, I couldn't figure out why you were going around in circles."

"The fog." Was all Erin said.

"You mean the blanket? It's what we call that sort of thing around here. It's actually a witch's spell don't you know."

"You mean you can generate that kind of cover with a simple witch's spell?" Presta was all a wonder.

"Well, it's not a simple spell...but yes you can. Look I'll show you."

The old lady went back and opened a drawer in her kitchen cupboard.

"Where is...that...oh, here it is."

The lot of them followed her to the back of the cottage with their eyes.

"Here ya go."

She walked into the front room carrying a small red ball that resembled a radish.

"This would do the trick. It takes a good half a season cycle to produce this baby. When it is cast down and broken, the spell inside produces enough fog to cover a large area...very large area actually."

She spun the object with her fingers and then tossed it without warning to Koln. Koln reached with both hands and snatched it from the air.

"I'm sorry, where are my manners. Is anyone hungry?"

The call from hunger put on a unified front. The word "Yes." resounded loudly from all present. *"Excellent! I have a spicy cabbage stew and napple pie."*

All who sat at the witch's wooden table ate like Kings and Queens. The bread was freshly baked that morning, and the apple cider made the head swim and the soul sing. The conversation was light and airy until the old lady asked the question.

"I don't mean to state the obvious...but is there someone missing?"

Rathth threw down his wooden spoon and stood. Without a single word, he removed himself from the table, and placed his coat on, opened the front door and silently left.

"Where is he going father?" Kill asked.

"He's going to tend the horses' son. He is an excellent soldier."

Everyone stopped eating for they knew it was because his close friend was barbequed on the dragon's front door and not some draconian duty at suppertime. The crew resumed their supper with their heads down. Koln looked at Enndora and spoke softly.

"We had a hard time acquiring this precious blood."

He reached into his vest and unwrapped the glass tube.

"We lost one of our own in the process. It could have been a lot worse and I'm content knowing that my soldier and friend did his duty. Here's to Sammth!" Koln raised his glass of drink.

Everyone followed… "To Sammth!"

Kill stopped shoveling food into his mouth and copied everyone else.

"To Sammth!"

Koln picked up his spoon and started eating again. This action brought everyone back to a lighter note. "Do you think there is enough blood in here?"

He handed the tube over to Enndora. The old lady grasped the tube and lifted it towards the ceiling's candlelight. She shook the tube from side to side.

"*I won't know until I try. It looks like enough, I have ways of stretching a potion…we shall see.*" She continued to twist the tube in the soft light. Presta asked the main question now on everyone's mind.

"How long might it take to finish the potion, Grandma?"

"*Oh that sounds so nice…Grand…ma*

"Grandma?"

"*Oh, I'm sorry child…I'm back now. What was your question?*"

"How long before the stuff is ready?"

"*Well…I have never made this potion before, but my witch's book says it takes a neat two cycles to properly complete…yes that's about right. There is something about fermenting in the process. Not to worry, little one. I will hurry for my son's sake.*"

Dinner was finally over and the small crew managed to destroy two complete napple pies. Kill was holding his belly as if he was about to give birth and Koln retired to a rocking chair to finish his brew. Enndora brought Rathth some food and dessert out to the barn. When she came back, she winked and told us he was all right. The cider finally caught up to all of them. It slammed all who sampled its toxic spirit.

Koln tried to sing a few road songs, while Erin endeavored to dance a jig. Kill and Presta busted a gut laughing at the two drunken buffoons. Enndora watched from a distance while starting on the potion. She was also sucked into the merry moment and laughed a toothless laugh at the joyousness that abounded. It wasn't long after that Presta turned in. The warm bath her grandmother drew for her did the trick. The rest of them slept wherever they could. Koln never did get up from the moving chair and Erin and Kill lay in front of the warm hearth. Rathth stayed in the barn with the Cyclops as a friend, much to the dismay of the horses. The white owl was perched on the cottage's roof with both eyes open wide. Every so often, he would slowly blink them, one at a time. Enndora spent most of the night humming and stirring her potion in a great wooden bowl.

The next cycle passed by in the blink of an eye. Nothing memorable happened and no one remembered what they did. It was as if it never happened. The next sunrise was quite a different story. It was eight bells, early rise, and everyone was being exceptionally lazy. The lot woke to the terrifying sound of the owl screeching. Rathth burst into the cottage out of breath. "You're not going to believe this, it's that mother of a dragon, and she's…here! Now!"

Rathth drew his sword in the doorway and ran back outside towards the barn. Koln sprung up from his sitting position and strapped on his sword belt.

"You kids stay inside until I assess the situation. Enndora, is there a back entrance to this place?"

"Yes, behind the wall-hanging where we take baths."

"Good, everyone be prepared to respond. Erin and Kill strap on your weapons." Koln opened the front door and briefly looked up towards the blue sky. He exited and slammed the heavy wooden door behind him. Koln ran quickly towards the back barn to join Rathth and the horses. The Cyclops was bent over and covering his head. "What's wrong with him?" Koln ask

"He is deathly afraid of dragons." Rathth almost had a secret smile on his face.

"I think she is looking for food, remember that baby was insatiable. We may need to give up another packhorse in a gesture of peace. I am worried if we try to fight that thing, we may lose."

"I hear you Rathth, but I'm going to see if the old lady may be able to help us with a spell or some fancy weapon she can't remember she has. Stay here with the horses. I will be right back." Koln turned and high-tailed it back to the cottage.

Koln entered the cottage so fast that it made all inside jump with fright.

"Sorry! We believe she is in search of food more than revenge, but with that said, I don't believe we are safe, at least not while that beast can spray chemical fire. We have an option to sacrifice one of the packhorses in a sort of offering.

Kill sounded angry. "If we do that father, we will have to travel back to Delockth without enough supplies, like food and tents. I don't think I would like that."

"I hear you, little one, but we must save this home and our very own lives first." Kill nodded as if he understood the urgent logic. Erin turned to Enndora who looked like she didn't know what was going on.

"Do you have anything in your magical arsenal that we might use to our advantage? Without a word, the old woman went to the back of the cottage and rummaged around. The sounds of cupboards opening and closing were evident. A few old and dusty trunks were opened and looked through. An extraordinarily large book was pulled down from a high shelf. She walked into the main room's light and plopped the heavy, dirty and dusty book on the table. She placed both hands on her back and tried to straighten her back out after trying to haul that oversized book across her cottage. "Oh, my old back! I think there may be..."

She flipped through the yellowed pages slowly. Everyone gathered around the table. Koln reached up and with a lit candle and ignited a few more of the unlit candles. She looked up at the light. "Thank you, Sir, these old eyes...well you'll find out someday." Here... this might help."She left the book and walked back to the rear of the cottage. It wasn't two tics before she returned with a small red ball with a yellow bird painted on its surface.

"Okay...what do we have here?" Koln looked genuinely interested.

After the enchanted arrow, Koln was sold on the old witch's magical powers. "This object is as old as the mountain. It has...now that I remember, been used on many an occasion, but never one to best a dragon."

"What does it do Gran?" Presta asked.

"It...my dear, is a flyte ball."

"A what ball?"

"A flyte ball, my Princess. It will raise the host 100, maybe two hundred hands into the air and move them in a horizontal position. Not very fast mind you, but enough to prune trees, and mend tall worship buildings and such."

"Well how will this help us?" Koln asked.

"I don't know, Sir Killgreth, that is for you to figure out. It may only get you dispatched for all we know."

Koln gulped a mouthful of fluid. "How does it work?"

"You must swallow it. A few tics later…all you have to do is think and it will perform your desire."

"Does it dissolve?"

"No…it will pass in time."

"Pass?" Koln looked perplexed.

"You know…at the jacks…pass!"

"You mean this has been…through other bodies…before?"

"Yes…of course. There is only one. Don't worry, soldier…I've have had it disinfected thoroughly."

Koln took the red ball and placed it in his jacket pocket. A deafening scream emanated from the barn area. Koln broke into a dash and ran outside to find the barn on fire.

The dragon waited for combatants. When no one challenged her, she had lashed out with a stream of liquid fire. The roof of the horse stable was fully ablaze. The Cyclops pushed aside his mortal fear and started to throw buckets of water on the building. He didn't know the property of the fire and the water he threw actually made the fire spread. Rathth managed to pull the highly agitated horses out of the burning barn. Some of the animals bolted away in several directions. Rathth only managed to hold on to two of the scared animals.

Koln rushing to the dramatic scene was almost trampled by Erin's stallion. He had to perform a circus roll to save himself from being hit. Enndora watched the roll from the side window of the cottage.

"Nice one, old man."

She had a tooth less smile on her face.

Koln looked at her and yelled. "If I remove this thing from the world, will there be any repercussions."

"There has to be a balance." She yelled back.

"If you have truly ended the male's life, then it would be a balance to remove the female. Just hope that the young dragon survives. There is probably a dark dragon baby somewhere… we hope."

Koln saw a shadow appear over his head and he ducked under a napple tree to take cover. On one knee, he pulled the red ball out of his pocket and closed his eyes. Opened his mouth and tossed in the ball. Swallowing the thing was a different story. The ball wasn't big in the hand, but in the mouth it felt like a closed fist. It took all his strength to open his throat and swallow. His eyes bulged from the gag reflex being activated. Down the red ball went to much relief from Koln. He drew his long sword out and stepped out from behind the tree trunk. The female dragon swooped down on Koln. He thrust his sword high into the air and scratched the underbelly of the winged beast. The dragon flew up into the sky a good 400 hands away. Koln ran over to Raththt who was trying to tie up a third horse.

"The barn looks done." Koln sounded out of breath. They both looked at the Cyclops sitting on his butt all tired out.

"We still have a few horses unaccounted for." Raththt pointed out. "I don't think she wants food. I think she wants us."

Just then part of the roof collapsed. The noise scared Dogglopp and he pulled himself off the ground and ran into the nearby field with his arms in the air.

"He's going to get himself dispatched, he is."

Raththt saw another horse wander into the front courtyard of the cottage. "Oh, there's one…I'll get it."

Koln saw the shadow come from behind the tree and yelled towards Raththt who was running with short sword held high towards the untied horse.

"No! Get down…look out, soldier!"

The mother dragon came in hot with talons extended. Raththt didn't see her coming and knew not what had happened. The dragon grabbed Raththt with her left talon and flew straight up with him flailing to get free. Koln grabbed his crossbow and let one fly. It only managed to pierce one of the female's wings. Once hit, she circled the cottage area then descended over the top of the burning barn. Raththt, by this time, had stopped squirming in her grasp and had dropped his sword. She then expertly opened her talon and dropped the lifeless Raththt into the heart of the burning structure. With her appetite for vengeance sated, and the slight sting in her wing, the beast of legends flew off with nothing more than a pinch.

Koln opened the cottage's front door. He placed his long sword down at the entrance and stepped in. "The beast has gone…Raththt…is gone."

He hung his head. Presta gasped and exclaimed. "Oh, No!"

"Erin and Kill…get ye outside and tend to that fire. I don't want it reaching this cottage." Without a word they grabbed their coats and a cooking pot for a bucket and left. "What happened?" Presta asked Koln after he sat down at the table.

"I think I contributed to Rathth's demise."

"How can you say that?"

Enndora brought Koln a cup of cider. "*Here.*"

"I took a shot at the big ugly bird and he dropped Rathth into the fire."

"Stop that thinking. It won't bring him back, and it certainly will not make you feel good every time you think of the man he was."

Presta made sense to Koln. He had to keep strong for the young ones. He wiped his aged eyes and took a long drink. Under his breath, he whispered to himself, "I shall miss the man…the soldier." He raised his glass in a silent toast.

Ψ

CHAPTER 11

The Witch's Broom

IT WAS TWO FULL BELLS later before Erin and Kill reentered the warm cottage. They were both covered from head to toe in black soot. Enndora gasped and started to immediately draw the bath in the back to wash them up. They both sat heavy at the table. "I am tired," Kill said while empting his lungs fully.

Erin added. "We didn't save much. That dark dragon's fire is the darndest stuff. The water we threw on only seemed to make it come…alive. We eventually had to shovel dirt to smother the burning devastation."

Erin was equally spent. Presta handed them each a napple and a warm drink of chocolate.

"Did you see Rathth's body in the fire?" Presta wanted to know. Erin shook his blackened head.

"There is nothing left…the fire was so hot. I could have forged 100 swords from the heat. Rathth has been successfully transferred to the next great world."

This information satisfied Presta.

"How are we going to get home, father?" Kill inquired sensitively.

"What do you mean, son?"

"Well…we don't have all the horses, and we have no more front or rear guards."

"I tell you what…go get cleaned up and have some warm food, and later by the fire we can discuss this problem like men…okay?"

Kill didn't say a word. He just acknowledged his father and went to the back of the cottage to get a well deserved bath. Erin poured himself another cider and hung his head from fatigue.

The next morning slowly rolled in. The total coverage of dark grey clouds that never appear, dominated the entire sky. Enndora standing on her front stoop, looked up in amazement.

"It has been thirty full season cycles since I've seen this kind of weather. There is something dark at hand; I can feel it in my bones. The last time...I remember, was the Great War."

She came inside. *"I think that's when your father became a hero fighting off the dark invaders."*

She looked directly at Koln. She pushed the door tight behind her as if she was keeping something bad out. "You do know we have only seven full cycles left to go to administer this potion." Koln was holding the blue sparkling magic ball that Enndora gave him between his fingers.

"I don't know if we can make it within the amount of time we have remaining." Koln looked worried. Presta looked at her grandmother as if she wanted to say something.

"What is it dear? What's on your mind?"

"This might sound funny, but since you practice witchcraft...do you have a flying broom or something like that?" Presta started to laugh with nervousness from the outlandish question.

"Why, yes, child, I have a witch's broom. Why does that sound irregular?"

"Does it really fly?" Her voice sounded excited.

"Of course it does...Why?"

"Could I fly it?" Presta asked.

"What are you thinking, princess? Koln stood up.

"What if...just hear me out." She put up her hand to ward off interjections.

"What if I could fly this broom thing...straight to Delockth castle and administer the potion ball to the High Wizard Kem, before it's too late."

The look on her face was priceless. Her eyes were wide open as was her mouth. "Well...what if?"

Koln looked seriously at Enndora. "Is this even possible?"

"Yes...only because of her family connection and her natural inborn abilities. It is very possible."

"Well, if you're up for the risk? I don't see any other way at this time, to travel the miles in time, for the potion to be effective. It will take us a good seven full cycles of hard riding to get home. Don't forget once we enter the land of Delockth, it will be deep in its winter season and will make horseback slow and treacherous. Being able to fly will avoid all that…except the cold."

"Can I…see it?"

"*If she lets you.*"

Presta cocked her head in wonderment. Enndora walked to the back of the cottage with everyone in tow. She stood in front of a tall, thin cupboard door. She paused then slowly opened the creaking door. "*It's been some time, it has.*"

Cobwebs were draped from one end to the other sealing in the broom.

"*Hello, Valda.*" Was all the old witch said.

"What do I do?" Presta asked. Presta looked in the closet. She pulled aside most of the webs and looked in.

What she saw was an old straw broom. It looked like every broom a street sweeper owned. "That's it…that's a flying broom?"

The old woman opened her withered hand and demanded, "*Come hither, Valda…a good witch calls ye.*"

The broom jumped from the closet and smacked sharply into Enndora's hand.

"Ok! Easy girl…easy girl. I believe she smells an adventure."

The broom started to shake and vibrate with the exciting prospects of flight. Enndora walked into the front room carrying the broom. Everyone followed her like sheep. She held the broom over her head with a mask of pride. "*This is Valda! She has been in our family since the first. She was also your mother's broom and mine. If she will have you…she will be yours and yours alone.*" The old woman put the broom beside her and stood as straight as she could.

"Come here, child. You need to be pure of heart to ride this beauty. You need to respect each other. Place your open hand thusly and repeat after me; Valda will you have me as your master, to ride and cherish, until I pass to the next great world?"

"Valda…will you have me as your master…to ride…and cherish…till I pass to the next great world?"

The broom left Enndora's hand and snapped tightly into the waiting young girl's tender hand. "She has accepted you, sweetheart…I am so happy."

Enndora started to cry and Koln had to bring her a piece of cloth to empty her wrinkled nose. Presta turned in circles holding the plain looking broom.

179

If someone just walked in the room, they would think she was off her wagon. "Can I ride her? Can you show me how, Grandmother?"

"Yes child…yes, but we will wait until the weather clears…ok."

Presta held on tight to Valda for a full three bells, until the clouds dispersed and the sun reclaimed its rightful place. Enndora lead Presta outside for an impromptu flying lesson in broomery. Everyone else present held a drink and rallied outside to cheer on their royal pilot.

"Okay, this is still all pending that Valda gives you permission to fly the friendly skies. The cold fact that she jumped into your hands earlier, leads me to believe you're a shoe in. Okay, so…here we…or should I say, you go! Oh my! It's been a while."

The old lady tried to lift her old hairy leg over the broom's length. She first had to desperately try to lift her heavy wool full-length multi-layered skirt out of the way. The two young boys had to turn their heads to one side to not get busted for giggling. With great effort she finally made the vault and successfully mounted the cleaning steed. Kill at this point had to turn right around. Koln looked back at his son's shoulders jiggling up and down silently. She started waving one arm as if she was riding a bucking bronco. "Up! Up! And away, good Valda."

She said at the top of her dusty lungs.

"Rise above the ground… for a true flight is profound."

Koln just knew at this point she was enjoying herself for the first time in a long while, and was overacting. He had a smile on his face for he had to admit he was enjoying watching her have the time of her life. Her big black boots started to rise off the ground, finger by finger. The boys now were fully engaged with the event and had their mouths wide open in astonishment. Kill managed to swallow a fly with his mouth wide, much to his father's amusement. Presta clapped her hands together in anticipation for her turn. Higher and higher she rose, her happiness seemed to equal the height attained. She suddenly tilted her head down and raised her voice.

"Listen, sweetie, I forgot to tell you…Valda extracts a price for flight. She will extract your natural powers and life energy, in exchange for flight. It's a moderate drain, but a drain none the less. So make sure you're fully rested if you need to do greater distances."

She straightened her old tired body and managed a few laps around the hibernating napple trees before coming to hover in front of Presta. The boys followed the old lady with their necks all a swivel. Presta looked quite intrigued by the whole deal. Enndora was feeling the purchase of Valda, so she cut her personal demonstration short. She touched down in front of Presta rather roughly. "Ooooh! It's been too long. Okay, your highness, I do believe it's your turn." The old lady stood straight-backed and canted.

"I relinquish this good broom…to your controlling hands…never to ride again…for I am resigned."

Presta opened her soft hand and Valda jumped from one generation to the next.

She looked at the broom closely. "My mother once flew this broom. Why did she stop?"

She looked at Enndora for an answer.

"Your mother gave up her magic to be with your father. For two to be one, all must be the same. She gave it willingly child. She loved your father so."

Presta wiped the single tear from her eye.

"Okay, child…there will be time for reflection once you get your wings."

"Oh, my grandmother…the handle is warm."

"Yes…well."

With the ease of a court tumbler, Presta kicked her leg over the shaft of Valda. All the boys took a drink as if they were watching live theater.

"Up! Up! And away…good Valda. Rise above the ground… for a true flight is profound."

Valda rose swiftly and contacted Presta's crotch with indifference. The effect was etched in the young girls face. "Ooooh! My." Was all the onlookers heard.

Erin leaned over to his dad and whispered.

"That's going to leave a mark."

Koln had to cover his own mouth with his hand. The expression changed on the Princess's face from surprise to euphoria when Valda lifted Presta into the air. Her small feet left the ground. Her gentle knuckles bore the tell tale color of white.

"Oh my goodness!" formed on her silent lips. She continued to lift until she was a strong forty-five hands high in the cool air. Presta yelled for instructions. "How does it go forward Gran?"

Enndora yelled back with her hand cupping her toothless mouth.

"Just tell her…dear, just tell her."

"Go forward, Valda!"

The broom swooshed forward at an incredible rate of speed. Presta's long hair trailed behind her like it was trying to catch her. This was too much too soon for the little girl and she tried to slow the broom down.

"Slow down, Valda! Slow…Down…Valda!"

The broom didn't respond, so the princess smacked the broom with an open hand on top of its wooden shaft."Stop!"

The broom stopped so suddenly that Presta almost slid off the end of the good broom. Presta wormed her way back to a more proper seating position. Kill looking up said to himself, with an almost inaudible whisper."Splinters"

"Now, let's begin again." Presta demanded.

This time the broom knew who was in charge. Slowly the broom moved forward at a manageable speed.

"Turn right, Valda dear, now Down ten hands good Valda."

Smooth as a hot knife through butter. "Now circle the cottage, a little quicker dear." The broom responded wonderfully. Enndora turned to Koln and said.

"She rides like her mother, she does. She's going to be just fine…yes indeed."

After one more complete circle around the tortured-looking trees, Presta landed effortlessly in front of all concerned. Without hesitation, she removed the broom from her person and gave one successful hop in place."Ta da!"

She shook her stiff hands and commented.

"I must learn not to grip the broom…so tightly. That was fun grandmother…Valda was wonderful."

Erin took the opportunity to rush over to Presta and give her a well-done hug.

"You were amazing. I've never…seen anything like…like that before. What was it like?"

Presta at a loss for clever words said,"It was very uplifting."

After a tic of silence, everyone burst out laughing. The old lady seized the momentous occasion and called out, "Okay everyone…inside for some tea and napple bread."

On the way inside the warm cottage, Presta grabbed her Grandmother's arm."Was I really good, Gran…was I?"

"You are so much like your mother, you are. I am so proud of you. The fact is, the first time your dear mother tried to fly she fell off. Of course we all had a great laugh, but she was a fighter like you and got back on."

"Really?"

"Yes, child! Now put Valda away and eat one of the napples in the wooden bowl on the side dresser."

The night felt festive for in the morning the team would be going in separate ways. The boys even managed to coax Presta into a few songs, which Kill almost ruined by trying to sing along. The witch was feeling the love of all, and expressed she would miss their company greatly. Their last night together was a good moment, for a long to be remembered memory.

After a hearty breakfast of rare found eggs, Enndora packed Presta a shoulder bag containing dried napples. She said on a long trip, they transported better. She fashioned her a scratchy wool dress from one of her own. Something she said would be needed for by the time she hit Delockth, the winter there would chill the warmest soul. Just in case, Enndora gave Presta a few spells and objects of power.

"I packed you some special objects, sweetie. If you hold them tightly...they will communicate what they are, and how to use them. Keep this one in your vest pocket...it is a warm pill I made. If you're really cold just swallow it...Its effect will last one complete cycle."

Enndora touched her cheek. Presta turned to Enndora and touched her weathered cheek. "I will be back someday and with my sisters."

"I know you will, you're Highness."

Presta hearing those words smiled warm and loving. Erin and Kill both got a kiss on the cheek. Koln pulled her privately aside.

"I don't know what to say...without you...the days are not going to be as bright. You will be instantly missed."

Koln had to break off the speech for his eyes were tearing. With a more authoritative tone he spoke.

"Now go straight home! Tell the Queen...with any luck, we will be home shortly after, and ask Korana for a favor. It's about the four guards...could she get hold of their loved ones and extend...some kind of remittance in my name. I will make amends when I see them in person."

"I shall, Sir Killgreth."

He bowed respectfully and kissed her hand. She reciprocated and embraced him like a father. Once outside she took a deep breath and checked to make sure the potion for Kem was in her flight bag. Pulling the bag around her back, she expertly jumped on Valda.

She turned her head and waved then without any more hesitation, rose into the air and swooshed away leaving all behind envious and heartbroken. Kill asked his father. "Does she know which direction to go?"

"Enndora told me the broom knows where she is headed… I will have to believe that." No one saw the dark shadow pass over the sun's face…heading in the same direction as the Princess.

Ψ

Presta and Valda: clear blue skies

My goodness the rush of flight was invigorating to say the least. I was too scared to fall off to wave back to my friends and my Gran. The sun in the sky was so bright I had to narrow my eyes to see where I was going. I verbally told Valda to stay just above the treetops unless I wanted a bigger view. I wasn't gone more than half a cycle when I started to get sore betwixed my legs. At first notice, it was oddly pleasurable, then increasingly not so much. Now I know why painted witch's in children's books, rode side saddle on their magical brooms. I made a mental note to change my style the moment I had to mount my broom in the future. Oh, well "live and learn" as my uncle Kem used to say.

I followed the river for a bit then noticed the Dark Wolf Forest coming up in the distance. I released one hand from my broom and drew my collar closer to my exposed neck. Gran was right the closer I got to home, the colder it was going to get. Just as I replaced my hand over my broom's neck a shadow passed directly over me. I craned my head left and right to see what was toying with me. When I looked up into the sun, a giant tail side swiped me hard. I had to hold on for dear life. Valda and I lost our symbiotic stabilization and went spiraling down towards the solid ground. Just before we hit the dirt, I saw a mental flash of the dragon mother's outline against the blue sky. Her leathery wings were in full spread, trying to achieve more elevation. What came next was nothing less of my sure demise. Sunlight…ground…sunlight…ground…sunlight…grou…

Ψ

CHAPTER 12

The Little People Of Dwell

RESTA'S EYES OPENED, BUT DIDN'T register a scene. The place where she awoke was either void of light, or she was blind. The wave of pain she felt in her tender body was only enhanced by the flips her stomach was making. The pain and discomfort washed in and out like the waves on her father's beach. She tried to sit up from the prone position but felt the ties of human intervention. The smell of smoke and fire was heavy in the air. Not the kind you commonly associate with cooking and supper, but the kind where you panic and run. The smell was buildings and rooftops, crops and even people. What Dark and goodless place was this? Is this where you go when you are no more? These questions rolled over in her confused mind.

Suddenly a great burst of light entered her dilated eyes. The pain in her head instantly tripled. She turned her head sideways and saw the outline of a small person standing in a doorway. Her focus was way off and had to fill in anything she didn't know with imagination. The small diminutive figure drew closer to where she was tied. Her vision was adjusting rapidly. The figure was a small man with a pointy hat and a long white beard. The smell of stale cabbage permeated his being. She could see behind him and noticed small people running in every direction in a frenzied panic.

"Ah! The She Devil is awake. Call the Magistrate…Call the guards."

They didn't waste any time, several smelly little men dressed as soldiers stormed the tiny dark room. A couple held small pikes and some brandished crudely made swords. Either way the little folk looked dangerous. Two of the closest untied me from what I now saw was a small dirty bed. My royal feet dangled over the edge a good four hands. They handled me roughly for a small girl and I got the impression they were actually scared of me more than they were angry.

When they hauled me into a standing position, I noticed the full extent of my injuries. My right shoulder hurt and my right ribs were ever so tender. They tugged on me and successfully pulled me outside. My eyes narrowed in the bright sunlight. My full vision returned quickly, but my poor head pounded smartly. I was in big trouble…I knew that for sure. Then I realized that my shoulder bag was missing carrying the potion to free Uncle Kem…and where was Valda?

Once more, the little darkies tugged on my sore arms. Some young one yelled, *"It's her!"* For a brief moment, I thought someone actually recognized me. Then the jeering started…punctuated with hate and condemnation. I soon learned they didn't.

"This is her…this is the little witch that brought the evil one."

I could hear shouts from a distance.

"Throw her on the fire!" "Take her head!" "Remove her from this place!""She's the one that brought the beast!"

"What beast? What were the crazy little folk talking about?"

As I looked around, I could see what the burning smell actually was. Giant swaths of destruction. All the buildings around me were burnt either to the ground or quickly on their way there. Their flimsy homes and buildings were made of wood and were soon defeated by the dark hot flames. I put two and two together and deduced that the mother dragon was the cause of my crash and the demise of this tiny town.

"Was it the dragon that did this to you?"

"Aye girl…the one you brought upon us."

"That I brought?" she asked.

"That Dark dragon was the reason I was put down."

Presta thought for a moment and decided to retract the reason she was down. If they thought she was a witch, she could be in more trouble than she was.

"We have been dragon-free for three generations and you…you brought this destruction down on us."

"Get her!" Someone yelled.

"*She's the one, she is!*" Screamed another.

One of the guards decided to throw me into another cell-type room. This one had wooden bars on a small window. As I was being forced down the burning street, I noticed a woman holding Valda. This made me wonder where my shoulder bag was with the potion for my uncle's freedom, and possibly his very life. I tried to use my vanishing power but the ride, plus the crash seemed to relinquish me of all magic. I was tossed into the small, unclean cell.

Ψ

Koln Killgreth: parting of the ways

Koln kept waving even though Presta was clean out of sight. "Dad…don't worry. She is pretty good at stuff…you know like a guy."

Kill tried to make his father feel better about his loss of control over Presta's well being. Koln smiled at Kill's words of encouragement.

"Okay, then, son."

Koln took a deep cleansing breath.

"Right…let's get the show on the road. I want to leave in half a cycle."

Koln barked out his wishes as if he was commanding seasoned warriors. Erin and Kill did their best to do what their father expected of them.

Koln thanked Enndora, "*I really want to thank you for all you've done for our cause, and of course your son…our High Wizard. Presta was really taken with you and finding that she had a Grandmother was like touching a part of her mother. Her sisters will be equally impressed with you, and I'm certain…will readily accept you into their family.*"

Enndora didn't know what to say, so she didn't. However…a tell tale tear rolled reluctantly down her wrinkled face. It was enough for Koln to see she understood his words. Koln and the boys mounted their over-packed horses and headed out. They headed towards the trail they had taken to reach the cottage. Looking back over their shoulders, they saw the old woman waving. Koln noticed the great white owl pass over their heads as they left the glen.

Ψ

The Sea of Shasath: The Black ship, Captain Vargas.

The first twenty ships were only a few cycles into the voyage across. The weather was cold and the winds were strong. But they seemed to be magically in their favor. The Admiral, who was one Captain Vargas, stood on the bow of the lead ship. His figure was rigid and the pipe he smoked graced the nose of the ship with a pungent smell. His collar was turned up to ward off the wet damp sea weather. He squinted his narrow eyes against the crosswinds, as he daydreamed of glorious battles soon to come. He pulled his smoking pipe out of his mouth and looked to the crow's nest. The unfortunate sailor freezing in the nest signaled to the Admiral that all was clear ahead. He smiled with his yellow and mostly brown teeth and then replaced his pipe amongst their ruin. His eyes narrowed as he stared into the distance.

Ψ

Presta Atlas: The little Dwell's cell.

The guard made certain I knew, that as soon as the fires were out they would be coming back to deal with me. I didn't like the way that felt and had to act fast to free myself from this Dark situation. The cell that I was roughly thrown into reeked of stale urine and cabbage. I had to concentrate not to retch on the spot. As I sat on my very small cot and tried to reel in my dignity, I noticed a presence in the dimly lit room. *"Who…Who's there?"*

A tiny voice bounced back to me. *"Looma"*

"Looma…did you say…Looma?"

"Yes…it is my name given."

"Why are you here?"

"Hungry I am, stole a Krugen, I did. Now I'm here."

The little girl moved her face into the small amount of light that wandered into the stinky cell. It was the face of a little doll. Perfectly round, with rosy red cheeks to boot.

Her face was covered in soot but her bright blue eyes shone through like beacons in the night. *"What's a Krugen?"*

"A small round food…red and sweet."

"I am Presta."

"What's a Prestha?"

"No…I'm Presta, and it's my given."

"Ooooh! You be not from around here…are you?"

"No…I am from the other side of Wolf Forest."

"Oh!"

"I need to get out of this room and this village."

"You are the one who brought the dragon fire?"

"I guess so…I don't know, I was (I was about to say I was flying, but I thought it would tax the little girls mind). I was traveling when I was attacked by the dragon, then brought here. Strangely enough…I find myself hungry."

"Do you want a Krugen? I have Krugen…you want try?"

"Well…I guess it couldn't hurt."

The tiny girl reached her dirty hand into a pocket on her equally dirty frock and pulled out a shiny red napple. The tears began to well up in my eyes. I wiped them dry with my own unwashed hands and reached out across the tainted divide for the miracle fruit. My hands were shaking from the knowledge of what a Krugen really was. I brought the napple to my slender nose and smelled the perfect fruit. *"Are there more where these came from?"* The girl pulled out another, similar in color but smaller. I reached for the second one. *"Oh my! This could make a difference."*

I ingested the small napple, core and all. Then I immediately called for Valda. I had called earlier but assumed that with the mayhem outside my captive cell, Valda could not respond. I needed a plan and with the diversion still going on outside, it had to be soon.

The plan I devised was simple. Looma and I would scream and carry on in the cell to attract the attention of the guards. Then I would use my invisibility to walk out of the sick smelling cell with Looma in tow. Then with any luck, we would be able to call for our ride. This had to work for time was fleeting. I ate the last Krugen, core and stem, burped and giggled.

Once I connect with Valda, I will fly away from this good forsaken place. It wasn't the best plan, but it was sound in theory.

"Here we go, little one. Don't be scared, just hold my hand. When the guards open the cell, just walk out with me."

"Scared I am!"

"Don't be, I have a few tricks up my sleeve and in no time…we will be home."

"A home…I have not my lady. Me elders are no more, and no kin have I to mention." She hung her head in the finality of what she had just said. Presta had a thought. *"Whatever happens…trust me…Ok?*

The little girl looked up with tears and nodded her acceptance. I grabbed her little hand and gave it the slightest squeeze, just enough to transfer the magic. *"Now scream, Looma!"*

We mounted a verbal distraction. As the pitch started to climb, the guards had to put their soot covered hands over their pointy little ears.

"Whaa going on tis that?"

The bigger of the two shouted. The other one shrugged his shoulders multiple times.

"What do you want to do?"

"See waa tis...open te door!"

The littlest one had to take a hand off his ear to grab the latch. The piercing noise made him place his lifted shoulder to try and block the sound, while he used his hand to work the latch. The smaller of the two peered around the slightly open door.

"I don't see any ting."

"Whaa...nothing?"

"I mean no a bodies."

"Whaa?"

The biggest one was getting frustrated, so he grabbed the handle of the latch and pulled hard to reveal no prisoners inside. They both comically scratched their heads in astonishment. Then for no apparent reason other than they had flipped their lids, spun in a circle like Whirling Dervishes.

By this time I was already out of the stinky cell with Looma in tow. Brave little Looma never uttered a sound. The two of us made it out to the streets, which were still in chaos.

Burning buildings were still being feverishly extinguished and little people were running every which way for no apparent reason. I noticed a few females spinning in circles like the two foolish guards. I wasn't as strong as I thought and heeded the warning call of my invisible powers. *We need more Krugen!* I demanded down at Looma.

"This way, you should follow." Said Looma.

Looma led Presta to a market that seemed to be miraculously untouched by the mayhem that engulfed the quaint village. The girls, while maintaining a grip on each other's hand, manage to pilfer a baker's dozen of napples, which they stuffed anywhere they could. Presta ate a shiny green one where she stood and marveled at how fast the effect could be felt. As she was chewing on the core, she spotted Valda in the hands of an older woman who was trying to put out a relatively small fire with the sentient broom. Presta without delay called for her broom.

"Valda! Come here! Valda...Now!"

The slightly damaged broom flew out of the old woman's hands, which sent her crashing down on her backside. Once the broom snapped into Presta's hands, it vanished like the two girls. Presta turned to Looma and told her, okay this is going to get weird, just trust me. Looma nodded the affirmative. Presta let Looma's hand go and she became visible. Then without hesitation, kicked her leg over Valda and picked up Looma like a child's doll placing her on the broom sideways. Looma disappeared again.

"Up! Up! And away, good Valda."

This was all the encouragement the broom needed. The thought of being used to put out fires, scared her to her walnut core.

Higher and higher Valda rose. Presta noticed that Looma and she became visible again once flying on Valda. Higher…still higher. Presta was high enough now to see the path of destruction the vengeful dragon had cut.

"Oh my…I caused this?"

"No, ma Lady…the fire beast burnt the village, he did."

Three quarters of the village was destroyed. Presta only hoped that one day she would return to help the little people. She held no grudge for their hostilities towards her. It was only the ancient fear of the dragon that had sent them spinning.

Valda was happy to obey her master's wishes and leave that good forsaken place. Presta realized in a flash that her shoulder bag with the High Wizard's cure wasn't on her person. She commanded Valda to visit the sight of their accident. Without too much crawling and moving of the local brush, Presta found her bag intact. She looked inside to make sure all was in order, then placed the bag over her shoulder. "Ah! okay, we are back in business."

They were soon on their way after a quick napple, but the direction was back to her Grandmother's cottage for a rest and recovery. She needed to have a rest before she could continue with her trip. Valda made a straight line for Enndora's cottage. Valda could feel Presta's power draining so she flew as fast as she could.

As Presta and her rider neared the cottage, dark plumes of smoke could be seen just over the tops of the Lotus Blossoms. Presta feared for the worst. As they flew closer, Presta could clearly see what was burning. The gnarly grove of napple trees had been burned to a crisp. Parts of the grove were still aflame and even closer still the Cyclops could be seen trying to put out a smoky patch on the cottage roof. Presta did not see her Grandmother out in the yard helping the Cyclops. Then her spirits lifted when she saw her toting buckets of water from the stream at the rear of the cottage. Presta commanded Valda to land just in front of the cottage's front door. When Enndora saw her, she dropped her buckets and ran in a sort of a gallop motion to her granddaughter. Her arms were wide and her eyes carried water. "Oh, my baby, you're safe."

The two embraced and gently rocked back and forth for several tics.

"Are you all right, Grandmother? Is the beast gone?"

"Well, it's gone for now. I still have a few tricks up my old sleeve. I guess she wanted vengeance for stirring up her peaceful nest."

The grandmother looked over Presta's shoulder at her smoldering trees.

"She's ruined my precious napple grove, she has. I really don't know what I'll do? They have always been here."

"Don't worry, Gran, I'm here now. I want you to meet someone. This little girl saved me...which I will tell you about later. Her name is Looma."

"Welcome, my dear...I wish everything was in order...like it used to be." Enndora started to cry. Both girls came close to comfort her. Presta turned to see Dogglopp still frantically trying to save the cottage and decided it would be time for comfort later. *"Come on girls!"* Presta shouted. We have a cottage to save. With that cry, Enndora ceased her tears and each grabbed a pail and joined in the fight to save the smoky cottage.

Thirty tics of hard work paid off, for the girls and a big one-eyed monster managed to save the cottage from destruction. The three girls sat on an unburnt cart together.

"Is it bad, Gran?" Presta asked with a face full of black soot.

"Not as bad as it looks, honey. Part of the roof is finished and the west wall could use some shoring up, but that won't take Dogglopp long to fix both. Despite his outer appearance, he is quite the worker, he is."

Dogglopp heard the positive comment the old woman threw his way and smiled through his spoked teeth.

"I have some roofing materials in that back shed. I use it to keep out the rainy season leaks. The wall will take more time...oh well, I'm just glad you're safe. It's my trees that I don't know what to do about. They were planted here way before my time by a good witch from very far away, I was told. I have some dried napples stored in my fruit cellar but after that...I don't know."

Looma looked like she wanted to say something, but it wasn't her place to speak. *"Is there something you wish to say?"* Presta asked Looma.

"Just say it, we're are all friends here," Enndora leaned forward.

"Growers my people are… I can help you restore the loss you see. Do you have the bremen for your Krugen?"

"What's that, honey?" Enndora asked.

"Krugen is their name for napple, Gran."

"Oh I see…do you mean seeds?" Looma nodded.

"Yes I do…a whole sack full in the cold cellar."

Looma smiled with beautiful white teeth. "Then what you need…I can do."

"Can she stay with you? She has no family and no place to call home."

"I would love that, child, and possibly my loneliness would be tossed away for good. Enndora reached for Looma's little hand and grabbed it with both of hers. She then started to pat the little girl's hand softly. Looma had a tear in her eye. She jumped off the cart and jumped into Enndora's arms. It was so precious to see Looma's head pressing against Enndora and only reaching her formidable belly.

The night was spent in the small utility shed while Dogglopp worked around the cycle to finish the roof for his friends. The old woman lit a small fire and cooked an old-fashioned meal of napple soup and barbecued chicken. It was Looma's first time for both treats and soon came to be her most favorite meal. Presta was sure it was the memory more than the meal. The girls sat back and listened to Presta's accounts of the village events, and wondered at the sheer magic of the tale. The three women finally drifted asleep dog tired, and sufficiently comforted beside each other.

Ψ

The morning seemed to come too fast for the three. The unmistakable smell of wet, burnt roof-straw and napple trees instantly brought back the traumatic events of the day before. Presta pushed open the shed door to see Dogglopp asleep against the side of the cottage. His large back was pressed up against the damp wall. Presta let him sleep, but Enndora started to cook a breakfast in the cottage's undamaged part and woke the ugly, but admirable beast. The roof had been repaired sometime while they slept. Enndora made sure Dogglopp ate extra food for his unselfish services. After breakfast, the Cyclops started on the damaged west wall.

"Well…I must go Gran…The High Wizard still is trapped and his time is running out."

"I know, child…you will be greatly missed. I hope I get to meet your sisters one day."

"You will…once we have eradicated this dark threat against our land, we will journey back to you."

Presta had no more time to waste. She fired up her broom's spirit and after a few hugs and kisses, flew off through the crisp morning air in a straight line towards Delockth.

Ψ

Koln, Erin and Kill: Heading towards an escarpment

The fearful concerns of the two boys came into play on the desired route home. Koln being the only true warrior in the group decided to take a longer but safer path home. The boys didn't really want another slice of the Dark forest. The dreaded Wolf Forest would have taken two cycles less but the risk of another canine encounter was too great. Even with Volzanth on their side, there was no guarantee that the other rogue wolves would follow his dominant lead. The control for a pack that big is always plagued with underdogs trying to step up. Koln chose a northern route that steered clear of the Dark Forest. This fortunately moved them through a great ridge on a high escarpment.

Kill asked. "Will this really take an extra two cycles to see our home, father?"

"Yes and maybe more. I only have these old roughly drawn maps Enndora gave to me. I don't know how accurate they are, or the quality of the detail. To me it looks like the information here was told from the view point of an owl."

The boys laughed but the owl, unnoticed sitting in the tree they passed by, didn't.

"For all I know…this could take six or seven cycles to see our old castle."

Erin didn't say much, all he could do was think about Presta and her unknown fate as she flew her magic broom solo towards home.

Koln kept the first leg short and set up a temporary camp on the northern edge of the Wolf Forest. "Why are we stopping here?" Erin asked.

"Well…I'm cutting the first part short because this place gives us ample wood for our fire, and possibly some fresh meat for our spit. Not to mention the shelter from the winds."

"Ok, that sounds good to me."

"I thought you'd agree."

"I'm hungry!" Kill almost whined when he confessed to the world.

"*Take my crossbow and go get us something to brag about in our recanting of this trip.*"

"But we have fresh provisions from the cottage," Kill tried to make a point. "Go…Now!"

The tone of Koln's voice left no room for any interpretation of the orders. Kill didn't speak again. He quickly shot Erin a worried look and took his father's crossbow from his hands. A few tics later, he was heading into the waiting forest.

Erin and his stepfather had set up a temporary camp and had a healthy fire blazing, when young Kill came back with three large grouse. Koln took the time and the opportunity to show the two boys how to gut and prepare wild fowl for the spit. It wasn't more than thirty tics before the plump birds were being cooked on the clean fire.

"This is good." Erin sounded surprised.

"*You'll have to thank the hunter for his keen aim,*" Koln suggested.

Erin held up a chunk of meat in a form of salute to his brother. Kill was too busy eating to notice. After the evening's food, the three tended to the welfare of their horses and the customary weapons inspection and sharpening. This was enough to make the boys sleepy. The three slept peacefully through the night, save for the moments they were disturbed by a lone wolf howling in the far off distance.

Ψ

Marideath Insertion force: General Mott Mansth, Plains of Volarin

Fifty elite men and horses rowed in on three long boats and a small barge for the horses and supplies. The provisions they traveled with were few, as the campaign wasn't designed to last very long. The large vessel specially designed for this operation was eventually moved out of sight. For this plan to work, stealth and concealment was the order. The fact that Delockth sympathizers were everywhere caused extra precautions to be taken.

The person in charge of the operation was General Mott Mansth of Blackshire. He was the son, of a son, of a soldier. Military life was natural for him and he was good at it. Marideath rewarded Mott with this latest mission. He dangled the carrot of retirement and titles in his soon to be newly acquired Delockth estates in front of the old warrior.

Marideath trusted his General to do whatever was necessary to complete this mission. What Marideath didn't realize, was that the General was getting older and subjected to frequent miscalculations. Most of the Generals past experiences were with the odds in his favor, and this was quite different, to have such a small force to do such a big job.

The fifty men lined up just a short distance back from the beach awaiting the commander's orders. The short-statured General stood on an erratic boulder to command the troop's attention. He took a deep breath.

"Dark warriors of Blackshire…we have an important mission given to us by our Dark Lord and master. I can tell you now, that we are going to be attacking the Castle of Delockth. Our mission is to try to remove the Queen and disrupt her unprepared army. This we will do…while another loyal Dark force… attacks by their sea front. You are…the best of the best. Our small numbers will help us to arrive unnoticed, and therefore have the powerful advantage of surprise. The young and inexperienced queen shall fall…and this ripe and fertile country…will be ours."

The men all raised an arm in the air and gave a rousing cheer. The general used his arm motions to silence the invigorated men. The fifteen full cycles at sea drastically took their fighting spirit down a notch or two. These were infantry…and not sailors. The winded General continued, *"I won't fool you…this is a tough and treacherous journey. The time of season this is…makes the Plains of Volarin…almost impassable. The mud and moisture will hamper our best efforts. The good news is…that the enemy will never expect us to cross at this time…and this will help our chances for surprise."*

The soldiers looked at each other with mixed emotions.

"I am expecting a solid five cycles to reach our destination. May the Dark Lord be with you." The General turned to his Sergeant and extended his hand for a help down from his sermon boulder.

"Give the order to mount up and move 'em out."

"Yes, General."

"And bring me another sweater; this good forsaken place is damp and cold."

"Yes, General. Okay…you heard the General, look sharp and MOVE OUT!"

Ψ

Koln and the two boys: High on the northern border of Delockth

After a good ten cycles of travel, Koln and the boys started to climb a high ridge. The ridge overlooked the Plains of Volarin.

"Father, its cold, can we make a fire?" Little Kill was violently rubbing his hands together.

"Put on those gloves I gave you awhile back and tie up your neck piece. That will help your body temperature."

"But…I'm cold too, Sir, and I'm wearing that stuff."

Erin lifted his hands to show Koln he was on Kill's side.

"The higher we go…the colder it is," Kill added.

"Can we camp soon?" Erin sounded like Kill's seven full-seasoned voice.

Koln removed his spyglass from his saddlebag and looked up at the ridge ahead.

"Okay…I can see a clearing a cycle ahead where we can make camp. I suppose we made good progress and my legs are starting to protest some. Come on men… let's keep moving."

Both boys were charged with the anticipation of warm food and drink. Their enthusiasm was shown in the speed in which they pushed their mounts towards their new camp. Koln chuckled to himself how easy it was to motivate the young men with just food and warmth.

The fire was tall and wide from the extensive amount of fuel just behind them. The Wolf Forest at their backs also provided several rabbits, which were highly coveted by the hungry three. The cooking turned out excellently and the warmth was gold. Kill had a smile on his handsome face again. Erin was also grateful, but was more subdued in his outward expression of the necessities he was receiving.

"I wish Presta was here with us," Erin divulged.

"What…you don't like…just boy time?" Koln said jokingly.

"No actually…I was hoping for a song or two. She was in fact…quite good. Don't you think father?"

"I wish she was here, too." Kill interjected.

Koln started to sing to the boy's dismay.

We…will…Fight to the last, we will drink until no more,
we will kiss all the women and take all the hor…

"Dad! Please! Save it for battle or something." Kill stood up.

"I am all for a good education, but don't put thoughts in my head before I'm ready…Okay?" Koln's face looked as if he had just seen a ghost.

"Whaa...Oh... for certain. I am sorry son. I was just reminiscing."

Erin started to laugh at the look on Koln's face, which made Koln burst into a belly laugh. Then finally, Kill joined them. The flames danced in their eyes while they all emptied their lungs of joyous air.

"Do you think she's home, Pa?" Kill asked. Koln had to wipe the laughter tears from his eyes.

"What?"

"Do you think she is home?"

"Oh...most likely. Especially if her path was straight and true."

Kill put his head down and grabbed a long twig. He poked the fire's coals and sounded distant. "What do you think of all that witchery stuff anyway?"

"I really don't know son. I guess when it benefits us it's good. When it's against us...well you know."

Hoot! Who! Hoot! Who!

All three instantly recognized the sound and spun their collective heads around trying to find the white owl. "Do you see it?" Erin blurted out.

"No, you?" Kill answered. Koln grabbed a flaming stick from the fire and held it high.

"There he is!" He pointed to the top of a short evergreen tree 150 hands away.

"What does he want, Pa?" Kill asked.

"I guess it's just Enndora's way of keeping tabs on us."

"But aren't we out of her range...so to speak?" Erin stood and looked closer towards the noise as he scratched his messy hair.

"I guess not. As far as that bird can fly...she can see."

The owl without provocation launched itself off the tree and headed in the direction of the Volarin plains.

"Why is he going that way, there is nothing out there?" Erin asked.

Koln asked himself the same question. He threw the burning stick back into the fire, which released a shower of sparks into the night's air. He rummaged through his saddlebags and pulled out his spyglass. At first, he saw only black in his seeing device, and then to his utter astonishment he saw what looked like several fires far off into the distance.

"That's strange...That many fires usually are associated with fifty to sixty men."

"What's so strange about fires?" Kill asked innocently.

"That's the Plains of Volarin; it's a flood plain in the summer seasons and a mud bath at this time of the season cycle. No one in his right mind would venture across at this particular time. Especially with that many people. There is something not right here."

Koln had the clear tone of worry laced through his gruff voice. He handed the spyglass to Erin who fumbled with the placement of the eyepiece.

"Here! take a look…over there, that direction. That my son…is a whole legion of men." Erin looking at the small lights asked, "Ahhh! If we can see them…can they see us?"

"Good point son. Kill, downsize the fire…right now."

Kill used his foot to scatter some of the logs making it easier to put them out. Erin removed the spyglass from his eye. "Did the bird head in that direction?"

"I believe it did." Koln stroked the hair on his chin as he thought.

"How many full cycles to the castle from here?" Erin asked.

"Two full cycle's hard ride."

"How many for a legion of fifty or more across mud and water?"

Koln paused. "Three and a half…maybe four cycles, slow and hard."

Kill asked the obvious question, which stopped Erin and Koln in their conversation. "Are they on our side father?"

"No son…I don't believe they are."

Their sleep was light and disturbing. Visions of deathly scenes circled about their nocturnal dreams. Morning came too soon.

When the two boys awoke, they found their father standing on the edge of the canyon with spyglass pressed up to his knowing eye. Kill wiped the sleep from his eyes and proceeded to poke at the fire, trying to coax it into to dancing for him. Erin must have found the sweet spot in his sleep, because Kill had to throw something at the Van Winkle to wake him up. Kill turned his attention back to the stubborn fire and fed the soon to be flames its morning breakfast of twigs and logs. The moment the fire produced heat, Kill found an away spot to relieve himself. Erin pulled himself together and heated up some napple cider. He walked over to Koln, who seemed to be contemplating their next move. He did this while trying to balance the hot liquid in the wooden cup he held in front of him. Koln turned to him and said, "Hmmm! Thank you I could smell the brew from way over there."

"Any change?"

"Yes actually…it looks like they're on the move."

"Where do you think they're going?"

"They seem to be moving slowly in the direction of Delockth. I'll tell you... Any force attempting to enter from this direction, are up to no good...that I know for sure. We have a real problem here."

"Do you know who they are?" Kill joined them on the canyon's edge. He had his own drink with him. Koln raised the spyglass to his eye with one hand.

"I'm almost certain its Marideath's troops. There are no other challenging forces anywhere near here, and if there were, they would send more than fifty or sixty men."

Koln walked back to the healthy fire, while the two boys gave each other a grave look. Koln sat down on a sideways log and threw the rest of his cider into the fire. Erin sat beside him.

"How do you know its Marideath's troops?"

"I could just make out the banner and armor. The easiest give away is the three a breast marching, it's a standard marching formation from Blackshire."

Koln stood abruptly. "I know now what I must do."

The two boys didn't like the tone of what their father said. Erin finished his drink and Kill gulped.

Ψ

Volarin Plains: General Mansth

The supply wagons were slow going. It took four large soldiers to constantly push from behind the wagon so it didn't get bogged down in the cold, wet mud.

"Keep them moving! Sergeant."

The first Lieutenant kept the verbal whip to their damp backs. The Lieutenant pulled up beside the General who was equally having a hard time with the unforgiving mud.

"I am sorry, my General...this ground is unbelievable. I mean if there was another route..." The General cut him off with a look of disgust.

"Do you think...I didn't know we were going to have a hard time, Lieutenant? Do you think I'm happy about this...mud? I suggest you concentrate on keeping your men motivated, and spend less time telling me...what I already know."

The Lieutenant slowed his horse's movement and let the General move ahead alone. One of the mounted soldiers pulled up beside the Lieutenant.

"I know you do not want to hear this...but we have a problem."

The Lieutenant gave him a look of despair. "What now?"

"The main food wagon has just lost a wheel in this dark mud."

The lieutenant held up his hand and stopped the troop. The General sensing the troop stopping, turned around. As he passed by the Lieutenant, he said in a somber and quiet voice. *"Make camp Lieutenant…fix the problem."*

Thirty tics later, the Lieutenant was summoned to the General's tent.

"Sit down lieutenant. How goes the repair?"

"Not so good sir…we had to send four men back to get another wheel. We will be delayed by a full cycle at best."

The general didn't say anything. He just poured himself some wine and didn't offer his Lieutenant any. The Lieutenant noticing this wiped his dry mouth with his dirty hand.

"You wanted to know why we are here… I'll tell you. Our great Dark leader thought that no one would ever believe we, or anyone for that matter, would attack at this time of the season over these very floodplains. He knew it would be impassible but he thought the element of surprise would greatly outweigh the hardships the men would bear. Do I think he was right? No! I love the honor of battle, the right-up-in-your-face kind of battle; not this sneaking around, wizardly kind of shit."

The general pounded the rickety table with his closed fist and startled the Lieutenant with his useless bravado.

"If we could have waited just thirty full cycles…we might have had a frozen mud bed to cross…instead of this shit. Please excuse my language. I'm just frustrated with the delays and… the mud. My horse has seen better days and this terrain is making her grumpy."

"I must tell you, the men are complaining. They are an elite force but they can't keep their feet dry and the misery is starting to build in them as well."

"I can't help that soldier, war is a dark business."

"Can I order double rations of wine for the men as long as we are stuck here?"

"Yes! Yes! See to it at once and for darkness sake…let's see how fast we can get out of the good forsaken mud. You know…I think it is very admirable that you care for your men, Lieutenant."

He raised his half-full glass to the soldier still without offering him a drink.

Ψ

CHAPTER 13

The Volarin Effect

KOLN AND THE TWO BOYS: Canyons edge

Koln sat with his head propped up with one hand while he poked at the mocking fire with a switch. Erin and Kill passed around some hard cheese that Enndora had packed for their journey home. Koln waved a piece off, not wanting to indulge at that particular moment. Kill pushed a piece at Koln.

"Here! The way Erin is consuming this stuff there won't be any left to eat."

Koln begrudgingly reached over and took the piece out of Kill's hand, which he then popped into his mouth.

"What are we going to do?" Erin asked.

Koln looked at Erin with the reflection of the flames in his black eyes. *"What do you mean?"*

"What are you going to do pa?"

Koln spoke sternly, *"I'm going to go down there and try to stall their progress, or at least try and talk some sense to them. We need to warn Delockth of their threat before they are surprised. I know it's a small force, but it's probably an elite force. That's where the two of you come in. You are to head straight to Delockth and warn the Queen of the invaders. I will try to slow them down."*

"They will put you down!" Erin stood quickly and kicked dirt at the fire.

"No they won't...they were my people...and they think I am a hero and a respected warrior."

Erin tried to walk away but Koln grabbed his arm.

"I know you're worried...but I can take care of myself."

Erin pulled his arm away with force.

"We will…never see you…again."

Erin walked into the dark. Kill stood and Koln said quietly and calmly.

"It's okay… let him go."

The two sat down again in front of the fire.

"We don't have any options. We are only men…not wizards."

"Will you be okay?" Kill asked softly.

"I don't know. All I know is what's important right now, and that's duty. You need to warn the Queen."

"Don't worry, father, I feel the call to duty as well and I will do what is expected of me." Koln patted Kill solidly on the shoulder and then squeezed his arm. Kill smiled back feeling the bond.

The next morning came swiftly and sadistically. A storm blew in before the sun rose to laugh in its great yellow eye. The storm showed no mercy for the travelers or anyone else for that matter. Bitter winds galloped across the flood plains and reached high into the escarpment. No creature was spared the wrath of nature. Koln and the boys were hard-pressed to keep their tents from turning into small sails.

"Dad we can't leave like this," Kill pleaded.

"No…you're right, but I'm going to use the blowing dirt for cover. Here! You take the map Enndora penned and my spyglass. I will need to travel light."

Kill blurted out just under the storm's volume, "I'm scared!"

Koln turned and grabbed his little face with one big hand.

"Good…very good! Scared will keep you alive. Now help me pack my tent."

There was no hot breakfast for anyone that morning. The bitter winds saw to the flame's sudden demise. The boys divided with themselves and their father, a napple each and some dried cookies Enndora baked. Oddly enough the simple fare made them feel invigorated, which made the boys argue that they were enchanted or something of that nature. Erin made sure the horses were secure. He tied them behind the camp in a small stand of trees to protect them from the dark winds. He wisely saved a napple for each horse. As he was hand feeding the animals, he heard the howl of a lone wolf in the distance, far inside the forest behind them and sorrowful as any sound he had ever heard. He felt the small hairs on the back of his dirty neck stand tall.

Koln pushed the last article into his saddlebag while the boys stood right beside him watching. Koln pulled his hood up and tied it off at the open neck hoping to stave off the ferocious winds. He turned to his brave sons. *"Ok…so* we know the plan. It won't be easy, but I have faith you can do it. Please have faith in me."

He hugged Kill who ran into his powerful arms. He shook Erin's hand and gave him a lame salute, which made Erin crack a smile. Without further ado he mounted his warhorse and snapped its rear with his long leather reins. The horse squinted his large eyes and reluctantly headed into the wind. He headed back down the path whence they had come. After thirty tics of hard travel, he reached the fork in the trail. This road led him down the escarpment serpentine style, until he reached the Volarin planes.

Ψ

Plains of Volarin: Marideath's Elite strike force

The next morning came with a bitter storm, which showed no signs of letting go. The special party to retrieve the wagon wheel parts had not made it back yet and was seriously making the General rethink his plans. Some of the soldier's tents didn't make it through the night, which forced some of the men to share accommodations. The good carts they had left were starting to sink from the extra weight of the men sitting on them to try to escape wet feet. Most of the fires had long since blown out, which readily left many men huddled around small struggling fires for unfeeling warmth. The General at this point made his fatal error. He ordered his crack troops to break camp and start to push forward slowly. He was hoping the repair party would return, fix the wagon and follow the tracks. He had to leave the broken wagon where it met its untimely death. Fifty percent of all the food rations plus pots and cooking pans remained bogged down in the life-sucking mud. Even the General's precious wine was left behind. As the soldiers started to march, they were immediately hampered with the combination of mud up to their knees and a bitter cold, blowing wind in their disgruntled and twisted faces. The General stayed at the back of the line, this time hoping the troops would shield him from the cold wind. The Lieutenant dropped back to talk to the bundled up General.

"Excuse me, General, Sir…Do you wish to reroute the troops around this mess?"

"No! Lieutenant…I have an important timeline to uphold. If we don't reach Delockth at the same time as the water attack, the master will literally have us for lunch. Do…I…make…myself clear,…Lieutenant?"

The general gave the soldier a look that meant he had no choice.

"I understand your dilemma, Sir…but if we keep this up, we won't have a force to do whatever it is we need to do. The men are professional…but they are only men,…Sir."

"Good point Lieutenant. I tell you what; in the interest of survival…send two good advanced scouts forward to try to find a raised spot that might be drier. We might be able to wait there for the food wagon."

"Yes, general…the men will be pleased with this idea and anything to lift their spirits right now…would be a good thing." The Lieutenant saluted the General and galloped off into the moisture-filled wind to fill out his new orders.

Ψ

Erin and Kill: Edge of the escarpment

"There he goes…I hope this is not the last time we see the man."

Erin tried to rise to the occasion by sounding like the scenario didn't bother him anymore.

"I have a good feeling we will." Kill said to himself.

Kill recognized Erin's posturing, and tried to follow in Erin's positive lead. Erin pulled his coat top closer around his exposed neck.

"Wow! If this cold don't get me…this hunger will. Let's try and birth a big fire so we can have warm food to eat. Maybe the wind won't blow a bigger flame out."

"Maybe dad would be able to see we are okay," Kill added.

Both boys pulled together and fortified their shelter the best they could for the night. For it wouldn't be long before early rise came, and they made their journey to warn the Queen of the possible threat from the great flood plains. Soon the flames were dancing in their favor and their bellies were warm with food. Erin turned his ear to a familiar sound coming from the forest. One lone wolf…far off in the distance.

Koln Killgreth:

The passage down was a real treat. Twice I had to physically convince my horse to endeavor the steep grade of the trail. Once I hit the flood plain the travelling got increasingly more difficult. The mud seemed to rise as high as my horse's first leg joint. He wasn't pleased with this terrain at all. It was times like these I wish my old war horse Rantor was with me. He wasn't scared of any challenge. I don't really blame this horse for protesting, the mud was relentless. It was a sad day when I had to put Rantor down on humanitarian grounds. Trying to look into the distance made me regret leaving my spyglass with the boys. My old eye's had much trouble judging how far away I was from the advancing troops. This fact made me estimate it would take a full 10 cycles to reach them. I managed to find a patch of raised dry ground about 6 cycles into the tiring trip. The winds died down somewhat and was replaced by colder temperatures. There was nothing to hitch my horse to so I drove my long sword into the ground and tied the four legged wonder to the hilt. I didn't want to risk a fire, but I didn't want to freeze either. I tried to place my tent between the small fire and the oncoming invaders. I also had to wait till dark so the advancing army's forward scouts could not see my rising smoke plume. Marideath had the best forward scouts in modern warfare. They were usually of aboriginal descent from a not too distant land to the east of Blackshire.

> I used my time well by tending to a loose horse shoe and sharpening my main weapons. I was hungry, but I had to wait till I could light my night fire. I had a very brief visit from our white owl friend. He perched himself on my tents front pole and blinked his eyes once or twice. I didn't know if he understood my words, but I told the bird to go and tell the Queen of Delockth that she was being invaded from the Volarin plains. The bird blinked again then flew off. The bird flew in the direction of the opposing army. So much for any wizardly intervention. That bird was probably a forward scout for the dark army. The light grew dim and I lit my fire. The hot food will be a welcome friend tonight.¥

General Mott Mansth: Generals tent:
The general was trying to eat some hastily prepared food but his stomach ulcer was giving him grievous repercussions. He placed one tired hand over his unclean shirt and closed his eyes hoping that the gut ache would disappear. The tent flap opened without warning, making the General's head snap back with anxiety. The Generals two personal guards used an arm each to make an entrance for the Lieutenant.

"I beg your pardon my General. I have some important and interesting news and I didn't want to wait until our scheduled meeting."

The General signaled with his hand for the Lieutenant to approach. He took a drink trying to wash down the mouthful of food he was working hard at chewing. He swallowed.

"Please sit down, Lieutenant, you're making me uncomfortable. Here…have a glass of wine, it's quite good."

"Thank you, Sir."

The Lieutenant placed his official cap under his left arm and pulled up a small collapsible stool. He sat down very cautiously because the stool was much too small for his rear end. The Lieutenant took a drink of the fine wine and smiled at its flavor.

"It's all the way from the province of Kullist, in the most southern part of Blackshire."

"What is?"

"The wine."

"The wine…Oh yes! The wine… but of course."

"They have no grapes to speak of, but the fruit they do ferment does make one's pallet jump with joy."

The Lieutenant looked at the General as if he was cracked in the head.

"What do you want?" The General's tone switched drastically.

"Oh…yes…well I have some good news. The rear scouts can see the men coming up the rear with the wagon-wheel supplies."

"Oh, very good. How long before we can move out?"

"It will be in the morning I believe."

"Anything else?"

The Lieutenant felt like he was being rushed and pushed out of the General's sight. "The forward scouts have seen a smoke plume far away, high on an overlooking escarpment."

"If it's far away what's bothering you?"

"If we can see it…they can see ours."

"Oh! Right…right you are. Send the forward scouts out farther to investigate. I wish to know if our position and surprise has been given away. This could greatly affect our plans."

The Lieutenant rose sharply and saluted the still seated General. He turned on his muddy heels and exited the General's tent to carry out his orders. As he walked away, he ran his tongue over his yellow teeth wishing he had taken another drink of the General's superb wine. The General opened a rolled map he pulled out from a leather tube. He slowly rubbed his stubbly rounded chin as he poured over the map's particulars.

The two specially assigned scouts bolted out of the make-shift camp in search of the unknown smoke trail. Their two horses didn't seem to mind the heavy mud; it almost looked like they were running on water. Fortunately, they didn't notice the owl flying 500 hands above their lowered heads.

Ψ

Kill and Erin: The next morning.

Morning came early for all. Massive thunderclouds covered the entire Volarin landscape. The damp strong winds blowing through the delta moved and tossed anything that wasn't tied down or rooted. The two boys woke up startled with a cold torrent of rain pouring into their half- baked tent.

"Ah! Son of the Dark," Erin shouted as he took most of the big leak directly on his sleepy head. His side of the tent looked more like a bath than a tent. Kill was a little wet but not as drenched as his stepbrother. Erin had had enough; he put on his overcoat and left the tent with the intent of walking a few paces, then relieving his bladder. He pushed the tent flaps aside and stood up straight in the rain.

Three full-grown wolves, no more than fifty hands away were staring right at him. Erin froze out of instinct. Remembering his training, he slowly reached down his body to his belt in search of his short sword. He quickly remembered taking it off to go to sleep. A sudden wave of panic shot through him as he started to whisper, *"Kill…Kill…bring my sword…Kill…wolves, hurry!"*

Kill must have heard him and understood the situation. He slowly pushed the sword handle through a slit in the flap's opening. Erin reached back behind him grabbing the cold hilt of his short sword. Kill lifted the rear edge of the tent and moved it enough to roll out from under its quasi protection. He managed to roll into a small depression in the ground filled with dirty cold water. Kill suppressed his anger and didn't curse out loud so as to alert the wolves of his circling plan. He stood up very slowly with his short sword gripped tightly in his ready cold hand.

Along the left side of the tent he crept, heel to toe. Kill managed to walk right up to and just beside the shaking Erin without engaging the wolves in any form of attack. Kill put his empty hand on Erin's back and whispered.

"Why aren't they attacking?"

"*I don't know.*" Erin was answering out the side of his mouth.

"What do you want to do? There are only three of them."

The moment that Kill spoke those words, thirty more large wolves walked onto the scene and surrounded the boys.

Ψ

Koln Killgreth: Volarin Plains,

Early the next morning, I thought the inclement weather took a turn for the worse. The falling rain turned to freezing rain, and then sleet was ordered like some macabre feast of tortures. My dry little hump of sand soon turned to a soupy bottom and I and my possessions were wet. The sun was trying desperately to poke its face from under a massive system. In or out of my poor tent didn't seem to matter much but I did have to relieve the drink I had been holding all night. I pushed back the tent flaps and stood up in the rain. I remember taking two large steps away from my tent as not to have it wash back to me later and that's when the lights went out. I am certain that I fell face first into the good mother earth.

Erin and Kill: Surrounded,

"*Is this…how it ends?*"

Erin directed his pertinent question to his petrified step-brother. Kill didn't answer right away; he was too frightened to talk. The wolves drew nearer, while still others joined the furry party. Then Kill broke his silence.

"Wait! This isn't what it seems. It's scary…but it's not what you think. Wolves don't congregate like this. They want something all right, but it's not our lives."

When Erin calmed down, he too noticed that something was amiss.

"*You may be right, little brother.*"

The boys lowered their weapons so as to show the pack that they didn't want to fight. Kill looked around and noticed that the horses weren't reacting as they should. "The horses aren't agitated. They should be spooked right out of their hides. Erin turned his head slowly while trying to keep an eye on the advancing wolves. "*Yaaa! You're right.*"

One extremely large wolf walked from the rear of the pack straight towards the boys. As he drew nearer, Kill exclaimed with an excessive amount of air, "Volzanth!"

The large wolf's tail started to wag when it knew it had been recognized. Erin tried something silly and kneeled down while snapping his fingers.

"*Come here, boy…come here.*"

"Are you for real?" Kill said under his breath.

The wolf drew nearer and then unceremoniously sat before the two boys.

"I wish you would not do the whistle thing. You have no idea how demeaning it really is."

The two boys just stood there with their mouths agape.

"What are you doing now, catching flies?"

The great wolf turned his head to one side like a playful puppy.

"*You can…you can talk.*" Erin sounded dumbfounded.

"Ooooh! You must be the bright one," the wolf said in true sarcasm.

"Yes…and rather well I might add. Enndora thought it best in her infinite wisdom, that it might come in handy. She thought you might need some reinforcements. Oh, that's a hard word to form. Reinforsssmentss…re…enforcements."

The wolf started to lick the roof of his mouth like something sticky was lodged there.

"It's not easy let me tell you using this mouth to form human words. I only hope I'm not a canine long enough to get good at it. Unfortunately this spell that Enndora granted me is relatively short and I will soon run out of human words."

Kill looked up and was the first to notice that the prior unforgiving rain had ceased to fall.

"Okay, that's more like it. I'm going to start a fire…I'm hungry."

Volzanth stood on all fours and barked several times, then sat down again.

"*What was that about?*" Erin asked.

"I told them to hunt rabbit. It won't be long before you can clean them. I find us to be excellent hunters."

Not a full cycle later, a roaring fire burned in front of the boy's damp tent. Kill found the fire spell that Enndora gave him helped immensely with all the abundant wet firewood hindering their campfire igniting. Erin had a big smile on his dirty face while he turned a spit with three large rabbits cooking. Volzanth lay between the boys drinking up all the fire's warmth. He was also enjoying the boys' company, longing to be human again.

"*Thank you for the food, Wolf,*" Erin said with meaning.

The great wolf just lifted his head and panted.

Halfway through the boy's simple meal, two large black wolves entered the boy's camp and stood either side of Volzanth. They barked several times each and immediately departed into the dark and wet woods.

"What did they have to say that…seemed so urgent?" Erin asked with his mouth full.

"It seems Killgreth…your father was captured and taken by two large men."

"DAD!" Kill cried out loud.

"Hold on brother…he could still be all right. When they find out it's the hero of the Northern Wars, they will show him leniency."

"What are we to do now?"

"Hold on… I might have a plan." Erin turned to Volzanth and grabbed his dog-like head caringly.

"I am going to ask of you a tremendous favor. I will also swear on my mother's life, that I will do everything in my power to return you to your human self."

The wolf tilted his furry head and said, "I'm all ears."

Kill had to turn his head away to snicker. The great white owl pushed off from a treetop overlooking the boy's camp. The inclement weather didn't seem to bother the enchanted bird. He was happy just to be wanted and useful.

Ψ

CHAPTER 14

For Love of Country

THE WIZARD'S TOWER: THE LIBERATION of Kem

Presta was still drained and mentally tired from her cold and stressful flight. The two napples she ate seemed to do nothing for her strength or general health. She found it difficult to push out of her mind the fact that Koln and the boys could be in danger and she wasn't there to help them. Erin's image reappeared over and over in her mind's eye. She knew what she felt was real and the worrying was part of her power drain. She had to constantly wipe her eyes from stressful moisture. She turned what little power she had towards freeing her High Wizard Uncle. She looked up at the long winding staircase which protruded from the cold stone wall. She had made this climb as a small child countless times before but never for such an important task. She used to count the stairs on her way up and today was no exception.

"Seventy-seven, seventy-eight! There! Wow…I'm pooped."

She stood in front of the great, tall wooden doors and gave a hard shove. The doors gave the tell tale cry of rusty hinges. As she walked into the room, the familiarity smacked her in the unblemished face. It had been some time since she was last there and even the cornucopia of smells, brought back fond memories. Most of her childhood memories were spent here being tutored within these purple and gold walls by her powerful Uncle. The fact that they knew Kem was really their Uncle, drew him even closer to her and her sisters. As she walked through the larger open room, she dragged her open hand over objects of fond memory. Upon spying a few large candles, she took the opportunity to try one of the secret spells her Grandmother had taught her.

Wish I may…wish I might
light these waxen…candles bright
for in the dark…the light does rest
now with my hand…I passed the test

As Presta waved her arm, all the large candles lit one by one, until all seven danced to her tune. Standing before her was a large figure draped in a white dust-cloth. Presta slowly bent over and grabbed the bottom of the white sheet.

"Sister may I help?"

Presta almost jumped out of her skin.

"What!?" Presta turned around clearly startled.

"Oh! It's you …Korrin. You scared the dark out of me, you did."

"I am sorry, I just want to help."

"Fine! Just stand back while I pull this sheet off."

Presta turned around and started again to relieve the tall figure of its covering. The dust-sheet slowly pulled away from the figure to reveal the High Wizard in a shocking pose. His arms were still in the defensive position he was frozen in on the King's Beach.

"Is it true?" Korrin asked.

"*Yes…he is Enndora's son, which makes him our uncle on our mother's side.*" Korrin walked up to the horrific green statue and placed her gentle hand on the green coating over the Wizard's face.

"I can't feel to heal."

"*I know…I have something here from our grandmother. This should do the trick.*" Presta pulled a glowing bluish ball out of her small purse that was around her slender waist and held it in the air in front of her green covered Uncle.

"What do we do now?"

"I don't really know. I am assuming…I throw it at the figure and hope for the best. We should stand back a bit."

The two girls measured back until they felt safe. Presta looked at Korrin.

"*Do you want to do it?*"

"Can I?"

Presta handed the glowing blue ball to Korrin. "What do I do?"

"Throw it at the Wizard…but don't miss."

Korrin drew her right arm back and stuck her tongue out of her mouth for some sort of accuracy trigger. The launch was true. The blue ball hit the green statue and splattered all over its surface. Immediately steam rose from the entire surface. The green coating was in effect...melting. First, his head was exposed, and then his shoulders and so on, until he was free of the green coating. The smell released from the process was putrid and acidic. Both little girls ran to separate windows and managed to push them open a few micro measures, just enough for a clearing cross-breeze. Korrin stood there in amazement while pinching her tiny nose. Presta had a smile on her face, as the High Wizard revealed himself once more.

The puddle on the floor quickly drained through the slightly separated floorboards to the unexpecting floor far below. Kem stood there wet in the same horrific pose.

"Now you may try." Presta said to Korrin.

Korrin walked up to her Uncle and placed her loving hands upon both sides of the tormented expression on his face. Korrin knew right away that she needed help. She signaled for Presta to come join her. Presta didn't touch Kem, she touched the back of Korrin's head. She knew she had to shelter Korrin from the effects of healing. Korrin absorbed the affliction during a healing session, but Presta could heal without absorbing. Kem took a deep shocking breath and collapsed on the floor in front of the two girls. Korrin slumped over into Presta's arms. Presta led her sister over to a dusty couch and sat her down.

"Stay here...you will be okay."

Korrin sat quietly with her chin to her chest while Presta tended to Kem. Small-statured Presta managed somehow to drag the old Wizard to a big ornate armchair. With a few minor incantations and the flick of a wrist, she lifted the dead weight onto the waiting chair. Oddly enough, Kem's chin also touched his chest. Presta looked at both. *"Oh! You make a fine pair you do."*

She walked back to stand in front of her sister. Then she lifted her sister's head with both of her hands. Korrin's eyes were shut. Presta concentrated and Korrin's eyes opened and she smiled. *"That feels good...how did you?"*

"You will learn our Grandmother is an amazing power. She has shown me my true potential and how I can achieve it. When we have time, I will travel there with you and you too should be able to unlock your true potential."

Presta dashed over to the table where she had placed her shoulder bag earlier. She pulled out two impressive red napples. She handed one to her tired and spent sister and bit into the other. *"Hey...you're splashing me!"*

"Go on! Take a bite. It will give you back a bit of your strength."

Korrin reluctantly tasted the napple.

"Oh...this is a nice taste. I love it," Korrin said.

"Finish it. I will be over here with Uncle."

Korrin had no problems with those instructions. Presta lifted her Uncle's head and bit off a chunk of sweet napple. She then forced the fruit into his closed and protesting mouth.

"If you don't chew this on your own, I will chew it for you."

Presta could see the old man needed a jump-start. She tried to think of magic or anything mystical that might wake him up enough to allow her to administer some power fruit. She hauled off and slapped the High Wizard in the face. *"Smaaack!"* The old man threw his head back and started to choke on the piece of napple wedged in his stinging mouth.

"Whaaap dib juuu doo nat hoor?" He spit the napple chunk on the floor.

"What...did you do that for?" He said clearly, as he rubbed the side of his weathered face.

"To what, do I owe the pleasure of your company?"

Korrin looked at Presta who looked at Korrin. *"You don't know?"* Presta asked.

"All I know...is that you just slapped me in the face."

Presta looked back at Korrin who was about to devour the napple core.

"Korrin and I just freed you from the Green coating."

"No! I thought I was dreaming that. You mean...it was real and I...?"

"You don't remember the fight on the beach...with the Dark Wizard?"

Kem looked down trying to recall. He rubbed his pointy white beard and then hoisted a crooked finger in the air.

"Ah ha! I remember now! Oh...but...I must have lost the battle...didn't I?"

The two girls just nodded their heads.

"How long was I frozen in the coating?"

"More than twenty full cycles," Presta said quietly.

"How did you free me?" He said with more enthusiasm.

"Enndora gave me a glowing blue ball."

"You went to see my mother? You made it through the Dark Wolf Forest and...back? You met your Grandmother?

You know...everything." He said that under his breath.

"Why did you do so much for me?" Presta looked at Korrin.

"Because we love you like a father. You practically raised us, you did."

Presta and Korrin looked over their shoulders to see their sister who spoke the words of love and devotion. Korrin stood and agreed. Korana walked into the scene with outstretched arms as the High Wizard made an attempt to stand.

"Sit ye down Uncle. I but say this once."

She drew closer and bent over to hug the old man were he sat. The other two girls joined in a warm group hug. The old man shut his eyes as he felt the power of life and love rejoin his spirit. Presta handed the Wizard a napple from her dress pocket, after they stood back.

"Here…do you remember these?"

"Napples! Yes I do. As a young man…I brewed a fine napple cider, I did."

"I want you to eat this now," Presta demanded.

The old man shook his spinning head.

"No I don't…" Presta looked at Korana.

"I…am still your Queen, and I am commanding you to eat the fruit."

The Wizard came to his senses and proceeded to eat the napple. The first bite flooded his taste buds with memories. The second bite was just sheer pleasure.

The thirty tics that Korrin was gone to fetch food and drink, Korana brought the good Wizard up to speed on some of the past events that led him to his predicament. After some hot food and a few goblets of castle wine, Korana explained the situation that the state and the country was in. Kem knew he wasn't up to full power and he knew it could take a few cycles of intense healing before he could take on his nemesis once more. The color soon returned to his cheeks and the three sisters had to ask a few questions.

"How long has it been since you've seen your mother… our Grandmother?" Presta asked.

"It's been over twenty-five full season cycles."

"Why so long?" Korana looked puzzled.

The girls could see the old man was reluctant to answer.

"I don't have the strength to get into details, but it has to do with what she did to my father. I found it hard to forgive her."

He stood and walked to the diminished fire in the stone fireplace. He grabbed a blackened poker and started to poke and prod at the glowing log arrangement until it grew brilliant with flame. Then he put the poker back in its metal holder "You have to understand girls, I love my mother…it's just."

The girls could see it was bringing him great pain and Korrin changed the subject. "Did you ever have your own broom...like Presta does?"

Kem looked at Presta with delight and surprise all rolled into one.

"Valda...Valda! My mother's broom." A slight touch of jealously tainted his voice.

Kem looked all reflective. "I remember being a small boy and borrowing Valda for a joy ride. Than darn barn broom...picked me up and dropped me in the river... head first. Of course, the river was much deeper then. My dear mother took a switch to my rear and I had trouble sitting on anything for quite a while."

The old Wizard sat back down in his throne-like chair cautiously, remembering the tanning he received, while looking distant in thought. Presta filled a goblet with fine wine and handed it to her Uncle. Kem looked at the girls.

"Can you bring me up to speed now with details? I'm feeling better...what happened to Seth?"

"Korana sent him packing." Presta said with deep pride, while Kem looked at Korana.

"Very impressive, my lady."

He raised his goblet towards her, and she smiled.

"So now Marideath knows she has powers?"

"Not really." Korana said.

"I destroyed the boat one of his men was escaping on. They tried to kidnap several of our children while he confronted you on the beach...a well-played diversion if you will. Kill...Koln's son, was one of the abducted. Fortunately he is as strong-willed as his father and made it back to shore with some help from me." Kem looked impressed.

"Seth did get away, but I felt he could sense something of my powers. He just doesn't know to what extent the powers are."

"What can I do?" Kem said with vigor.

"There is nothing you can do at this moment in the condition you are in. You are to rest and gain your strength. If the dark force is approaching from the rear, you can be sure that there will be one directly in front of us. This is probably why Seth invaded with such a small force."

"They were just being forward scouts, and possibly tried to take you out in the process." Presta added.

"Well they almost did." Kem added.

The girls ran to their Uncle and hugged him where he sat. The fire roared in the hearth and all who felt the love, also felt the warmth on their backs. The girls left the High Wizard to his sleep. Korana posted a double guard on both the upper and ground-floor doors. They needed their Wizard's guidance and wanted to insure no foul play would befall him.

☥

Delockth Castle: Korana's bedroom balcony.

The winter season blew colder than most could remember. The warming influence of the sea brought little relief to the bitter winds. The Prophesy was blamed for everything that went wrong in the land, even the bitter cold nights.

It was late four bells night fall. A large snowy white Owl landed on the Queen's stone balcony ledge. The powerful bird whooed and clicked while ever blinking one intense eye at a time. Korana felt a connecting and on-looking presence. She looked through her balcony door windows to see the mystical flyer staring intently back. She couldn't help feeling a strange family connection to this bird of wonder. She set this feeling to one side and placed on her slender body, a royal fur robe. She clapped her hands smartly and her chambermaid burst through the chamber's side door. "You wish my attention, my Queen?"

Without taking her eyes off the large white bird, Korana asked for her sister Presta to be summoned immediately.

"*Tell her it's an Owl…she will understand.*"

"Yes, my Queen." The chambermaid scooted off. Korana thought to herself, "*An owl in the daylight…how peculiar.*"

It wasn't very long before Presta bounded into her sister's chamber.

"Are you kidding me…Where? If you're making jest…I will."

Then Presta saw Enndora's bird. The smile on her face seemed to touch both of her ears. Korana had to hold Presta back until she had placed a heavy robe on her to shield her from the bitter cold. The two girls opened the doors together and stood in front of the blinking white owl. Korana, feeling no fear only some strange bond, tried to reach out to stroke the bird. Presta also reached out and stopped her. Korana looked at Presta. "*Something's wrong… That's why it's here.*"

Presta said. "I know."

Presta shut her seeing eyes and used her middle eye. She jumped back in horror. She looked at Korana. "My goodness…its Killgreth. He is in despairing trouble…and there is a small force of dark soldiers surrounding him."

Korana looked into the distance from her balcony. She drew her robe closer around her open neck to shield herself from the cold. She outstretched her two arms like a human divining rod and let the magic flow through her. With her eyes still closed she spoke.

"We have a situation sister…I can feel fifty or more dark figures at our back door."

She whispered to herself, "*Volarin Plains. We must act swiftly…why didn't I see this before?*"

"Maybe…Maybe because you were not looking, my sister."

Korana agreed with a nod of her head.

"*This won't happen again, my bright sister, not on my watch. I want you to go and prepare the Master Wizard while I tend to our forces. We will be swift… yet merciful.*"

The great white owl leaped into the air backwards and glided down and out. He made a large circle and swooped down beside the two girls on the balcony. Presta understood this as a goodbye, and message delivered. Korana, after touching her sister's cheek made haste into her warm chambers to get dressed to summon the Army's commander. Presta shivered a bit and then convinced herself she was warm. She could feel the heat trickle into her extremities and she started to smile. She thought…what a wonderful new power she had just found that she owned. She only wished she had stumbled upon it sooner. Maybe even on that very cold broom ride from her Grandmother's. She squinted her eyes and concentrated on the two boy's fate. There they were… alive! She pulled her emotions together and went to tell the High Wizard of the newly acquired information.

Ψ

Queen Korana's council chamber: Five Bells afternoon.

The large double doors were struck and the Queens special guard poked his weathered head around their great stature.

"They are here your Highness, shall I…?"

"Yes…Yes! Send them in for goodness sakes."

The overdressed guard stepped fully into the Queen's council chambers. He stood as rigid as he could and tried to impress all who could hear him.

"Your Highness...General Bassenth and Captain Vestran Delrayth."

Both uniformed men bowed deeply and respectfully in front of their young Queen. The General gave the overzealous guard a slight nod, which sent his confidence a flutter.

Korana had grown quickly in her short time as monarch and as the Supreme Commander. She had learned the ways of the court from watching her masculine and authoritative father. A couple of gritty lessons from the High Wizard also sharpened her court wit. Even her personal assistants, who knew her mother and father, constantly drew comparisons to them and her, with the very manner in which she dispatched her newly acquired governing powers. They who now grew with the little Queen were highly impressed. She stood up from her throne while they bowed, then she sat back down ever so gently. She quickly took control of the little get together.

"General Bassenth...Why do we have vermin on our back porch?"

"I beg your pardon, my Queen. What are you asking me?"

"I have just received intelligence...that a small force of Dark soldiers, whose mission we could only guess...are trying...as we speak, to approach us from the rear. The Volarin Plains...to be exact."

The general started to laugh. "The Volarin Plains...please your Majesty... impossible. The Volarin Plains at this time of season are impassable. Why the mud would be up to your neck."

Korana reached out her hand and mentally squeezed the General's throat, effectively cutting off his breathing. His thrashing about became a dance of the macabre. The General wheeled around like some enchanted puppet, flailing his arms from side to side around his stout and protruding mid-section.

"Do you actually doubt my sensitive information,...General? I have but merely to think of your dispatching... and how should I say; you would be a memory in some record book as the first to feel the Queen's rage. What say you, good General?"

Korana watched in amusement as the General's purple head swelled from a lack of air. She did not want to be dark and hurt anyone anywhere, but she needed her loyal followers to be just that...followers. She let the good General breathe again. The old man fell to his knees clutching his throat with both hands and gasping for air like a gold fish out of water. Korana had practiced some of Korrin's healing powers while Presta was away, and was able to accomplish small feats of healing from a distance. She closed her eyes and concentrated on the General's compromised airway. His breathing was less laborious and his normal color of pale white soon returned.

"Thank you, my…Queen. I surly…meant no… disrespect. I will take this… as a lesson learned."

Korana sat in her throne more relaxed and waved to her attendant for refreshments for the three of them. The General stood slowly, just in time for a guard to bring in two chairs for the General and the Captain to sit on in front of their powerful Queen. *"Please Gentlemen…sit!"*

The Captain tried to direct the Queen's attention to him and off his friend the General. "What information if any…do you have on Killgreth's whereabouts."

The Captain reached to his left and received a goblet of superb wine. He tipped his head in appreciation to the servant. The Queen received her special drink of buttermilk and took a small sip. When she pulled the goblet away from her face, a white creamy mustache was left to tell the tale. The Captain pointed to his face as his cheeks blushed at his amusement. Korana figured out what he meant quickly and then wiped her mouth with her long fashionable sleeve like a child. She tipped her head towards the Captain in appreciation.

"He is three quarters away through the mud bath from our castle side. That is all I know. We only assume he is still alive. He most likely will be used for their amusement, or will be currency…for some kind of exchange."

"How do you know that?" The General asked politely.

"I have studied the ways of my enemy, and they love to repeat themselves…even their mistakes. I believe it's their true weakness."

The old General looked impressed, and was gaining respect for his Queen by leaps and bounds.

"His two sons are not back from their journey, and are close to that area. Do we have any military exercises in that area?"

The General and captain looked at each other and simultaneously said, "No!"

"How soon can we get a defensive force to that area without leaving the castle defenses weakened?"

"Why…do you believe this is a pawn move? Are they are just trying to draw us out?" The Captain asked.

"No, not this time, they usually play an upfront advance and commonly use brute force to gain ground. I don't want to take chances. Can we afford to send eighty cavalry into the interested area?"

The general answered quickly, "Yes, my Queen."

"How fast?"

"We could be there in fourteen cycles or bells, whichever time measurement suits your fancy…, your highness."

"I want you there in ten Bells, or whatever."

The General wanted to complain about the unrealistic time given and was in the process of rising to protest. Half-way standing, the Queen mentally pushed him back into a seated position. The General without any more hesitation said, "I will push the troops and make this happen."

"Very good, General Bassenth…you may leave."

The General stood with a slight hesitation thinking he was going to be shoved once more. He quickly bowed and scurried out of the Queen's Council chambers.

"You were a little hard on the old man," the Captain said amused.

Vestran rose and casually walked over to the wine decanter and poured himself a drink. He raised it towards the Queen.

"Very good, your Highness…your parents would be very proud of the take-charge monarch you've become."

He raised the goblet to his red lips and tasted the fruity nectar. She rose from her working throne. "I have had many great tutors, Captain. Take my newly found Uncle, he taught all three of us to earn our respect and not just assume that we posses it."

The Captain stood directly in front of Korana and looked into her eyes.

"What do you see, my Queen?"

She looked down at the floor as if she had been caught taking liberties. She looked up slowly and Vestran saw a young beautiful woman…not the Queen of Delockth. His eyes sparkled and his knees did shake. He knew he could never play on the feeling he possessed for her.

"I am taken aback by your sudden emotions towards me, good Sir. However… this is not the time for such thoughts. You have my permission to start again when all has settled down. I apologize for being so bold and up front, but my position in this realm does not leave me much time to learn the ways of courting. I am looked at as a very young body…but I assure you, I am an old soul and will be a quick study."

She flashed him a smile and scurried out of her own room. The Captain felt as if he had just been thrown from an agitated horse and he had landed on his soft head.

He smiled to himself and finished his wine.

The Captain put his goblet down as Korrin entered the chamber. She had been eyeing the Captain and had her designs on him.

"Well, good Captain…are we officially at war?"

"It hasn't been coined war, but we believe we are being attacked from the rear."

"Ooooo! I like the way you say that."

The Captain had a perplexed look on his face. She walked right up to Vestran and placed both hands upon his armored breastplates.

"How cold these things are. I need to touch flesh in order to heal."

"Fortunately, my lady…I am in perfect health."

He forcefully turned to one side and walked away from the Princess. She turned her body to follow his movements and looked at his behind.

"Yes…you are a specimen of excellent health."

The captain was getting highly agitated.

"Is there something you wish…pertaining to our urgent predicament…, you're Highness?"

Korrin changed her tone. "No! My sister asked me to tell you to bolster the castle troops and double the elite guard."

"Will that be all,…my lady?" The Captain spent his most charming smile on the Princess.

"Yes, Captain…I will not detain you from your duties any longer."

The Captain bowed and the Princess bowed her head. Presta walked into the grand room as the handsome Captain was making his getaway. She looked at Korrin and had to ask, "What's wrong with him?"

"Nothing sister…absolutely nothing."

"Now cut that out. We have big problems and have no time for affairs of the heart, or bedroom for that matter."

Korrin seemed to pop out of her lurid dream world on the snap of Presta's fingers. "Marideath is definitely up to something big."

"Why do you think that, because he has an insertion force at our backs?"

"Yes…but not only that, we have knowledge of someone making large purchases of lumber over the last eight full season cycles from the forested country of Alpinees. We are going to assume it's for ship building, and based on the information that Killgreth gave seasons back, we know Marideath's fleet of ships were either destroyed, or have the rot."

"Are we to think…he is going to attack from the front and the rear?"

Korana entered the room.

"Yes, this is what we need to prepare for."

Both sisters bowed their heads respectfully towards their reigning sister.

"Relax…there is only us."

The Queen walked over and sat on a large window-sill. Her two sisters joined her for a talk. "What are you thinking?" Presta asked.

"I'm thinking that the Prophesy is actually heading quickly towards its end game. We need to be very vigil on all fronts. I fear our High Wizard has not fully recovered, and may be no match for the Dark wizard. However…the three of us have grown stronger in our own rights, especially Presta here. Her magic is strong. I believe if we stand together Marideath will be no match for us."

"Do you really believe that?" Korrin asked quietly.

Korana stroked her sister's long hair with her soft hand and smiled lovingly at her.

"Yes, I do, sweetheart. We also have the advantage of surprise. No one outside our close circle has any idea how powerful we actually are together."

Korrin touched her sister's face in return. Korana pulled herself off the stone window-ledge. She was heading out of the room, when she stopped in her tracks and turned.

"I will get an immediate message to our illustrious Navy to prepare for a Dark war. I suggest you ladies inform the staff what they need to know. They are relatively new and might not know what is expected of them during a siege or a clandestine attack."

Korana spun on her heels and headed out with barely a wave. Her head poked back around the door's edge and with a clearly evil look she said, "By the way Korrin…He's mine."

The two sisters could hear her giggling as Korana continued on with her personal mission. Presta and Korrin stared to laugh.

Ψ

Presta: High Wizards Tower

Presta went back to see how her uncle was doing. She noticed at once that he had better color on his withered cheeks but still shuffled his feet as if they were constructed of led. The two door guards bowed as she approached. They didn't announce her presence on her request and just opened the two large doors.

"Uncle! Uncle, are you up and about?"

"Is that you, Presta...oh, please come in; it's so quiet and boring here. Come here, child." Presta entered the open chamber and found Kem with his half glasses on sitting by a window trying to read a very large dusty book. He looked at Presta approaching over the top of his half glasses perched on the end of his nose.

"What is it child? I sense the urgency in your voice."

Presta sat on a rickety stool in front of her Uncle and leaned forward. In a clear and steady voice, she brought her Uncle the latest update.

"We believe that Marideath has sent a considerable sized elite force around our flank, into the Volarin Plains. Our loyal troops as we speak are racing to the very location in question. We also found out that Killgreth was taken prisoner."

Kem sat up straight in his chair.

"The Volarin Plains are virtually impassible at this time of the season. I fear for Killgreth, they may not treat him with kindness."

"We don't know his fate, but anyone worth their scratch would interrogate the prisoner for up to date information about the place they are about to attack. I guess they figured we wouldn't watch the plains because of their impassibility."

"It was fate that put Killgreth in their path."

The Wizard sounded worried. Kem placed the heavily gilded book down and took a deep breath. "Be careful...I feel the forces of Dark moving and I don't mean in the plains. I can feel the movement of many a dark soul and I would suggest you patrol the seas... and keep your swords sharp."

"Is this the beginning of a war, Uncle?"

"This is the Prophesy as it was written...but not in stone as we say. There can be slight movements to the left and to the right. This isn't the beginning child...it's more the end, but for whom I cannot tell. Only time will tell."

"What were you reading when I came in? I know all the books and I didn't recognise the large golden covered book you were buried in."

"It is a Black Magic book, and something I suggest you stay away from as it is very intoxicating. It can pull you in physically if you don't know the proper incantations to protect yourself. This is why I have hidden it from you girls."

"*The book is Dark…is that what your trying to say?*"

"I am saying stay away. It will destroy you if you're not prepared."

The Wizard covered the top of the large book with a piece of cloth that was lying beside it.

Ψ

Marideath's first twenty: Sea of Shasath

An energetic knock sounded on the Captain's door.

"*Come in*" The first mate poked his weathered face around the door's edge.

"Aye, Cap…you wanted to be knowing when we reached that certain place."

"Yes, I did…good work mate. See that the men check the powder…I want to be sure that it's dry."

"Aye, Aye, Captain."

The Captain thought to himself that these coordinates meant that they were within three cycles of their destination, providing the prevailing winds were in their favor.

"Is that all, Cap?"

"No! Also make sure you signal all the other ships accordingly and see to it the men get a double ration of food. It could be a while before we eat again."

The Captain thought to himself…full men fight better.

The first mate walked away from the Captain's quarters with a toothless smile and thoughts of the food he was about to consume and not the battle he would probably perish in. Maybe if no one was looking, he might commandeer himself a splash of rum and a taste of the brew for the boys as well.

The Captain had the confidence he needed to get the job done. He poured over the sea charts and decided to change the route slightly to avoid fishing trolleys from the island of Vectorth. He wanted the attack to be as much of a surprise as his Lord Marideath prescribed. He headed topside to check on the powder himself. With extra rations filling the first mates head, he could possibly forget to do so. That would be disastrous if they attacked with damp powder. Once topside, he looked to the stern of the ship. He could see the sails of fourteen of the twenty ships in the Dark armada.

Ψ

Koln Killgreth: Enemy camp, Plains of Volarin

I woke with an ache in my head that would stop a charging bull. I tried instinctively to rub the sore spot, but found my hands were shackled. This realization made my head hurt more. When I opened my eyes to view my predicament, I found myself to be tied and shackled to a pole in the middle of a large commander's army tent. The pole that was inserted into the ground was usually used as a battering ram, but for today, it was the catalyst of my detention.

I was a prisoner... of that I was certain. With little or no food in my stomach, I felt very weak and vulnerable. I have been in battle feeling like this many times before, but I am older now and a little softer. I was afraid this play would be my undoing.

My keen observational skills told me I was in a tent commanded by Marideath's Dark forces. The design was obvious and the smell of the damp canvas was indeed memorable. I was thankful that the Delockthian tents were made of a heavy cotton weave and did not carry the pungent odors of these old-style tents. I could barely see out of the tent flaps, which I was facing. The odd gust of wind taunted me with a quick view of my internment's surroundings. It gave me enough opportunity to see that it was light out...maybe morning, and there were two heavily- armed guards stationed out front of my prison tent. The first duty of any prisoner is the duty to try to escape so I searched the room with my eyes to see any possible means at my disposal.

The tent flaps flew open, and in walked the commanding general.

"Well! I see you're awake...have a nice sleep?" The general threw his riding gloves on the top of a wooden clothes trunk.

"I know what you're thinking, a clothes trunk on a short campaign? I assure you this very subject came up a few times. I am General Mott Mansth...and a brilliant general of my stature... needs to be presentable when he rides victorious into his defeated enemy's camp. Don't you agree...Sir Koln?"

Koln looked at him in disgust. *"I remember you. You are unworthy of any rank."*

Koln said this with a dry and cracked voice.

"Now! Now! Temper! You're lucky you even survived our two overzealous scouts." The General took off his wet overcoat and placed it meticulously on a chair back. He pulled up another chair and sat a few paces in front of Koln. The General turned his head on a slant and looked more closely at Koln's head wound.

"Oh…I can see now they cracked you a pretty good one." Koln saw that he almost dared to chuckle. The General clapped his hands and one of the guards entered the tent. He gave the General a snappy salute. "Sir!" Untie this man! Don't you know he was the hero of the Northern Wars?" The General's tone was of certain mockery.

"But Sir…He."

"Oh, don't worry Captain; he will be on his best behavior. He is a soldier of the highest caliber." The General had a smirk on his face. All that Koln could think was that this could be his only chance to save himself. The edgy guard sat Killgreth down on an overturned barrel. Koln rubbed his sore wrists hoping for some magical relief from the agonizing tenderness. The General pulled his collapsible chair up to the table at the other end across from the prisoner. Then he waved the sour faced Captain back to his menial guard post. The General's aid pushed through the tent flaps and placed a pitcher of wine on the table with three goblets beside it. He immediately turned and left without uttering a word.

"You've got it soft here."

"It's merely the perks of being an all-star General."

Mott cleared his throat. "It's something you'll never know."

"Actually…I have a beautiful wife and two strapping sons who love me…that's something you'll never know."

The General raised his half-full goblet.

"Touché, Sir Killgreth…Touché. How unfortunate that you shall never see again. You see, he who laughs last, laughs best…or something to that effect."

The General reached out and took hold of the pitcher of wine. He refilled his glass pouring a sufficient amount in an empty goblet. He pushed the goblet towards Koln.

"Here…amuse me for old time's sake."

Koln was parched and found it hard to refuse. The cool wine was from Blackshire, and tasted of fond memories of a life past. For an instant, he forgot his predicament and the duty that was his to complete. Koln put the empty goblet down gently as if in respect. The General didn't hesitate to refill the goblet while he talked.

"This drink is the best of the best."

"What's the special occasion?"

"You are, my old friend…you are a highly sought after human being. My lord Marideath will grant me whatsoever I wish for your return. Maybe even your old village and surrounding shires as a reward." The General looked pleased.

"Back in your home…they say you are worth a King's ransom."

"I am…in my home."

"Not for long my old friend…not for long."

The General was feeling the wine and starting to speak more freely.

"The King of Delockth is dead and those three little bitches are no match for the all- powerful Dark Lord."

Even Mott's words were starting to slur.

"Really is that what you believe? I think you are in for a shameful surprise my friend." Without warning, an out of breath, over enthusiastic soldier burst into the General's tent unannounced. He looked to be in his late teens, his boyish features stood out from under his oversized, regulation leather helmet. He straightened out his helmet with a push and began to speak before being spoken to.

"Sir! General, Sir. We have movement…you're not going to believe this."

"Stand at attention soldier and tell me what is going on."

The General was truly startled, but didn't give the exciting news enough priority to even stand. He just waved an arm at the boy. The one with the wine goblet in it, and wine sloshed everywhere.

"There is something headed our way…Sir."

"What do you mean by something,…Private?"

The General finally stood up which made the soldier cringe.

"The perimeter guards said…and I quote. It looks like a large pack of dogs… Sir. There also looks to be two mounts following the so called pack,…Sir."

Killgreth knew immediately it was Volzanth and his two boys coming to his rescue. He couldn't figure how they got the forest wolves to enlist in such a folly, but it gave Koln exactly what he needed…a diversion of staggering proportions.

"How long before they reach our encampment soldier?"

The General started to pace.

"At the current rate of advancement, we expect the enemy within the bell, Sir." The General paced and scratched his chin.

"Set up a defense perimeter and have the Lieutenant, send out two soldiers to test their strength and resolve."

"Yes, sir!"

The young man snapped off an explosive salute; turned on his heels and left the same way he had entered.

"You've got to admire the enthusiasm," the General said as he started to snicker to himself.

"Well, my old friend, it looks like…someone or something, thinks you're important enough to die for."

The General started to laugh. Then he called for the guards to tie Killgreth back up to the pole in the centre of the tent. They tried to forcefully tie the big man back to the pole, but he acquiesced and made it easy for them. In the process, they didn't tie the bonds on his feet as tight as before, and gave Koln an access point for his hopeful escape. With the thought of an imminent battle, the General and the guards went scurrying off to prepare for who knows what and left Koln alone to his own predicament.

Getting free again was his first and only priority. He moved his feet back and forth in a semicircle pattern trying to loosen the already compromised knot. Several tics later, he felt a small victory in the act of removing his legs from bondage. He lifted his left leg and snagged the edge of the General's flimsy table. He pulled with vigor and coerced the table close enough to side-swipe a knife off the surface. With the paring knife on the ground, Koln used his heel to toe method, and removed one of his wet boots.

He wiggled his big toe as it was looking at him through the hole in his wet wool sock. Oddly enough at that moment, he thought of his wife and how much he missed her. He had the drive to put her memory aside and use all his faculties in times of personal danger, but the sight of his big toe made him want for better times. Koln laughed silently and grabbed the small knife with his talented toes. He bent his leg at the knee and lifted his leg as far behind him as it would go. With his searching fingers, he managed to pinch the pointy tip and manipulate the blade around in his favor. With a few well-guided rubs his bonds fell to the floor. It was at this time he counted his blessings that the inept guards had tied him with rope, and not the shackles he had previously donned. Once freed, he replaced his wet boot and grabbed the General's short sword conveniently hanging from his coat rack. Koln looked around the room while listening for any guards near the entrance to the tent. He spotted a map laid out on the General's bunk. He snatched the map and spread it out on the table before him. He traced the points that interested him with his finger while he stroked his furry chin. He grunted an acknowledgement to himself, then quickly folded the map up and placed it in his open shirt for safe-keeping. He stepped to the tent's opening and pushed aside one flap just enough to see what the situation was. Killgreth patiently waited for the right time to strike.

Ψ

Erin and Kill: Volarin Plains

Kill yelled at Erin from his sweaty horse. Steam blasted from the nostrils of the powerful beast. "Are you sure these horses can keep up this pace?"

"They don't have a choice…now do they."

The boys were in a full speed gallop behind their new four legged wolf friends. The wolves were stretched out themselves, hungrily trying to get at their new enemy. The soft obsessive mud didn't seem to hold back the pack's advance. The large wolf never did reveal what motivated the pack to listen to him. Erin hoped that one day Volzanth might shed some light on the question. The boys got caught up in the frenzy and followed without hesitation. "How long before we engage the enemy?"

Erin raised his head from behind the horses, squinted his eyes and narrowed his vision.

"We still have thirty tics…as long as the ground doesn't bog out."

Erin put his head back down and spurred his horse for more speed.

Ψ

Killgreth: Armed camp

I decided quickly that it would be better to try to blend in. I left the illusion of my protective spot and entered the one directly across from the General's tent. A soldier of rank was in the middle of placing his armor on as I ran inside. I didn't give him a chance to even turn around and acquaint himself with his attacker. I just hit him with the flat side of the short sword and put him to rest. Luckily, for me, he was near my size; therefore, I didn't have to cut off any critical circulation to complete my ruse. As I turned over the downed soldier, he punched me in the face and I believe he broke my nose. The little flashy lights that accompany that dance were prevalent for my obvious entertainment. There was a great need to be silent, so I followed through with my borrowed short sword and stabbed his waiting and exposed throat. There was a bit of a gurgle but not much more. The arterial spray washed me in warm blood. I was covered from face to waist in the vital red nectar and for a brief moment in time, I was transported back to Blackshire and a scene from the great Northern War.

Koln's flashback:

The large men of the North kept coming in waves of endless beastly humanity. There wasn't much finesse in that type of battle. For the most part, you just swung your long sword at anything coming at you from one direction. The smell of blood and entrails was derailing, especially on a young unbattled soldier. The large mad like swings of your enemy, falling friends and comrades, put you in a slow motion and dream-like state. The mindless effort of so many for no apparent reason other than to simply vanquish the people whose land you wanted. We obeyed orders without thought or morals for the sake of our Dark Lord. The sound of bones being broken by heavy swords still haunts my nights and sometimes blinds my days.

The soldier's tent came back into my view as I wiped my blood-spattered face with my dirty hand. The taste of the blood was sour and tainted.

I was sitting on the soldier's stomach. I ripped of a piece of cloth, which covered his bunk and tried to clean my face as best as I could. I hastily started to remove his protective armament and strap it to my person. I also placed his red signature Sergeant's cape over the metal armor. This would be my ticket around the camp, or at least until someone recognized me. I stood straight and welcomed the fit and weight of the excellent protective gear. I found his full-faced red plumed helmet and urgently crushed it on my head to protect my identity. I pulled the torn sheet off his bunk and covered the half-naked soldier, then pushed him into a corner and covered him with some of his personal gear to help conceal his lifeless corpse.

Without warning a ranking soldier burst into the tent and yelled at the uniform I was wearing. I tilted my head down a bit to help my concealment.

"Sir, we need to move! In coming…less than ten tics."

I could tell he was beneath me in rank, so I tore a few strips off the man for barging in without proper etiquette. Then I replaced my stolen short sword with the fallen soldier's long battle sword and ran out into the camp. I made my presence look urgent by running through the frenzied camp and thus helping with my diversion and concealment. I managed to find my horse and my personal objects, which were miraculously still attached. I mounted my steed that somehow recognized me even under someone else's stinking clothes. The moment I was mounted, I felt complete. I rode to the front of the camp and waited for the fight with everyone else.

Ψ

Delockth Navy: Routine maneuvers

"Sir...we need you topside."

"What is it lieutenant? I was just about to have me tea."

"We see unidentifiable vessels sir."

"What do you mean...unidentifiable sailor. You mean there is no flag or insignia present?" The Captain sounded agitated at the lack of another captain's sea protocol from the oncoming ship.

"No, Sir! We have Willth in the crows...sir. He is the best pair of eyes in this person's Navy..., Sir."

"Yes, Yes! I know that! Okay...I'll be right up. Damn...Dark! A body can't have a simple brew of tea."

The Captain murmured to himself as he pulled on his thick coat and screwed his hat on to his balding head. He reached back for a last sip of his favorite black tea. The Captain pushed the doors hard to the topside and begrudgingly stepped onto his clean deck. The cold damp air hit him squarely, so he did up the remaining buttons on his heavy coat. He then smashed his dry hands together and rubbed them like two sticks trying to make a fire.

"Okay, where's me spyglass? Which one of you scum dogs...has me sight?"

A small, older sailor rushed up to the Captain and handed him the tool as if he thought he was going to be hit for doing so. The Captain took the spyglass and then growled at the poor sailor. This reaction made the man scurry off like a kicked puppy.

The Captain climbed the stairs to the prow of the ship and placed himself on the very edge of the rail. He opened his personal glass and scanned the distant horizon. Nothing appeared in the Captain's view and as he was getting frustrated, he heard the man in the crow's nest yell down with a distant voice.

"Captain! Captain! It looks to be fifteen to eighteen large sails. They look like Manowar class,...Sir!" The human sound on the deck rose as the words they were hearing from the nest resembled fighting words. A nervous frenzy riffled throughout the ship. The Captain moved to the stern of the large ship pushing sailors unceremoniously out of his way. When he reached the stern, he reopened his spyglass and focused on twenty or more tall sails. Quietly the Captain said almost under his breath, "I think ye be right…Manowar class most of them as well. Is no good, this is no good indeed."

Then at the top of his lungs, the old Captain yelled and commanded his attention. "Bring us around…bring me the homing pigeon. I need to alert the entire fleet. Hurry man! We are out gunned if we try to do this alone."

With everyone aboard making haste, no one noticed the large white owl perched on the main sail's crosspiece. As the pigeon was released, the great owl followed the fast flying bird with little effort back to shore.

Ψ

Queen's Special Troops: Southernmost tip of the Volarin Plain

The Captain raised his leather and chainmail glove. The eighty mounted men behind him stopped and tried to hold their horses still. The beasts had ridden hard to get to the position they were in but they wanted more.

"Lieutenant!"

The very young-looking officer galloped from mid-pack to where the Captain was. He pulled back hard on the horse's reins and the horse almost threw him off the back when its front legs went into the air.

"Control your mount, Lieutenant!"

"Yes Sir."

The soldier patted the horse's neck and the great animal calmed down sufficiently.

"Give me the spyglass."

The Captain reached out his hand waiting for the desired object while the Lieutenant fumbled around in his pack for the spyglass. Without a word, the soldier placed the tool in the Captain's hand like a nurse in a fancy operation. The Captain extended the glass and hemmed and hawed.

"Ok! Give the men ten tics to relieve themselves and give the horses water. We have a situation and we will be entering a very difficult conflict."

"Why difficult…Sir?"

"Mud, Lieutenant…unbelievable amounts of cold, wet mud. Horses hate mud. That is all!"

The Captain continued to look while he waved the young Lieutenant off to see to his duties.

Ψ

CHAPTER 15

The Battle for the Plains of Volarin

KOLN WAS STILL UNDETECTED WHEN *he saw the wolves near the perimeter of the Dark Troop's camp. He pulled right up behind General Mott and listened in to his conversation. "The scouts didn't come back, Sir."*

"Damn! What I don't need now is a morale breaker. Get the mounts to the rear…I don't want them in on this dog pack thing. I want the archers up front. Let's see how many we can take out before we engage with swords."

The first wave of wolves hit the outer perimeter and was dispatched with little or no effort by the professional archers. The large wolf seeing the play commanded the next wave to split up and flank the overconfident soldiers. The third wave hit directly on and managed to get 80% through the rain of arrows. The General had to cut back on the archers. He wanted to save some of the punch for the real battle that supposedly lay ahead and would be fought by a well equipped opposing Delockth army. Koln could see his two boys off in the distance approaching at a full gallop. The pride in his heart made his eyes fill up with water, which he had to desperately wipe away. He started his diversion and made his horse kick over the burning fires, which made several tents catch fire and create the diversion he needed. Once that was achieved, he started galloping through the centre of the camp lopping off heads of anyone caught in his path. The enemy didn't know what was going on and created their own circus of confusion and mistakes.

Killgreth removed five surprised heads before someone of rank recognized him and made him the focus of attention. The invading army feared Killgreth more than a hundred angry and desperate wolves. The invading troops swung their swords while they ran in every conceivable direction. Koln had no cover, but kept swinging his newly acquired long sword until an archer's arrow found an opening in his back armor near his armhole. This hit was sufficient to dismount Koln from his warhorse and lay him flat on his back in the cold mud. A young boy with a ranking insignia rushed over to the fallen threat to finish him off. He stood over Koln and with his boyish face aghast. He slowly raised his long sword and was readying his mind for the dispatching strike. At the instant of commitment, a very large wolf jumped at the boyish figure and grabbed him fatally by the throat. Koln witnessed this with wide eyes. He went to say thanks to the Wizard wolf, but passed out from weakness and loss of blood.Kill was struck with an arrow on his assault charge. The bright red feathers on the shaft bristled in the wind as he continued with his attack. The pain was sharp but manageable. Erin rode beside his smaller brother and snapped the red end of the arrow off giving him some measure of fighting comfort. The adrenalin flowing through Kill's young veins was overabundant and strong. His horse had to jump over several dead wolves and a handful of lifeless armored soldiers. He managed to get a few one-on-one confrontations but the advantage was clearly his. Most of the Dark Lord's cavalry was sent to the backside of the camp for protection, thus leaving only the tired and bewildered foot soldiers.

Erin managed to escape the dreaded archer's points. He clearly was on top of the situation in his warring confrontations and displayed an uncanny ability to think one step ahead of his opponent. The General and his men started to retreat away from the attacking wolves and the two boys. Erin was amazed until he realized that the Delockth army was approaching directly behind him at a full gallop. Half of the enemy threw down their weapons and put their empty hands in the air hoping for some form of mercy with the approaching force. The remainder of the wolves didn't feel that they owed the invading army anything and continued to tear at the vanquished and retreating men. The large wolf sat at one end of the camp and tried to call off the frenzied attack. He had no feelings for the invading army, but didn't want to lose any more of his four legged brothers. A white owl landed on a tent close to the great wolf. He recognized that this was a creature like himself, a lost soul trying to get home. Erin and Kill came together and took each other's hand.

"Brother…you fought well."

"As did you my older brother…as did you. We need to find our father."

Without another word, the two dismounted and waded through the carnage and mud looking for Koln. The shadow of a bird placed its mark on the roof of a large tent. Volzanth barked at the owl and the owl answered by spreading his impressive wings. One loud screech and Volzanth had his answer. The great white owl retreated to the unchallenged skies.

Ψ

The General's Tent: Killgreth

Koln opened his scratchy eyes and beheld Presta staring sadly into them. He tried to sit up but Presta's small hand was no match for his surrendered weakness. He felt the sharp pain below his left lung and had to breathe slow and shallow. Korrin leaned in but Koln through his disadvantage barely recognized her. Presta drew close enough that Koln could feel her tender and sweet breath upon his dirty face. "Can you hear me, Sir Killgreth? Tis I…Presta. Do you know where you are?"

Presta looked at Korrin and shook her head in doubt. Koln tried to speak but the words took too much of his precious breath. A grunt was all he could afford the Princesses.

"Never mind brave one…we will take care of you now."

One of the Princess's personal guards handed Presta a clean cloth, which she put to good use relieving Koln of the mud mask he was wearing.

"Sister…shall I relieve him of his pain now?"

"No! You must not do this alone. I will assist you. We will stop the bleeding and keep back the infection. I will not risk you or me at this juncture. We don't know what great battles lie just ahead and we need to conserve our strength and abilities."

Korrin gave no opposition for Presta to lead in this matter. She could feel Presta's power growing day by day and knew she was right in this affair. Together they preformed a laying on of hands. Korrin's hands radiated a creamy white, while beneath Presta's hands glowed a brilliant yellow. After several tics, Presta pulled away and Korrin did the same.

A Sergeant from the Delockth regiment entered the tent.

"We have the General, your majesties. What do you wish us to do?"

"Put him in one of those wagons they brought and we shall take him back to our Queen. I am sure she will have a few words for him and possibly some important questions. As for the survivors of the Dark invaders…tend to their wounds and *feed them. We will house them at the penal facility at the naval base. Tell the good Captain to arrange for their transport…that is all."*

As Presta was waving the soldier on, Erin and Kill burst into the tent.

"Father! Father!" Kill was sporting a shoulder bandage and a muddy face almost like his father's. Presta moved to block Kill from waking Koln from his medical intervention. She quickly but gently placed an open hand on the advancing boy's chest. Kill stopped in his tracks and looked at Presta.

"Presta,…your majesty!"

With his focus directed at the Princess, he reached for her in a brotherly embrace. Erin stood there with his eyes tearing, looking at his object of affection held tight within his brother's arms. He placed a smile of anticipation upon his face patiently waiting for his turn to be in the arms of the one he loved. Korrin watched this all go down with a general understanding that the trip they had just recently completed had drawn the four of them very close together in mind and spirit. She took comfort in knowing all was well. Korrin staggered and one of the inside guards grabbed the weakened Princess. She was placed on one of the General's wobbly chairs. Presta and Erin broke their intimate hug and rushed to Korrin's side. Presta kneeled down in front of Korrin.

"Oh, my heart,…I hate this part…the part that punishes you for giving relief from suffering for whom you heal. I will now in turn give to you my new found gift."

Presta reached forward, still squatting down in front of her brave sister and put both her cold hands on each side of her head. Presta tilted her head down in concentration. A yellow glow emanated from her hands and sandwiched the young girl's head. Korrin's eyes widened and mouth began to open.

"Oh, sister! What have you given me? I feel wonderful…I feel renewed. Thank you." The two sisters hugged as soon as Presta released her hands. Presta stood and turned to the guard.

"Retrieve me a napple from my saddle bag. Actually bring the last three placed there…now hurry!" As Presta turned, she saw Erin beside the bed and Kill draped over his now awakened father. Koln turned his head towards Presta and asked, "Where am I?"

"You are in the former General Mott's tent, situated inside the defunct enemy's camp."

She took his cold and bloody hand as Kill tore himself away from his father's chest. Koln looked at Kill, then at Erin. Korrin drew nearer and Koln smiled as he recognized her beautiful face.

"What happened...I...I was fighting one tic...then?"

"You took an arrow under your armor and it damaged your lung."

"No! I mean to the enemy...what happened?"

"I will explain in more detail around a warm campfire one night, but for now all you need to know is that the Plains of Volarin have seen its first battle and the two sons of Killgreth and the Delockth army were the victors. You have a very big wolf to thank and a large white owl."

Koln started to laugh which caused him pain. Koln looked lovingly at his two mud covered sons. "You boys...sons of Killgreth, have a real battle under your belts. It shall be written and told about for all time. I am very proud."

The napples were brought and Presta and Korrin indulged to recharge their energy for the ride back to the castle.

Erin stood close to Presta.

"With your permission...Kill and myself, wish to accompany you fine princesses back to the castle."

Korrin bowed to the two boys. "The honor and enjoyment would be ours but we need to get back right away and Valda is only a two-seater at best."

The boys understood the urgency. Killgreth rose from the flimsy bed and tried his arms and legs in a movement that looked like some drunken dance.

"I feel like new...Ladies, shall we take our leave of the infernal mud bath and retreat to the warmth of our castle?"

Both princesses curtsied, while Presta took Koln`s hand. The Captain arranged for the twenty prisoners to be escorted to the Prison at the naval base. Ten of his best saw to that action, while the rest took the storehouse of weapons and horses they had just acquired and headed for the Delockth castle in a double convoy. Koln pulled himself together with the help of his powerful friends. He rode out a ways beyond the edge of the camp to thank the great wolf for whom he owed a great debt.

Not far beyond the camp's sight stood the great Volzanth. He was surrounded by the remainder of his loyal pack. With a few spicy barks and one long growl, the defensive line parted and Koln and his horse entered the pack. Koln dismounted from his steed carefully because the mud was about ankle high at this location. Koln stood before the great wizard wolf and went down on one knee.

"You are above all others…with your sacrifice and unwavering service to your land and your Queen…and to me. I hold you totally responsible for the lives of my children and mine." Koln bowed his head and put his left hand over his heart. The great wolf sat up with his head back and started to change and morph into a naked old man. Slowly and not without pain his face showed the transformation. When the metamorphosis was complete, the old man stretched his hands east and west in an apparent remembrance of the simple act. He tilted his head back and yelled in a very parched voice, "*YES!*"

All the wolves took several steps back fearing the demise of their alpha leader. Koln had the look of wonderment smeared across his dirty face.

"You…you changed! But…how? Why?"

Without another word, the old wizard kneeled down and embraced several of the wolves who seemed to recognize the naked man as a master or even a differently shaped wolf. With great love and over-abundant affection the old man hugged and petted every beast. He looked up at Koln who stood up to stretch his stiff legs. "You sir…have repaid any debt you might have believed you had towards my person. You gave me the opportunity to act in a way that released my canine bindings and trapments. I don't even know if that's a word, but it will take some time to reclaim my humanity…I'm sure. You owe me nothing."

Koln noticed the old man start to shiver and pulled the thick horse blanket off his mount. He walked over to the Wizard and draped it over his bony shoulders. "You cannot stay here Sir Wizard, for the elements are now your enemy. I will take you back to camp for we are about to depart for Delockth. The Princesses feel something is wrong and we must return immediately." The old man gave the dog-like creatures one last touch and wiped the tears from his eyes.

"Surely, you do not weep for these creatures?"

Koln asked while preparing his horse for a second rider.

"*I have been…how you say, a four legged creature for a very long time and I have sired many offspring. These are my children sort of speak…do you understand that, Sir Killgreth?*"

"Now that you put it that way…I do. I wish I could give you more time…we…"

"It's okay. They actually understand. They are very smart creatures. I will be traveling with one companion."

One of the larger wolves with different markings from the pack moved through the animals towards the old man. The wolf stopped directly in front of him and put its tail between its back legs.

"This is my mate…Korell. I don't know if they have names but in my mind, all these years as a wolf, my human influence dominated my thoughts and ideas. She will be with me always."

The wolf's tail started to wag dramatically. Koln never said a word. He mounted his horse and offered the old wizard a hand up. The old man struggled with his inferior legs, but managed the mount with a few well-placed grunts and ouch's. The two set off back to camp with the lone female wolf following close behind.

"Why did you change back?" Koln turned his head to ask.

"I believe it was the unselfish act of love for another human which broke the spell. I have to admit…it was a strong spell. But most spells can be broken with the right act of unselfish love. Your need…was the perfect opportunity for me to prove my theory."

The old man pulled himself close to Koln's back hoping to snag some desperately needed body heat. Volzanth already missed the fur, which had kept him warm on so many cold nights. Presta was waiting for them when they returned. She looked at the blanket covered old man behind Koln and the wolf beside them.

"It looks like you have a fantastic story for tonight's fire,…Sir Killgreth."

"That I do your grace …that I do." The old man just smiled.

"We need to leave now, Sir Killgreth. I feel the tide turning and we need to make ready."

Presta entered the ex-General's tent wishing to tell the two boys that they were breaking camp for home. The two boys were lost in a heated debate on who did what to whom on the wolf littered battlefield. When Kill saw Presta enter the tent opening behind Erin, his words stopped dead in their tracks. Erin put his readied hand over his sword hilt and turned to see what had startled his brother.

"Boys…having a bit of a word with each other?"

"Ah!...yes, my princess. We were discussing the virtues of the recent battle field."

"I'm sure you were. We are about to leave; would you like to travel with my personal guard...both of you? Or would you rather travel with all the virtuous soldiers?"

"Erin looked at Kill for a micro tic."We will take our place among the many."

"Oh good! You will be safe within the fold."

The smile on Presta's face told all. She was acting like a royal, but the undercurrent of little girl in love bubbled to the surface once in the presence of her love interest. Erin could see the want in Presta's flushed face and put his strong arm around her waist and smartly pulled the little girl into his arms for a spontaneous, full out hug. This overt act of affection, even made the young Kill blush. How could his brother be so brazen? Just as the two appeared to merge to be one, Korrin entered the tent like a sudden gust of wind.

"Well, what do we have here? I think you have been holding out on me, sister. There are a few stories I believe you have left out of your tales of wonderment and adventure. Yes indeed!"

"You want in your Highness?" Kill said.

Kill put his arm around Presta and offered Korrin a way in. Korrin ran into the three with a smile on her face yet to be described by the three. The four young people enjoyed the moment and didn't say a word.

The trip back to the Castle Delockth was uneventful and cold for the young boys but the tales and friendship that were shared made for personal and memorable times.

Ψ

High Wizard's Chamber: Delockth Castle

A light rap tickled the round wooden door. A weak voice drifted through its solid composition."You may enter."

The door creaked open and in walked the Queen unannounced by the two semi-conscious guards. When the High Wizard spotted his unannounced guest, he tried to quickly sit up from his bed. She caught him halfway and gently with a wave of her slender hand forced him back down.

"Please! Please, Uncle...don't sit up for me. I need you to be strong when the time comes."

"So Presta told you. I am so sorry sweetheart...I wanted to tell you, but your father...rest his soul."

She cut him off with a finger to her lips. *"It's okay...we were children and all we needed to know was that we were loved. And you didn't hold back on that. The three of us always new father put you in charge for a good reason. Whether you were family or not made no difference in our education. We love you...I love you."* The old man couldn't hide his joy, his eyes told the tale.*"I will be a good Queen because you taught us how to love and care for others."*

"Oh my dear, you are more than your parents could have wished for. You will be our greatest Queen since recorded time. The Prophesy could not be clearer."

Korana placed her open hand on the old wizard's shoulder.

"How do you feel?"

"I am feeling not bad considering the spell I was under. I am still having a tough time concentrating on my magic and I feel scattered somewhat."

"Presta asked me to give you these."

Korana pulled three big red and juicy napples from her pouch hanging over her white shoulder. "Oh, my! Those are from the cottage...I can tell. It looks to me like they have some enhancements. It would be typical of my mother to do such a thing."

The old man received the fruit from the Queen and placed them on a simple nightstand beside his humble bed.

"I shall partake in the pleasures after you have left your majesty."

The Queen bowed her head in response. *"Make it soon."*

She suggested with a tone that lifted the old wizards head.

"Why such haste your Highness? I sense an urgency you have not yet spoken of?"

"We have a situation where I believe we will need your...how should I say... your talents, High Wizard of Delockth. I have just received a message from our fleet that twenty to thirty warships are heading our way. Our full force is on the water as we speak, but should they fail at keeping the invaders at bay we will have to defend ourselves from the beachhead."

"Its Marideath...isn't it?"

"You know it is, Uncle. He has waited for a chance to claim our land for himself. The Plains of Volarin was merely a feeble attempt to divert our attention. The only good news is that we won the battle on the plains. Our warriors will be home in two, maybe three cycles."

"How are the girls?"

"The girls are fine. They will be home via Valda quite soon. I also understand they saw no action. Killgreth however was wounded...as was Kill, but both will make a full recovery thanks to Presta's talent for healing."

"Presta! Don't you mean Korrin?"

"That's the strange thing...since her journey; she has grown in strength and ability. Our Grandmother has somehow unlocked hidden talents or instructed her how to grow what she already possesses."

The old man stood and straightened his stiff back. He reached for a napple and shined it against his robe. He turned to Korana.

"Why now in the middle of our winter? The timing seems...off."

"Maybe he was hoping to catch us off-guard...or maybe he is just being his arrogant, overconfident self," Korana said.

Kem took a big bite of the napple. The juice flew in every direction. From the smile on his face, it was clear the napple transported him back to a time he had forgotten. "Hmmm! I will be ready your grace. I feel better already."

She walked close and put her soft hand on his shoulder.

"Don't worry, we will get through this together."

She turned gracefully and walked out of the Wizard's chamber.

Ψ

Captain's Forward Ship: Delockth Navy

The lieutenant walked up behind the Captain as he pulled at his coat's lapels trying to close the gap exposing his neck to the bitter cold wind.

"It's cold today, sir."

"That's a fair understatement, Lieutenant."

The Captain put his dry and weathered hands into a pair of leather gloves in hopes of warming them.

"Yes...I'm figuring a sailor overboard would only last twenty tics before he met his ancestors."

"Yes, Captain...interesting way of putting it. I want to inform you the carrier pigeon has returned from the Queen's office."

"Yes ! yes!" The Captain turned to face the Lieutenant with a nervous look about him.

"Well, what does it say!?"

"It tells of a great battle won on the plains of Volarin and we have been instructed to fend off all invaders to the best of our ability. There are three more warships and a supply vessel heading our way as we speak. Our hearts are with you…signed, Korana Atlas, Queen of Delockth."

"So…that son of a no good sea cow sent a troop to the castle's rear at high flood. He thought we would not notice and he would have a diversion."

The Captain rubbed his white bearded chin.

"Do you want to send a response?"

The Captain turned his sights to the distant ships. He pulled out his pipe and began to stuff the bowl with tobacco.

"Captain?"

"No! There's nothing to say…ready the men. I want all powder double-checked and swords pulled a measure from their hilts."

The Captain lit his ornate pipe.

"I want an extra ration of rum and food for all the men. For all we know this could be the last great battle. See to it Lieutenant."

"Aye, Aye, Sir."

The lieutenant saluted and scurried off with thoughts of extra rations.

Ψ

CHAPTER 16

The Queens in Check

THE KINGS BEACH: KORANA, KEM and the Captain,

"My Queen…you requested my presence?"

"Yes, I did, my good Captain."

The Captain bowed with deep reverence. Vestran was in awe of his Queen's transformation into a proper and most powerful head of state. He then gave a more simple head nod to the High Wizard.

"I'm glad you're feeling better, Sir Wizard. You had us worried."

The High Wizard nodded in return but offered no words. With the attention to the Queen returned, she began to speak.

"The High Wizard and I were trying to speculate on this dramatic naval battle which is about to take place. We wish to know what your thoughts are on this matter should our navy fail to deter or defeat Marideath's forces?"

Without hesitation the Captain began to speak.

"Your Majesty…we have been preparing for more than ten full season cycles. Our stock-pile of weapons…thanks to Killgreth's village, are up to the rafters…so to speak. Our young men have grown into fine, practiced soldiers and our food rations are at capacity. We couldn't be more ready for the fight. We are 10,000 strong and eager to defend,…my Queen."

The Captain bowed again.

"May I point out your Grace that you and your two sisters are much stronger now than ever. This will surely be a surprise for our would-be invaders."

"He is truthful on that fact your highness. The three daughters of Delockth are a force to be reckoned with."

The Queen bowed her head towards her Uncle.

"Our navy is the best your majesty…fear not." Vestran smiled broadly. Presta and Korrin ran down the road towards the beach were the three stood. Three exhausted guards foolishly tried to keep pace with the young girls. Presta waved, as she got closer. "Korana…it's us!"

"How did they get back so soon?" Vestran inquired.

"Most likely Valda helped in that department." The Queen interjected.

The Captain looked at the High Wizard.

"Valda?"

"I will explain later," Kem said.

Korana opened her arms wide to receive her sisters. They came together as one. A loud thunderclap sounded over the beach area to everyone's surprise. There was not a cloud in sight.

The Captain of the Queens Navy turned his head around to see what had made the noise.

(In a ship at sea.) The Captain of the Dark Navy narrowed his reddened eyes and took a nervous breath.

Marideath looked out the porthole of his cabin, and instantly knew something was not right.

The King's Beach:

The sisters shrugged off the thunderclap and enjoyed a group hug. When they pulled away, Korana asked, *"Where are the others?"*

"They are a full six bells away and should be here this late evening, give or take a few bells."

"Why didn't you stay with them?"

Presta's face turned a serious shade. "I felt something…something is not what it seems. I…I mean…we were worried, so I used Valda to get here sooner."

"And what of the boys?"

"All are well…they long to be home."

Korana put her hand on Presta's shoulder. *"I heard you had something to do with their recovery."*

"Yes…well, I did pick up a trick of two in my travels."

"A trick or two! Healing without repercussions is no trick, my sister, it is a blessing."

Korana gave Presta a crushing hug. Korrin stood back and watched. She was a bit jealous of Presta's new-found power. She thought to herself, "What now could I bring to the table that isn't already done better." She knew she had to push this bad thought aside and rejoice in her sister's gift. A loud explosion sounded at the sea's horizon...then another. Everyone standing on the King's Beach stared at the horizon in horror.

The three sisters spoke in unison. *"It has begun."*

Presta added, *"Oh, My!"*

Korrin pulled her shawl tighter over her slender body. The Captain seizing the moment put his arms around her and started to escort her back to the Castle.

"Come...there is nothing we can do here at this time." Korana took Presta's hand and followed the Captain and Korrin. Korana stopped and turned to Kem.

"Are you coming Uncle?"

"I will see you inside soon, my Queen. I need a few moments to think. I will be with you at supper. Go on now...before you catch a cold."

Korana continued on up the road to the castle. She only looked back several times.

Ψ

The Admiral's Ship: Delockth Navy

The Admiral stood a good step closer to the pot-bellied stove located amidship. He removed his wet gloves and held his hands out in hope of reaping it's obvious benefits. He moved his crooked fingers about wishing he had more circulation as in his youth. A cannon fired from the port side of his flanking ship. The report startled the old man and he lashed back with a profusion of curse words that would embarrass a seasoned sailor.

"Hold your fire, Captain!" He shouted.

He held up both his arms to signal ceasefire.

"We seem to be falling short, Admiral."

"Yes, Captain!" He yelled back.

"I can see that! I am too old to yell."

He signaled his first mate to tell the Captain of the flanking ship to double the powder and try again. The Captain of the Admiral's ship hurried from below to see what all the noise was about. "What did I miss, Sir?"

"Nothing...that darn fool of a Captain...underpowered his cannon and the shot dribbled out the end like an empty barrel of brew."

"How long before we are in range, Admiral?" (BAMM!)

The Captain placed his hands over his ears too late. The Admiral rubbing his hands directly over the stove exclaimed, "*Good! Much better.*

"*Captain make note to double the powder. I think we may have a case of wet or inferior powder.*

"Aye, Aye, Captain, I will signal all the ships to this effect. How long do you figure it will be…before we engage the enemy sir?"

"*Could be daybreak before we see any action. That's if the wind be in our favor. I will be in my cabin, Captain. Call me just before we are in accuracy range.*"

"Aye, Aye, Admiral."

The Captain of the Admiral's ship rubbed his hands together. "It's going to be a cold one tonight it is," he said to himself.

He pulled his collar up and proceeded to call his first mate.

"Bring me my spyglass and be quick about it."

The Captain was handed the brass device. He raised the tube up to his good eye and closed the other. He twisted the tube until the lead Black ship came into focus in the small circle of the spyglass.

Ψ

The Black Ship: Marideath's Warship forward deck

The Captain banged his ivory pipe bowl against the railing at the bow of his ship. His over bushy eye brows wavered in the strong wind. He physically signaled for his first mate to come closer. With the foul mood he has been in of late, the first mate was a little apprehensive on what he actually wanted of him.

"*Bring me a hot drink. It's colder than a witch's tit out here. Hurry now… before I make you inspect the underside of me hull.*"

"Aye, Aye, Cap."

The Captain took the time to reacquaint himself with his spyglass. He started to talk to himself under his tainted breath. "*Come…just a…little closer you…water logged excuse…for a warship.*"

"Here's your drink,…Cap."

"What? Oh ya!"

"Do you want me to hold it?"

"Oh, for dark sakes…just put er there."

The Captain kept his eye on the approaching vessels. Even though they outnumbered the Delockth ships in sheer firepower, he knew from experience that the Delockth ships were superior in many ways.

It was well-known in their country that the Delockth Navy was to be respected. If it were not for the gigantic flotilla just out of sight behind him, he would have had major reservations about challenging such an opponent. The Captain put the device down and grabbed the steaming mug. He carefully placed it on his bottom lip and slowly tipped the mug. The look on his etched face was a moment in pleasure. He took a second sip then wiped his bearded face with his Captain's jacket sleeve. He looked at the first mate and paused.

"Load all the cannons on the starboard side."

"All the cannons?"

"That's what I said you fool. Are ye daft? Go on! Do it!"

The first mate bounded off without a word. The Captain took another sip of his brew. It wasn't long before the first mate returned.

"Sir...we are standing by."

"Take aim at the closest ship...and fire simultaneously."

"Aye, Aye, Captain."

The first mate turned the ship so the starboard side faced the oncoming ship, and with one arm-motion fired all the starboard cannons. Twelve long-range cannons sounded almost in unison. The recoil from the cannons shook the very boat to its lower timbers. The twelve cannon balls fell short of the first ship by a distance of several ship lengths. The Captain was watching in his spyglass as the balls entered the turbulent sea.

"Load them again," he yelled.

"But hold your fire," he yelled right after.

A good fifteen tics went by while all held their breath. Then the Captain signaled for the second volley. Once again, the cannon's report was thunderous. This time the cannon balls found their mark. The man in the crow's nest on the Admiral's ship yelled down. "IN COMMING!"

Seven of the twelve hit the Admiral's ship solid. Many men were thrown into the icy waters from the initial explosions. The main mast took a direct hit and started to tilt to one side. The man in the crow's nest was thrown, but managed to grab onto one of the cross ropes and traverse the rigging and make it to the deck in one piece. The main sail fell under the weight of the compromised main mast failure. The deck was littered with lifeless bodies and small fires that were scattered about when the deck heaters were thrown about by the force of the incoming projectiles. Two cannon balls pierced the main hull twelve micro measures above the ever changing waterline. The two gaping holes were taking in water at an alarming rate. The men below the decks started a bucket brigade, but were over-taken when the large ship started to list to one side.

The ships directly behind the Admiral's vessel pulled alongside and tried to extend planks to receive any survivors. Many of the men met their watery grave just trying to walk the heaving plank to the sister ship. Those who survived the initial strike were plagued with panic and madness. The ship was lost and soon to vanish. The first mate from the sister ship crossed over in hopes of retrieving the Admiral. The ship was on its side as the keel was almost out of the water. The sailor found the Admiral clinging to a rope just above the waterline. His face was white as a ghost and expressionless.

"Come, Admiral…give me your hand…Hurry!"

"No! Leave me!"

"Give…me …your …hand!"

The sailor was holding on to a rope himself and leaned out as far as he could stretch.

"Leave me alone! I must go down with my ship. I should have seen this coming."

"The war is just starting and we need your experience. You must survive this ship, Sir. You need to take my hand."

The boat started to turn and the nose began to point up. The Admiral looked into the sailor's eyes and with no expression on his face, let go of the rope that was holding him. The sailor yelled.

"NO!" As the Admiral slid into the icy cold locker of the Shasath Sea. The sailor bowed his head for a brief moment and then struggled to save his own life as the downed boat did its final pirouette into the sea. The Captain of the sister vessel cut off all ties just before the ship sank. A few good men were plucked from the icy waters, but most followed their ship down as the first casualties of the watery war. The first mate ran up beside the Captain.

"Sir, with the Admiral lost, this is now your command. What are your orders?

The other ship's Captains are looking to you for their orders,…Sir."

The Captain scratched his beard and reluctantly accepted the responsibility that was thrust upon him.

"Have them spread out. I want one on one if possible."

"But Sir…isn't there safety in numbers?"

"I don't want to lose multiple ships with one volley of fire. We will fight to the last man, but I want a fight not a duck shoot at some local carnival."

The sailor smiled. "Right you have it, sir. I will get the flagman on it smartly."

"Oh…and I want double the powder in those cannons. Bring us around…I want to answer with a play of my own."

"Aye, Aye, Sir."

The Delockth Navy spread out and approached the oncoming Dark threat wide and thin. The enemy stayed true to their plan and stayed bunched together in hopes of punching through the spread out Delockth Navy. It wasn't long before the exchange of fire was prevalent from both sides. The lead Black ship took extensive damage and the men had to abandon to a sister ship. The Captain stood on his bow and puffed on his ivory pipe. He looked back at his ship still afloat but smoking with fire and lifeless sailors. His first mate was lifeless at the wheel. He turned and looked straight at the Captain of the enemy ship approaching fast. He pulled his collar closer to ward off the bitter cold. The approaching Captain lowered his arm and the bow cannon fired. The Captain of the Black ship's eyes widened as he saw the incoming shot. He had just enough time to blow one of his famous smoke rings into the chilled air. The projectile struck just micro measures before the Captain's feet. The explosion was tremendous. It shattered the deck and the Captain, sending wood and flesh all over the doomed ship. Several more shots were received by the Black ship ending its illustrious career and any hope of seeing this battle complete. It sank so fast, the men on the opposing boat thought some mythical sea monster was pulling it down to feed.

The exchange of firepower was noteworthy. Men were being blown off on either side and consumed by the frigid waters. The malodorous smell of freshly burnt gunpowder was in everyone's nostrils. The sound of pain and agony echoed in the ears of the survivors. The tactical advice to stay in one battle group proved fatal for the Dark Navy. By mere chance or divine intervention, seven ships of the Delockth Navy survived. Outgunned and out-manned, the victors savored no joy or enthusiasm. For the loss of their friends and comrades was overwhelming. Most of the invading ships were fatally damaged or sunk. Only time would heal the wounds received on this day. The Captain found a moment to light his pipe and watch in amazement as a great white owl circled curiously overhead. "Captain! Captain! What are your orders,...Sir?"

The first mate had a bandaged arm and a head wrapping with a large stain of fresh blood oozing from its centre. "See to the survivors mate." He put his hand on the first mate's arm.

"You did the service proud. You did your Captain proud. Now be off with you and break open another barrel of rum...ya hear!"

"Yesss! Sirrrr!"

The smoke could be seen from the Castle's walls. Korana and the High Wizard were standing there out of sight from the formidable sea battle, but through their wizardly insight could see the end result. They didn't speak a word to one another. They walked back inside to the warmth of the Queen's Chamber fire. Presta and Korrin were sitting there waiting for their sister to join them. Korana sat between the two and all the sisters joined hands. The High Wizard lit his long metal pipe as Vestran pour wine from a decanter. The large white owl landed on the windowsill and spread his gigantic wings. The three sisters shut their eyes and started to sway gently.

"There is a Dark wave fast approaching...can you feel it?"

Korana spoke as if it was a forced whisper.

"No...I cannot," Korrin answered.

Kem blew a smoke ring in the shape of a dragon.

"I can feel it sister...I am scared." Presta had a waver in her voice.

"It's Marideath himself. We have won the first battle, but the second test won't be quite so easy."

A knock sounded on the Queen's chamber door.

"*Enter!*" The Queen commanded.

The door creaked open and in walked Erin, Kill and Killgreth. The three girls stood explosively and ran towards the men.

Ψ

Crow's Nest: Captains lead vessel, Delockth Navy

The night was about to fall, but the Crow's man thought he saw lights twinkling in the distance. He rubbed his eyes with his dirty hands and looked again.

"Oh! My!....... Captain! Captain!"

"What is it you fool? The Captain is in the lower levels tending to the wounded."

One of the sailors put his hands around his mouth so the crow's man could hear him.

"Get him top side now…you son of a pig farmer."

The insult was strong and knowing Jimth the crow's man, he knew he wasn't fooling around. The sailor pulled the Captain topside, almost against his will.

"What is it you…you!" The Captain was not pleased.

"More ships, Sir…approaching."

"How far man? How far?" The Captain put his bloody hands to his mouth.

"A good twelve bells behind us…Sir."

The Captain put his hand to his beard and stroked the dirty grey hairs. After a few tics of thought… he called up.

"How many do you see sailor? How…Many?"

"Hundred…defiantly over a hundred!"

The Captain's mind went blank, as he stood silent with his mouth agape.

EPILOG

VERY EARLY, AT FIRST LIGHT, Koln commandeered a small two-person sailboat. With the help of Kem, he used a spell to conjure up a personal breeze that took him safely and quickly to the Island of Vectorth. He arrived in a short time and had no problems finding the departed spice trader Laval's family. The widow was torn apart with the news of her husband's demise, but was grateful for knowing his true fate and not left to wonder her remaining years of his whereabouts. Koln expressed Laval's love for them all and gave the strange Dragon ring to his son Maraculas, thus fulfilling the promise he had made to the dying man. The boy was about seventeen full cycle seasons of age and of strong mind and body. He felt indebted to Killgreth for the return of his father's ring and swore allegiance to the great warrior. Before he left the good people to grieve, he found out that the Island had never been invaded in its long history. The only export they had to survive on was fish. The only import they needed was salt. Koln devised a secret plan with the promise of endless supplies of quality salt, in exchange for his idea. The leaders of Vectorth agreed and Koln headed back with a sense of well being and a plan.

The great cave with the large door fashioned from salt, showed signs of a disturbance. A small puff of steam drifted around its outer edge.

Korana and her two sisters stood together on the castles high tower looking towards the sea. All three shared the same vision of what was to be. Taught by their teachers not to be over confident in war, but prepared instead. As they grabbed each other's hands a familiar clap of thunder appeared from a clear sky. The three girls didn't know from where it came or for what purpose. They felt the Dark presents on their door step and if only slightly, feared for their realm and their loyal people.

Watch for the conclusion of; Three Daughters of Delockth (The Three Orbs of Radiant-Flux)

In the Fall of 2013

CPSIA information can be obtained at www.ICGtesting.com
Printed in the USA
LVOW040109301012

305016LV00001B/1/P

9 781460 202371